THE CORPSE READER

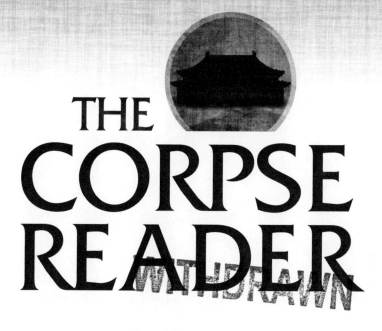

THE CORPSE READER

ANTONIO GARRIDO

TRANSLATED BY THOMAS BUNSTEAD

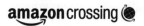

amazoncrossing

MYS

Text copyright © 2011 Antonio Garrido

English translation copyright © 2013 Thomas Bunstead

All rights reserved.

Printed in the United States of America.

Published by Amazon Crossing

PO Box 400818

Las Vegas, NV 89140

ISBN-13: 9781612184364

ISBN-10: 1612184367

Library of Congress Control Number: 2012923020

To my wife, Maite. She is all my happiness.

PROLOGUE

1206, Tsong dynasty. Eastern China.
Fujian Circuit.
Jianyang Subprefecture farmlands.

Shang didn't know death was coming for him until he tasted the blood spurting up into his throat. He covered the wound with his hands to try to stem the bleeding. He tried to speak, too, but before he could make a sound, his eyes opened wide and his legs crumpled beneath him like a worn-out marionette's. If he could have uttered the words, he would have spoken his killer's name, but the blood in his throat, along with the cloth the killer had stuffed into his mouth, prevented him.

On his knees in the mud, before breathing his last breath, Shang felt the warm rain on his skin and smelled the wet earth beneath him. Both had been with him his whole life. Then, soaked in blood, Shang's body collapsed into the mire, and his soul drifted away.

PART ONE

1

Cí got up early that morning to avoid running into his brother Lu. He could barely pry his eyes open, but he knew that, like every morning, the paddy field would be awake and waiting.

He got up and began putting away his bedding, smelling the tea his mother was brewing in the main room. He entered the room and greeted her with a nod. She replied with a half-hidden smile that he noticed nonetheless, and he smiled in return.

He adored his mother almost as much as he did his little sister, whose name was Third. His other sisters, First and Second, had died very young from a genetic disease. Third was the only one who had managed to survive, though she remained sickly.

Before breakfast, he went over to the small altar the family had erected in memory of his grandfather. He opened the wooden shutters and inhaled deeply. Outside, the first rays of sun were filtering delicately through the fog. The breeze moved through the chrysanthemums in the offering jar and stirred the spirals of incense rising in the room. Cí closed his eyes to recite a prayer, but the only thought that came into his mind was this: *Heavenly spirits, allow us to return to Lin'an.*

He cast his mind back to when his grandparents were still alive. This backwater had been paradise to him then, and to his brother Lu, who was four years his elder, his hero. Any child would have worshipped Lu. Lu was like the great soldier in their father's stories, always coming to Cí's rescue when other children tried to steal his fruit rations, always there to deal with shameless men who tried to flirt with his sisters. Lu had even shown him how to win a fight using certain kicks and punches. He'd taken him down to the river to splash around among the boats and to fish for carp and trout, which they'd then carry home in jubilation. He had also shown Cí the best hiding places from which to spy on their neighbors.

As Lu got older, though, he became vain. At fifteen, he was stronger than ever, as well as boastful, and was unimpressed with anything other than a good right hook. Lu began organizing cat hunts so he could show off in front of the girls. He'd get drunk on stolen rice liquor and crow about how he was the strongest in the gang. He became so arrogant that even when girls were making fun of him he thought they just wanted his attention. Eventually, all the girls began avoiding Lu, and Cí gradually became indifferent to his former idol, too.

In spite of everything, Lu had generally managed to steer clear of any serious trouble, apart from the occasional black eye from fighting or from riding the community buffalo in the water races. But when their father announced his intention to move to the capital city of Lin'an, Lu, who was sixteen at the time, refused to go. Lu didn't want to move to *any* city; he was happy in the countryside. In his eyes, the small village had everything: the paddy field, his braggart group of friends, even a few local prostitutes for his amusement. Although his father threatened to disown him, Lu refused to back down. So that year the family split up: Lu stayed in the village and the rest of them moved to the capital, in search of a better future.

Cí had found it difficult adjusting to Lin'an life, though he had a routine. He was up every morning with the sun to check on his sister. He'd make her breakfast and look after her until their mother came back from the market. Having wolfed down his bowl of rice, he'd go to classes until midday, and after that he would run all the way to the slaughterhouse to help his father in his job clearing away carcasses. In the evening, after cleaning the kitchen and praying to his ancestors, he studied the Confucian treatises for recitation in class the next morning. Month after month this was his life. But one day, everything changed. His father left the slaughterhouse and got a job as an accountant for the prefecture of Lin'an under Judge Feng, one of the wisest magistrates in the capital.

Life improved rapidly. The salary his father was now earning meant that Cí, too, could give up the slaughterhouse and dedicate himself to his studies. Thanks to excellent grades, after four years in school Cí was given a junior position in Judge Feng's department. To begin with, he was given straightforward administrative tasks, but his dedication and attention to detail set him apart, and the judge himself decided to take the now seventeen-year-old under his wing.

Cí showed himself worthy of Judge Feng's confidence. After just a few months he began assisting in taking statements, interviewing suspects, and preparing and cleaning the corpses of anybody who died under suspicious circumstances. It wasn't long before his meticulousness, combined with his obvious talents, made him a key employee, and the judge gave him more responsibility. Cí ended up helping with criminal investigations and legal disputes, and thus learned both the fundamentals of law and the basics of anatomy.

Cí also attended university part time, and in his second year Judge Feng encouraged him to take a preparatory course in medicine. According to the judge, the clues to a great many crimes lay hidden in wounds. To solve them you had to develop not a magistrate's but rather a surgeon's understanding of trauma.

Everything was going well until, one night, Cí's grandfather suddenly fell ill and died. After the funeral, as was dictated by Chinese custom, his father was obliged to give up his job as well as the house they had been living in, since the owner, Cí's grandfather, was dead. Without a home or work, the family had to return to the village, the last thing Cí wanted to do.

They came back to a very different Lu. He had built a house on a plot of land he'd acquired, and he was the boss of a small crew of laborers. When his father came knocking at his door, the first thing Lu did, before he would allow him to cross the threshold, was make him get down on his knees and apologize. He made their father sleep in one of the tiny bedrooms, rather than give up his own, and treated Cí with the same disinterest. Soon after, when Lu realized his younger brother no longer worshipped him and cared only for books, Cí became the target of all Lu's anger. A man showed his true value out in the fields, Lu maintained. That was where your daily rice came from, not from books, not from studying. In Lu's eyes, his younger brother was a twenty-year-old good-for-nothing, just one more mouth to feed. Cí's life became little more than a series of criticisms, and he quickly came to hate the village…

A gust of wind brought Cí back to the present.

Going back into the main room, he ran into Lu, who was at the table beside their mother, slurping his tea. Seeing Cí, he spat on the floor and banged his cup down on the table. Without waiting for their father to wake up, he grabbed his bundle of work things and headed out.

"No manners," muttered Cí, taking a cloth and wiping up the tea his brother had just spilled.

"And you should learn some respect," said his mother. "We're living in his home, after all. The strong home—"

"I know, I know. 'The strong home supports a brave father, prudent mother, obedient son, and obliging brother.'" He didn't need to be reminded of the saying. Lu was quite fond of it.

Cí laid the table with the bamboo place mats and bowls; this was supposed to be Third's job, but recently her chest illness had been getting worse. Cí didn't mind filling in for her. According to ritual, he lined up the bowls, making sure there was an even number of them, and he turned the teapot so that its spout pointed toward the window. He placed the rice wine, porridge, and carp meatballs in the center of the table. He cast his eyes over the kitchen and the cracked sink all black with carbon. It looked more like a dilapidated forge than a home.

Soon, his father hobbled in. Cí felt a stab of sadness.

How he's aged.

Cí frowned and tensed his jaw. His father's health was deteriorating: He moved shakily; his gaze was lowered and his sparse beard looked like some unpicked tapestry. There was barely a shred left of the meticulous official he had been, the man who had bred in Cí such a love of method and perseverance. Cí noticed that his father's hands, which he used to take such care of, were anemic-looking, rough and callused. He imagined his father must miss the time when his hands *had* to be immaculate—the days he'd spent examining judicial dossiers, doing proper work.

Cí's father sat at the head of the table, motioning for Cí and his mother to sit as well. Cí went to his place, and his mother took her seat on the side closest to the kitchen. She served the rice wine. Third didn't join them because of her fever.

"Will you be eating with us this evening, Cí?" his mother asked. "After all this time, Judge Feng will be delighted to see you again."

Cí wouldn't have missed it for anything. He didn't know why exactly, but his father had decided to curtail the mourning period and return to Lin'an. Cí was hoping Judge Feng would agree to take him back into the department.

"Lu said I have to take the buffalo up to the new plot, and after that I was thinking of stopping in on Cherry, but I'll be back in time for dinner."

"Twenty years old and still so naive," said his father. "That girl has you wrapped around her finger. You'll get bored of her if you carry on seeing so much of each other."

"Cherry's the only good thing about this village," said Cí, eating his last mouthful of food. "Anyway, you were the ones who arranged the marriage."

"Take the sweets I made with you," said his mother.

Cí got up and put the sweets in his bag. Before leaving the house, he went into Third's quarters, kissed her feverish cheeks, and tucked her hair back. She blinked. Cí took out the sweets and hid them under her blanket.

"Not a word!" he whispered.

She smiled, too weak to say anything.

Walking along the edge of the muddy field, Cí felt goaded by the rain. He took off his drenched shirt and urged the buffalo on with all his might. The beast took its time, as if it knew there would only be another furrow after this one, and after that another, and another. Cí looked up and contemplated the green, watery field.

His brother had ordered him to dig a drainage ditch along its edge, but it was hard going because of the dilapidated stone dikes separating the properties. Exhausted, Cí scanned the waterlogged paddy. He cracked the whip, and the buffalo plunged on through the mud and water.

He'd worked only a third of the day when the plow got snagged.

"Roots." He cursed.

The buffalo lifted its head and bellowed but wouldn't move; Cí shook it by the horns to no avail. He tried to make it go backward, but the harness was caught on the other side. Resigned, he looked the animal in the eye.

"This is going to hurt."

He tugged on the ring in the buffalo's snout and pulled the reins. The animal jumped forward and the harness creaked. Cí realized it would be better just to dig out the root with his hands. *If I break the plow, Lu will give me a real beating.*

Taking a deep breath, he sunk his arms in the muddy water until his hands hit a tangle of roots. When after a few yanks he couldn't dislodge it, he took a knife from his knapsack, knelt down, and began working beneath the surface. He tossed away a few small stumps and started on the thickest, central root. It was then that he noticed he'd cut himself. Though his finger didn't hurt, he examined the cut with great interest.

From birth, the gods had cursed him with a strange disorder. He first became aware of it when he was four years old and his mother stumbled and tipped a saucepan of boiling oil over him. He had barely felt it—no more than if he were being washed with warm water—and it was only the smell of his flesh burning that had told him something terrible was happening. His torso, upper arms, and hands were scarred, and those scars were reminders that he was different. Though he felt lucky to never experience physical pain, it also meant he had to be extremely careful of any injury. While it wouldn't hurt if he were ever beaten up, and fatigue barely affected him, he often pushed himself beyond his body's limits.

Lifting his hand out of the water, he was alarmed now at the amount of blood, which he was sure had to be from a sizable wound. He ran for a cloth to wrap around it. But having wiped the blood away, he discovered the cut was, as he'd first thought, tiny.

"What the…"

Confused, he went back to where he'd hobbled the plow and, parting the roots, saw how red the boggy water had become. He loosened the reins, freed the buffalo from the plow, and moved the animal aside. As he looked at the water, his heart began to pound. The only sound was that of the rain falling on the paddy.

Stupefied and afraid, he walked over to the small crater where he'd left the plow. Nearing the spot, he felt his stomach contract. He almost turned and ran away but contained himself. Then he saw bubbles rising rhythmically to the surface, mingling with the raindrops. He slowly kneeled down in the mud and lowered his face to the water. Another bloodshot bubble floated up.

Something suddenly moved under the water. Cí jumped to his feet, pulling his head sharply back, but when he realized it was only the fluttering of a small carp, he breathed a sigh of relief.

"Stupid thing."

He kicked at the carp, trying to compose himself. But then he caught sight of another carp, this one with a shred of flesh in its mouth.

"What on earth?"

He began backing away but lost his footing and fell facedown in a whirl of mud and bloody water. Feeling something bump against his face, he opened his eyes. His heart skipped a beat. There in front of him, with a cloth stuffed in its mouth, was a decapitated head floating between the plants on the surface of the water.

He screamed until he was hoarse—but no one came to help.

He remembered that the plot had not been used for a long while, and that the peasants were mainly on the far side of the mountain. He could abandon the buffalo and look for help. Or he could wait in the paddy until his brother came.

Neither option was appealing, but knowing that Lu wouldn't be long, he decided to wait. There were all kinds of robbers and ruffians on this side of the mountain, and a buffalo was worth much more than one human head.

While he waited, he finished cutting the roots and freed the plow's blades. Luckily, the plow wasn't damaged, which meant Lu would only be angry that he wasn't yet done plowing. At least, that was what Cí hoped. He reset the plow and got back to work. He tried whistling to distract himself, but all he could hear were his father's words: "Avoiding problems solves nothing."

Yes, but this isn't my problem.

However, he plowed only two more furrows before halting the buffalo again.

He cast a wary eye on the head as it bobbed on the water, then looked a little closer. The cheeks were caved in, as if someone had viciously stomped on them. There were tiny lacerations on the bruised skin from the carp bites, the eyelids were swollen, the flesh beside the trachea was in tatters…and there was the strange cloth coming out of the wide-open mouth.

Never in his life had he looked on something so horrifying. He shut his eyes and vomited. Then, with a start, he recognized the face. It was old Shang. The father of Cherry, the girl Cí was in love with.

Recovering a little, he looked at the strange expression, the mouth forced unnaturally wide by the cloth. Taking hold of the cloth's edge, he pulled and unraveled it, bit by bit, like a ball of string. He placed the cloth in his sleeve and tried to shut the jaw but couldn't. Cí vomited again.

He washed the face with the muddy water. Then, getting up, he retraced his steps over the plowed land in search of the rest of the body. It was midday before he found it, on the far eastern side of the plot, a few *li* from where the buffalo had gotten stuck. The corpse's trunk still had the yellow sash and the five-button gown that identified the man as an honorable person. There was no sign of the blue cap Shang always wore.

Cí couldn't go on. He sat down in the stone ditch and nibbled at a stale bit of rice bread but found it impossible to swallow. He looked at poor Shang's headless body, abandoned in the mud like that of some common criminal.

What on earth am I going to say to Cherry?

What kind of person could have cut short the life of someone like Shang, a dedicated family man who was respectful of tradition and performed all the proper rites? All Cí knew was that whoever was responsible didn't deserve to go on living.

⚜

Lu didn't arrive until late afternoon. He had three workers with him, and each carried a sapling, which meant there must have been a change of plan: they were going to plant the rice without waiting for the field to drain. Cí left the buffalo and ran over to his brother. He bowed in greeting.

"Brother! You won't believe it—" His heart was beating hard.

"What do you mean, I won't believe it?" Lu roared, pointing to the untilled plot. "I can see it with my own two eyes."

"I found a—" Before he could finish, his brother punched him in the face, knocking him to the ground.

"Slacker!" spat Lu. "What makes you think you're better than everyone else?"

Cí touched the cut on his brow. It wasn't the first time his brother had hit him, but because Lu was older, according to Confucian customs, Cí was forbidden to fight back. He was the one with the swelling eye, but he still had to apologize.

"Brother, forgive me. I was delayed because—"

But Lu kept going.

"Because the puny little bookworm doesn't have it in him to do a little hard work! Thinks the rice will plant itself! He leaves it for his brother Lu to break his back!"

"I…found…a…corpse," Cí managed.

Lu raised an eyebrow.

"A corpse? What are you talking about?"

"There, in the ditch."

Lu turned toward the spot, where a couple of rooks were pecking at the head. He walked to it and pushed the head with his foot. Frowning, he came back.

"Damn it! You found it here?" He picked up the head by the hair, holding it at arm's length in disgust. "Confucius! It's Shang, isn't it? What about the body?"

"Over there."

Pursing his lips, Lu turned to the workers.

"What are you waiting for? Go and pick it up! Dump those saplings and put that head in the basket. Damn it! We're going back to the village."

Cí went over to the buffalo to take its harness off.

"And what the hell are you up to?" asked Lu.

"Didn't you say we're going back?"

"*We* are," he spat. "You can come back when you've finished your job."

2

For the rest of the afternoon, choking on the stench given off by the laboring buffalo's hindquarters, Cí tried desperately to imagine what crime Shang could have committed to get his head chopped off. As far as Cí knew, Shang didn't have any enemies and had never given anyone any trouble. His worst offense, it seemed, was to have fathered several daughters, which meant he had to slave to make enough money for remotely attractive dowries. Shang had always been honest and respected.

The last person someone would think of killing.

In addition to the plowing, Lu had ordered Cí to spread a pile of black earth made up of a mix of fertilizers—excrement, earth, ashes, and weeds. Before Cí had realized it, the sun had set. Climbing on the buffalo's back, he set off wearily in the direction of the village.

Cí considered the similarities between Shang's body and cases he'd seen during his time in Lin'an. He had accompanied Judge Feng to the scenes of several violent crimes and had even witnessed the results of brutal ritual killings carried out by various sects, but he'd never seen such a savagely mutilated body. It was good that Feng would be at the house; Cí knew *he'd* find whoever was responsible.

Cherry and her family lived not far from Lu's house in a hovel that was precariously balanced on worm-eaten stilts. Cí arrived there deeply anxious. He'd thought of a few different ways of telling her the news, but none of them seemed right. It was pouring with rain again, but he stopped outside the door and racked his brain for what to say.

I'll think of something.

As he lifted his hand to knock, he realized his arms were trembling.

No one answered. He knocked again without receiving a response, then gave up and headed to his house.

⟿⟆⟆⟇⟇⟻

Cí had barely opened the door when his father began reprimanding him for being late. Judge Feng had been there for some time, and they'd been waiting for Cí to begin dinner. Seeing their guest, Cí brought his fists together in front of his chest and bowed in apology, but Feng wouldn't allow it.

"By God! What have they been feeding you? Only last year you were still a boy!"

Cí hadn't noticed it himself, but it was true: he was no longer the scrawny boy people used to make fun of in Lin'an. Working in the fields had transformed his body, and his lean muscles were like a bunch of tightly woven reeds. He smiled shyly. Feng didn't seem to have changed at all. His serious, furrowed face contrasted with his carefully arranged whiskers and his silk *bialar* cap—an indicator of his rank.

"Most honorable Judge Feng," said Cí. "Excuse my lateness, but—"

"Don't worry yourself, boy," said Feng. "Come in, you're soaked."

Cí ran to his room and came out with a small parcel wrapped in delicate red paper. He'd been looking forward to this for a whole month, ever since he'd heard that Feng was coming. As was custom, Feng rejected the gift three times before accepting.

"You really shouldn't have." He put the gift with his belongings without opening it. To do so otherwise would mean he valued the object over the act of its having been given.

"He's grown, yes," said Cí's father, "but he's still as irresponsible as ever."

Cí tried to speak. The rules of courtesy meant he shouldn't burden a guest with issues that weren't related to the visit, but a murder surely transcended all protocol. The judge would understand.

"Excuse the discourtesy, but I have some terrible news. Shang has been killed! Someone cut off his head!"

His father looked at him gravely.

"Your brother has already told us. Sit down now and let's eat—our guest has waited long enough."

Cí was exasperated by how coolly his father and Feng took the news. Shang had been his father's closest friend, but the two older men began eating, unflustered, as though nothing had happened. Cí followed their lead, seasoning the food with his own bitter feelings. His grimaces didn't go unnoticed.

"There's nothing we can do," said his father eventually. "Lu has taken the body to the government offices, and his family will be holding a wake. And as you well know, Judge Feng is out of his jurisdiction here. All we can do is wait for them to send the relevant magistrate."

Cí knew all this, but his father's levelheadedness upset him. Feng seemed to read his thoughts.

"Don't worry yourself," said Feng. "I've spoken to the relatives. I'm going to go and examine the body tomorrow."

The rain battered the slate roof, and the conversation moved on to other topics. Summer typhoons and floods often took people by surprise, and that day it was Lu's turn. He arrived drenched, reeking of alcohol, his eyes glazed. He stumbled straight into a chest and then kicked the piece of furniture as if it had stepped into his path. He babbled an incoherent greeting to the judge and went straight to his room.

"I think it's time I retired," said Feng once he'd cleaned his whiskers. To Cí's father he said, "I hope you'll consider what we discussed." And to Cí, "As for you, I'll see you tomorrow at the hour of the dragon. I'm staying at the sergeant's house."

As soon as they shut the door, Cí scrutinized his father's face, his heart pounding.

"Did he—did he talk about our coming back?"

"Take a seat. Shall we have some more tea?"

Cí's father poured a cup for each of them. He gave Cí a sorrowful look before dropping his gaze.

"I'm sorry, Cí. I know how much you've been looking forward to going back to Lin'an." He took a sip of tea. "But sometimes things don't turn out the way we want."

Cí stopped with his cup halfway to his mouth.

"What happened? Didn't the judge offer you your old job back?"

"Yes, he did, yesterday." He took another long sip.

"So?" Cí got up.

"Sit down, Cí."

"But Father, you said—"

"I said sit down!"

Cí obeyed. Tears came to his eyes. His father poured more tea, to the point that the cup overflowed. Cí started to wipe it up, but his father stopped him.

"Look, Cí. There are things you're too young to understand..."

Cí didn't know what it was he wasn't able to understand: That he would have to go on taking the way his brother treated him? That he would have to accept not going to the Imperial University of Lin'an?

"What about our plans, Father? What about—"

His father stiffened. His voice was unsteady, but his look was uncompromising. "Plans? Since when does a child have plans? We're staying here, in your brother's house. And that's how it will be—until the day I die!"

A poisonous rage ran through Cí, but he was quiet as his father left the room.

⚜

Cí cleared away the cups and went to the room he shared with his sister.

As he lay down next to Third, blood pounded at his temples. From the moment they'd come back to the village, he'd dreamed of returning to Lin'an. As he did every night, he shut his eyes and began thinking about his former life. He remembered the competitions with his schoolmates and the times he'd won; he remembered his teachers, whose discipline and determination he so admired. Judge Feng came to mind, and the day he had taken Cí on as his assistant. Cí wanted so much to be like him, to be able to take the Imperial exams one day and become a member of the judiciary. Not like his father, who, after years of trying, had only become a humble functionary.

He racked his brain as to why his father would not want to return. Feng had offered him the position he'd so badly wanted back, and then, in the space of a day, something had changed. Could it be because of Cí's grandfather? Cí didn't think so. Six months had passed since his grandfather's unexpected death. The ashes could just as well be transported to Lin'an, and the filial mourning period observed there.

Third coughed, making Cí jump. She was half-asleep, shivering and breathing with difficulty. Cí tenderly stroked her hair. Third had shown she was more resilient than First and Second; she'd already lived to the age of seven. But she wasn't expected to live beyond ten; that was her fate. If they were in Lin'an, they might be able to care for her better.

Closing his eyes again, Cí thought about Cherry, who would be shattered by the death of her father. Cí wondered what impact it would have on their future marriage; then he instantly felt miserable for thinking something so self-centered.

It was suffocatingly hot, so Cí got up and undressed. Taking off his jacket, he found the bloody cloth. He looked at it with renewed astonishment before placing it beside his pillow. He heard cries from next door; their neighbor had been suffering from a toothache for the past few days. For the second night in a row, Cí didn't sleep.

✦

Cí was up before dawn so he could meet Judge Feng at the residence of Bao-Pao—where government officials stayed whenever they were in the area—to examine the corpse. In the room next door, Lu was snoring loudly. By the time he awoke, Cí would be long gone.

Cí dressed quietly and left the house. The rain had stopped, but the air was muggy. He took a deep breath before diving into the labyrinth of tight village roads, where a series of identical worm-eaten huts were laid out like carelessly aligned domino tiles. Every now and then there was the tinted light from a lantern in a doorway and the smell of tea brewing, and Cí could see the ghostly outlines of peasants on their way to the fields. But the village was still mostly asleep; the only noise was the occasional wailing dog.

It was dawn when he reached Sergeant Bao-Pao's residence.

Judge Feng was on the porch, dressed in a jet-black gown that complemented his cap. Though stone-faced, he drummed his fingers impatiently. After the usual reverences, Cí thanked him again.

"I'm only going to take a quick look; don't get your hopes up. And don't look at me like that," he said, seeing Cí's disappointment. "I'm out of my jurisdiction, and you know I haven't been taking on any criminal work lately. And don't be so impatient. This is a small place. Finding the culprit will be as simple as shaking a stone out of your shoe."

Cí followed the judge to an annex where his personal assistant, a silent man with traces of Mongol in him, kept watch. Sergeant Bao-Pao was inside, along with Shang's widow and sons—and Shang's corpse. Seeing it, Cí couldn't help but retch. The family had positioned it on a wooden chair as if Shang were still alive, the body upright and the head stitched to the neck with reeds. Despite the fact he had been washed, perfumed, and dressed, he still resembled a bloody scarecrow. Judge Feng paid his respects to the family and asked their permission to inspect the body, which the eldest son granted.

"Remember what you have to do?" Feng asked Cí as he approached the body.

Cí remembered perfectly well. He took a sheet of paper, an inkstone, and his best brush from his bag. Then he sat on the floor next to the corpse. Feng, commenting that it was unfortunate they'd already washed the corpse, came closer and began his work.

"I, Judge Feng, in this, the twenty-second moon of the month of the Lotus, in the second year of the era of Kaixi and the fourteenth of the reign of our beloved Ningzong, Heaven's Son and honored emperor of the Tsong dynasty, with the relevant family authorization, undertake the preliminary investigation, auxiliary to that which should be carried out no less than four hours after the notice of death to the magistrate of the Jianningfu Prefecture. In the presence of Cheng Li, the deceased's eldest son; the widow, Mrs. Li; and the two other male children, Ze and Xin; as well as Bao-Pao, the local sergeant; and my assistant Cí as witness."

Cí noted down the dictation, repeating out loud each of Feng's words.

Feng continued, "The deceased, name Shang Li, son and grandson of Li. According to his eldest son, fifty-eight years of age at the time of death. Accountant, farmworker, carpenter. Last seen the day before yesterday, midday, having attended to his work in Bao-Pao's warehouse, where we are now. His son declares that the deceased did not appear to have been ill, showed only the normal signs of aging, and had no known enemies."

Feng looked over to the son, who confirmed the facts, and then Feng asked Cí to recite his notes.

"Due to an oversight by his family," continued Feng disapprovingly, "the body has already been washed and clothed. They have confirmed that when it was brought to them, the body had no wounds other than the large cut that separated the head from the body—undoubtedly the cause of death. The mouth is exaggeratedly wide open, and"—he tried, unsuccessfully, to shut it—"there is rigidity in the jaw."

"Aren't you going to undress it?" Cí asked, surprised.

"That won't be necessary," Feng said, pointing to the neck cut and waiting for Cí to answer.

"Double cut?" suggested Cí.

"Double cut, the same as with pigs when they're bled out..."

Cí leaned forward to look at the wound. At the front, where the Adam's apple would have been, there was a clean, horizontal notch. Then the cut grew wider and showed teeth marks like those of a slaughterhouse handsaw. He was about to say something when Feng asked him to relate the circumstances in which he had found the body. Cí did so with as much detail as he could remember. When he finished, the judge gave him a severe look.

"And the cloth?"

"The cloth?"

How could I have forgotten?

"You disappoint me, Cí, something you never used to do." The judge was quiet for a moment. "As you *should* already know, the open mouth is not that of someone crying out for help or in pain; if it had been either, the mouth would have shut with the loosening of the muscles that follows death. An object must have been introduced into the mouth before or immediately following the death and must have remained there until the muscles seized up. With respect to the type of object, I presume—noticing the bloody threads still between the teeth—we are talking about some kind of linen cloth."

The reproach hurt Cí. A year earlier he would never have made that sort of mistake, but he was out of practice. He rummaged in his jacket pocket.

"I meant to give it to you," he apologized, handing over the carefully folded piece of material.

Now it was Feng's turn to examine it carefully; the material was gray, stained with dried blood, and about the size of a head scarf. The judge tagged it as evidence.

"Conclude the notes and put my stamp on it. Then make a copy for the magistrate when he comes."

Feng bid farewell to the others and left the annex. It was raining again. Cí hurried after him and caught up just as they reached the Bao-Pao residence.

"The documents..." stammered Cí.

"Leave them over there on the night table."

"Judge Feng, I—"

"Don't worry yourself, Cí. When I was your age I couldn't tell the difference between a murder by crossbow and one by hanging."

Cí felt sure the judge was only saying this to make him feel better.

He watched the judge as he organized his certificates. Cí wanted to have even half Feng's wisdom, decency, and knowledge. He wanted Feng as his teacher again, but there was no chance of that as long as he was trapped in this village. He had no idea how to get out. When Feng put the last piece of paper away, Cí asked about his father's taking his old job back, but the judge shook his head resignedly.

"That's between your father and me."

Cí moved hesitantly among Feng's possessions. "We talked about it last night and he told me…The thing is, I thought we'd be coming back to Lin'an, but…"

Cí was on the edge of tears. The older man took a deep breath and placed a hand on Cí's shoulder. "Cí, I don't know if I should tell you this—"

"Please."

"All right, but you must promise to keep it to yourself." Cí nodded, and Feng collapsed into a chair. "I only made this trip on account of your family. Your father wrote to me a few months ago communicating his intention to take up his post again, but now that I've made the trip to see him, he won't hear of it. I tried to insist; I offered him a comfortable job with a good wage; I even offered him a house in the capital. But he refused, and I have no idea why."

"Why can't you take me, though? If it's about forgetting the cloth, I promise I'll work hard. I'll work myself to the bone if I have to; I won't shame you again! I—"

"Truly, Cí, the problem is not you. You know how highly I think of you. You're loyal, and I'd be more than pleased to have you back as my assistant. I said the same to your father; I talked about your prospects. He won't budge. I'm truly sorry."

Cí didn't know what to say.

There was a clap of thunder in the distance. Feng slapped Cí on the back.

"I had big plans for you, Cí. I even reserved you a place at the university."

"Imperial University?" Cí was wide-eyed; this was his dream.

"Your father didn't tell you? I thought he would have."

Cí thought his legs might collapse. He felt utterly cheated.

3

Judge Feng was needed to help interrogate some of the village residents, so he and Cí agreed to meet again after lunch. Cí wanted to visit Cherry, but he needed his father's permission if he was going to miss work.

Before he went into the house, Cí commended himself to the gods and then entered without knocking. Startled by Cí's return, his father dropped some documents, which he quickly gathered from the floor and put in a red lacquer chest.

"Shouldn't you be out plowing?" he asked angrily, shoving the chest under a bed.

Cí said he wanted to visit Cherry, but his father wouldn't hear of it.

"You're always putting pleasure before duty."

"Father—"

"She'll be fine. I have no idea why I let your mother talk me into letting you two get engaged. That's girl's worse than a wasp."

Cí cleared his throat. "Please, father. I'll be quick. Afterward, I'll finish the plowing and help Lu with the reaping."

"Afterward? Perhaps you think Lu goes out in the fields for a nice stroll. Even the buffalo is a more willing worker than you. When is afterward, exactly?"

What's going on? Why is he being so tough on me?

Cí didn't want to argue. Everyone, including his father, knew full well that Cí had worked tirelessly the last few months sowing rice and tending to the saplings; that his hands had become callused reaping, threshing, and panning; that he had plowed from sunup to sundown, leveled the soil, transported and spread the fertilizer, pedaled the pumps, and hauled the sacks of produce to the river barges. While Lu was off getting drunk with his prostitutes, Cí was killing himself in the fields.

In a way he hated having a conscience; it meant he had to accept his father's decisions. He went to find his sickle and his bundle, but the sickle wasn't there.

"Use mine," said his father. "Lu took yours."

Cí gathered up the tools and headed to the fields.

⊱🙰⊰

Cí hurt his hand whipping the buffalo. The animal roared at the treatment but then pulled as though possessed in a desperate attempt to evade Cí's blows. Cí clung to the plow, trying to push it into the sodden earth as the rain poured down. He whipped the beast and cursed, furrow after furrow. Then a thunderclap stopped him in his tracks. The sky was as dark as mud, but the suffocating heat was unrelenting.

Suddenly there was a flash of lightning and an earth-shuddering boom. The buffalo cowered and tried to leap away again, but the plow held fast in the ground, making the animal fall on its hindquarters.

The buffalo was flailing in the water now, trying to get to its feet. Cí heaved but failed to help it up. He loosened the harness and hit the beast a couple of times, but it only raised its forehead out of the water as it tried to escape the punishment. Then Cí saw the terrible open fracture in its hindquarters.

Dear gods, what have I done to offend you?

Cí approached the buffalo with an apple, but it tried to gore him with its horns. It tired itself out writhing and bellowing, and rested its head to one side for a moment, dipping a horn in the mud. Looking in its panic-stricken eyes, Cí sensed it was trying to convey that it wanted to escape its crippled body. Snot streamed from its huffing nostrils. It was as good as meat for the slaughterhouse.

Cí was stroking its muzzle when he was grabbed from behind and pushed into the water. Lu, brandishing a staff, stood over him in a rage.

"Wretch! This is how you repay me?"

Cí tried to protect himself as the stick came down on his face.

"Get up." Lu hit him again. "Time for a lesson."

Cí tried to get up, but again Lu struck him, then grabbed him by the hair.

"Know how much a buffalo costs? No? Time for you to learn."

Lu thrust Cí's head underwater. Once Cí had flailed for a bit, Lu yanked him up and pushed him under the harness.

"No!" cried Cí.

"Don't like working in the fields, eh?" He was trying to tie Cí into the harness. "You hate that Father loves me best."

"Hardly! Even though you're a bootlicker!"

"What?" roared Lu. "You'll be the one licking boots when I finish with you."

Wiping away blood from his cheek, Cí looked hatefully at his brother. Custom dictated that he not fight back. But it was time to show Lu he wasn't his slave. Cí got up and punched Lu in the gut as hard as he could. Lu, not expecting the blow, was winded for a moment, but his return punch knocked Cí to the ground. Cí had years of pent-up hate, but Lu was bigger and a much better fighter. When Cí got up, Lu knocked him down again. Cí felt something crack in his chest, but he wasn't in pain. Then another blow, this time in the gut. Still on the ground, he took another blow. He couldn't get up. He felt the rain on his face. He thought he heard Lu shouting at him, but then he lost consciousness.

⧉⧉⧉

Feng was with Shang's corpse when Cí stumbled in.

"Cí! Who's done—" But before he could finish, he had to leap forward to catch Cí as he fainted.

Feng laid Cí down on a mat. One of Cí's eyes was swollen shut, but the cut on his cheek didn't seem too bad. Feng touched the edge of it.

"You've been striped like a mule," he said, examining Cí's torso. The bruise on his side was alarming, but luckily none of the ribs were broken. "Did Lu do this?" Cí shook his head groggily. "Don't lie! That animal. Your father did well leaving him behind in the countryside."

Feng was relieved to find Cí's pulse still rhythmic and strong, but he sent his assistant to get the local healer. Soon a small, toothless old man came bearing herbs and concoctions. He examined Cí and then applied ointments, gave him a tonic, and recommended rest.

⧉⧉⧉

Cí woke to a buzzing noise. Managing to sit up, he realized he was in the annex with Shang's body. Shang's dead flesh had begun to rot in the monsoon heat, and the stench was unbearable. Once Cí's eyes adjusted to the dark, he saw that the buzzing was coming from a swarm of flies, contracting and expanding like a ghostly shadow, attracted by the dried blood at the corpse's throat.

"How's that eye of yours?" asked Feng.

Cí jumped. He hadn't noticed Feng still there, seated in the dark a few feet away.

"Not sure. I can't feel anything."

"You'll be OK. No broken bones and—" A thunderclap sounded nearby. "By the Great Wall! The gods are certainly stomping around."

"I feel like they've been angry with me for a while," said Cí.

Another thunderclap boomed in the distance.

"Shang's family will be here soon. I've invited them, along with the village elders, so that I can share my findings."

"Judge Feng, I can't stay in the village. I beg you, take me with you to Lin'an."

"Cí, don't ask the impossible. You owe your father your obedience and—"

"My brother will kill me—"

"Wait, here come the elders."

Shang's family entered carrying a wooden coffin on their shoulders. Shang's father, clearly distraught over losing the son who should have been honoring him at his death, headed the procession. Other relations and neighbors followed. When they were all inside, they gathered around Shang's body.

Feng greeted them, and each bowed. He waved the flies clear, but they returned immediately. To keep the flies away, Feng ordered that the wound be covered. Then he sat down next to a black lacquer table in a chair his aide had brought for him.

"Honorable citizens, as you already know, the magistrate from Jianningfu will be here later. Nonetheless, according to the family's wishes, I have already started the investigation. I will therefore bypass the protocol and present the facts."

Cí observed from the corner of the room, admiring the shrewd wisdom in everything Feng did.

The judge began: "Everyone knew that Shang had no enemies, and yet he was brutally murdered. What could the motive have been? I have no doubt that it was a robbery. His widow, an honored and respected woman, confirms that when he disappeared he had three thousand *qián* on his person. Young Cí, however, who demonstrated his perceptiveness this morning by identifying the cuts to the neck, assured us that when he found the body there was no money at all." Feng got to his feet and, fingers interlaced, walked among the family and the elders. "Cí found a cloth stuffed in the oral cavity. I have marked it as evidence." He took the cloth from a small box and spread it out for everyone to see.

"Justice!" cried the widow, sobbing.

Feng nodded and was quiet for a moment.

"At first, it might look only like a piece of linen with blood on it. But if we look carefully at the bloodstains," he said as he ran his fingers over the three main marks, "we see a pattern."

Whispers broke out—what could it mean? Cí asked himself the same question.

Feng continued: "In order to reach my conclusions, I've conducted tests that I'd like to repeat for you." He called his assistant forward. "Ren!"

The aide stepped forward holding a kitchen knife, a sickle, a bottle of tinted water, and two cloths. He bowed, placed the objects on the table, and withdrew. The judge soaked the kitchen knife in the tinted water before drying it on one of the cloths. He did the same with the sickle, and then held up the results.

Cí saw that the marks left on the cloth used to dry the knife were straight and tapered; on the cloth used to dry the sickle, the marks were curved—just like on the cloth found in Shang's mouth.

The murder weapon was likely a sickle. Cí marveled at Feng's brilliance.

Feng continued: "I had my man, along with Bao-Pao's men, go around this morning and collect all the sickles in the village."

Ren came forward, this time dragging a crate full of sickles. Feng went to the corpse.

"The head was separated from the body with a butcher's saw. And Bao-Pao's men found one in the field where Shang was killed." He took a saw out of the crate and placed it on the ground. "But death itself came from something different. The instrument used to end Shang's life was, without doubt, a sickle."

The group murmured over the news.

"The saw has few distinguishing marks," continued Feng. "The blade is made from base iron and the handle from an unidentified wood. But, as we all know, sickles are always inscribed with their owner's name. Once we match the marks made by the weapon, we'll have the murderer." He gestured to Ren, who opened one of the annex doors and led several peasants into the room. They gathered at the far end where it was too dark for Cí to see any of their faces.

Feng asked Cí if he felt up to helping. Cí nodded, though he was still having trouble standing. He took a notebook and a brush as the judge went over to examine the sickles. He meticulously placed the blades against the marks on the original cloth and held them up to the light. He dictated every action, and Cí transcribed.

Until that point, Cí had found Feng's resoluteness somewhat strange: The majority of the sickles would have been forged using the same mold. Unless the blade they were looking for happened to have some peculiar notch, it was unlikely they would find anything conclusive. But now he understood: since it was prohibited under the penal code to condemn the accused without prior confession, Feng had come up with a way of flushing out the criminal.

There's no evidence; he's got nothing.

After finishing his tests, Feng pretended to read Cí's notes before handing them back. Then, stroking his whiskers, he approached the peasants.

"I'll say it only once!" he shouted. "The blood marks on the cloth identify the murderer. They match one sickle only, and the sickles have *your* names on them." He peered into frightened peasants' eyes. "You all know the punishment for such a terrible crime! But," he bellowed, "what you don't know is that if the murderer does not confess now, the execution will be by *lingchi*, and it will happen straightaway."

The group murmured again. Cí was horrified. *Lingchi*, or death by a thousand cuts, was the bloodiest death imaginable. The condemned was stripped, tied to a post, and chopped up into pieces— literally filleted. Then the pieces were laid out in front of the condemned, whom was kept alive until a vital organ was extracted.

The peasants' faces were etched with terror.

"But because I am not the judge charged with ruling in this prefecture," continued Feng, standing no more than a foot from the group now, "I am going to give the criminal a chance." He stopped in front of a young peasant who was on his knees whimpering, gave him a disdainful look, and carried on. "I am offering the mercy that Shang was not afforded. And the chance to regain a shred of honor, the chance to confess before being accused. This is your only chance to avoid disgrace, as well as the worst of deaths."

To Cí, Feng looked like a hunting tiger, with his slow gait, his curved back, his taut gaze. The peasants cowered.

Time seemed to stand still. There were only the sounds of the thunder and rain, the hush in the annex, and the stench of the body. No one stepped forward.

"Come forward, you fool! This is your last chance!"

No one moved.

Feng clenched his fists, digging his nails into his hands, and cursed under his breath. Cí had never seen Feng like this. The judge snatched the notes from him and pretended to read them again. He turned back to the peasants and then unexpectedly went over to the corpse, where the flies still swarmed.

"Damned bloodsuckers!" he said, swiping his hand to disperse them. "Bloodsuckers…" Feng waved his hands again, directing the cloud of insects toward the sickles. A bunch of flies settled on one particular sickle. Feng let out a satisfied sound almost like a growl.

Feng crouched over the sickle and looked it over carefully. He noted it was the same as all the others, and apparently, clean. Nonetheless, this was the sickle that attracted the flies. Feng brought a lamp beside the sickle, revealing some red flecks on it. Then he turned the light on the handle and the letters marked there. Reading it, Feng's face froze. The tool he held in his hands belonged to Cí's brother, Lu.

4

Cí looked in a bronze mirror and tentatively touched the wound on his cheek. He dropped his head and walked away.

"Don't worry about it, boy," said Feng. "Soon you'll have a scar to be proud of."

And what about my brother? How can I ever be proud of him?

"What's going to happen?"

"To your brother? Be relieved to be free of that animal," said Feng, chewing on one of the rice cakes they had just been served. "Try one."

Cí wasn't hungry.

"He'll be executed?"

"My goodness, Cí! What if he is? You saw what he did to Shang."

"He's still my brother…"

"And a murderer." Feng pushed the food away in annoyance. "I can't say what will happen. Another judge will sentence him. I presume a wise man will be put in charge of the case. I can speak to him, ask him to be merciful, if that's what you really want."

Cí nodded, but was unconvinced. He didn't know how to persuade Feng to take more interest in Lu. Flattery, he thought, might be an option: "It was magnificent, sir. The flies on the sickle…the dried blood…I'd never have thought of it!"

"I made it up as I went along. It was only when I shooed the flies and they flew to that sickle that I realized they wouldn't do that by chance. They went to the one with blood on it, the murder weapon. Your help was key. Don't forget, you found the cloth."

"Mmm," said Cí regretfully. "Do you think I'll be able to see my brother?"

"Well, first we have to catch him."

Leaving Feng, Cí wandered through the narrow streets, trying to ignore the windows that shut as he walked by, the neighbors who turned their backs and shouted insults. What did it matter? The rain-slicked stone paths seemed to be a reflection of his soul, his empty, desolate spirit. He could still smell Shang's putrefying flesh. Everything he saw—the tiles blown from roofs by the wind, the rice terraces snaking up into the mountains, the empty barges bobbing uselessly on the river—reminded him of his ill fate. The wound on his face made him feel diseased.

He hated the village, hated his father for tricking him, hated his brother for his brutality, hated the neighbors for spying on him, hated the incessant rain, which seemed to soak him inside as well as out. He felt near hatred for his dead sisters—for dying and leaving him with Third. He hated himself. What could be worse than betraying your own family?

The downpour intensified. Cí hurried toward a building for shelter; as he went around the corner, he almost ran straight into an entourage of men led by a coolie who maniacally beat a tambourine. The man behind him brandished a sign that read: BEING OF WISDOM—JIANNINGFU MAGISTRATE.

Eight porters followed, carrying the magistrate's litter. Four slaves with the luggage came next. Cí bowed, but the retinue ignored him.

He watched fearfully as they passed. It wasn't the first time he'd seen the magistrate, who came to the village from time to time to resolve disputes over inheritances or tax issues. But he had never been called to deal with a murder, nor had he ever arrived so promptly. Cí hurried after the retinue, which headed in the direction of Bao-Pao's. He overtook the group and positioned himself by an open window so he could observe what was about to transpire.

Sergeant Bao-Pao received the magistrate as if he were the emperor himself, bowing low in deference. Once the formalities were over, Bao-Pao told him about Feng's investigation.

"You still haven't managed to capture this man Lu?" Cí overheard the magistrate ask.

"The storm is making it difficult for the tracker dogs. But we'll catch him soon enough...Shall we eat?"

"I thought you'd never ask!" He sat down at the head of the table, and Bao-Pao sat opposite him. "Isn't the accused the son of your civil servant?"

"Yes. Your memory is as prodigious as ever."

The magistrate laughed heartily. Bao-Pao was serving him more tea as Judge Feng entered.

The judge excused his late arrival with a bow. "I was only just advised of your arrival."

Beneath Feng in both age and rank, the magistrate got up and offered him his seat, but Feng waved it away and sat next to Bao-Pao. Feng updated them on his discoveries, though it appeared to Cí that the magistrate was more interested in the carp than the information.

"It is—"

"Delicious!" said the magistrate.

Feng raised an eyebrow.

"As I was saying," continued Feng, "it is a tricky case. The accused is the son of a former employee, and unfortunately, his own brother discovered the body."

"Ooh, Bao-Pao told me about that," said the magistrate, helping himself to more food. "What a stupid kid."

Cí wanted to kill him.

"I've prepared a detailed report," said Feng, "which you'll want to see before your examination."

"Eh? Well, all right. But I mean, if it's so detailed, why do we need a second investigation? Especially," he said with a laugh, "seeing all this food we've got to get through!"

Feng signaled to his assistant that he would retire with his reports. He asked the magistrate if he wanted to interrogate Cí, but the magistrate said no and continued wolfing down his food. Suddenly he stopped chewing and looked Feng in the eye.

"Let's forget the bureaucracy and go out and catch this bastard."

<hr>

Before dinner was over, a group of bloodhounds led by Bao-Pao's men found Lu on Green Mountain, on the road to Wuyishan. He had 3,000 *qián* in his pocket, and he defended himself like a cornered animal. Bao-Pao's men managed to subdue him, but only by giving Lu the beating of his life.

<hr>

Word that the trial was scheduled for that night arrived at the house while Cí was still explaining to his father what had happened.

"Lu would never..." Cí's father howled. "And you, how could you? You *helped* accuse him?"

"But I had no idea…" Cí hung his head. "Feng will help us. He promised…"

Cí's father, furious, didn't wait for Cí to finish, but gathered Third in his arms and, along with his wife, left the house.

Cí followed at a distance. It was strange that the trial was set so quickly, but it seemed as if the magistrate was in a hurry for resolution. The judicial flag was up at the assembly hall when they arrived, and silk lanterns hung on either side of an empty desk and chair.

Bao-Pao's men brought Lu in—his head and arms in a *jia*, the heavy wooden stocks used for criminals; the shackles on his bloody feet and the pine handcuffs signaled that he was dangerous. The magistrate, wearing a silk gown and a *bialar* cap, entered. A sheriff introduced the magistrate and read the charges.

"If the accuser is in agreement…" boomed the magistrate.

Shang's eldest son touched his forehead to the ground to indicate he agreed. The sheriff asked him to confirm his place in the proceedings, and he read haltingly from the document in front of him before thumbprinting his signature.

"By the grace of the Supreme Emperor Ningzong," began the magistrate, "heir to the Heavenly Empire. In his honorable and praiseworthy name, I, his humble servant, the Being of Wisdom from Jianningfu Prefecture and magistrate in this tribunal, have read the charges against the abject criminal Lu Song, who robbed, murdered, and profaned the body of Shang Li. I declare that, in accordance with our thousand-year-old *Songxingtong*, there are a number of facts in Judge Feng's astute report. The certainty of these facts is such that I now hand the floor to the accused so that he can declare his own guilt. If he does not, he will be made to suffer until he offers a full and complete confession."

Cí's heart sank.

The sheriff shoved Lu to his knees. Lu's eyes were sunken and blank. When he opened his mouth to speak, Cí saw he was missing a number of teeth.

"I didn't kill anyone..." Lu managed to say.

Lu had been badly beaten. No matter what he'd done, Cí thought the abuse was too harsh.

"Consider your words carefully," said the magistrate. "And be advised that my men are very handy with certain implements."

Lu didn't respond. Cí thought that maybe he was drunk. One of the guards shoved Lu again, and he toppled forward, striking his head on the floor.

The magistrate calmly read Feng's notes. His gaze settled on Lu.

"The accused has certain rights. His guilt has not yet been decided, so we therefore give him the chance to speak for himself. Tell me, Lu, where were you on the day in question between sunrise and midday?"

"Working," said Lu, though without much conviction.

"Where?"

"Don't know. In the fields."

"Ha! But two of your workers have already contradicted this. According to them, you were nowhere to be seen all morning!"

Lu stared dumbly back at the magistrate.

"You won't remember, but Lao, the innkeeper, says you were drinking late into the night. You got drunk, played dice, and lost a lot of money."

"Not possible," said Lu scornfully. "I never have anything *to* lose!"

"The innkeeper confirms that you lost it all anyway."

"Which happens when you play dice."

"Be that as it may, when you were apprehended and searched you had three thousand coins on you!" The magistrate squinted.

"Let me refresh your memory—with something other than liquor. That afternoon, when you fled following the murder—"

"I wasn't fleeing; I was on my way to Wuyishan market. I—I was on my way to buy a new buffalo. My imbecile brother managed to break the other one's leg!"

"With three thousand *qián*? Everyone knows a buffalo costs at least forty thousand!"

"It was going to be a down payment."

"It was money you'd stolen! You just agreed you lost all your money at dice, or that you never had any, and your own father has confirmed that you're in debt."

"I won that three thousand off someone after I left the inn."

"Oh! And who might that have been? I imagine they'd be willing to testify?"

"No…I don't know…I'd never seen him before. Some drunkard who wanted to play, and I won. He told me they were selling buffalo cheap in Wuyishan. What should I have done? Given him his money back?"

Judge Feng approached the evidence table and asked permission to speak. Then he turned to Lu, untied the purse from the accused's belt, and showed it to Shang's eldest son, who didn't look at the coins but stared at the purse itself.

"That was my father's," he spat.

As terrible as the situation was, Cí couldn't help but admire Feng's shrewdness. There was a custom among peasants to personalize their purses.

The magistrate nodded and looked over the documents again. "Tell me, Lu," he said, "do you recognize this sickle?"

Lu had shut his eyes in seeming disinterest.

"According to the report," continued the magistrate, "Judge Feng concluded that this is, without a doubt, the murder weapon.

Even though this, along with the money, would be sufficient to condemn you, the law still obliges me to ask you to confess."

"But I've already said—"

"Damn you, Lu! Out of respect for your father you haven't been tortured yet, but you're leaving me little choice."

Lu laughed maniacally. "I couldn't care less!"

A guard hit him across his back with a cane. The magistrate made a gesture, and two guards dragged Lu over to a corner.

"What now?" Cí asked Feng.

"He'll need the gods on his side if he hopes to resist the Mask of Pain," replied the judge.

5

Cí was trembling. He knew about the Mask of Pain, yet he also knew that if someone was accused but didn't confess, any proof against them would be worthless.

The sheriff came forward with the sinister-looking wooden mask; it was reinforced with metal and had two leather straps hanging down. At his command, two of the guards grabbed Lu, who writhed and kicked as they tried to tie the contraption to his face. Cí went numb as he watched his brother howl and bite. Several of the women turned away in fright, but when the guards secured the mask, applause broke out. The sheriff approached Lu, who, having been struck a few more times, had stopped struggling.

"Confess!" shouted the magistrate.

Although he was in chains, Lu was stronger than the guards restraining him, and he suddenly lashed out, hitting the nearest one with the stocks and rushing toward Cí. The guards intercepted Lu and subdued him with another beating before chaining him to the wall. The sheriff struck Lu across the face.

"Confess, and you might be able to eat rice again!" said the sheriff.

"Take this off me!"

At a gesture from the magistrate, the sheriff tightened a handle on the mask, making Lu howl. The next turn of the handle applied pressure directly to his temples, and Lu let out another cry. A couple more turns, Cí knew, and his brother's skull would crack like a nut.

Just confess, brother.

With the next turn, the contraption creaked. An animalistic wail shook the room. Cí couldn't watch. When he opened his eyes again, blood was pouring from Lu's mouth. Cí was just about to shout for mercy when Lu crumpled over.

The magistrate ordered the guards to cease. Lu signaled to the magistrate, who ordered the guards to take the mask off.

"I...confess..." croaked Lu.

Hearing this, Shang's eldest son rushed over and kicked Lu, who barely seemed to notice. The guards pulled the son away and then raised Lu onto his knees to thumbprint the confession paper.

"In the name of the all-powerful Heaven's Son," the magistrate announced, "I declare Lu Song has confessed to the murder of the worthy Shang Li. Execution will be by decapitation."

The magistrate stamped the sentence and concluded proceedings by ordering the guards to take the defendant out. Cí tried to say something to his brother, but Lu pushed him away. Their father was prostrate before Shang's family, begging forgiveness, but they ignored him and left. Cí went over to help his father, who waved him away before getting to his feet and dusting himself off. Without a word, he exited the hall, leaving Cí alone with his bitter thoughts.

But then he felt a hand on his shoulder. It was Cherry, who had crept away from her family.

"Try not to be too upset," she whispered from beneath her hood. "My family will see you're not all like Lu."

ANTONIO GARRIDO

"Lu has dishonored us," Cí managed to say. He tried to push her hood back.

"I have to go," she said. "Pray for us."

Although he knew he'd now be free of his brother, Cí felt overwhelmed with remorse. He felt in his brother's debt. Because he'd protected him when they were younger? Because he worked hard for the family? The tragedy of the moment made Cí forget how Lu had abused him, and all his ignorance and roughness. Cí didn't even care, just then, that Lu was a criminal. He was his brother, and that was all. The Confucian teachings had drummed into Cí respect and obedience for his elders; he somehow couldn't acknowledge the idea that Lu was a murderer. Violent, yes, but a killer?

When Cí woke the next morning, everything seemed the same at first—it was still raining, and lightning could still be seen off in the distance—but then he remembered: Lu was gone.

He found Feng and his aide at the stables. Feng told Cí that he was leaving immediately on a mission that would last several months; he would be traveling overland to Nanchang, and from there they'd take boats along the Yangtze River to the northern frontier.

"But how can you go now, with Lu about to be executed?"

"That won't happen straightaway," said Feng, explaining that, in cases of capital punishment, the Imperial High Tribunal in Lin'an had to confirm the verdict. "Lu will be at the state prison until the confirmation is sent. And that won't happen before autumn."

"And what about an appeal?" implored Cí. "Could we lodge an appeal? You're the best judge in the land, and—"

"Cí, there's nothing to be done. The magistrate knows about these matters, and he'd be deeply offended if I tried to interfere."

Feng passed a bundle to his aide and paused a moment. "The one thing I could perhaps do is recommend they transfer your brother to Sichuan, to the west. I know the governor at the salt mines there. If they work hard, prisoners are allowed to live longer."

"But what about the proof? No one in their right mind would kill for three thousand *qián*—"

"You said it: *in their right mind*. Do you really think that's what Lu is? That story about winning money when he left the tavern…" Feng made a dismissive gesture. "Is an angry drunk able to make rational decisions?"

"Will you speak to the magistrate?"

"I'll try."

"I don't know how to thank you." Cí knelt down.

"I've never told you this, but I think of you like a son, Cí," Feng said, making him stand up. "The God of Fertility has never given me one of my own. All small-minded people want are possessions, money, fortune, when the most valuable thing is a descendant to look after you in your old age and honor you once you're gone." Lightning flashed outside. "Damn this storm! That was nearby," he muttered. "I must go. Say good-bye to your father for me." He placed his hands on Cí's shoulders. "When I'm back in Lin'an, I'll make the appeal."

"Promise you won't forget about Lu."

"Don't worry."

Cí knelt and touched his forehead to the ground—to hide his bitterness, as much as in respect. When he got up Feng was gone.

Cí wanted to speak to his father, who had shut himself in his room. Cí's mother told him to leave his father alone, that anything they did to try to help Lu would only bring more dishonor to the family. Cí decided it was up to him to do something about the appeal.

He asked for an audience with the magistrate, and when he was ushered in to see him, Cí was surprised to be offered something to eat.

"Feng has told me a lot about you," said the magistrate. "It's a real shame about your brother; such a sad affair. But these things happen—don't dwell on it. Take a seat and let me know how I can be of service."

Cí was shocked by how pleasant the magistrate was being.

"Judge Feng said he'd talk to you about the mines in Sichuan," said Cí, bowing. "He said it might be possible to send my brother there."

"Ah, yes, the mines…" The magistrate popped a piece of pastry in his mouth, then licked his fingers. "Listen. In the old days there was no need for laws; it was enough to have the five audiences. The background to a case was presented, the changes on the faces of the audience members were observed, their breathing and their words listened to, and in the fifth audience their gestures were scrutinized and counted. You didn't need anything else to discern the blackness of someone's spirit." He took another mouthful. "But things are different now. Nowadays, a judge may not, let's say…*interpret* events with the same…*informality*. Understand?"

Cí didn't entirely, but he nodded politely anyway.

"Now, in terms of your request for him to be transferred to Sichuan…" He wiped his hands on a napkin and got up to look through some documents. "Yes, here it is: in certain cases, the death penalty can be changed to exile if, and only if, a family member pays sufficient compensation."

Cí listened attentively.

"Unfortunately, in your brother's case, there's no room to maneuver. He is guilty of the worst of crimes." He paused a moment to reflect. "In fact, you should be thanking me. If I had decided that Shang's decapitation had anything to do with ritual magic, not only would Lu be facing death by a thousand cuts, but your whole family would be exiled forever."

I could think of worse fates.

Cí pressed his fists together. He understood that in the eyes of the law the convict's parents could share the guilt, but he wasn't sure what the magistrate was getting at.

"Bao-Pao mentioned to me that your family has property. An area of land worth quite a lot."

Cí nodded.

The magistrate cleared his throat, chuckling. "Bao-Pao also suggested that, under the circumstances, it might be better for me to speak with you than with your father." The magistrate shut the door and then settled down again at the table.

"Apologies," said Cí, "but I'm not sure I understand."

The magistrate shrugged. "The first thing on my mind is a decent meal, but perhaps while we eat, we can come to some agreement on *the sum* that might be needed to free your brother from his predicament."

***

For the rest of the afternoon, Cí thought about the magistrate's proposal—400,000 *qián* was exorbitant, but at the same time it was nothing if it meant saving Lu's life. When Cí entered his house, his father was looking through some papers. His father hid them away in the red chest and turned on Cí.

"The next time you come in without knocking, you'll be sorry."

"You keep a copy of the penal code, I presume?" replied Cí. Cí knew his father would think him impudent, so he continued before any rebuke could come. "We have to talk. There might be a way to help Lu."

"Says who? That swine Feng? Buddha! Why don't you forget about your brother? He's brought shame on this family."

"It doesn't matter who told me. The important thing is that we might be able to use our savings to spare Lu's life."

"*Our* savings?" said Cí's father, his eyes wild. "Since when have you saved any money? Forget about your brother and keep away from Feng."

"But father! The magistrate told me if we bring four hundred thousand *qián*—"

"I said forget it! You have no idea! In six years as an accountant I didn't make more than one hundred thousand! From now on it's just us, so you'd be better off saving your energy for the fields." He crouched down and covered the chest with a cloth.

"Father, there's something about the crime that doesn't add up. I can't just forget Lu—"

Cí's father slapped him. At that, Cí turned and left the house, ignoring his father's shouts to come back, and trying to understand how his father had become a menacing old man.

He walked through the rain to Cherry's house. The funeral altar had become a soggy pile of candles and flowers. He straightened it a bit, then walked past the main entrance on his way to the shack where Cherry often went. He knocked three times with a stone—their code—and waited. He waited for what felt like forever, but then she knocked back.

It was difficult for them to spend time together. The strict rules governing engagement defined precisely the events and festivals at which they were allowed to see each other. Nonetheless, they managed to cross paths from time to time, arranging to go to market on the same day, or brushing hands at the fishing platforms, or stealing looks when no one else was watching. Even though he was never allowed inside, the visits at the shack gave them privacy.

He wanted her. He fantasized about the touch of her pale skin, her lovely round face, her full hips. But it was her feet that he dreamed most about—they were always hidden. He knew Cherry's feet had been bound by her mother since birth to make her seem like she was from an upper-class family, and he imagined they were as small and graceful as his young sister's.

The hammering rain brought Cí back to the present—a night when not even dogs would have been sleeping outside. It was raining as though the gods had burst the banks in the heavens. As he sat in the darkness, he was sure it must be the worst night of his life. He remained there, preferring being drenched to returning home and confronting his father again. He whispered to Cherry through the slatted wall that he loved her, and she knocked once to signal she had heard. They couldn't talk much for fear of waking her family, but it was enough that she was so close. He curled up against the wall, preparing to spend the night sheltered under the eaves of the shack. He fell asleep thinking about the magistrate's offer.

6

Cí was woken by a crack of thunder. He rubbed his eyes and tried to get his bearings, then heard shouting toward the north. He turned and saw a plume of smoke coming from his family's home. Panicking, he ran to the road and joined the large number of villagers also rushing to see what was happening.

Near his house, the smoke grew so thick that Cí could hardly see. Although he was surrounded by screams and cries, he could only vaguely make out some ghostly figures. Suddenly he stumbled into a boy whose terrified eyes stared out from a bloody face. It was his neighbor Chun. Cí went to take him by the arm to ask what had happened, but the limb was only a stump, and before he knew it, Chun had collapsed.

Cí leaped over Chun's body, going deeper into the mess of rubble and logs scattered on the path. He couldn't see his own house, and Chun's had disappeared, too. Everything was in ruins. Panic surged through him again. What suffocated him more than the dense smoke was the certainty that all this rubble could only signify death.

He ran up the mound of beams and debris and heaved aside stone and wood, calling out for his parents and Third.

They must be alive! Dear gods, please!

Pushing on a joist and shifting the remains of a chair, he slipped on a piece of glazed slate but barely noticed when it cut his foot. He scrabbled through the rubble. Suddenly he saw a hand—one of his family's? Then he realized there were others groping in the same spot, and he assumed villagers had come to loot the place. He was about to drive them off when someone began shouting that he'd found something. Cí realized the villagers were only trying to help.

He ran over, pushing people aside, and immediately wished he hadn't. There, in a gap in the wreckage, were the burned corpses of his parents. He lost his footing, falling and striking his head. All became smoke and darkness.

When Cí came to, he was lying in the middle of the street surrounded by strangers. He tried to get up, but someone stopped him. Instead of his worker's rags, he was dressed in white—the color of death and mourning. The taste of smoke was in his throat, its smell in his nose. He tried to remember what had happened, but his mind whirled, and he had no idea what was dream and what was reality.

"What happened?"

"You hit your head," a voice said.

"But what *happened*?"

"Lightning, probably."

"Lightning?"

He tried to remember. Suddenly, a crack—the same sound that had woken him at Cherry's. His family…

It can't be real. I must have dreamed it.

He leaped up and ran down the street. Though it wasn't yet dawn, he could make out the remains of the destroyed house. He screamed until he was hoarse, but for all he implored the gods, the nightmare didn't end.

People were crouched in a circle outside another house, across from the ruins. As Cí approached, they let him through. The smell of death was mixed with the gloomy, bitter aroma of charred wood. He moved forward slowly as his eyes became accustomed to the low light filtering through the ruins. Then he came to a group of corpses on the ground. He recognized Chun and a number of other neighbors. And his parents. Upon seeing their scorched and bloody bodies again, he let out a cry.

He wept for them, but his tears gave him no relief.

Drained, he left the remains. Neighbors told him what had happened: Lightning had struck the hillside behind the village, causing a landslide, and this had been followed by fire. Four houses had been damaged or destroyed, six people dead—but his sister wasn't one of them. Third had been found curled up under some joists, and she had suffered only a sprained ankle.

Cí felt guilty that his last conversation with his father had been in anger, and he wondered whether, if he had returned home from Cherry's, he might have saved his parents. But maybe he had been spared so that he could look after his sister.

Third had been taken in by old No Teeth and his wife. He ran all the way to No Teeth's house and, bursting in, found Third peacefully sleeping under a blanket, far away from all the pain and sadness. He thanked the couple and asked if they would look after Third while he attended to his parents. No Teeth's wife muttered something, but they didn't protest, and Cí went back to the ruins.

He accompanied his parents' bodies to the shelter that Bao-Pao had erected, and he stayed there praying until midday. Then he hurried back to the ruined house to remove anything valuable before the place was looted.

In the light of day he could see that the landslide had damaged six of the twenty or so houses nestled into the hillside; the four in the middle had been completely destroyed. Several of his neighbors were clearing the rubble of their ruined homes. As he approached, a number of them pointed angrily at Cí and accused him of bringing ill fortune upon them.

He gritted his teeth and set to work. He spent hours in the mud and ash, sorting through the jumble of broken furniture, tattered clothing, chunks of wood, and tile. He stopped at times, flooded with tears as he excavated prized family possessions: his mother's porcelain dishes, which had been smashed to pieces; iron pots and pans, battered and dented; and his father's paintbrushes, which, miraculously, were still intact. Cí remembered learning to write with them. He set a few things aside and kept going.

Suddenly he heard laughter behind him. He turned and saw a shadow poking out from behind a wall. Cí went over and found Peng, his neighbors' six-year-old son, known for being a rascal and brighter than most. Cí offered the boy some nuts from a package he'd found in the wreckage, but Peng refused, smiling wickedly. Cí repeated the offer and Peng inched closer.

"You can have some if you tell me what happened." Peng glanced around as though frightened of someone catching him eating treats—no doubt because of his bad teeth.

"There was lightning and the mountain fell down," he said as he tried to snatch some nuts. But Cí held them high so he couldn't get any.

"Are you sure?"

"And I saw men…"

"Men?"

The boy was about to answer when a shout stopped him. It was his mother, and he hurried off in her direction. He was about to disappear around the corner when Cí called out and threw the package of nuts to him. Peng caught them and turned, his mother already beside him. She gave the little boy a smack and led him away.

Cí shook his head and went back to his task.

By midafternoon, Cí had moved everything but the largest rocks. He was looking for the chest containing the money his father had saved to return to Lin'an so he could use it to pay the magistrate's blackmail. He was beginning to lose hope that he would be able to move the very largest rocks, or that he would find the chest, when suddenly he glimpsed the chest poking out from under a large pillar.

I'll get you out from under there if it's the last thing I do.

He positioned a beam between a rock and the pillar for leverage and pushed down on it as hard as he could. He tried a few more times before making a higher ridge with another rock and then yanking on the makeshift lever. Finally the pillar gave way; as it did, Cí fell on his back. When the dust settled, he saw that the lock on the chest had been broken, and inside he found no money, just clothes and rags. He couldn't believe it.

Then he heard a voice behind him. "I'm sorry. My wife says we can't look after her any longer."

It was No Teeth, with Third beside him. His sister was frowning, looking confused, and clinging to a cloth doll.

"My daughter has another one that's the same," said No Teeth, pointing to the doll. "She can keep it if she wants."

Cí bit his lip. He was beginning to feel it was him against the world, but he brought his fists together and bowed, thanking No Teeth. No Teeth didn't return the bow but instead left as stealthily as he'd come.

Third looked at Cí as if he might have some kind of explanation. Expectant, quiet, obedient—she was always lovely, Cí thought, even though she was so ill. He looked at the ruins and at her again. What could he do with her? He found a thick branch and put her astride it, playing giddyap horsey for a minute. In spite of her cough, she laughed. He laughed, too, though he was gripped by sadness.

Cí managed to get them some boiled rice before nightfall, and he fed Third, saving only a few grains for himself. That and a drink of water would have to do. Next to the ruins, Cí used dry branches to construct a bed with a little roof over it, and as he put Third to bed, he explained that their parents had gone on a long journey to heaven. He told her he'd be looking after her from now on, and that she'd need to be good and listen to him. Then he said he'd build them a new house, a big one, with a garden full of flowers and a swing.

Once Third was asleep, Cí went back to work in the failing light, sifting through the rubble in search of the red chest. Eventually he gave up, exhausted. Someone must have stolen it.

He collapsed next to his sister with the impossible problem of money on his mind: If it had taken his father six years to save up 100,000 *qián*, how on earth would he get together the 400,000 that the magistrate was demanding?

7

Before the night was through, Cí was cursing the storm gods again. Woken by a fresh downpour, he checked to make sure Third was staying dry and then ran to try and save what he'd salvaged, hoping he could sell it. Once he'd put it all under the shelter, he considered the assortment of objects: his father's books, a stone pillow, a couple of iron cooking pots, some singed woolen blankets, a few pieces of clothing, two sickles with charred handles, and a chipped scythe. The whole lot probably wouldn't fetch more than 2,000 *qián* at the market. There was Third's medicine, too. Plus, a sack of rice, another of tea, a jar of salt, and some smoked ham, all of which his mother had bought for Feng's stay and were probably worth more than the rest put together. These basics would help them survive while he got organized. He'd found 400 *qián* in coins and an exchange note worth another 5,000; added to the possessions, it might have been worth a little more than 7,000 *qián*—about the same as a family of eight would earn in two months. He still couldn't figure out where the savings had gone.

As the sun came up, he had one last search around. He went through the pieces of wood again, pulled aside the pillars, and looked under a bamboo bed base. Nothing. He laughed in desperation.

Until he found Shang's body, all he'd had to worry about was getting up early; he'd sulked about having to go out plowing again and spent his time yearning to be back at university. But he'd had a roof over his head and his family around him. Now he had only Third and a few bits of loose change. He kicked a beam and thought about his parents. He hadn't been able to understand his father recently—always an upright man, possibly a little severe, but honest and far more fair than most people. Cí couldn't help but feel guilty for having been rebellious and for not returning that night.

Finally, after turning over a nest of cockroaches, he gave up on the search and woke Third. She'd barely opened her eyes when she started asking for their mother. While cutting her a strip of the ham, Cí reminded her about their parents' long journey.

"They're still watching over you, so you have to make sure you're good."

"But where are they?"

"Up behind those clouds," he said, looking off into the distance. "Quickly, eat up. Otherwise they'll get angry. You know what father's like when he gets angry."

She nodded and took the meat to chew. "The house is still broken," she said.

"It was such an old house. The one I'll build will be new and big. But you'll have to help me, OK?"

Third swallowed, nodding. As Cí buttoned her jacket, she sang the song their mother had sung every morning.

"*Five buttons represent the five virtues that a child should aspire to: sweetness, a good heart, respect, thriftiness, and obedience.*"

"That wasn't mother saying that, was it?" asked Cí.

"She just whispered it in my ear," said Third.

He smiled and kissed her on the cheek. His thoughts turned to the Rice Man, who he thought might hold the answer to their problems.

Raising 400,000 *qián* wouldn't be easy, but during the night Cí had come up with an idea that he thought just might work.

Before heading out, he took the copy of the penal code he'd rescued from the debris and consulted the chapters on capital punishment and the commuting of sentences. Once he understood, he made an offering to his parents—a strip of the ham on an improvised altar. When he finished praying for them, he picked up Third and walked with her on his hip to the Rice Man's ranch. The Rice Man owned the vast majority of the land around the village.

A well-built man covered in tattoos stood at the entrance to the ranch. He looked distinctly unwelcoming, but when Cí told him what he'd come for, the man led them through the gardens and up to a small pavilion that looked out over the rice fields on the mountainside. An old man was resting on a couch, being fanned by a concubine. He looked at Cí disdainfully, but his attitude changed when the guard announced Cí's intentions.

"Here to sell Lu's lands? Well, in that case!" The Rice Man offered Cí a seat on the floor. "I am sorry about your family. But you have to understand, that doesn't change the facts. This is still a difficult time to be doing business."

Especially for someone in my position.

Cí bowed in response before sending Third off to feed the ducks. Then he sat, careful to appear relaxed. He was prepared.

"Many people speak of your intelligence," Cí told the Rice Man. "And I have also heard about your head for business." The old man nodded vainly in agreement. Cí continued, "Doubtless, you think my situation obliges me to undersell my brother's properties. But I haven't come to give anything away for free; I know what I have is valuable."

The old man leaned back. Would he hear Cí out, or send him for a flogging? Eventually he gestured for Cí to carry on.

"I happen to know that Bao-Pao was trying to make a deal with my brother," Cí lied. "He has been interested in Lu's property since long before my brother came to own it."

"I don't see how this could be of interest to me," the old man said with contempt. "I've got plenty of land as it is—I'd need to make slaves of the people of ten villages to cultivate what I already have."

"Clearly. And that's why I'm here, rather than speaking to Bao-Pao."

"Boy, get to the point, or I'll have you thrown out."

"You have far more land than Bao-Pao. You are richer, but he is still more powerful than you. He's the sergeant. You, sir, with all due respect, are only a landowner."

The old man grunted. Cí, sensing he was on the right track, went on.

"Everyone in the village knows of Bao-Pao's interest in the lands. And that Lu refused to sell, time and again, because of a family enmity."

"Your brother won the lands one night at the tables. Do you think I don't know this?"

"And my brother refused to sell them for the same reason as the previous owner: the creek passes through his borders, so there's irrigation even when there isn't much rain. You own the lower lands, which are supplied by water from the river, but Bao-Pao's lands are on the higher slopes, so he has to use the pedal pumps for irrigation."

"Which he can't use because they pass through my property. And? I have all my land and plenty of access to water, too. Why would I be interested in your miserable little plot?"

"To stop me from selling to Bao-Pao."

The Rice Man was silent.

"Think about it. The power he already has, plus how much he'd be able to grow if he had access to Lu's stream…"

The Rice Man seemed to be trying to think of a comeback. He knew Cí was right. How much it was going to cost him was another matter.

"That property is worth nothing to me, boy. If Bao-Pao wants it, he can be my guest."

He's bluffing. Keep going.

"Third!" Cí shouted, getting to his feet. "Leave those ducks, and let's go!" Turning back to the Rice Man he said, "Fair enough. I suppose it's to be expected that the sergeant gets his way, and the landowner is powerless to stop him."

"How dare you!"

Cí didn't answer. He began making his way down the steps from the pavilion.

"Two hundred thousand *qián!*" the Rice Man shouted. "I'll give you two hundred thousand *qián* for the land."

"What about four hundred thousand?" asked Cí calmly, stopping and looking back at the Rice Man.

"Are you serious?" the old man sneered. "That land isn't worth half what I've offered; anyone would know that."

You might know it, but your green-eyed monster doesn't.

"Bao-Pao has offered three hundred and fifty thousand," Cí lied again—it was all or nothing now. "The price of getting one up on him will be another fifty thousand on top."

"No child tells me how much I should pay for a piece of land!" roared the old man.

"As you wish, sir. I'm sure it will make you happy looking out over Bao-Pao's lands in the future."

"Three hundred thousand. And if you try and go a grain of rice above that, you'll be sorry."

Cí began down the steps again but stopped—300,000 *qián* was at least one and a half times the worth of Lu's lands. Turning, he found the Rice Man on the step immediately above him. They both knew it was a good deal.

"One last thing," said the Rice Man when they had the lease papers in front of them. "You can be sure that I'll measure the property, down to the very last *mu*. And I swear, if there is even the tiniest bit missing, you'll regret it."

By midmorning Cí was at the market with the objects he'd saved from the house, but getting anything like the 500 *qián* he needed was going to be difficult. He reached the 500 *qián* by throwing in the iron pots and the knives, which he had hoped to keep. Hardly anyone in the village could read, so the books were desirable only for burning. In exchange for them, he got the use of an abandoned barn—a place for Third to rest. He kept only the food and his father's copy of the penal code. After the market, he left Third at the barn and charged her with guarding the ham.

"Watch out for cats! And if anyone comes, scream really loudly."

Third stood beside the ham and made a face like a ferocious animal. Laughing, Cí promised he'd be back soon. He closed the barn door and set off in the direction of Bao-Pao's residence.

When he arrived at the annex where the corpses were being kept, he began thinking about the funeral arrangements for his parents. His father's coffin had been made a long time before, as stipulated by the *Book of Rites,* the *Liji.* When people reached their sixties, the coffin and all the objects necessary for a funeral were supposed to be serviced once a year; when they were in their seventies, once every season; in their eighties, once a month; and when they were in their nineties, every day. His father had been sixty-two, but his mother had not reached fifty yet, so Cí would need to have a coffin made for her. He found the carpenter busy speaking with other victims' families; it was going to cost Cí a lot to get a coffin quickly.

He went over to his parents' bodies and bowed. They hadn't been washed, so he scrubbed them down using a bundle of wet straw. He hoped his parents would forgive the fact that he didn't have candles or incense. He prayed again for their spirits, promising them he'd look after Third. It hit him then that his life would never be the same, and he realized how very alone he was. But he was wasting time—time the Being of Wisdom had given him to negotiate his brother's release—and after bowing once more to his parents' corpses, he left the annex and headed out into the overcast day.

<hr/>

A servant led Cí to the magistrate's private apartments. The magistrate was in the bath, being washed by one of his aides. Cí had never seen such an enormously fat man. When he entered, the magistrate sent his aide away.

"Very punctual—just the kind of person I like to do business with." He reached out for a tray of rice pastries and offered them to Cí, who declined.

"I've come to talk about my brother. Your honor guaranteed me that you would commute the death sentence if I paid the fine—"

"I said I would try. Have you brought the money?"

"But, your honor, you promised—"

"Hold on! Have you got the money or not?" The magistrate got out of the bath, totally naked. Though somewhat embarrassed, Cí refused to be intimidated.

"Three hundred thousand. It's all I have." He laid out the notes on top of the rice pastries.

The magistrate counted the money enthusiastically. "We did say four hundred thousand..." He raised an eyebrow but held on to the money.

"But you'll set him free?"

"Set him free? Don't make me laugh. We only discussed transferring him to the Sichuan mines."

Cí grimaced. It wasn't the first time someone had tried to cheat him, but there was a lot more at stake this time. He managed to appear unruffled.

"Maybe I misheard, but I understood that the money corresponded to the compensation established by the Ransom Scale."

"The Ransom Scale?" The magistrate feigned surprise. "Please. The scale you refer to has entirely different quantities. Commutation requires *twelve thousand* ounces of silver, not the pittance you've brought."

Cí was quickly realizing there would be little point in appealing to the magistrate's good will. Luckily, he'd come prepared. He took some notes from his bag and read them aloud to the magistrate.

"Twelve thousand ounces if the offender is an official in the higher levels of government, up to the fourth echelon; five thousand and four thousand for anyone up to the fourth, fifth, and sixth echelons." He found himself gaining in confidence as he read. "Two thousand five hundred for anyone in the seventh echelon, as well as inferiors and those with degrees in literature; two thousand for any person with a degree." He tossed the notes down triumphantly on the rice pastries. "And one thousand two hundred ounces of silver for a normal individual, as in the case of my brother!"

"So!" exclaimed the magistrate. "A legal expert, all of a sudden."

"Looks like it." Even Cí was a little surprised at his own forthrightness.

"Your knowledge of numbers, however, is somewhat less impressive, seeing as twelve hundred ounces of silver is worth only eight hundred and fifty thousand *qián*."

But Cí kept on. "I knew that. Which is why I also knew you were never going to reduce the sentence. You just came up with a fee you thought I might be able to raise. Tell me, what will your superiors in Jianningfu think about this?"

"Quite the learned little man..." And the magistrate's tone hardened. "Let's see, then, since you know so much: Is there any chance that you might also have been involved in your brother's crime?"

Cí remembered what the magistrate had said about the murder having something to do with ritual magic.

Vermin. This man is pure vermin.

He changed his approach. "My humblest apologies, venerable magistrate—my nerves must have gotten the better of me. It was a bad night. I barely know what I'm saying." He bowed. "But please allow me to point out that the amount I've brought is more than the penal code asks."

The magistrate covered himself up and began drying the rolls of his belly with a black towel.

"I'll try and be a little clearer, boy: there is no way your brother's getting out of this, OK? I should really have had him executed by now, according to the wishes of Shang's family, so even if I were to send him to Sichuan, that would still be a lot. And what's more, the only person with the authority to allow such a thing is the emperor himself."

"I see," said Cí. "In that case, I'll take my money back and begin the appeal."

"Appeal? On what grounds would you appeal? Your brother has confessed, and all the evidence is against him."

"So you won't mind if it's the High Court Tribunal that decides the sentence."

The magistrate bit his lip. "I'll tell you what we'll do," said the man. "I'll forget your impertinence today, and you'll forget we ever had this conversation. I'll promise to do everything I can."

"I'm not sure that's enough," said Cí. "Either you authorize a commutation, or I'm going to need my money back. I'll have to take it to your superiors in the province prefecture."

Suddenly angry, the magistrate looked at Cí as if he were trash.

"Or maybe I just give the order for your brother to have his throat slit? Do you honestly think a little runt like you can come in here, threaten me, and get away with it?"

Now it was Cí's turn to be worried; this was getting out of hand. Why had he given the money up front?

"Please accept my apologies. I'm sorry if anything I've said has offended you, but I really need my money—"

Then there was another voice in the room. "*Your* money?" And Bao-Pao stepped into view. "You wouldn't be referring to a sum obtained by selling a lot of land, would you?"

Cí remembered the tattooed guard at the Rice Man's place. He had thought it strange, at the time, that the guard disappeared. The man obviously had more than one employer.

"Yes."

"Well then, what you mean to say is *my* money," said Bao-Pao menacingly, advancing on Cí. "Or did no one tell you? I altered Lu's sentence this morning, adding a clause that has to do with the expropriation of property—"

"But…but I'd already sold it."

"Property, unfortunately, that had already been ceded to me," said Bao-Pao.

Cí went pale.

Retrieve what you can and get out of here as quickly as possible.

Bao-Pao had joined in to outmaneuver him; if the magistrate had wanted to, he could have had the property confiscated during the judgment, but this way it meant Bao-Pao would end up with both the fine *and* the property.

Cí shrugged. "It's only a shame that you didn't get the second installment as well."

"What second installment?" Both men were suddenly interested.

"Oh, the Rice Man was extremely keen on the property. He knew how much you both wanted it, so to ensure the sale, he agreed to pay me a second installment. Another three hundred thousand *qián*. Yes. Once he'd had a check done of the lands and made sure of the legality of the transaction, another three hundred thousand *qián*. Of course, I'd be more than happy to pass that amount to you both, if you follow through on your promise."

"Another three hundred thousand?" Bao-Pao was astonished. He must have known that it was far more than the property was really worth, but greed was clearly getting the better of him, too. Then the magistrate stepped forward.

"And when did he say he'd pay you?"

"This afternoon. As soon as I showed him the deed of property—although he also wanted to see a copy of my brother's sentence to make sure the property doesn't have any debts, charges, mortgage arrangements, or other concerns attached to it."

"So, without the expropriation clause."

"If you want me to bring you that money…"

It took the magistrate only a moment to decide. He called for a scribe and told him to draw up a copy of the original sentence.

"With today's date," added Cí.

"Fine," said the magistrate, signing and handing over the document. "Bring the money, and I promise to release your brother."

It was obvious to Cí that the magistrate was lying through his teeth. Cí made an effort not to show it.

Cí had to make sure his parents were buried properly. Two of Bao-Pao's slaves wheeled the coffins to the Mountain of Rest, a nearby burial place planted with bamboo. Cí looked for a spot that would face the sunrise, and where the wind would whisper through the trees. When the last shovelful of earth covered the coffins, Cí knew that his time in the village was over. If things had been different, he might have rebuilt the house, taken work in the fields, gone through the mourning period, and then married Cherry. Maybe after a few years, if children, money, and all life's considerations had allowed, he might have gone back to Lin'an to take the Imperial exams and find a good husband for Third. But there was nothing left; it was time for him to flee.

He bade farewell to his parents' bodies and asked for their guidance wherever he went. He pretended to Bao-Pao's men that he was going to see the Rice Man, but when they could no longer see him, Cí went to the annex where his brother was being held.

Staying well hidden in the undergrowth, he checked to see how many guards there were; though there was only one, he had no idea how was he going to get past him. He had to speak to his brother before he went. For all the evidence against him, something in Cí's heart told him his brother was no murderer.

He noticed a small window at the back of the annex. He quietly rolled a barrel into position and climbed up on it; the window was too small to fit through, but he peered into the dark interior, and, as his eyes adjusted, he saw a figure curled up in the corner. He was tied up, his clothes bloody, and his face—his tongue had been cut out and there were no eyes in the sockets.

Cí fell off the barrel. His mind roiled with what he'd seen. He stumbled around for a moment, then vomited. There was no way that tortured, broken figure was still alive. There was nothing left of Lu—only the bitterness Cí would always carry.

He had to get out of the village. The Rice Man would be expecting property that wasn't his anymore, either that or money

Cí didn't have, and neither he nor the magistrate would care about his excuses. He ran to Cherry's to tell her his plans and ask her to wait until he'd proved his innocence. But her answer was unequivocal: she could never marry a fugitive, let alone someone who had neither property nor work.

"Is this about my brother?" cried Cí through her window lattice. "If that's it, you don't have to worry anymore. He's been punished. Do you hear? He's dead. Dead!"

He waited, but Cherry didn't reply. It would be the last time they ever spoke.

PART TWO

8

Cí found Third as he'd left her: content and oblivious to any danger. Cí praised her for guarding the ham and cut her a slice as reward. To stand out less, he changed out of his white mourning clothes and into a coarse burlap gown that had belonged to his father. He packed the few remaining coins, the penal code, some clothes, and the ham; then he hid the 5,000-*qián* note in the lining of Third's jacket.

"How would you like to travel on a boat?" He didn't wait for her to answer but began tickling her. "You're going to *love* going on a boat."

Cí tried to appear cheerful, even though he felt far from it as they walked to the river dock. Initially he had thought they would travel to Lin'an overland, along the northern road, but that was the busiest route. Even though the trip by river was longer, it would also be safer. At harvest time, numerous rice barges and smaller boats carrying precious wood left from the dock for the maritime port of Fuzhou. From Fuzhou they could follow the coast up to the capital. Cí planned to board one of these barges with Third.

To avoid the crowds, they went to the southern dock, where loading and unloading took place. He came across a large, half-sunken-looking barge where an old man with blotchy skin—the captain, presumably—was urinating over the edge as he watched his two sailors preparing the vessel. Having overheard someone saying Lin'an was its destination, Cí waited for the captain to disembark and then asked him if he and Third could travel on the barge. The captain was suspicious: though it wasn't unusual for villagers to travel on the barges, they usually negotiated with the shipping agents.

"The thing is," said Cí, "I owe the shipping agent some money, but I don't have it at the moment." He offered the captain a handful of coins.

"That's hardly enough!" said the captain. "And anyway, you can see how full the barge is already."

"Please, sir. My sister's terribly ill, and I can get the medicine she needs only in Lin'an."

"So go overland."

"Please...She won't survive the trip overland."

"Listen, boy, do I look like a charity? If you want to come along, you're going to have to come up with the cash."

Cí, keeping the 5,000-*qián* note secret, said the coins were all he had. The captain wouldn't budge.

"I'll work during the voyage," offered Cí.

"What good will you be?"

"I'll work hard, I promise. And I can get more money in Lin'an."

"Who's waiting for you there? The emperor with a sack of gold?" But then he glanced at Third, who was pale and tired after the night in the barn and the walk to the docks, and the captain's heart seemed to soften. He spat on the ground and turned away. "Damn it! All right, you can come. But you have to do everything I say, and when we get to Lin'an, you'll be the one unloading *all* the cargo, got it?"

Cí couldn't thank him enough.

The barge moved slowly, like a fish trying to extricate itself from mud. Cí helped the sailors guide the barge with thick bamboo poles, while the captain, whose name was Wang, stood at the rudder shouting and cursing. Cí wasn't convinced they'd ever get anywhere—the barge was so low in the water with cargo. Gradually, though, the current grew stronger, and they picked up speed. Cí felt briefly soothed by the thought of leaving the village behind, once and for all.

Cí spent the day helping steer the boat away from the banks with the barge poles and fishing with a borrowed line. A sailor at the prow checked the depth of the river, and another at the stern propelled them along with a pole whenever the current slackened. When the sun went down, the captain dropped anchor in the middle of the river, lit a lantern to attract mosquitoes, and, having checked to see that the cargo was all stowed properly, announced they would start again at dawn. Cí settled down between two sacks of grain next to Third. They ate some boiled rice prepared by the crew, honoring their parents' spirits before they began. The onboard conversation soon died down, until the only sound in the night was the lapping water. Cí continued to ask himself what he could have done to anger the gods, what it was that had provoked them to ravage his family.

Worn out by everything that had happened and by his own internal debate, he shut his eyes, comforting himself with the idea that his parents were still watching over him and Third. It wasn't that he was unacquainted with death—he knew of women dying in childbirth, stillborns, children dying young from illness or malnutrition; he knew of deadly floods and typhoons—but none of that had prepared him for the deaths of his parents and his brother. Either the gods were capricious, or he'd done something terribly wrong and this was his punishment. And the pain he felt—he had no idea how he would ever be rid of it.

And he didn't know what course his life would take next. Lost and overwhelmed, he knew all he could do was focus on the present—getting away from the village, protecting his sister. That was all.

By the time the sun came up the barge crew was already busy. Wang had hauled anchor and was giving instructions to his sailors when a small rowboat crashed into the barge. Wang shouted at the man at the oars, but he was an old fisherman with a foolish grin and didn't seem to care. Then a small fleet of fishing vessels appeared and swarmed past the barge.

"Damn them, they ought to be hanged!" said the captain.

"We've sprung a leak!" shouted one of the sailors. "The cargo will be ruined!"

Cursing, Wang immediately ordered them to move close to shore, just in case. Luckily, they weren't far from Jianningfu, the main confluence of rivers in the region where there was a large town; they'd be able to get repair materials there. Being near the shore, though, would also make them easy prey for marauding bandits; the captain told everyone, Cí and Third included, to keep their eyes peeled.

The Jianningfu jetty, when they got there, was a hive of dealers, hawkers, livestock, beggars of all kinds, prostitutes, and peons. The stench was of rotten fish, cooking oil, and unwashed, rancid bodies.

As soon as they docked, a small man with a goatee rushed over demanding the docking fee. Wang drove him off with a few kicks; they weren't stopping to do business, Wang roared, but because some idiot, probably a local, had damaged the barge.

After leaving the younger of the sailors to guard the boat with Cí and sending the older sailor, Ze, to buy bamboo and hemp for the repair, Wang went for provisions. The younger sailor grumbled over being left behind, but Cí was pleased since he wouldn't have to wake Third, who was fast asleep again, nestled between two sacks of grain. There was a bracing breeze coming off the mountain, and Cí covered his sister with an extra blanket. The younger sailor stood watching the prostitutes go by with their makeup and bright clothes, and he soon spat out the straw he'd been chewing, announced he was going for a stroll, and jumped down to the dock. Cí didn't mind being alone; he decided to make himself useful by scrubbing the deck.

When he looked up, a girl was standing beside the barge. She wore a threadbare red robe that made no secret of her curves. Her smile showed off a full set of teeth. He blushed when she asked if it was his barge.

She's even prettier than Cherry.

"I'm just, um, looking after it," he stuttered.

She made Cí nervous. Aside from Cherry, the women in his family, and a few glimpses of the courtesans in Lin'an when he went to the tea shops with Judge Feng, he'd barely had any contact with women. The girl strolled a few steps away from the barge, and Cí watched her hips sway. When she turned and approached again, with her eyes fixed on his, Cí didn't know where he was supposed to look.

"So, is it just you traveling?" she asked.

"Yes…I mean no!" Cí noticed that she was looking at the burn scars on his hands, so he hid them behind his back.

"But you're all alone now," she smiled.

"Y-yes. The others have gone to buy tools."

"What about you? Don't you get to go ashore?"

"They told me I have to watch the barge."

"So obedient!" She came closer. "And have they also said you aren't allowed to play with the girls?"

Cí couldn't think of an answer; he was being pulled into the girl's spell.

"I…I don't have any money."

"*You* don't need to worry about that." She smiled. "*Good-looking* guys get a special. Wouldn't you like a nice cup of hot tea?" She pointed to a cabin nearby. "My mother makes a peach tea—that's how I got my name: Peach Blossom."

"I really can't leave the barge," said Cí.

She smiled and walked slowly to the cabin. A few minutes later, she emerged with a teapot and two cups. Blushing as he was, Cí couldn't hide how much he wanted her.

"Don't just stand there," she said. "Give me a hand up."

He offered her his hand while trying to hide the worst of his scars beneath his sleeve cuffs. One quick heave and she was aboard. She leaned over the side to get the tea, took a seat on a bale, and offered him a cup.

"Come *on*, I'm not going to charge you for it."

Offering tea, he knew, was a tactic used by all "flowers," as the prostitutes liked to call themselves. Surely, he told himself, he could accept a cup of tea without any obligation, and anyway, he was thirsty for one. As he drank the tea, which was spicy, he looked at the girl—her painted-on eyebrows, her rice-powder makeup. She began to sing while using her hands to make motions like those of a flying bird.

As the melody floated up around him, he took another sip of the hot tea. Cí felt caressed by the song, the tea, the air, the lapping of the river. He began to feel very drowsy, and sweet sleep soon swallowed him whole.

Cí woke to cold water being thrown at his face.

"Slacker!" shouted Wang, hoisting him off the dock. "Where's the damned, damned, *damned* boat?"

What is happening?

Cí's head pounded and spun. The old man shook him, but he couldn't talk.

"Drunk! Where's my sailor? And where in damned hell is my boat?"

The older sailor threw another bucket of water on him, and Cí began to feel less dizzy. A series of images: docking at the jetty... the captain and the sailor going off...the girl...the tea...and then, nothing. He understood in an instant he'd been drugged and the boat stolen—and with it, his little sister.

Desperate, he pleaded with the captain to help him find Third. Wang shouted that all he really needed to do was throttle Cí for abandoning the barge.

9

Wang could have threatened to tear him to shreds, but Cí would have done anything necessary to find his sister.

He scrambled after Wang, who had dived into the crowds looking for a boat to rent. He didn't have any luck until he came across a couple of young fishermen next to a skiff. They said they'd rent their boat, but when Wang tried to hire them to row, and when they heard he was going after bandits, they changed their minds: no way would they risk their lives or put their boat in danger. They would agree only to sell the boat—at a massively inflated price. Wang couldn't change their minds, so he paid them and hopped onto the skiff with Ze. Cí tried to get aboard, too.

"Damn! What the *hell* do you think you're doing?" cried Wang.

"My sister's on your boat," he said.

Wang looked over at Ze—clearly they needed Cí's help.

"Fine, but if we don't recover that damn cargo, I swear you'll pay for it in blood, which I'll beat out of you myself. Both of you, get the damn skiff ready, and I'll go and find us some weapons—"

"Boss," Cí interrupted. "Is that a good idea? Do you know anything about weapons?"

"By God, I know enough to cut out your damn tongue and eat it grilled! How would you suggest we stop them, eh? Offer them a cup of tea?"

"But," reasoned Cí, "we have no idea how many there are, or if they're armed. They probably have a better idea about fighting than a couple of old guys and a country boy like me. If we try and attack them with bows and arrows we have no idea how to use, they'll slaughter us."

"So we just go and ask nicely?"

"While you argue," said Ze, "they're getting away."

"Damn you, Ze! Why don't you just do what I say?" screamed the captain.

"The boy's got a point," said the old sailor. "And if we head off right now, we'll find them within an hour. They're bound to unload downriver. They'll be in a rush, and they won't have any transport. It will be easy to corner them."

"And how do you know all that? A prophet as well as a sailor now!"

"They'll see their cargo is wood, won't they? And they must know that upriver, wood's worth nothing, whereas down at Fuzhou they'll get a good price. Plus they'll want the easy way out—downriver, *with* the current."

"And finding them in an hour?"

"The leak. The barge won't stay afloat long," said Ze.

"Yes! The leak!" said the captain. "They'll have to make for shore, and as you said, how would they have transport—"

"Who knows, boss, but I think we should just look for the first inlet or tributary where they might be able to hide from prying eyes. If you happen to know of any—"

"I damn well do, as it goes! Come on, let's get going!"

Cí loaded the materials they'd bought for the repair and jumped on board. Each of them grabbed a pole and began pushing the skiff in pursuit of the bandits.

Just as Ze had predicted, within an hour they caught sight of the barge making its way up a tributary. It was listing badly, and it moved slowly and close to shore. They had no idea how many were on board, but only one person was at the helm, which Cí thought was a good sign.

They pushed the skiff faster.

During the pursuit they had considered different strategies, and whether to board the barge as soon as they caught up to it or wait until it had been unloaded. When they saw that there were three bandits, they decided on Cí's plan: he would pretend to be a sick merchant to awaken the robbers' greed, and they would get as close to the bandits as possible. "The last thing they'll expect," Cí said, "is for two old men and one so ill to attack them."

"Then, on my signal," Wang said, "we'll hit them with the poles and try to knock them into the water. But we've got to reach them before they dock."

As they approached the barge, Cí covered himself with a blanket, and Wang smiled broadly in greeting to the three bandits and the prostitute.

From under the blanket, Cí could hear Wang asking the robbers to help with his wealthy master, who had suddenly fallen ill. They began discussing a price. Heart hammering, and nearly overcome by the rancid smell of fish in the skiff, Cí waited for the signal. But suddenly, silence.

Something's wrong.

"Now!" shouted Wang.

Cí sprang to his feet, swinging a pole at the man nearest to him and hitting him in the gut. Wang did the same with the man at the stern. Both wobbled on the edge of the barge and, after receiving another blow each, toppled into the water.

Ze wasn't so lucky: the third man had drawn a dagger and was advancing on him. But Cí and Wang used their poles to push him into the river. Ze slapped the prostitute, pushed her to the deck, and stood over her. While Wang used his pole to keep the three robbers from reboarding, Cí ran through the cargo shouting for Third. He quickly grew desperate, but then heard a tiny voice from among the sacks. Under a sheet, there she was, clinging tightly to her doll. She looked even more ill than before and very frightened.

When Cí asked that the prostitute be allowed to stay aboard, Wang rolled his eyes in disbelief.

"They made her do it. And she saved my sister."

"It's true," said Third, who was hiding behind Cí's legs.

"You'll believe anything! Open your eyes! This 'flower' is bitter and thorny—they're all the same. She'll say anything to try and save herself."

They had pushed off from the tributary, staving off the bandits with the poles and heading to the far side of the river, where the current was too strong for the bandits to swim through.

Cí tried again to persuade Wang.

"Why should I?" continued Wang, exasperated. "She probably only looked after your little sister so she could sell her to a brothel. I ought to throw her in the water for the robbing, lying serpent she is. Stop arguing and help me with this wood."

Cí looked at Peach Blossom, who was crouched down, appearing so pitiful she reminded him of a stray dog that had been beaten so mercilessly that it could trust no one. Her suffering seemed a reflection of his own.

"I'll pay for her passage," said Cí.

"Wait, is my hearing playing tricks on me? Did I just hear you say that?"

"I guess so," said Cí, turning to his sister and taking the 5,000-*qián* note from her jacket. "This," he said, thrusting it at Wang, "should get the three of us to Lin'an."

"Why…you said you didn't have anything else! Well, it's your money. Do what you want with it. The harpy is your problem, but when she plucks out your eyes, don't come crying to me."

By midday, they'd repaired the barge: the bundles of reeds had been assembled and the straw and tar caulks had stopped the leak. Wang and Ze each took a celebratory swig of rice liquor. Meanwhile, Cí continued to bail the water that threatened to rot the wood cargo. He was almost done when Wang came over.

"Hey, kid. I wanted to say thanks."

"I don't deserve your thanks, sir. I was an idiot to let the girl come aboard like that…"

"Enough, enough. It wasn't all your fault. I made you stay aboard, and my other sailor just wandered off. On the bright side, I'm rid of one useless sailor, we've got the boat back, and," he said with a laugh, "we've been saved from a fair bit of paddling!"

Cí agreed. "The robbers did a good amount of that work for us!"

Wang examined the side of the boat. Looking concerned once more, he spat in the river.

"I don't like the idea of stopping in Xiongjiang. There's nothing to be gained hanging around this county—a slit throat maybe, if you're lucky." Parting his jacket, he showed a long scar running across his chest. "Robbers and whores, the lot of them! Not a good place to buy supplies, but we'll probably have to do it anyway. That caulk won't last much more than a day."

After a quick meal of boiled rice and carp, they set off toward the City of Death, Wang's name for Xiongjiang. As they traveled along the river, Cí's thoughts turned to Feng—how much he admired the judge, and how he hoped Feng's mission wouldn't keep him away from Lin'an for too long—and then to his parents, the memory of whom saddened Cí immediately. Third came over to where he was sitting, and she could see something was wrong. He said he just felt a little ill and then cut her a slice of the ham. He carried her to the stern, where they sat together.

Soon the prostitute joined them. "I heard you before," said Peach Blossom. "When you were defending me, I mean."

"Don't get involved," he said. "I did it for my sister." The prostitute's proximity made him uncomfortable.

"Do you still think I'm going to trick you?"

"Who wouldn't?"

"This is exactly what I mean!" she said, standing up. "I thought for a moment you might be different. That perhaps you'd seen something in me. You have no idea what a girl like me has been through. I've worked since I was a child, and all I have for it is this dirty, battered body, lice in my hair, beggars' rags…"

She broke down crying, but Cí was unmoved.

"I don't need to know," he said, getting up and looking back along the boat at Wang. The old captain stood at the rudder; with his chin lifted and eyes half-closed, he radiated calm. Cí didn't want to get into an argument with the prostitute. He didn't feel like doing much at all.

As he watched over Third, Cí was surprised to catch himself glancing furtively at Peach Blossom every now and then. He was increasingly captivated by her graceful movements, the apparent delicacy of her gaze, the softness of her complexion, the very faint flush to her cheeks.

Why have I wasted the last of my money on her?

The next time he glanced over, he was shocked to find her looking straight back at him; it was like a sudden flash of light in the dark, illuminating his most intimate depths. He couldn't break free of her gaze.

She seemed to float toward him in the dark, then took his hand and led him to the empty skiff, which was tied up alongside the barge. His heart trembled as she moved her hands underneath his shirt, and he quivered as they moved down his body. She trapped him with her kisses, absorbed him through her lips. Cí failed to understand anything—why he felt suspicious even while all his pain was being quenched, why he felt afraid when her sweet, honey-eyed body seemed to be dissolving his very senses—

"No!" cried Cí as Peach Blossom tried to take his shirt off.

She didn't understand how embarrassed he was by his scars, but he let her take his pants off. Then she was astride him.

He thought he was going to die as the girl's hips moved slowly and deliberately in a deep, continuous sway. She pushed down on him as though she would take every last bit of him inside her. She guided his hands onto her small breasts and moaned as he caressed her, sparking something in him, making him drunk with delight, transporting him somewhere unknown.

The next morning, Wang found Cí in the skiff, sleeping as deeply as if he'd been drunk. Wang woke him, laughing heartily.

"Now I see why you wanted to keep her, eh! Come on, get yourself together and help with rowing. The City of Death won't wait forever."

10

Cí shuddered at the sight of the City of Death. In Wang's view, to dock there was to engage in a dangerous game of chance. The place was infested with outlaws, fugitives, traffickers, cardsharps—all of them ready to bleed dry any foreigner. But as the barge approached, the wharf area, swathed in mist, looked abandoned, and the crews of the hundreds of docked boats were nowhere to be seen. Even the water lapping against the boats' sides seemed particularly gloomy.

"Be on your guard," whispered Wang.

They glided toward the primary dock and began to see people running between the warehouses. Cí looked down just as a dead body, surrounded by a bloody spew, floated past. Other bodies floated nearby.

"The plague!" cried Ze.

Wang nodded, and Third and Peach Blossom came and huddled next to Cí. He tried to discern the shore, but the mist was too thick.

"We'll go on downstream," Wang said. "You," he added, addressing Peach Blossom, "grab a pole and help."

Instead of doing as she was told, Peach Blossom grabbed Third and made as if to throw her into the water. Third struggled hard and began to cry. The prostitute's face had become a wicked mask.

"The money!" she shouted. "Give me the money or I swear I'll throw her in!"

"What are you doing?" cried Cí, stepping forward.

"One more step…" warned Peach Blossom.

"Careful, Cí!" cried Wang. "The water's poisonous!"

Cí stopped; he'd heard about the terrible illness contained in this area's river water. He begged Wang to give Peach Blossom the money, but the old man stood firm, glaring at her.

"I've got a better idea," the captain said, taking a pole and pointing it at her. "Let the girl go, and scram. Otherwise I'm going to stick this pole right up inside you and throw you in the water."

"The money!" she screeched.

"What are you doing?" cried Cí. "Give her the money!"

Wang dropped his head and began lowering the pole, but then he deftly swung it, catching Peach Blossom on the side of the head and knocking her off balance, though not into the water. Third jumped away, but Peach Blossom managed to grab Third's ankle and push her into the water. Third had never learned to swim, and she sank like a stone. Cí dived in after her.

He swam down, thrashing underwater until his lungs burned. He came up for air screaming Third's name. He saw her surface between a couple of bodies, but then she disappeared again under the hull of a trawler. He swam desperately toward her and found her with her shirt snagged on the trawler, keeping her from sinking again. But she was limp; her eyes were shut and a stream of bubbles escaped from her nose. Cí unhooked her shirt and swam with her toward the barge, shaking her at the same time and pleading, "Please don't die!"

Something prodded at his back. It was Wang. Cí hoisted Third up to him and then clambered onto the boat himself. Third lay unconscious across the captain's lap, and he rubbed her arms vigorously.

Cí tried to help, but Wang pushed him away. He sat Third up and patted her back hard until she vomited the water she'd ingested and began to cough. When the coughs subsided, the tears came—Third's as well as Cí's.

As Cí held Third in a tight hug, Wang told him that the moment Third went overboard, Peach Blossom had jumped into the skiff and rowed away. She'd just been biding her time until she had the opportunity to do so.

"I don't know what you got up to with her last night," said Wang reproachfully, "but whatever it was, she charged a high price."

"And what about him?" said Cí, pointing to Ze, who was on the deck, his shin bleeding.

"He tried to stop her and fell on the anchor." Wang threw Ze a cloth. "Wrap that before you sink us with your blood."

Cí took off Third's wet clothes and bundled her up. As he dried himself off, he saw images of Peach Blossom, and of Cherry. He swore he'd never trust a woman again.

They continued downstream. Cí watched Third carefully; he knew that if the waters gave her any sort of illness, she was unlikely to overcome it. She didn't seem to have a fever, and her coughing had subsided. But their luck ended there: Wang, fed up with all the problems, announced he was going to off-load them at the next village.

Cí wasn't given long to dwell on this newest setback. Ze shrieked, and when Cí turned around, the old sailor was on the ground clutching his leg. Not wanting to delay the others, he hadn't been honest about how bad the wound was. When he finally let

Wang near and the captain removed the cloth wrap, they saw that the cut on his shin went all the way to the bone.

"I can carry on, boss," gasped Ze.

Wang shook his head. Cí knelt down to examine the wound more closely.

"Luckily it hasn't hit any tendons," Cí said. "But it is deep. We're going to need to sew it up before it starts rotting the leg."

"I see, doctor!" said Wang. "And how do you propose we do that? Tie him up like a pig?"

"How far to the next village?" asked Cí, remembering Wang's threat to throw him and Third off the boat.

"If you're thinking about taking him to a witch, forget it. I don't believe in those charlatans."

Country people tended to look down on witches—it was a position that passed from father to son but was an unhappy inheritance. Healers were better thought of—they knew about herbs, infusions and ointments, acupuncture and moxibustion. People usually were taken to a witch only once the healer had declared the person dead, and since the Confucian laws made it illegal to open up bodies, this only cast witches in a worse light.

Cí, from his time working with Feng, knew that a human's body—its innards, bones, and flesh—didn't differ much from that of a pig. He continued to probe the wound, but Wang stopped him.

"Careful! He's more useful to me lame than dead," said Wang.

"I know a bit about medicine," said Cí.

When it came down to it, there would be no one else who could do anything for Ze until they reached Fuzhou.

Remembering what he'd learned, and being careful of the motion of the boat, Cí cleaned the wound with freshly boiled tea. The liquid helped wash away all the stuck fibers so Cí could assess it better. The wound ran from just below Ze's knee to nearly the top of his ankle. Cí was concerned by how deep it was and by the fact that it was still bleeding. Once he'd finished rinsing it, he asked Wang to take them over to the riverbank.

"Is that it? Done already?"

Cí shook his head grimly. Without needle and thread, the only thing he could think of to stop the bleeding was the "fat head" ant. He explained to Wang how he'd seen them used on a corpse as sutures.

"They live in the bulrushes. It won't be hard to find them."

Wang frowned. "All I know is their bite is supposedly bad enough to wake the dead. I'm not sure about this, but let's go. At least I can check the caulk while you gather bugs."

They cast anchor in a dirty-yellow sand delta at the mouth of a tributary, where the ocher mud contrasted with the deep green of the bulrushes. In different circumstances it would be idyllic. Just then, all Cí wanted was to do a good job.

He found an anthill and knelt down beside it. It wasn't long before the ants began to attack his legs and arms, but he, of course, didn't feel any pain from their bites. He thrust his forearm into the mound, and when he pulled it out the maddened ants had their disproportionately large mandibles sunk into his skin. Sometimes it was great to not be able to feel pain, he thought, as he waded back over to the barge.

"Dragon shit, boy! Doesn't that hurt?"

"Of course," said Cí. "They pinch like devils!"

Over time, he'd learned to hide his unusual gift. When he was a young boy, the fact he didn't feel pain had won him attention—neighbors lined up to marvel at how he could withstand pinches on the skin and even moxibustion burns. Once he was in school, though, things changed. The teachers were astonished at the beatings he could tolerate without the slightest cry; his schoolmates envied him at first but then began to see him as aloof. So they tried to prove that if they hurt him enough, surely he'd cry at some point. Previously playful kicks and slaps turned cruel and increasingly violent. And that was when Cí began to learn that, to protect himself, he'd have to perfect the art of *pretending* he felt pain.

He looked Ze in the eye. "Ready?"

Ze nodded grimly. Cí took an ant between his finger and thumb and, with the other hand, pressed Ze's wound shut. He laid the ant against the wound's edge, and it clamped its mandible shut. Cí then tore off the ant's torso, leaving only the head. He repeated the operation, with great care, along the length of the wound.

"That's it," Cí said. "In two weeks you can take the heads off—it isn't difficult. And after that a scar will form…"

"Him?" said Wang. "How's he going to do it with those huge mitts?"

"Well, I mean, you could use a knife…"

"In your dreams. You're not leaving him like this."

"But you said you were going to throw us off."

"If I did say that, you can forget it. You're taking Ze's place. There's plenty of rowing to be done between here and Lin'an, and Ze's in no fit state."

Cí was so grateful that he found himself speechless.

"And if you even think about trying to get a wage out of me, I'll throw you in the river before you can say Confucius."

The captain might not be the friendliest, thought Cí as Wang walked away, but he had saved their lives.

***

For the next week Cí kept a close eye on Third. She developed a fever, and while her medicine helped some, he was worried it was going to run out. The first thing he would have to do when they got to Lin'an was stock up.

When he wasn't looking after Third, Cí worked hard—cleaning the deck, moving and refastening the cargo. Sometimes Wang would have Cí check the river depth or push aside branches, but the current did most of the work of propelling the barge. One afternoon he was cleaning the deck when Wang called out to him.

"Ahoy! Hide the girl and keep your mouth shut!"

Wang's warning worried Cí. Looking up, he saw a barge coming toward them; there were two men aboard along with an enormous hound. Wang whispered to him to leave the cleaning and grab a pole.

"My name is Kao. I'm a sheriff," called one of the men, holding out the badge that identified his office. "You wouldn't happen to have anyone aboard by the name of Cí Song?" The man had a pockmarked face.

"Cí?" Wang laughed. "What kind of stupid name is that?"

"Just answer the question. Otherwise you'll feel my baton! Who are the other people aboard?"

"Apologies. My name is Wang, native of Zhunang. The cripple over there is Ze, my crewman. We're on our way to Lin'an with a cargo and—"

"I couldn't care less where you're going. We're looking for a young man who boarded a boat at Jianyang. We believe he's with a girl who is unwell."

"A fugitive?" asked Wang, sounding intrigued.

"He stole some money. And who's this?" he said, gesturing at Cí.

Wang hesitated. Cí gripped the pole and got ready to defend himself.

"My son. Why?"

The sheriff looked him up and down disdainfully.

"Out of the way. I'm coming aboard."

Cí bit his lip. They wouldn't have to look very hard to find Third, and if he tried to impede them, they'd take him in for sure.

Think fast or you're done for.

Suddenly, he screwed up his face in pain and collapsed forward as if his spine had snapped. Wang reached a hand out in surprise, but Cí began to cough violently. His eyes bulged, and he began beating his chest as if he were dying; then, he stood partway up and coughed again, letting out a spray of blood. He straightened up with some difficulty and reached a hand toward the sheriff, who looked with horror at the boy's blood-spattered mouth.

"The water..." Cí croaked, advancing on the sheriff. "Please, help me..."

The sheriff backed away, terrified. Cí staggered forward another step before falling flat on his face, knocking over a sack of rice.

"The water sickness!" cried Wang.

"The water sickness," repeated the sheriff, turning pale and leaping back onto his own barge.

"Row, damn it!" he howled at the other man.

The barge pulled away and was soon far downriver.

Cí stood up, completely recovered, as if by magic.

"But...how did you manage that?" stuttered Wang.

"What, that?" He spat a little more blood. "I mean, it hurt a bit biting my cheeks, but the look on that guy's face was worth it!"

"You rascal!"

They both fell down laughing.

Wang glanced downriver at the sheriff's barge as it disappeared into the distance, and turned back to Cí, his expression serious.

"No doubt they are heading to Lin'an. I don't know what you've done to attract his attention, and I honestly don't care, but bear this in mind: When you get off there, be very careful. That sheriff had the look of a prison dog. He won't stop until he's got you in his teeth."

PART THREE

11

Cí had yearned for months to be back in Lin'an, and now that the capital was in sight, silhouetted against the surrounding hills, his stomach churned. Life was waiting for him in Lin'an.

The barge moved slowly through the mist toward the enormous Zhe estuary, where the river met the filthy western lake, announcing, with an unbearable stink, the richness and misery of the queen of cities: Lin'an, the great prefecture's capital, old Hangzhou, the center of the universe.

Weak sunlight softly illuminated hundreds of vessels—imposing merchant ships, half-sunk barges like Wang's, and smaller, worm-eaten wooden skiffs clinging desperately to rotten foundations. The boats tried to maneuver past each other and through the swarm of sampans and reeds for a clear course toward port.

After the calm along the river, now all was frenzied shouts and gasps, warnings, insults, threats, and collisions, and as Wang steered through the churning river traffic, he quickly lost patience. Cí tried to follow Wang's orders, but the captain was so worked up it wasn't easy.

"Damn you! Where did you learn to row?" he roared at a passing sailor. "And you, what are you laughing at?" he added, rebuking Ze. "I don't care how bad your leg is—stop thinking about your whores and lend a hand. We'll dock farther up, away from the warehouses."

Ze complied, grumbling, but Cí kept quiet; he had enough to deal with just keeping hold of the barge pole and pushing along.

When the crush of boats had cleared somewhat, Cí looked up. He had never seen Lin'an from the river, and its grandeur struck him all the more. But as they came closer to the docks, the familiarity of the scene also gave him the feeling of a distant family welcoming him home.

The city stood implacable and proud, sheltered by the wooded hills to the west and open to the river on its south side. An enormous flood ditch and a magnificent stone and earth wall prevented access directly from the water.

A slap around the ear from Wang brought Cí to his senses. "Stop gawking and row."

It was another hour before they found a place to dock; they stopped across from one of the city's seven great gates, where Wang had decided it would be a good place for Cí and Third to disembark.

"It's the safest option," he assured them. "If anyone's watching for you, it would be near the rice market or the Black Bridge on the north side, where goods are unloaded."

Cí thanked Wang for his help. During the three-week voyage, the captain had done more for them than all the people in their village ever had. Moodiness aside, Wang was the kind of man you'd trust with your most valuable possessions. And Cí had done just that by trusting him with his and Third's lives. Wang had gotten them safely to Lin'an, given Cí work, and hadn't asked questions. In many ways, the captain reminded Cí of his father, and Cí knew he'd never forget him.

Cí took one last look at Ze's leg and the progress of the scarring under the pressure of the ants' mandibles. It looked good, but Cí left a few mandibles in place.

"You can pull the rest of the heads off in a couple of days—make sure you leave your own on, though!" Cí slapped him on the back and they both laughed in farewell.

He took Third by the hand and shouldered his bag. Before he got off the boat, he looked back at Wang, wanting to thank him again, but before he could, Wang stepped forward.

"Your wages," he said, handing Cí a purse of money. "And one piece of advice: Change your name!"

In any other circumstance, Cí would have refused the unexpected money, but he needed it badly to stand a chance of surviving in Lin'an. He tied the purse to his belt and hid it beneath his shirt.

"I…" Before Cí could gather himself to respond, the old captain had turned around and begun to push the barge away from the dock.

Cí trembled as he reached the gigantic wall with its whitewashed bricks and the Great Gate set in its center. Now that his dream to return to Lin'an was within reach, unfamiliar fear gripped him.

Don't think, or you'll never do it.

"Come on," he said to Third. Diving into the vortex of people entering and leaving the city, they stepped across the threshold of the Great Gate.

Everything was exactly as Cí remembered: the shanties lining the banks, the overwhelming smell of fish, the noise of carts rumbling along the streets, food and drink at every turn, sweating youths struggling with bellowing animals, red lanterns swaying on workshop porches, shops selling silk and jade and trinkets, brightly colored stalls clustered together like carelessly stacked tiles, boister-ous stall keepers vending their wares and shooing away children.

They were wandering through all of this when Third started tugging at Cí's sleeve. She had caught sight of a colorful candy kiosk, presided over by a man who looked like he might be a for-tune-teller. Cí was sad that Third was so excited; there was no way he could waste money on a handful of candy. He was just about to say so when the fortune-teller came over.

"Three *qián*," he said, holding out two pieces of candy to Third.

Cí considered the little old man and his toothless smile as he shook the pieces of candy in his hand. He was wearing a donkey pelt, which gave him a half-repulsive, half-extravagant air and com-peted as an oddity with his cap, which was made from dried sticks and little windmills. He had a shock of gray hair that made him look like the closest thing to a monkey Cí had even seen.

"Three *qián*," he insisted, smiling.

Third reached out for them, but Cí stopped her.

"We can't," he whispered to her. "Three *qián* would buy us enough boiled rice to feed us for a whole day."

"Oh!" said Third, turning very serious. "But I think candy might be the only thing I can eat!"

"She has a point," said the old man. "Take one, try it."

"Please, we don't have any money." He pulled Third's hand away. "Come on, let's go."

"But he's a fortune-teller," whimpered Third. "If we don't buy from him, he'll curse us!"

"He's a fake. If he really knew the future, he'd know we can't spend any money."

Third nodded. She cleared her throat, but this became a cough, and it stopped Cí cold. It was a cough he knew all too well.

"Feeling all right?"

She coughed again but said she was OK. Cí didn't believe her, not for a moment.

They made their way toward Imperial Avenue. Cí knew this area near the gate, between the old interior wall and the outer wall. Not a day had passed when he worked for Judge Feng that he hadn't been down to these slums, the city's poorest and most dangerous quarter. It was a frightening place, where women sold themselves on corners, men rolled around drunkenly, charlatans and robbers roamed the streets, and if you looked at the wrong person you'd risk having your throat slit. It was also where informants could be found.

Cí began to worry about where they'd sleep that night. He cursed the law that meant government officials were obliged to work somewhere different from their place of birth. It had been put in place to try to stop the nepotism, corruption, and bribery that had been so commonplace. But it also meant government officials were cut off from their families—and that Cí and Third had no one to turn to in all of Lin'an. In truth, they didn't have any people anywhere—their father's siblings had emigrated south and died in a typhoon, and they didn't know their mother's family.

They had to hurry. When night came, the area would quickly become even more dangerous. They had to find shelter somewhere else.

Third complained, and with good reason. She'd been hungry for quite a while, and Cí hadn't gotten her any food yet, so she sat down on the ground and refused to go on.

"I'm hungry!"

"We don't have time now. Get up or I'll have to drag you around."

"If we don't eat, I'll die," she said, crossing her arms. "Then you'll have to drag me around anyway."

Cí looked at her remorsefully. Yes, they should rest for a bit. He looked around for a food stall, but they all looked too expensive; then he caught sight of one with a small crowd of beggars around it. He approached and asked the prices.

"You're in luck," said the vendor, who smelled nearly as offensive as the food he was selling. "Today we're giving it away."

In fact, a portion of noodles cost Cí two *qián*—a rip-off.

When he brought the food to Third, she glowered. She'd never liked noodles; they were what the barbarians in the North ate.

"It's all there is." Cí sighed.

She placed a few noodles in her mouth but spat them out immediately.

"It tastes like wet clothes!"

"How do you know what wet clothes taste like?" Cí asked sternly. "Stop complaining and eat up."

But when he tried some, he couldn't help but spit them out also.

"Filth!"

"Stop complaining and eat up," sang a rather smug Third.

No sooner had Cí thrown the leftovers to the ground than the nearby beggars were devouring the mush. He grabbed Third and soon found some boiled rice; seeing Third was still hungry after wolfing hers down, he gave her the rest of his.

"What about you?" she said through a mouthful.

"Oh, I had a whole cow for breakfast," he said, letting out a burp.

"Liar!" she said, laughing.

"I did. When you were still asleep, lazybones."

Her laughter turned into a coughing fit. Clearly, her cough was getting worse, and the thought of her dying like his other sisters terrified him. He patted her back, and gradually the coughing subsided some, but he could see how much it hurt.

"We'll get you better. Hang in there."

He rummaged around in the bag for the dried roots that were her medicine—there were barely a few sprigs left. She chewed and swallowed them, and soon after, the coughing stopped.

"That's what you get for eating too quickly," he said, trying to make a joke.

"Sorry," she said seriously.

Cí's heart sank.

***

Racking his brain for a place they could go, he took a street toward Phoenix Hill, a residential area in the south of the city, where they'd lived before. They obviously wouldn't be able to go back, as the houses were all assigned to current government officials, but he remembered Grandfather Yin, an old friend of his father's. Cí thought perhaps he would take them in for a few days.

Gradually the five-story buildings of the Imperial Avenue area gave way to detached mansions with curved roofs and ornate gardens; the racket and odors of the crowded area near the gate were replaced with a breeze through trees and the sweet, clean smell of jasmine. Cí briefly savored the feeling of being back in a world where he might dare to belong.

By the time they knocked on Grandfather Yin's door, it was sunset. Grandfather Yin's second wife, a haughty, unfriendly woman, opened the door. As soon as she saw them she screwed up her face.

"What are *you* doing here? Do you want to ruin us?"

Cí was dumbstruck; it had been more than a year since they'd seen each other, but it was as though the woman had been expecting them. Before she could slam the door in their faces, Cí asked after Grandfather Yin.

"He isn't here! He won't see you!"

"Please. My sister is unwell."

She looked at the girl in disgust.

"All the more reason for you to go away."

"Who's there?" Cí recognized Grandfather Yin's voice coming from inside the house.

"Some beggar! He's going already," she shouted, stepping outside and leading Third by her arm to the street so that Cí had to follow. "This is a decent house, get it? We don't need thieves like you coming around and muddying our name!"

"But—"

"Don't play dumb! Sheriff Kao went through the neighborhood earlier today, and he had an enormous dog with him. He snooped around the whole house and told us what you did in the village, get it? He said you'd probably try here. I don't know what possessed you to flee with that money, but if it weren't for the memory of your father, I'd march you straight to the police and report you myself." She let go of Third's arm and pushed her toward Cí. "Make sure you don't come back. If I catch you anywhere near the house, I swear I'll make every single gong in the city ring out, and then there'll be nowhere for you to hide."

Cí took his sister's hand and backed away, stumbling with worry and doubt. Clearly the magistrate had followed through on his threat to implicate Cí in Shang's murder—or the Rice Man had reported him for stealing the 300,000 *qián* the magistrate had appropriated. Sheriff Kao was the man they'd sent to get him.

The sheriff had probably warned the rest of the neighbors in the vicinity, so they walked near the walls to avoid being seen. Cí considered staying in one of the inns near the gate. It obviously wasn't the most suitable area, but the rooms would be cheap, and no one would come looking for them there.

They came upon a dilapidated building with a sign advertising inexpensive rooms. Its uneven walls abutted a restaurant that stank of rot. Cí parted the threadbare drape at the entrance and went over to the manager, a brute of a man, half-asleep and reeking of alcohol. The manager didn't even look at Cí; he just extended a palm and said it was fifty *qián* up front. This was all Cí had. He tried to barter, but the drunkard spat—he couldn't have cared less. Cí was wondering if they had any other options when Third began coughing again. This ill, she couldn't sleep on the streets, but if he accepted the price, there would be nothing left to buy her medicine.

At least until I find some work.

He wanted to think he'd be able to find some work. He paid and asked whether there was a key.

"Ha! You think the people who stay here have anything valuable enough that they'd need a key? The room is at the back, third floor. And one thing: I don't care if you're having sex with that child, but if she dies, you'd better get her out of here. We don't want problems with the law."

Neither did Cí, so he squelched the impulse to give the man the punch he deserved.

They walked along the hallway, where voices and laughter filtered through the drapes covering the doorways of the rooms, and went up some rickety stairs. The rancid smell of sweat and urine made Cí retch. There was hardly any light, though their room faced the river, which could be seen through cracks between the bamboo reeds that had been used to patch a wall. There was a stained mat on the floor—the last thing someone would want to sleep on. He kicked it aside and took a blanket out of his bag. And again, Third started coughing.

I must get medicine now.

The ceiling was so low he could barely stand up straight. How could that swindler charge so much for such a tiny space, filled only with trash and the bits of broken bamboo left over from the wall repairs? He took some of these pieces and stacked them up, making an arch and covering it with the mat to form a shelter. Then he wiped some of the floor dirt on Third's face in the hope that this would camouflage her in the dark.

"Listen, this is really important." Third's wide eyes were like lights embedded in her grimy face. "I have to go out, and I'll be back really soon, but while I'm gone…do you remember how you hid the day the house burned? Well, I want you to do that again now. Don't make a peep until I get back, OK? If you do a good job, maybe I'll bring you some of that candy the fortune-teller had."

Third nodded. Even if Cí didn't entirely believe she'd do as he said, what choice did he have?

As they were covering her up, Cí said a prayer for his parents to watch over her. Then he rummaged through his bag for anything he might be able to sell. He'd get nothing for the four cloths and the knife he'd brought from the village. The only thing he had of any value was the *Songxingtong*, his father's copy of the penal code. But he'd need to find someone interested in buying something so specialized.

He had to go to the book market stalls around the Summer Pavilion at the Orange Gardens. The network of canals was the quickest way to get around the mazelike city, so to save time, he hopped on a barge along the Imperial Canal.

He arrived at the market at the best time of day, when the students left class to drink tea and browse the recent arrivals from the printers in Hionha. Cí recognized himself among these aspiring government officials, who were dressed neatly in loose-fitting black shirts and hungry for knowledge—at least he recognized the person he'd been a year ago. He was envious of the conversations he overheard about the importance of knowledge, the invasions in the North, the most recent thinking on neo-Confucian trends. He had to remind himself what he was there for at that moment.

There were many copies of the penal code at the stalls specializing in legal texts. He found an edition similar to his, bound in purple silk, and he held it up to the vendor.

"How much?"

The vendor picked up the book and opened it admiringly.

"Hmm. I see you know a true piece of art when you see it: a handwritten *Songxingtong*, in Master Hang's distinctive calligraphy, no less…ten thousand *qián*. I'm virtually giving it away."

Cí refused with a smile—he'd forgotten how everything for sale in Lin'an was being "given away"—but judging by the number of noblemen browsing at this particular stall, the books probably were quite valuable. An old man with an oiled mustache and wearing a bright red gown and cap—the attire of a great master—picked up the edition Cí had been looking at. He asked the vendor the price and grimaced at the answer. But he kept looking at it, and then announced he'd get some money and come back to buy it.

Cí didn't think twice.

"Please excuse the intrusion, venerable master, but I saw the book you were interested in."

The old man stopped, looking somewhat alarmed.

"I'm in a hurry. If you want to know about joining the academy, you can speak to my secretary."

"It isn't that," said Cí. "The book you were looking at—I have an almost identical copy I can sell you for far less."

"A handwritten *Songxingtong*? Are you sure?'

Cí took it out and showed him. "Five thousand *qián*," he said.

The old man examined it carefully before handing it back.

"I'm very sorry, but I don't buy from thieves."

"Sir, the book was my father's, and I swear I wouldn't be selling it unless I really had to."

"Right. And your father is…?"

Cí frowned; he was worried about revealing his identity. The old man started to walk away.

"Sir, I swear I'm not lying…I can prove it!"

The old man stopped again. Cí knew it was risky enough to address a stranger this way, let alone detain him. The old man could easily shout out to the police, who were always patrolling the market. But he turned around and challenged Cí.

"Go on, then."

Cí shut his eyes and took a deep breath.

"The *Songxingtong*, Section One." Cí began to recite the opening paragraph. A few sentences later, the old man interrupted him.

"Yes, yes, yes. I've seen this trick a hundred times. What about a part that isn't right at the beginning?"

"Anything!" said Cí. "You can pick, or even ask me a question! Any part you like."

The old man squinted at Cí and, seeing he was serious, began leafing through the book. Holding it open at a certain point, he cleared his throat.

"Very well, wise man: On the division of days…"

That part! It's been months since I've read it.

"OK," he said, stalling for time. "No problem…"

He shut his eyes again, and could hear the old man begin to tap his foot.

"The days are divided into eighty-six parts!" Cí almost shouted. It came flooding back. "A workday is made up of the six hours between sunrise and twilight. Night is another six, making a total of twelve hours every day. A legal year has three hundred and sixty full days, but a person's age is counted based on…the number of years since his birth was announced at the public register—"

"OK, OK."

"I swear, sir, the book belongs to me. And I need the money for my sick sister. Five thousand *qián*, please."

The old man looked the book over again. Cí knew it was beautifully bound and handwritten with the most careful of brushstrokes—the lettering was almost vibrant. Aside from the words, just looking at it was an emotional, poetic experience.

"I'm sorry," the old man said, handing the book back finally. "It's truly magnificent, but I can't buy it. I promised the vendor I'd buy his, and keeping my word is worth more to me than saving some money. It would also be wrong to buy it cheap because you're desperate. Here's what we'll do: take a hundred *qián*, and keep your book. I can tell it would pain you to sell it. And don't be offended about the money; consider it a loan. I'm sure you'll get it back to me when you've figured out your situation. My name is Ming."

Cí didn't know what to say. He felt ashamed but knew he had to take the money anyway; he swore he'd repay Ming before the week was out. The old man nodded with a knowing smile before going on his way.

Cí took off in the direction of the Great Pharmacy, which he knew was the only place he had any chance of buying Third's medicine for less than a hundred *qián*.

When he arrived, there were a number of families shouting and complaining. Going past the private entrance, he went up to the charity counters, where there were two groups, the second of which included children who were running all over and making noise.

As he lined up in this second group, his heart skipped a beat: there was the sheriff with the pockmarked face, Kao! He was inspecting the parents with children, one by one. He must have learned of Third's illness.

Cí was about to sneak away when he bumped into the sheriff's hound. It turned to sniff him, and Cí feared someone in the village had given it a piece of his clothing to smell. Cí backed away, and the hound began to growl. It thrust its snout toward Cí's hand, and

Cí was on the verge of turning and running when the dog began licking his fingers.

The noodles! Cí hadn't washed his hands since eating the noodles. He let the hound lick him, then turned and made his way slowly toward the first group.

A shout made him jump. "Stop right there!"

Cí obeyed, heart in mouth.

"If you're here to get medicine for a child, go back to the other line!"

Cí breathed a sigh of relief—it was just the attendant. But as he turned to go back to the other line, he found himself face-to-face with Kao, who recognized him instantly.

The second it took for the sheriff to shout a command seemed to last an eternity. The hound leaped up to tear a strip out of Cí's throat, but Cí was already off and running. He dove into the crowded street, knocking over carts and baskets to try and block Kao and his dog. He sprinted in the direction of the canal.

Swerving between carts, he crossed the bridge, but just when he thought he was safe, he slipped and fell, dropping his father's book. He tried to grab it, but a beggar appeared out of nowhere and snatched it up. Cí thought about pursuing him, but the sheriff and the hound were close behind. He got up and started running again.

He grabbed a hoe as he ran past a tackle stall, and then leaped onto an abandoned barge on the canal, thinking he would cross it and jump onto a moving barge, but the hound leaped after him. It looked possessed as it bared its teeth and growled. Kao was coming up behind. Cí gripped the hoe tightly and swung it at the dog, but the animal dodged, then lunged forward and sank its teeth into Cí's calf. Though he didn't feel any pain, Cí saw the teeth going in deeper, and he brought the hoe down on the dog's head. Its skull cracked, and when he hit it again its jaw loosened. Kao stopped, dumbfounded.

Without thinking, Cí jumped into the river. He broke through the surface layer of old fruit, reeds, and scum and felt water rush through his nose. He dove under a barge, and when he resurfaced, he saw that Kao had grabbed the hoe and was following him along the bank. He dove again and swam to the far side of the barge, holding on to its edge. Then he heard shouts announcing the opening of the sluice gates, and he remembered how dangerous it was to be in the water when the locks were opened, how people died that way...

It's my only way out.

He let go of the barge, and a torrent of water whipped him downriver, tossing and buffeting him around. Once he was through the first sluice gate, the main danger was being smashed against the side of a barge. He was carried toward the second gate, convinced that any minute he'd be crushed. But he got through the second gate and then managed to grab onto a loose cable. The water level rose rapidly around him, and the barges and boats squeezed close together, threatening to squash him.

He tried to use the cable to climb up one of the canal walls, but his right leg wasn't working. Lifting it just above the surface of the water, he saw how bad the bite was.

Damned animal!

Using only his left leg and his arms, he scrambled up to the edge of the dock. He turned and collapsed, then saw Kao on the far side. With no way of reaching Cí, Kao kicked the ground in obvious frustration.

"Run all you want! I'll find you! I'll get you! No matter what!"

Cí didn't reply but dragged himself up and went off, half-hopping, into the crowds of Lin'an.

12

Limping along backstreets, Cí cursed his bad luck and worried about Third. With the Great Pharmacy no longer an option, he had to find a private herbalist, and the medicine would be expensive. He stopped at the first he came upon. The counter was cluttered with dried roots and leaves, mushrooms and seeds, chopped-up vines and stalks, and minerals, but there were no customers. Although the shop was empty, the two owners barely acknowledged Cí. He asked if they had any of the medicine, and the men whispered to each other before telling him—at some length—how scarce that particular root had become recently. It came as no surprise to Cí when they claimed that the price had gone up to 800 *qián* for a handful.

He tried bartering. All he had was the 100 *qián* from the old professor. He showed them his money.

"I don't need a whole handful. A quarter's enough."

"That will be two hundred, then," said one of the owners. "And here," he added, pointing at the coins, "I see only a hundred."

"It's all I have." He looked disdainfully around the run-down shop, as if to suggest business clearly wasn't very good. "It's better than nothing!"

They didn't look impressed.

"And bear in mind I could get it for free at the Great Pharmacy," said Cí.

"Look," said one of men as he began to put the medicine away. "Do you honestly think we haven't heard it all before? If you could've got it for less, you would have. It's two hundred *qián*, or you can go back under whichever rock you crawled out from."

Cí took off his sandals.

"They're good leather, you could get at least a hundred *qián* for them. Really, it's all I have."

"Do we look in need of footwear? Go on, get out!"

Cí thought about grabbing the medicine and running, but he knew the wound to his leg would make that impossible. Leaving the shop, he wondered how things could possibly get any worse.

❦

It was the same story at the other herbalists he visited. The last, a godforsaken place near one of the city gates, tried to sell him some powdered bamboo. But he'd bought Third's medicine so many times before that its sticky texture and bitter taste were unmistakable to him; he dipped a finger and knew immediately that the owners were cheating him. He managed to get his money back but then had to flee because the owners, cunningly, tried to accuse him of breaking the sale agreement.

Not knowing what else to do, he spent the rest of the afternoon trying to find work—even though he knew he'd probably be paid only in rice. He went to all the nearby stalls asking for a job, but seeing how worn-out he looked and the way he was limping, no one was even remotely interested. He went to several of the smaller jetties, but they were crowded with people clamoring for jobs.

He asked anyone he could for work, and said he was willing to do anything, but no one listened. All the while, he knew, Third would be deteriorating.

He became so desperate it seemed difficult to breathe. He thought of stealing, or even selling his body down by the canal bridges like other paupers did—but for that, he'd need connections with the gangs.

He sat on the sidewalk and tried to pull himself together. Looking up, he spotted the fortune-teller who had tried to sell Third the candy. He still wore the donkey skin but had swapped his stool for a small stage on which he now stood, offering people a chance to win some money. A small crowd was gathering, and Cí, though extremely skeptical of such displays, drifted over.

The fortune-teller had quite a setup. On a table behind the stage lay a huge assortment of knickknacks and trinkets: old turtle shells used for fortune-telling, badly painted clay Buddhas, cheap paper fans, kites, rings, belts, sandals, incense, old coins, lanterns, spiders, and snake skeletons. It looked to Cí as if someone had spilled a bag of the strangest trash on the table and was trying to sell it off. But he couldn't imagine the pile of junk was what was attracting the crowd.

As Cí came a little closer, it became clear.

The fortune-teller had set up a cricket race: a table with a maze of concentric marks on it, and six channels, each painted a different color, each ending at the mound of sugar in the center of the table. Bets were being laid on which of the crickets would reach the center first. The citizens of Lin'an loved to bet.

Cí pushed his way to the front just as the fortune-teller was announcing the last chance to bet, egging on the crowd.

"Come on! Money to be won! Your chance to escape your misery and your poverty! Win, imagine it, and you'll have so much money you can marry the woman of your dreams—or go out whoring instead!"

The mention of flesh prompted a few more bets. The crickets waited in their boxes, each daubed on the back with paint matching the colors of the channels.

"Is that it? No one else has the balls to challenge me? Bunch of cowards! Afraid of my old cricket? Fine...I'm feeling *crazy* today!" The fortune-teller picked up his cricket, which was marked with yellow paint, and pulled off one of its front legs. Then he put the insect down in the labyrinth so everyone could see it stumble around. "What about now?" he cried.

A few people found this to be sufficient proof that the fortune-teller had in fact lost his mind, and they raised their bets. He knew it was a bad idea, but Cí was also seriously considering betting. All he could think about was getting enough money for Third's medicine.

The bets were about to close when Cí slammed his money down.

"A hundred *qián*! Eight to one."

And may fortune protect me.

"Betting closed! Stand away!"

The fortune-teller placed the six crickets at their respective gates and checked to make sure the silk netting that prevented the insects from hopping away was secure.

"Ready?" asked the fortune-teller.

"Ready yourself?" echoed one man. "My red cricket's going to *destroy* yours."

The fortune-teller struck a gong and lifted the gates. The crickets hurried into their respective channels—all except the yellow one, which tottered feebly forward. Soon the men were roaring with excitement, growing even louder if one of their crickets stopped. The red cricket was doing well, charging ahead of the others, but then, barely a hand's length from the finishing line, it stopped. The men fell silent. The insect hesitated, as if some invisible obstacle had sprung up in front of it. Then, in spite of its owner's cries, it went back the way it had come. At the same time, the fortune-teller's cricket was miraculously scurrying forward at top speed.

The shouting became deafening again. The yellow cricket caught up, but then also stopped, wavering, as if unsure. And just when the blue cricket, whose owner was a giant of a man and was shouting louder than anybody, looked as though it had taken the lead, the yellow one shot forward, overtaking the blue at the last possible instant.

No one could believe it. It seemed like the devil's work. They were all rubbing their eyes when the giant turned to the fortune-teller.

"Cheating bastard!" he roared.

But the fortune-teller wasn't flustered. Moving the silk net aside, he picked up his cricket and held it out for all to see: its front left leg definitely was not there. In a rage, the giant knocked the insect from the fortune-teller's hand and stomped on it. He spat and, before turning to leave, promised the fortune-teller he'd be back. The rest, grumbling, gathered up their insects and followed the giant away.

Cí went nowhere. He urgently needed that money, and he couldn't see *how* the fortune-teller had won without some kind of trick. It also struck him as strange that the man didn't seem to care that the cricket was dead, even though it had just made him all that money.

"You can get out of here as well," said the fortune-teller.

Cí ignored him and crouched down to examine the squashed remains of the cricket. Using a fingernail, he dislodged some bright plating still attached to the abdomen. It looked like a sliver of iron or a similar metal. And he found traces of glue on the underside. What could it have been for? Wouldn't it just weigh the creature down and make it go slower?

He was astonished when the dead insect suddenly flew from his palm and attached itself to the knife at his belt. Suddenly it all made sense...

By now the fortune-teller had gathered up his things and wandered off in the direction of a nearby tavern. Cí carefully placed the insect's remains in a cloth and headed after him.

There was a boy at the door to the Five Pleasures Tavern looking after the fortune-teller's folded-up betting table. Cí asked him how much he was being paid, and the boy held out two pieces of candy.

"I'll give you this apple if you let me look at that table."

The boy thought for a moment.

"OK. But only to look."

Cí gave him the apple, which one of the men had dropped at the bet, and opened the table.

"I said don't touch," said the boy.

"I need to look at the underside."

"I'll tell him—"

"Eat your apple and shut up, will you?"

Cí opened and shut the channel gates, sniffed the channels, and looked closely at the underside, pulling out a small sheet of metal about the size of a biscuit, which he hid in his sleeve. Putting the table back as it had been, he nodded to the boy and entered the Five Pleasures Tavern. He had everything he needed to get his money back.

Though Cí didn't see the fortune-teller when he first walked into the tavern, a couple of prostitutes were whispering excitedly about a man throwing money around. Cí followed their glances to the curtains at the back of the room.

He took a moment to consider his approach. The tavern was a dive like all the others near the gates—thick with greasy smoke and customers eating plates of boiled pig meat, Cantonese sauces, and Zhe fish soups. The smell of the food mingled with the stink and sweat of the fishermen, dockers, and sailors who were celebrating the end of the week as though it were their last day on earth—drinking, swinging, and swaying to the rhythm of flutes and zithers.

On the far side of the bar, on a makeshift stage, a group of "flowers" sang melodies that were barely audible over the din and tried to catch the eye of their next customer. One of them came over to Cí and made a show of concern over his wounded leg before she began rubbing her flabby rump up against his crotch. Cí pushed her away. He marched to the back of the tavern, parted the curtains, and there was the fortune-teller, shaking his pale ass over a young girl. He was clearly surprised to see Cí but seemed unbothered. He smiled foolishly, showing his rotten teeth, and then carried on. Doubtless he was drunk.

"Having fun with my money?" Cí asked. He shoved the old man, and the girl grabbed her clothes and scurried out.

"What on earth?" said the fortune-teller.

Before the old man could get to his feet, Cí grabbed him by the shirt.

"You're going to pay me back, right down to the last coin! And I mean now!"

He was about to start rummaging through the fortune-teller's purse when he was picked up, dragged out of the cubicle, and thrown against some tables in the middle of the dining area. The music stopped.

"No bothering the customers!" roared the manager.

The man was as big as a mountain; his arms appeared to be thicker than his legs, and he had the look of an enraged buffalo. Before Cí could respond, the manager punched him in the ribs.

"He's a cheat!" Cí managed to say. "He swindled me!"

"As long as he pays his way when he's in here, I don't care."

"Leave him. He's just a kid," said the fortune-teller, coming out from behind the curtain as he buttoned his pants. He looked down at Cí. "You get out of here before you really get hurt."

Cí struggled to his feet. The wound in his leg had started to bleed again.

"I'll go," he said grimly, "when you've given me back my money."

"Don't be stupid. Do you really want your head cracked open?"

"I know how you do it. I inspected your maze."

A flicker of worry crossed the fortune-teller's face.

"Hee-hee, I see. Come now, have a seat. Tell me what you mean."

Cí pulled out the sliver of metal he'd found attached to the cricket and threw it on the table.

"All I know is you must have lost your mind," said the fortune-teller, but he was staring at the metal all the same.

"Fine," said Cí, taking out the biscuit-size metal sheet and placing it under the table. "Watch and learn, since this is all new to you."

When he moved the sheet beneath the table, suddenly, as if propelled by an invisible hand, the sliver began moving around, too. The fortune-teller shifted uncomfortably on his stool.

"Magnets," announced Cí. "Not to mention the camphor repellent at the ends of the other crickets' channels! Or—what else?—the trapdoor where the first cricket disappeared and the second cricket, the one with the metal sliver attached, was released? But you don't really need me to explain all this, do you?"

"What do you want?" whispered the fortune-teller.

"My eight hundred *qián*—which I would have won from the bet."

"Ha! You should have figured this out a lot earlier. Now get out."

"Not till I have my money."

"Listen, kid, you're sharp, I'll give you that, but you're starting to bore me. Zhao!" He called the manager over. "Give him a bowl of rice and show him out."

But Cí wasn't giving up that easily.

"My money," he growled.

"Enough!" said the manager.

"No," a voice behind them boomed, "it isn't enough!" Everyone in the tavern turned to see who it was.

A man stood in the middle of the dining area. It was the giant, the owner of the blue cricket that had nearly beaten the fortune-teller's yellow one. The fortune-teller looked terrified as the man, who was even bigger than the manager, strode purposefully over, pushing people aside. The manager stepped forward, and the giant took him down with one punch. Then the giant grabbed the fortune-teller by the neck, and Cí, too.

"Now," he growled, "let's hear this little story about magnets one more time."

Cí hated swindlers, but he hated violent people even more. Moreover, this man seemed perfectly prepared to take his money.

"This is between us," said Cí obstinately, even though the giant had him by the neck.

"The devil with both of you!" said the giant, flinging them against an old lattice screen, which broke into pieces.

As Cí struggled to his feet, the giant got astride the fortune-teller and began choking him. Cí leaped on the giant and punched him in the back, but it was like punching a brick wall. The giant threw him back toward the screen. Cí tasted blood on his lips.

The other patrons gathered around, eager for a fight. They started laying bets.

"Hundred-to-one odds on the giant," announced a young man who appointed himself deposit taker.

"Put me down for two hundred!"

"A thousand!"

"Two thousand if he kills him!"

Cí knew that none of these wolves would help him; his life was in serious danger, and running wasn't an option. Aside from his injured calf, he was surrounded, and the giant was on his feet, looking down at Cí as if he were a cockroach there to be stomped on. The giant spat on his hands and encouraged the crowd. Suddenly, Third popped into Cí's mind, and he decided what to do.

"Well," said Cí, "it won't be the first time I've smacked a woman down."

"What?" roared the giant. He swiped at Cí, who managed to hop out of the way, causing the giant to stumble.

"I'll bet you're more girl than man."

"I'm going to rip out your guts and feed them to you!" Again the giant swiped at Cí, and again Cí dodged him.

"You're worried about an injured man beating you. Bring us some knives!" Cí shouted.

"It's your own grave you're digging!" the giant sputtered as he grabbed someone's gourd of liquor and downed it. Wiping his mouth on his sleeve, he brandished one of the knives that had been brought from the kitchen.

Cí checked his. It was razor sharp.

"What about a bet on the little guy?" called the boy taking bets. "Come on! I have to cover the bets. He moves quick…he might survive one attack."

Laughter went around.

"*I'll* bet on me," said Cí, to everyone's amazement. "Eight hundred *qián*!" he said, staring directly at the fortune-teller.

The fortune-teller looked amazed, too. But after a moment, he nodded his assent. He rooted around for the money, and gave it to the taker.

"Fine," said the deposit holder. "Anyone else? No? OK…Strip to the waist and get ready to fight!"

The giant smirked, then winked and bragged to someone in the crowd about how he was going to crush Cí. He dramatically removed his robes, revealing an alarmingly muscular torso, and then took a bowl of oil and poured it over his chest for greater effect.

"Shit yourself, have you?" said the giant.

Cí didn't answer. With a ritual air, he placed his belongings in a neat pile. Knowing what he was about to do, he emanated calm. He took off his five-button tunic, and there—from waist to neck and all along his arms—was the thick tangle of scars for all to see. Proof of some atrocity. A stupefied murmur went around. Even the giant looked stunned.

"Ready!" said the taker, and a roar went up.

"Before we start," yelled Cí, and the noise died down, "I want to offer this man the chance to save his life."

"Save it for the grave!" said the giant.

"You'd be better off listening," he said. "Or do you think someone with these scars would be easy to kill? I take no pleasure in executing my opponents. How about the Dragon Challenge instead?"

The giant blinked. The Dragon Challenge would put them on more even footing, but not many people dared take it on: it required having a pattern cut into oneself with a knife. The cut had to be both deep and long. And the first to cry out was the loser.

"I'll do mine right over my heart," said Cí, hoping to get the crowd on his side.

"You must think I'm stupid! Why would I want to be cut when I can crush you without suffering a single scratch?"

"Yes, yes—I don't blame you." Turning to the crowd, Cí raised his voice. "I've come across plenty of cowards just like you before!"

The giant could see from the people's expressions what was at stake. If he turned down the challenge, his manliness would be in doubt.

"Fine, shrimp. But you're gonna be swallowing your words along with your teeth."

It was the bravado Cí had expected.

Another cheer went up.

Cí set out the rules: "The cuts start at the nipple, trace the outside in loops, carry on outward, going deeper all the time. We only stop when one of us cries out."

"Agreed," said the giant. "On one condition." He looked at each person in the crowd, savoring the moment.

"Whoever wins gets to sink his knife into the other's heart."

13

"Ten thousand *qián* on the boy!"

Everyone, Cí included, turned around in astonishment to see who was placing this bet.

A murmur went around: "He's mad! He'll lose it all!"

But the fortune-teller wasn't deterred. He took a bill from his wallet. The youth taking the deposits checked the bill's authenticity. Once the amount was matched by other bettors, he struck a gong, signaling the preparation for the duel.

Cí and the giant stood a few feet apart, facing each other. The two cooks marked the knife blades to indicate how deep they should sink them. The giant, eyeing his blade as if it were a snake and he had to work out how venomous it was, drained the last of his liquor. He slammed the gourd down and ordered another.

Then the cooks painted on the combatants' bodies the pattern their knives had to follow. The cook who was painting on Cí trembled when his brush crossed over a particularly thick scar.

Cí shut his eyes and prayed for the spirits to protect him. He'd taken part in a Dragon Challenge three years earlier. He'd won then, but it had nearly cost him his life. He knew there was a chance now that his lung could be punctured long before his opponent, with his thick layers of muscle and fat, was seriously injured. But in his mind it was still worth it: Third needed him to be victorious.

And so it began.

⋘⋆⋙

Cí swallowed. He didn't feel the incision, but watched the blood bubbling out of his chest, dripping down his belly and onto his legs. While pain wasn't an issue, the tricky part was staying calm: the slightest jolt and he'd lose the bet. He took slow, even breaths as the tip of the knife sliced through his skin.

He watched the other cook cut the giant, who flinched, but his sardonic smile showed Cí he was a serious opponent. The longer it went on, the closer death came.

The grooves grew increasingly deep, parting fat and flesh, beginning to slice the muscles and fascia. Cí feigned pain. The giant's mouth was jammed shut, the strain in his jaw and neck apparent. He kept his enraged, pained eyes locked on Cí.

Looking down, Cí saw that the knifepoint had stopped directly over his heart. The cook had pushed too hard and hit a rib, and the knife was caught between it and the tough scar tissue. Seeing this, the giant seemed to think victory was almost his, and he shouted for yet another drink. Cí told his cook to continue—if he stopped for too long, that also could be taken as defeat.

"Sure?" said the cook, trembling.

No!

But Cí nodded.

The cook gritted his teeth and pushed down. The skin stretched like resin and then, with a pop, the knife sunk deeper. It was almost at his heart—Cí could feel his heart hammering and held his breath. The cook glanced up for a signal to stop.

"Go on, you bastard!"

The giant laughed. Cí looked up. The giant's torso was bathed in blood.

"Who's the coward now?" he roared, lifting another gourd to his lips.

Cí knew that, any second, it could all go terribly wrong. He shut his eyes and thought about the money and Third.

Cry out, for god's sake!

And it happened—as if the giant had heard his thoughts. His eyes clouded before opening horrifically wide.

The crowd fell silent. The giant tottered toward Cí. The knife was in to the hilt—in his heart.

"It...it was him...he moved!" stuttered the cook.

"De...vil...boy!" croaked the giant, before crashing straight through a table and collapsing on the floor.

A number of men rushed forward to try to revive him, while others crowded around the taker for their money.

Cí didn't even have time to put his clothes on. The fortune-teller grabbed his arm and dragged him to the back door. They went as fast as they could, given Cí's wounded leg and the bleeding from all the cuts, and went down an alley that led to a canal. There, they ducked under a stone bridge, out of sight.

"Take this. Cover yourself and wait here."

Cí took the man's jacket and put pressure on the worst cuts. He began to wonder if the fortune-teller would come back and was amazed when the little man appeared not long after, carrying an over-full bag.

"I had to get the kid at the door to hide the rest of my things. Are you in much pain?" Cí shook his head. "Let me see. Buddha! I have no idea how you managed it."

"And I don't know why you bet on me."

"I'll explain later. Use this." He handed Cí a bandage. "How on earth did you get those burns?'

Cí didn't answer. He hadn't forgotten about the fortune-teller's cheating him. The fortune-teller took off his donkey pelt and put it around Cí's shoulders.

"Do you have any work?"

Cí shook his head again.

"Where are you living?"

"None of your business. Did you make your money back?"

"Of course. I'm a fortune-teller, not an idiot. Is this what you're after?" He held out a purse full of coins.

Cí took his winnings—800 *qián* transformed into 1,600. It was hardly adequate return for what he'd been through.

"I've got to go," he said, standing up.

"Why the hurry? Look at you. You aren't going to get far on that leg."

"I need to get to a pharmacy."

"At this time of night? They can't do much for a wound like that in a pharmacy. I know a healer—"

"Not for me!" He tried to walk but stumbled. "Damn!"

"Shh! Sit down or they'll see us. Those men bet their week's wages, and I can promise you they're no Buddhist monks. They'd kill you for less."

"But I won fairly."

"Right—as fairly as me with the crickets. You don't fool me, boy. We're made of the same stuff, you and I. When the giant was squeezing your neck you hardly even flinched. I didn't think of it then, but then when I saw your scars, and especially the ones that looked like they were from another Dragon Challenge...Come on! There's no way that was the first time you'd played. I'll say it again: I have no idea how you managed it, but you tricked a roomful of people. All except me. Xu, fortune-teller and cheat. That's why I bet on you."

"I have no idea what you mean."

"Mmm. And I have no idea what a magnet is. Here, let me have a look at that leg." Peering at Cí's shin, he swore. "Whoa! Been playing with tigers, have you?"

Cí gritted his teeth. He was losing precious time. He hadn't put his life on the line just so Third could spend the whole night hidden in that hovel alone.

"Do you know of any pharmacies around here?"

"I know a few, but they won't open unless I'm with you. Can't you wait until morning?"

"No. I can't."

"Fine, let's go."

A thick fog hung over the backstreets near the gate. Cí knew they must be getting close to some warehouses by the smell of fish. They came by several ruffians, who eyed them hopefully, but between Cí's limp and the fortune-teller's threadbare donkey pelt, they obviously didn't look worth mugging. The fortune-teller took them down a fish-bone alley, where filth and fish guts were dumped. Stepping from the soup of putrid, sticky blood coating the ground, he knocked on the second door of a shady-looking building. A man with boils all over his face peered out.

"Xu? Got the money you owe me?"

"Damn you! Can't you see this man is injured?"

The man spat.

"Got my money or not?"

Xu stepped past the man and went in. The room was a sty. Once they had pushed aside piles of junk and found somewhere to sit, Cí asked if he had any of the root Third needed. The man with the boils on his face nodded, disappeared behind a drape, and returned with the medicine. Cí checked to make sure it was the right one with a dab on his finger and asked if there was more than the small amount he was offered, but the man said that was all he had. They haggled, and the man finally accepted 800 *qián*.

"Hey," said Xu, "give us something for the boy's leg, too."

The man handed Cí some ointment.

"I'm fine—"

"Don't worry, I'll get it." Xu paid, and they left the hovel.

It had begun to rain, and the wind had picked up. Cí began to say good-bye.

"Thanks for—"

"Don't mention it. Listen, I've been thinking...You said you don't have any work."

"That's right."

"My real job is as a grave digger. It's decent pay if you know how to treat the deceased's families. I work in the Fields of Death, in Lin'an's Great Cemetery. The fortune-telling, all that, is just something I do on the side. You cheat a couple of people, like with the crickets, and word gets out. I always have to work different neighborhoods...and then there are the gangs to deal with. They take most of my profits anyway. I've got family! And the whores and the wine, they cost, too!" he said and laughed.

"Sorry, but—"

"OK, I get it. You have to go. Where are you headed? South? Come on, let's go. I'll go with you."

Cí said he'd be getting a barge, now that he could pay for a ride.

"Money's a great thing! Sure you don't want to earn more?" Laughing at his own joke for some reason, Xu slapped Cí on the back, forgetting about his wounds.

"Do you really have to ask?"

"Like I said, the crickets and everything, that's just to cover costs...But you and me together...I know the markets, all the corner spots. I know how to reel the people in, and you, with this gift of yours…Hmm…We could be rolling in it."

"What do you mean, exactly?"

"Hmm, yes…We'd have to be smart…Not like with that giant, no. Get pimps, real street folk, preferably drunk! The areas around the gates are packed with idiots just dying to lose their money! A fresh face like yours would be just the thing. By the time they realize we've screwed them, we'll be long gone!"

"I appreciate the offer, but I've actually got other plans."

"Other plans? Are you trying to get more money out of me already? Don't worry, we'll split it right down the middle, fifty-fifty. Or maybe you think you could make more without me? Because if it's that, I can promise you you're wrong."

"No, I'm just hoping for slightly less risky work. I've really got to go," said Cí, stepping onto a barge that was just leaving. He tossed Xu his pelt.

Xu caught it and shouted, "Hold up. What's your name?"

Cí answered only by saying thanks, then turned and was lost in the fog.

His trip back across the city went slowly. Third weighed heavily on his mind, and he felt sure something bad had happened to her. Back at the hostel, he hurried up the stairs, ignoring his injured leg. There were no lanterns, so he had to feel his way along to the room. Pulling the drape aside, he called for Third. She didn't answer. It was deathly quiet. Rain had been coming in through the hole in the wall, and the floor was soaking wet.

His hands trembled as he moved aside the bamboo shelter in which he'd left her. There was some kind of unmoving bulk in there—Cí prayed she was just sleeping. He reached his hand out slowly, afraid of touching it…And when his fingers reached the pile of rags and blankets on the floor, he let out a cry.

There was nothing there. Just some soaked pieces of fabric, including the clothes Third had been wearing when Cí had left.

14

Cí ran down the stairs shouting his sister's name. He burst into the little room where the innkeeper slept, tore away the blanket the man was sleeping under, and grabbed him by the throat.

"Where is she?"

"Who?"

"The girl who came in with me! Answer me, or you're dead!"

"Shh…she's in there…"

Cí shoved him back down on his bed and rushed into the room the innkeeper had pointed toward. It was unlit, with pieces of broken furniture everywhere. He stumbled through to another room, where a lantern flickered. It was a mess, too, and though it was lit a dim orange, it was difficult to distinguish anything. Suddenly Cí heard labored breathing coming from a corner of the room. Squinting, he was able to make out the shape of a person. He went over and was met by the eyes of a girl peering at him from a filthy face. But it wasn't Third; Third lay in the girl's lap, curled up and trembling violently.

He was about to kneel down next to them when something struck him on the back of the head, knocking him unconscious.

Once again, that sensation of heaviness and dark.

He could hardly even clear his throat. He was tied up, and a rag that must have been gagging him had fallen down around his neck. His eyes began to adjust; he could see that the girl was still there and Third was still in her lap. The girl was mopping Third's sweaty brow. Third coughed.

"She's OK?"

The girl shook her head.

"Can you untie me?" he said.

"My father says you aren't to be trusted."

"You're his daughter? Gods! Can't you see she needs her medicine?"

The girl glanced nervously at the door. After gently laying Third down on a mat, she went over to Cí and was about to untie him when the door opened. She jumped back—it was her father, and he had a knife.

He knelt down next to Cí. "Right then, you little shit. What's all this about the girl being your sister?"

Cí assured him Third was his sister, explained her illness and how he'd gone out to get her some medicine, how when he'd come back and she wasn't in their room, he'd thought the worst—imagined she'd been taken to some brothel.

"Damnation! That hardly explains why you threatened to kill me!"

"I was out of my mind with worry. Please untie me. I really have to give my sister this medicine. It's in my bag."

The innkeeper reached into Cí's bag.

"Careful, that's all there is."

The innkeeper sniffed the medicine, recoiling at the bitter smell.

"And what about the money you had in here? Who did you rob?"

"No one. Those are my savings. And I need every last penny for my sister's medicine."

The innkeeper spat.

"Fine," he said to his daughter. "Untie him."

As soon as Cí was free, he rushed over to Third, mixed up the powdered root with some water, and gave it to her.

"How are you doing, little one?"

That she smiled, though only weakly, made Cí feel a hundred times better.

The innkeeper would give him back only 300 *qián* of the money he'd taken while Cí had been unconscious; the rest he was keeping as compensation for his daughter Moon's looking after Third, for the clothes they'd dressed her in when they found her coughing and soaked in sweat.

The amount seemed too much, but Cí didn't argue; he knew the man had to look out for his own. Soon, a voice in the entry called the innkeeper away, and Cí tried to talk to Moon, but she seemed reluctant. He took Third in his arms and turned to Moon.

"Would you be able to look after her?"

The girl didn't seem to understand.

"I need someone to be with her. I'll pay you."

Moon appeared curious but didn't answer. She got up and held the door, gesturing for him to go out now. But as he went past her, she whispered, "See you tomorrow."

Cí smiled in surprise. "See you tomorrow."

Cí ran his fingers distractedly over the wound on his leg and watched the light of a gloomy dawn breaking through the cracks in the wall of their room. Though Third's medicine had helped, it hadn't lasted long, and she'd coughed much of the night. Cí had saved a bit for the morning, but he had to get more. He woke Third and gave her what was left of the medicine; he told her that Moon would be looking after her and that she had to promise to behave.

"I could help her clean her house," said Third. "It's very messy."

Cí smiled, shouldering his bag. When they went downstairs, they found Moon polishing some copper cups.

"You're going already?" she said.

"I've got to deal with some things. In terms of the money…"

"My father deals with money, and he's outside at the moment."

"See you later, then…Third's had her medicine, so hopefully she'll be OK. She's a good girl; she'll help you if you need her to." He put his hand on his sister's shoulder. "Won't you?"

Third nodded proudly.

"When do you think you'll be back?" asked Moon.

"Around nightfall, probably. Here," he added, handing her a few coins. Those are for you—you don't have to tell your father."

They bowed to each other, and he left. The innkeeper was just outside the door, dragging a bag of trash. He stopped and looked disdainfully at Cí.

"Leaving, are we?"

"We're going to stay a bit longer." He reached in his pocket and, keeping some money aside to put toward more medicine, offered the innkeeper the rest.

"What is this? That room costs more than you look like you're going to be able to make."

"Please, I'll find a way. Give me a couple of days—"

"Right. Have you seen yourself? In your state I doubt you can piss straight!"

Cí took a deep breath. The man had a point, and he had no energy to negotiate a deal. He handed him a few more coins.

"Dearie me. This isn't enough to get you a tree to sleep under in this city. I'll give you the room for one night. Tomorrow, you're out."

Cí made his way toward the canals in the pouring rain. Judge Feng came to mind. If Feng had been in the city, he'd have helped, but he wasn't going to be back for months. Work. He had to get some kind of work.

⚜

Cí wanted to get a job as a private tutor at the Imperial University. He'd cleaned himself up as best he could, but the most important thing was to obtain the Certificate of Aptitude, which he needed to demonstrate his qualifications and give proof of his parents' integrity.

When he reached the university's main entrance, a vast number of students were milling around. He'd forgotten how busy it could get with students lining up for the documents necessary to take exams.

As he moved through the swarm, he noticed how really nothing had changed: the well-ordered paths through the gardens, the administrators' bamboo huts, the vendors selling boiled rice and tea, the groups of high-class prostitutes with their immaculate makeup and gowns, the police watching out for pickpockets.

Before Cí got very far, though, he saw signs saying that these huts were only for foreigners. Anyone like him, born in a nearby precinct like Fujian, was directed to the vice chancellor's office.

Cí knew he had no chance with the vice chancellor. The run-in with Kao was on his mind, and the police presence at the university worried him. But what else could he do?

A while back he'd found the gateway of the Palace of Wisdom inspiring and uplifting. Now, though, the dragons adorning the blood-colored gates unsettled him. They seemed to be there to frighten away those who didn't belong.

He reached the building where the vice chancellor's office was housed. Cí made his way to the Great Hall on the first floor, where he was greeted by an official with a friendly face.

"Is it for you?" asked the man, when Cí told him the document he needed.

"It is."

"You studied here?"

"Law, sir."

"Very well. And do you need a copy of your grades or just the certificate?"

"Both," said Cí, before providing his details.

"Wait here; I need to speak to someone in another office."

When the man came back, his face was hardened, and Cí's immediate thought was that he was going to be turned away. But the official's severe look seemed less for Cí than for the documents themselves, which he went through several times.

"I'm very sorry," said the man at last. "I'm not going to be able to give you the certificate. Your grades are excellent, but in terms of your father's integrity…" He didn't seem able to bring himself to say more.

"My father? What happened with my father?"

"Read it for yourself. During a routine inspection six months ago, he was…" The man glanced kindly at Cí before going on. "He was found to have embezzled funds. The gravest crime an official can commit. He was on mourning leave at the time, but he still had to be demoted and dismissed."

Cí trembled as he tried to make sense of the documents. His father…
corrupt! That was why he decided not to return to Lin'an. His change
of mind, the change in his attitude—it all stemmed from this.

He felt the shame transferring to him; he was dirty, contami-
nated by his father's dishonesty. He'd now have to bear all of this.
Feeling he might vomit, he fled from the Great Hall, down the
magnificent stairs and out.

He stumbled through the gardens, castigating himself for his
own stupidity. He had no idea where he was headed, or what to do
with himself. He bumped into students and professors as if they
were errant statues; he crashed into a bookstall, knocking it over,
and when he tried to help pick up the books, the vendor shoved
him away while shouting a few choice insults. A police officer made
his way over to see what the commotion was, but Cí was able to
disappear into the crowd.

Leaving the university grounds, he was nervous he'd be
stopped. He made his way to the nearest canal and took a barge
toward the trade square. All he had left was 200 *qián*. Now it was
impossible for him to be a tutor. He had to reconsider.

What jobs could he look for? In a market flooded with farm-
workers, his legal education would do no good. He didn't have
more skill than any other peasant in any kind of manual work,
he wasn't a member of any guild, and his injuries limited him. He
went to a number of shops anyway, asking if there was anything he
could do, anything at all, but had no luck.

He arrived at a salt warehouse and asked there. The man in
charge looked at Cí as if he were trying to sell him a lame mule. He
prodded Cí's shoulders to see how strong he was, then winked at
his assistant and told Cí to stay right there. From the top of a flight
of stairs, the man dropped a sack of salt for Cí to lift; he just about

managed it, though his ribs felt like they would crack under the weight. When he tried to lift a second sack, he fell flat on his face. The two men burst out laughing and sent Cí on his way.

Cí dragged himself along, trying to keep his spirits from sinking too low. Though he wasn't in physical pain, he was sure his injuries were preventing him from making a good impression. But he had to keep trying. He checked all kinds of warehouses, businesses, workshops, the docks, even the municipal excrement collection service, but no one was willing to give him a chance.

He wandered to an area outside the city walls. For a while he drifted aimlessly, but then he heard shouting and headed toward the commotion.

A small crowd had gathered beneath a filthy awning; four or five men were holding down a boy who was kicking and screaming. The boy grew more distressed when another man came toward him brandishing a knife.

Cí realized he was witnessing a castration. There were specialist barbers who were charged with "converting" young homeless boys—usually those deemed to be brimming with vitality—into eunuchs for the emperor's court. Feng had dealt with numerous corpses of boys who had died following the operation—from fever, gangrene, or blood loss. Judging by this particular barber's appearance and the condition of his implements, everything pointed to the boy's becoming one of those corpses.

Cí pushed his way to the front of the group. With a better view, he gasped at what he saw.

The barber, a toothless old man reeking of alcohol, had tried to remove the boy's testicles but had accidentally cut the small penis. Cutting off the penis entirely, which he was now faced with doing, was clearly well beyond this man's shaky abilities. The child wailed as if he were being split in two, and his weeping mother was begging her son to try and stay still.

Cí went over to the woman, and though it was risky to say anything, he turned to her and said, "Woman, if you let this man continue, your son is bound to die."

"Get out of here!" shouted the barber, clumsily taking a swipe at Cí with the rusty knife. Cí sidestepped it easily and held the man's gaze. The barber's eyes were wild, and Cí figured he'd probably drunk every last penny from his most recent job.

"And you," the barber said to the whimpering boy, "you're still a man, right? So stop all that crying."

The boy tried to comply, but he was in too much pain.

The barber, muttering that it was the boy's fault for not keeping still, tried to stanch the blood. Because the incision had reached the urethra, he said he'd have to cut deeper. He took a straw compress from his bag of implements and pressed down. Cí shook his head. The barber twisted the penis and testicles together, and the boy shrieked. The barber paid no attention, but instead turned to the boy's father and asked if he was absolutely sure. It was part of the rite: according to Confucius, not only would the boy become a "non-man," but also, after death, his soul would never find peace.

The father nodded.

The barber placed a stick between the boy's teeth and told him to bite down. As soon as he resumed his work, the boy passed out. It wasn't long before the barber was finished, and he handed the parents their son's amputated genitalia.

The barber, packing away his things, gave them instructions: As soon as he came to, the boy was to walk around as much as possible for two hours, then rest completely for the following three days. After that, the straw compress could be removed. He'd be able to urinate without any problem; everything would be fine.

As the barber started to leave, Cí stepped out in front of him.

"He still needs looking after."

The man spat on the ground and sneered.

"The last thing I need is children."

Cí bit his lip. He was about to reply but was interrupted by sudden cries behind him. Turning around, he saw that the boy lay in a pool of his own blood. And when Cí turned back, the barber had disappeared. Cí went over to try and help, but the boy was half-dead already. And then a pair of police officers arrived. Seeing Cí step back with blood all over his hands, they assumed he was responsible and tried to detain him. Cí dashed into the crowd and made his way to the canal, where he washed his hands and shook his head in disbelief at all that had just happened. He sat and looked up at the sky.

Midday already, and I still have no idea how I'm going to pay for the hostel or Third's medicine.

Just then, a small cricket clambered onto his shoe. He flicked it off. But as the insect was trying to right itself, Cí remembered the fortune-teller's proposal.

The thought of it made him nauseous; he hated the idea of making money from his unusual syndrome, but the situation with Third meant he might have to. Maybe it was the only thing of any value about him.

The canal's dark, turbulent waters made their way toward the river. He thought of throwing himself in, but the picture of Third in his mind held him back.

He jumped to his feet, suddenly decisive. Maybe he was destined to end up dead in the river, but even if that was his fate, he didn't need to give in so easily. He spat on the ground and headed off in search of Xu.

The fortune-teller wasn't at the market stalls in the fisherman's district or at the salting houses, nor was he at the brick market next to the silk shops along the wharves or the Imperial Market. Cí asked everyone and anyone, to no avail. It was as if the earth had swallowed up the fortune-teller and spit out a hundred other tricksters and charlatans in his place.

Cí was ready to give up when he suddenly remembered Xu's job at the Great Cemetery. He boarded a barge to get there.

On his way to the Fields of Death, he wondered if this was the right thing to do. Why try so hard to stay in Lin'an? His only interest here was in continuing his studies. Perhaps it would be better to flee to a city where no one knew him, and where there weren't the likes of Kao on his trail. Here he was, though, trying to prolong a dream any idiot could have told him was now unattainable.

How could his father have dishonored the family and condemned him and Third to their current state? The same man who had taught him about honor and being virtuous in society had apparently thieved and betrayed Feng's trust! It seemed unbelievable, but the man at the university had said the reports were beyond doubt. And Cí had read through them, memorizing the details of each accusation. For all his anger at his father, he still questioned whether his father could have been guilty of such acts.

He opened his eyes with a hard jolt of the barge as it moored clumsily at a jetty on the western lake near the cemetery.

As Cí made his way up the gentle incline to the Fields of Death, he was far from alone. It was a common thing to do at the end of the working week—to join together as a family and honor one's dead, and many people were walking up the hill. Third came into Cí's thoughts; the sun was starting to set, and he didn't know if Moon would have fed his sister, or if Third's cough had worsened. At the idea of Third going hungry and needing her medicine, Cí quickened his pace. Overtaking a number of people, he reached the huge gate at the cemetery's entrance. He asked a group of groundspeople if they knew where he could find Xu, but they didn't, so Cí continued up the hill, to the highest part of the cemetery. The higher he went, the better kept the lawns were, and here in the most exclusive part of the cemetery, there were large gravestones and gardens with family mausoleums. Groups of wealthy families, dressed pristinely in mourning white, made offerings of tea and incense. He saw a gardener by a pavilion that had a sweeping, winglike roof and asked again about Xu. The man pointed up higher, in the direction of the Eternal Mausoleum.

Cí reached a squarish temple swathed in mist. A small man was digging a grave, spitting curses with every shovelful of earth extracted. Seeing Xu, Cí was suddenly nervous. He watched as the man stopped to rest, and then he approached slowly, still unsure that this was a good idea.

Just as Cí considered turning on his heels to go, the fortune-teller looked up and caught his eye. He planted his spade in the earth and straightened up. Then he spat on his hands and shook his head.

"What the hell are you doing here? If you're after more money, I've spent it on women and wine, so you might as well go back to where you came from."

Cí frowned. "I thought you'd be pleased to see me. You seemed a bit more enthusiastic yesterday."

"Yesterday? I was drunk yesterday. And now I've got work to do."

"Don't you remember your offer?"

"Listen. Thanks to you, the whole of Lin'an knows how I worked it with the crickets. I have no idea how I got away this morning. If the others had caught up with me, I'd be in one of these," he said, pointing to the grave.

"Sorry, but I wasn't the one cheating people."

"Ah, right! So what do you call going up against a giant knowing that, even if they cut you in two, it wouldn't hurt a bit? Damn! Get out of here before you make me get out of this grave and kick you out."

"But yesterday you wanted me to do it. I'm here to accept your offer. Don't you get it?"

"Listen, the one who doesn't get it is *you*." The fortune-teller got out of the grave, brandishing the spade. "You don't *get* that you've made it so I can never go back to the market. You don't get that word's spread about your special talent, and now no one's ever going to bet against you. You don't get that you're cursed, you're bad luck! And most of all, you don't get that I've got work to do!"

Then a voice came from behind them.

"He bothering you, Xu?" An enormous man covered in tattoos had appeared out of nowhere.

"He was just leaving."

"Well, get on with that grave," said the man. "Otherwise you'll be looking for another job."

The fortune-teller grabbed the spade and began digging again. Cí jumped in beside him.

"What are you up to?" Xu asked.

"Can't you see?" he said, scooping out earth using his hands. "Helping."

The fortune-teller looked at him for a moment and sighed.

"Go on, take this," he said, handing him a hoe.

They dug side by side until the hole was the length of a body and half as deep. Xu worked silently, but when they finished, he sat back on the grave edge, took a dirty flask from his bag, and handed it to Cí.

"Not afraid to drink with someone who's cursed?" asked Cí.

"Go on. Have a drink, and let's get out of this damned hole."

The deceased and his family arrived. At a signal from a man who appeared to be the family elder, Cí helped Xu lower the coffin into the grave. It was almost in place when Cí lost his footing, and the coffin dropped the last couple of feet, its top coming half-open on impact and dirt falling inside.

Cí couldn't believe it.

Gods in heaven! What else can possibly go wrong?

Cí jumped down into the grave and tried to get the top back on, but the fortune-teller pushed him away. Xu tried moving the coffin himself, but when it fell he'd sprained his finger and could barely use it.

"Get away from him, you idiots!" cried the widow. "Hasn't he suffered enough?"

With the help of some of the men from the family, Cí and Xu lifted the coffin out. They all went to the mausoleum to repair the coffin and clean the body again. Seeing how swollen Xu's finger was, Cí took the jasmine-soaked sponge from him and dabbed at the dead man's muddy shirt. The family members were happy to let him; the general belief was that the bad luck from touching a dead body only affected the person doing the touching.

Cí had dealt with so many dead bodies that he wasn't superstitious. But as he continued with the sponge, he noticed some marks at the neck.

He turned to the family elder. "Did someone apply makeup to the body?" Cí asked.

The man shook his head, surprised.

"How did he die?"

"Fell off a horse. Broke his neck."

Cí checked the dead man's eyelids.

"Mind telling me what you're up to?" asked Xu. "Why don't you stop annoying them so we can finish this job?"

But Cí wasn't listening. He turned back to the elder and said, "Sir, there is no way this man died that way."

"What—what do you mean?" stuttered the man. "His brother-in-law saw it all."

"What you said may have happened, but it's clear that, perhaps after being thrown from a horse, he was also strangled."

He showed the elder the purple bruises on either side of the neck.

"These were hidden underneath some makeup. Not the best job, either. In any case, these bruises clearly correspond to a pair of powerful hands. Here and here," he said, pointing to the bruising.

The elder asked if he was sure. Cí said there could be no doubt about it. The family agreed to postpone the burial and go straight to the local magistrate to report the findings.

<hr>

Cí made a splint for Xu's finger. When he was done, Xu asked, "Are you crazy or something?"

"Clearly!" Cí said with a laugh.

"Fine! Let's talk business."

Cí raised an eyebrow. A short while ago Xu had told him no one would ever bet against him, but now the fortune-teller grinned like a beggar who'd been gifted a palace. Cí didn't care—his only concern was to obtain a few coins up front so he could pay the innkeeper and get medicine for Third. Night wasn't far off, and he was growing more and more worried. He told Xu the story of what had happened at the inn, but the man laughed it off.

"Money worries? We're going to be rich, kid!"

He handed Cí enough money to cover a whole week at the inn. Still chuckling, he took Cí by the hand.

"Now, swear on your honor that you'll meet me back here tomorrow, first thing."

Cí counted the money and said that he would.

"Am I going to be fighting?"

"Something far more dangerous, and far better."

15

For most people, the idea of never feeling pain would seem like a gift from the gods. But Cí knew it was also the stealthiest of enemies. Going along the canal on a barge, he prodded his ribs, checking for any breaks or serious bruising. Then his legs—first rubbing softly, before digging his fingers deeper. The left leg seemed fine, but there were violet-colored bruises all over the right, around the wound. There was nothing he could do but continue to apply the ointment, so he pulled his pant leg down and looked in his bag at the sweet rice buns he'd bought for Third. Picturing her happy face, he smiled. He'd counted the money from the fortune-teller several times now; he could hardly believe how much there was—enough at least for a week's stay.

When Cí got back he found the innkeeper outside arguing with a shady-looking youth. The innkeeper gestured that Third was upstairs and went back to his argument; Cí went straight up, taking the stairs two at a time. He found Third sleeping peacefully. He didn't want to wake her to eat, so he stroked her brow softly; she was still running a fever, but it wasn't nearly as high as it had been. He lay down next to her, said a prayer for his lost family, and, finally, shut his eyes to rest.

There was bad news when he woke up the next morning. The innkeeper was happy to let them stay but said neither he nor Moon could look after Third. Cí couldn't understand why not.

"What's to understand?" spat the man as he prepared his breakfast. "This is no place for a child—that's as clear as can be."

Cí thought he was after more money. He started to haggle, but this just made the innkeeper angrier.

"Haven't you seen the kind of people we get around here? They're scum. If she stays here, you'll come back one night and find her gone—either that or you'll find her with her legs akimbo, bleeding from her sacred little cave. Then you'll try to kill me, so I'll have to kill you. And really, I'd just prefer the money...Room, yes. Nursery, no."

Cí was trying to think of a way to change his mind when a half-naked man left one of the rooms—followed by Moon. That was that. Third would have to come with him.

"What do you think this is, an orphanage?" cried Xu when they arrived at the cemetery.

He grabbed Cí and Third by the arms and angrily led them away from the entrance. He shook his head in agitation and scratched at his beard as if he had lice. Then he knelt down and got them to follow suit.

"It doesn't matter that she's your sister. She can't stay."

"I never get to stay with you," Third whimpered at Cí.

"She's with me," said Cí. "Why can't she stay?"

"Because...because...What the hell's a little kid going to do in a cemetery? Do we leave her to play with the dead bodies?"

"Dead bodies are scary," said Third.

"You be quiet," said Cí. He looked around, took a deep breath, and held Xu's stare. "I knew it wasn't the best idea, but I had no choice. I still don't know what kind of work you've got in mind for me, but she'll have to stay with us until I find another solution."

"I see! Perfect! The destitute's giving his master orders now!" He got up.

"You're not my master."

"Maybe not, but you're a destitute, and…" He muttered to himself and kicked the ground. "Damn it! I knew this was a bad idea."

"What's the problem? She's a good girl. She won't bother us."

Xu knelt down again, still muttering. Then he suddenly got up.

"Fine. If it's the gods' will…Let's seal our pact."

⚜

Xu took them up to the Eternal Pavilion, where bodies were brought to be shrouded, to discuss business. The fortune-teller went inside with a lantern, leading them into a room that stank of incense and rotten flesh. Cí squeezed Third's hand reassuringly. Xu lit a candle and positioned it on a long, raised platform for cleaning bodies. He cleared a space among the essential oils and implements and swept away the sweets and clay pots that often accompanied the dead.

"This is where we'll do business," he said in a proud voice, lifting the candle. "I saw it right away," said Xu. "Your gift of sight—"

"Sight?"

"Yes! And to think I called *myself* a fortune-teller! You kept it well under wraps."

"But—"

"Listen. You'll install yourself here, and you'll examine the dead bodies. You'll have light, books, everything you need. You examine them. You tell me what you see, whatever occurs to you:

how they died, if they're happy in the next life, if they need anything. Make it up if you have to. I'll convey your findings to the families, they'll pay us, and everyone will be happy."

Cí was dumbstruck.

"I can't."

"What do you mean, you can't? I saw you yesterday with my own two eyes. The whole thing about strangulation? Word will spread. People will come from far and wide."

Cí shook his head. "I'm no fortune-teller. I just check for any marks on the bodies, any kind of sign—"

"Marks, signs, what does it matter what you call them? The fact is, you can *tell* things. And that's worth a lot of money! What you did yesterday, you could do it again, right?"

"I might be able to work some things out, but—"

"Well then!" said Xu, grinning. "We've got a deal!"

The three of them sat around a makeshift breakfast table—a coffin. Xu brought out containers of Longjing prawns, butterfly soup, sweet-and-sour carp, and tofu in a fish sauce. Since the dinner their mother had served when Judge Feng visited, neither Cí nor Third had eaten a real meal.

"I told my woman to cook," Xu said, sipping his soup. We've got reason to celebrate!"

Finishing the last of the food, he told Third to go and play outside.

"Right," said Cí. "Let's get our terms clear. What do I get out of this exactly?"

"I see you're no fool," laughed Xu. Then he turned serious. "Ten percent of any profits."

"Ten percent? For doing most of the work?"

"Eh! Don't get mixed up, kiddo. It's my idea. I provide the place, I get the bodies."

"And if I don't accept, that's all you'll have: bodies. Fifty-fifty, or no deal."

"What do you think I am, made of money?"

"It will be dangerous." Without the correct authorizations, doing anything with corpses constituted a serious crime, and this was all about examining corpses.

"For me as well."

Cí got up to leave, but Xu grabbed his sleeve and pulled him back to his seat. He produced a flask, poured liquor into two gourds, and drank both himself. Then he burped.

"Fine. Twenty percent."

Cí looked him in the eyes. "Thanks for the food," he said, getting to his feet again.

"Damn you. Sit for a moment, would you? This business has to benefit us both, and you must see I'm the one risking more. If anyone catches wind of me making money out of corpses, I'm out of a job."

"And I'll be thrown to the dogs!"

Xu frowned and poured more of the liquor, this time offering one of the gourds to Cí, then drinking and again refilling his own.

"You think it all depends on your special telling powers, but things don't work that way. The families will need convincing before we can even look at the corpses. When I talk to them I'll be getting as much information as I can. That way we can work out what they really want. The art of fortune-telling is one part truth, ten parts lies, and the rest pure illusion. We'll want to pick families with money and get to them during the wake, but we must be very discreet about everything. One-third: That's my final offer. That's fair to us both."

Cí stood again and, placing his fists together, bowed.

"When do we start?" he asked.

For the rest of the morning, Cí helped Xu with his tasks at the cemetery: straightening gravestones, digging graves, cleaning out vaults. While they were working, Xu mentioned he occasionally helped at Buddhist cremations—a practice reviled by Confucians, but one that was becoming more popular with Buddhism's increasing appeal and because conventional burial rites were so expensive. Cí said he'd be interested in going with him sometime.

Xu asked him where he'd learned about corpses, and Cí told him it ran in the family.

"The same with not feeling pain?"

"The same," he lied.

Cí spent the afternoon cleaning the Eternal Mausoleum. The room in which Xu kept his tools was an utter pigsty, and Cí imagined Xu's home was probably a mess, too. So when Xu proposed the idea of Cí and Third moving in with him, Cí wasn't exactly enthusiastic.

"But if we're going to work together, it's the least I can do, right?" Xu asked. Then he frowned. "Obviously, I'd have to charge you, but it would solve the issue of your sister."

"Charge me? What do I pay you with?"

"We'd take it out of your share of the profit. Ten percent, say."

"Ten percent!"

"Absolutely." Xu shrugged. "And don't forget, your sister would have to help at home, with the fishing and some chores."

It seemed exorbitant to Cí, but that Third would be looked after was appealing. Xu told him about his two wives, both of whom were in the house. He'd had three daughters but managed to marry them off. All Cí was worried about was Third's health, but Xu reassured him that it wouldn't be heavy work. This made Cí feel better. Everything seemed to be fitting into place.

Next they began to discuss how to organize their work. Xu told Cí that he'd try to go for the deaths that offered the best potential profit—accidents or even outright murders. But he had another idea as well: he wanted Cí to tell the surviving family members what was wrong with them.

"When it comes down to it, you know about illnesses, bodily problems. I bet you could take one look at someone, dead or alive, and know if something's wrong with their stomach, their intestines, their guts—"

"Guts and intestines are the same," Cí pointed out.

"Hey! Don't get smart with me! People always turn up in some kind of pain, including pangs of conscience. You know how it goes: something they said wrong to the deceased, some small betrayal, something they stole...Now, if we can establish a relationship between that and the deceased's tormented soul, they'll want to get rid of the curse immediately—and *that's* where we make some real money."

Cí rejected the idea. It was one thing to apply his knowledge to discern a cause of death, quite another to take advantage of living people in need of real advice.

But Xu wasn't giving up. "Fine. All you have to do is identify the ailment. Leave the rest to me."

<hr />

That afternoon they attended six burials. Cí wanted to examine one corpse whose inflamed eyelids seemed to suggest a violent death, but the family wouldn't allow it. When the same thing happened several more times, Xu began worrying aloud that this had been a bad idea. He told Cí he'd have to figure out a way to make his part work or the deal was off.

It was nearly nightfall, and the cemetery would be closing soon. Cí watched another cortege coming up the hillside. A beautifully carved coffin and a troupe of musicians playing funeral music indicated the family was wealthy. He scanned them to see who might be most susceptible and decided on a youth in full mourning garb with red-rimmed eyes. Cí was ashamed about what he was about to do, but he had to do it. Third's food, board, and medicine wouldn't pay for themselves. He walked up to the youth and asked if he could join him. Then he offered him an incense stick that he said had special powers. As he described all the wondrous properties of the incense, he searched the youth's face for a clue to any ailment—and there it was: a yellow tinge to the eyes that he knew was related to a liver condition.

"You know, of course," said Cí, "that it's normal for the response to the death of a family member to lead to vomiting and nausea. But if you don't do anything to cure it, the pain in your right side will eventually kill you."

Hearing this, the youth began trembling. He asked Cí if he was a seer.

"Yes," said Xu, appearing next to them, smiling. "And he's one of the best."

And Xu took over. Bowing spectacularly low, he took the youth by the arm and led him away from the cortege. Cí couldn't hear their conversation, but judging by the money he had afterward, it seemed his partnership with Xu was beginning to be profitable.

That night Cí was introduced to Xu's houseboat. A long way from being seaworthy, it was permanently moored, and the hemp ropes between it and the jetty were all that kept it from sinking. It creaked with every step and stank of rotten fish. In Cí's eyes it was everything but a place to lay your head, but Xu was proud of it. Cí pulled aside the sailcloth that served as a door drape and came face-to-face with a woman. She screamed and looked as if she were about to push Cí and Third over the side, but Xu intervened.

"This is my wife, Apple," Xu said with a laugh. Another woman appeared, bowing when she saw the visitors. "And this is my other wife, Light."

The women whispered all the way through dinner, clearly unhappy about the idea of taking in two people when there was barely space for them. But when Xu showed them the money they'd earned that day and gave Cí credit, the women stopped complaining and started smiling.

"I'll pay you your percentage soon," Xu whispered, taking Cí by the shoulder.

They went to sleep squashed together like canned sardines. Cí's face ended up right next to Xu's feet; it might have been better, he thought, to find some rotting fish to snuggle up with. Cí's inability to feel pain seemed to be counterbalanced by an overly acute sense of smell. Suddenly he remembered the bitter, intense smell after his house had burned…that smell…

He tried to let the lapping water lull him to sleep. Every now and then a distant gong marked the passing hours. Strong images of his university days took over, and he was calm. Then he was in a dream, seeing himself graduating…when he suddenly woke to an unknown man's hand clamped over his mouth and Xu shaking him awake. Xu's face was right up against his, and he motioned to him to get up quietly.

"We've got problems," he whispered. "Hurry!"

"What's happening?"

"I told you it would be dangerous."

16

They followed the man who'd woken them. Cí had no idea who he was, and only caught brief glimpses of the man's face beneath his threadbare hood. He stopped at every corner to make sure they weren't being followed before signaling them on. They kept to dark streets and headed westward, toward the mountains, where the main Buddhist monastery, the Palace of Chosen Souls, was located. By the time they reached the Great Pagoda with its tower of two thousand stairs, the night had grown particularly gloomy, with clouds almost entirely obscuring the moon.

The man signaled to them to wait while he identified himself to the entrance guard. Cí tried to get Xu to explain what was happening, but Xu just told him to keep his mouth shut.

In place of the unknown man, an old monk with pale eyes appeared. Xu bowed, and Cí followed suit. The monk returned the reverence and warmly asked them to come with him. Cí was surprised by the ornate gilding on the temple walls and its contrast to the dour solemnity of Confucian temples. After passing through the first rooms, they entered a hallway, plain in comparison, which led to the wing where cremations took place. The smell of burning flesh grew strong. Cí was strangely intimidated by it all.

They came to a cavernous room hewn out of the mountainside. A pall of ash hung in the air. A large pyre was burning up ahead, and, by Cí's count, there were about ten people in the room aside from the deceased.

Xu walked toward a body next to the pyre. He gestured for Cí to follow and asked the people present to give Cí room for his examination.

As Cí knelt down next to the corpse, Xu whispered to him. "Don't be nervous, but this was the boss of one of the city's worst gangs. And these men around us are his sons. They would like it if we could tell them who killed him."

"What makes them think we can find that out?" he whispered back, trying to appear calm by beginning to prod and examine the body.

"Because…I told them you could."

"You *what?*"

Xu signaled for him to keep his voice down.

"Well, tell them you got it wrong, and let's get out of here."

"Mmm…can't."

"Why's that?"

Xu gulped. "Because they've already paid."

Cí glanced at the family members. Their expressions were cold and cutting—just like their daggers, thought Cí. He knew if he didn't play this right, there could be two more corpses added to the pile.

He asked for more light and did his best to appear unconcerned, gruff even. Secretly he was praying he could remember Feng's teachings.

He brought the lantern up to the dead man's face: a mess of dried blood and cuts, one ear missing, and the cheekbones smashed in. This was gratuitous violence; none of these wounds looked mortal. The rigidity of the body and the coloration of the skin suggested he'd been dead at least four days. Cí turned to the family members to ask them what they knew about the circumstances of death, and whether any kind of official had looked at the body.

"No one's examined him," said one of the elders. "He was found at the bottom of a well in his garden, by a servant." The elder went on to remind Cí of the deal, in case he'd forgotten: he had to give them the name of the assassin.

Cí shot an angry look at Xu and took a deep breath. The most important thing, he knew, was to seem infallible.

"Remember, it isn't all down to me," Cí said, raising his voice so everyone could hear. "Yes, I have the gift of sight and telling, but first come the gods, and as we all know, their will is inscrutable." He looked toward the old monk for approval.

The monk agreed, bowing. The family members didn't look impressed.

Cí cleared his throat and returned to his examination. The neck was intact, but when Cí pulled back the sheet covering the body, he found the intestines exposed and covered with writhing maggots. The stench was so strong that Cí vomited immediately. When Cí recovered he asked for some cotton soaked in hemp oil, and he stuffed them up his nose the moment they were handed to him. Then he asked the attending monks to make a pit to lay the body in.

"But he was Buddhist," said Xu. "They will cremate him."

Cí explained that the pit wasn't for burying the body but to warm it. It was something Feng often did as part of his examinations, and it would buy Cí some time, too. As the monks dug, Cí began the more detailed part of his examination.

"With the firstborn's permission: We have here an honorable male of approximately sixty years. There are no scars or marks on the body to suggest that he had any sort of serious or even mortal illness." Cí looked around at the family members. "His skin is tender and gives easily under touch, but it is also brittle. He has thin, white hair, which comes out easily when pulled. The bruises to his head and face were likely caused by a blunt instrument."

He stopped, looking closely at the corpse's lips. He made a mental note, and then carried on with his commentary.

"The upper torso shows scratches, probably from having been dragged along the ground. In the abdominal area," he continued, trying his best to hide his revulsion, "there is a deep cut reaching from the bottom of the left lung to the right groin; the innards have spilled out of this incision." He broke off to force down another retch. "The intestines are distended, unlike the stomach itself. The penis looks normal. The legs don't have any scratches on them."

What have you got me into, Xu? It's not easy figuring out how someone died—what on earth made you think I could identify the killer, too?

He got the monks to stop digging for a moment and help him turn the body over; unfortunately, there were no marks on the back to help him complete a theory he'd begun to form, so he covered up the body.

"It would appear that the cause of death was the large gash across the gut. That led to the viscera—"

"Gods!" shouted one of the older men of the family. "We haven't paid you to spell out the obvious!" He gestured to a young, thin man with a scar down his face, who stepped forward and, without a word, grabbed Cí by the hair and held a dagger to his throat.

The older man took a stub of a candle and placed it on the ground next to Cí.

"You've got until this burns down to give us an answer. If you haven't figured it out by then, we'll be mourning you and your partner, too."

Cí shuddered; he still hadn't much of an idea of the cause of death. He glanced at Xu, who didn't return the look.

Cí had embers brought from the kitchen and spread out across the pit. Once they died down, Cí laid a wicker mat over them and sprinkled it with vinegar. Then he had the body laid on top of the mat and covered with a blanket.

Cí's stomach was in knots. He kneeled down to examine the corpse's ankles.

"As I was saying, it might *seem* as if the gash killed him, but all it actually proves is how cunning and depraved the killer was." He ran his fingers over the ankles. "The killer was cold, calculating, disturbed. He made sure he had plenty of time to carry out the crime, and he manipulated the body so that we'd mistake the cause of death."

He had the room's attention now. He tried to focus on what to say, and not on the weak, guttering flame.

"This man did not die from the incision. I know this because the skin immediately around the gash has not attracted worms; that is, when the incision was made, no blood flowed. And that means that when the incision was made, he had already been dead a few hours."

A startled murmur went around the room.

"Nor did he die from drowning. His stomach is empty, and there are no food particles in his nostrils or mouth, nor any insects or the kind of muck you usually associate with wells. Had he been dropped in the well *alive*, he almost certainly would have swallowed an amount of this kind of matter. I therefore conclude that he was dead before he was thrown into the well."

"He wasn't stabbed or drowned, and he wasn't beaten to death," said one of the sons. "So how *did* he die?"

Cí was all too aware that his and Xu's lives were on the line. The candle was almost burned down. He weighed his words carefully.

"My conclusion is that your father was poisoned." Another murmur went around. "Black lips and dark tongue—these are sure signs of one thing, and one thing only: cinnabar, also known as red mercury, the Taoist's fatal elixir and the demented alchemist's venom. After he was dead, under cover of night, your father was dragged by his ankles, face down, and thrown most disgracefully into the well in his own garden. But the killer hadn't finished. He still had time to open up the stomach and mutilate the face—both of which were intended purely to throw us off."

"How can you possibly know all this?" came a voice.

"The marks revealed by the vinegar vapor are incontrovertible." He pointed to the finger imprints on the ankles. "And then, the scratches on the stomach, and the nails, which have so much soil under them, complete the picture."

"This is all very impressive, but you still haven't given us the name. The name!" the elder bellowed suddenly, and the youth sprang forward again, grabbing Xu and putting the knife to his neck.

A few moments passed; the room was silent.

The elder wasn't bluffing; he nodded to the youth, who moved to slice Xu's throat.

"The Great Deceiver!" shouted Cí. It was the first thing that came to his mind.

The youth looked to the elder for direction.

"That's the name of the man you're after," said Cí.

He glanced at Xu, hoping he'd know what to do next. But Xu's eyes were pressed shut in terror.

"Do it," said the elder.

Xu's eyes were suddenly wide open. "Chang!" Xu shouted. "The Great Deceiver is also known as Chang!"

The elder went pale.

"Chang?" He reached a trembling hand into his robe and brought out a knife that glinted in the light. He advanced slowly on one of the men, who took a few terrified steps back.

The elder motioned to the others, and several of the men took hold of Chang. He denied his guilt at first, but when they started pulling out his fingernails, he burst out with the admission, but he said he hadn't meant to do it.

They took their time putting him to death; the elder slit Chang's neck veins, prolonging the process with great skill. Finally, Chang breathed his last and collapsed forward.

Then the men turned to Cí and bowed, and the elder handed Xu a purse full of coins.

"The rest of your money." Though Xu was still recovering from the shock, he managed to return the elder's bow. "Now, if you'll allow us, it's time for us to honor our dead."

Xu made to leave, but Cí stopped him.

"Hear me!" Cí exhorted the room. "The gods have spoken through us. It was their will that the murderer be revealed. By the power vested in me, I order you to never breathe a word of what has happened here this evening. Not another soul can know. If anyone shares this secret, all hell's devils and demons will pursue him, and his family, and death will be close on their heels."

The elder considered the words, pursing his lips. Finally he gave another bow and withdrew with his contingent. Cí and Xu were shown the exit by the monk who had brought them in.

The pair made their way back into the city, coming back down the hill atop which the Great Pagoda sat. There was a glimmer of the rising sun out to sea—a sun that barely seemed real to Cí. They walked in silence, each of them lost in thought over what had happened. As they approached the city wall, Xu turned to face Cí.

"What the hell did you think you were doing, threatening them like that? They know everyone. If not for your clever little sermon, everyone would be hearing about us; we'd be rolling in clients. We'd make enough to buy ourselves our own cemetery! You just threw it all away!"

Cí didn't think he could tell Xu that a sheriff was trying to track him down. But that didn't stop his stomach from churning with anger. Their lives had been on the line, and Xu didn't even see fit to thank him for saving them. All Xu cared about was the future of the business.

He had a sudden urge to get away from Xu—to take Third and get away, anywhere.

"Is this how you repay me?" Cí said.

"Hey, careful now!" shouted Xu. "Don't try and take all the credit. I named Chang!"

"OK, I get it," he said. "You'd have preferred it if I let that guy slit your throat. It would have been better, you reckon, if I'd said nothing about the corpse."

"I named Chang!" repeated Xu.

"OK! Who cares? When it comes down to it, this is going to be the last time we argue like this."

"Meaning?"

"Meaning I'm never going to get involved in another situation like that one just because you see a chance to make a bit of money. I still have no idea what the hell you were thinking. I've not even finished my studies, and you think it's a good idea to cart me out in front of those lunatics."

Xu had opened the purse and was biting one of the coins.

"They're real silver!"

"I don't need a silver coffin," muttered Cí.

"What would you like, then? One made of flax? Because that's what you're headed for if you carry on like you have been."

Cí started to walk away.

"Where are you going?" Xu hurried after Cí. "Here." Xu emptied out roughly a third of the money. "That's more than you could make in six months doing anything else."

Cí rejected it. He knew where avarice led—his father had taught him that much.

"Goddamn, boy. What are you about?"

"That man, Chang, maybe he—"

"Maybe he *what*?" roared Xu.

"Maybe he was innocent. What made you name him?"

"Innocent! Don't make me laugh. All of those men were more than capable of butchering their own children. And anyway, he confessed in the end, didn't he? I knew Chang—everyone knew Chang—and it was common knowledge he was out for the crown. And what does it matter, anyway? He was a thief, a lowlife; sooner or later he'd have ended up dead. It's better that you and I become a little less poor in the bargain."

"I don't care about any of that. You didn't know for sure. You didn't have the proof, and without that no one should be accused. Maybe it was only the torture that made him confess. No, I'm never doing anything like that again. Get it? I'll dig graves, probe patients, examine people dead or alive—but I'll never again accuse someone without proper proof. If you ask me to do that, the first thing I'll do is point my finger at you."

<hr />

For the rest of the walk, Xu shot poisonous looks at Cí. But Cí didn't care; he was agonizing over what to do next.

The money Xu had offered him changed things: it meant he could actually take Third and get out of Lin'an—away from all this danger. But Lin'an still held the promise of all his dreams: university, the Imperial exams, and the chance, if he passed them, to win back his father's honor.

He didn't want to submit to Xu's crazy whims; he'd seen what the consequences might be. And he didn't much want to wait around for Kao to come and finish him off, either.

He kicked a stone and cursed.

He bemoaned not having his father for advice. Or Feng. Someone upright and virtuous to help him through these troubles. He swore to himself that his children, if he ever had any, would never have to suffer this sort of disgrace. He'd do anything to make them proud of him. Everything that had been snatched from his father, he'd win back. That would be their inheritance.

When they arrived at Xu's houseboat, Cí still hadn't decided what to do, but Xu's stance made it easier for him.

"You've got two choices, boy," he said, stepping one foot onto the houseboat. "Keep on working like you have been, or get out of here. Simple."

Cí looked at Xu and gritted his teeth. He only had one option, really: to keep his sister alive.

17

The next few weeks weren't easy.

Cí would get up every night and go to the Imperial Market so he could help one of Xu's wives carry fish back to the houseboat and clean them. The fish cleaning had been assigned to Third, and it had to be done whether she was ill or not, so Cí tried to lighten the load. Then he would accompany Xu on a round of the markets and wharves to find out about the previous day's deaths and violent accidents. They also would stop by the hospitals and clinics, including the Great Pharmacy, where Xu would slip an attendant a little money in exchange for details about the most seriously ill patients. With this information, Xu would plan their next move.

On their way to the Fields of Death, Cí would evaluate the patients' backgrounds, looking for anything that could help make his pronouncements more believable. When they got to the cemetery, he'd put the tools in order and then help dig trenches, lug sacks of earth from one end of the cemetery to the other, place gravestones, help carry coffins. He and Xu would eat and then get ready for the performance; one of Xu's wives had come up with a necromancer outfit with a mask.

"We'll come across as more mysterious," said Cí, but he didn't mention that he was a fugitive and that the other advantage to the disguise was that it would hide his identity.

Xu wasn't wild about the costume, but Cí convinced him by pointing out that if he ever decided to give up the work, it would make it easier for someone else to take his place.

Their work included corpses at the Buddhist monastery. Cremations tended to bring them less money than burials, but it all helped to spread their reputation, and intrigue grew.

They'd return to the houseboat after dark, and Cí would always wake Third to check that she was feeling well and that she'd done her chores. He'd give her little wooden figures that he'd whittled between burials. Then it would be time to give her medicine, check her writing exercises, and recite the thousand words children had to learn to master reading.

"I'm tired," she'd say, but Cí would stroke her hair and insist they do a little more.

"You don't want to be a fisherwoman your whole life," he would tell her.

After everyone was asleep he'd go out into the cold night air and stare at the reflection of the stars in the water as he tried to recite *Prescriptions Left by the Spirits of Liu Jun-Zi*, an impassioned text on surgery that he'd bought secondhand. He'd study until overcome by sleep or until rain extinguished the lantern.

Every night he also remembered his father's dishonor and felt overwhelmed by bitterness.

❦

As the months went by, Cí learned to tell the differences between accidental wounds and those brought about in an attempt to kill; to recognize the incisions made by hatchets, daggers, kitchen knives,

machetes, and swords; to discern between a murder and a suicide.
He discovered that a murderer's methods would be sloppy when the
motive was jealousy or sudden anger, and more sophisticated when
the death was premeditated and based on revenge.

Each case challenged Cí differently, and required both knowledge and imagination. He attended most to the smaller details—
scars, wounds, inflammation. At times something as slight as a lock
of hair or a minor discharge could provide the key to an apparently
inexplicable case.

There was nothing he hated more than when he failed to find
the clues he needed. The more corpses he examined, the more he
realized how little he really knew. Everyone else thought he had
magical powers when he was actually learning the extent of his
ignorance. He'd grow desperate sometimes—if there was a symp-
tom he couldn't make sense of, a corpse that wouldn't give up its
secrets, a scar whose origin he couldn't figure out. Each time he
came to an impasse, he remembered Feng and the man's attention
to detail. Feng had taught Cí things he never would have learned in
university—but, surprisingly, he was also learning from Xu.

Xu had some expertise when it came to the dead. He knew how
to figure out how bruises might have come about and how to discern what job a person had done. He'd developed a familiarity with
corpses though years working at the cemetery and helping with cremations at the Buddhist monastery; he'd even worked at one time as
a gravedigger at the prisons in Sichuan, where torture and death were
commonplace. He had much of the practical experience Cí lacked.

"Did I see executions there!" he bragged. "Proper killings they
were—none of this kid stuff. If prisoners' families didn't bring
them food, neither did the government."

Of course, this reminded Cí of Lu's awful death. It was some
comfort to know it probably wouldn't have been any better for him
if he had survived and made it to Sichuan.

Cí, as hungry for knowledge as ever, tried to glean as much information from Xu as he could, but he also had to study if he was to stand a chance with the Imperial exams. As winter approached, he mentioned to Xu that he wanted to buy more books.

"Fine by me," said Xu. "But it comes out of your wages."

Even though the price of food and medicine was rising, Cí still had ample money to keep Third fed and medicated. He could get the books, but after working such long days he didn't have much time to study.

<hr />

Spring came to Lin'an, and Cí had become calmer and more confident in his work. He could immediately identify the purplish bruising from a blunt instrument; he could distinguish the smell of rotting flesh from the sweeter smell of gangrene; his fingers were more proficient in finding hard spots beneath skin tissue, the little ulcers of a rope burn on someone's neck, the tenderness of old age, moxibustion burns, even the tiny scars made by acupuncture needles.

He was feeling more and more sure of himself.

And that was his big mistake.

On a rainy day in April, a large retinue of well-dressed nobles made their way up the cemetery hill carrying a coffin. Two servants came ahead of them to ask Xu about determining the cause of death. The man, who had been an official in the War Ministry, had died following a long illness, but its cause was unclear, and they wanted to know if the death could have been avoided.

Xu negotiated a price and fetched Cí from the grave he was working to repair. Cí's clothes were filthy and he wanted time to change, but Xu told him they had to hurry and that he should get his mask and come immediately. Cí realized the gloves he'd been using to hide his scarred hands were covered in mud.

And I left the other pair on the houseboat.

He couldn't afford to let himself be identified by his scars.

"You know I can't do it without the gloves," he said.

"Damn it, Cí. Hide them—put them up your ass for all I care. You could do it with your hands tied behind your back nowadays."

He should have said no, but his increased confidence led him to agree. From what Xu had told him, Cí figured old age would probably be the cause of death, which would eliminate the need for much examination. He put the mask on in the pavilion and went out to receive the cortege while keeping his hands tucked into his sleeves. He took one look at the corpse and knew a stroke had killed the man.

Fine. We'll just do our routine.

He bowed to the retinue and approached the coffin. The neck was swollen, the wrinkled face was peaceful, and the funeral outfit smelled of incense and sandalwood. There was nothing out of the ordinary. He didn't need to handle the body. All the family wanted was something specific, and that was what he'd give them. Making sure his hands were well hidden, he pretended to examine the face, neck, and ears, passing his sleeves across them.

"Death by stroke," he announced finally.

The family members bowed in thanks, and Cí bowed back. Straightforward. But as he withdrew, there was a shout behind him.

"Take him!"

Before he knew it, two men had grabbed him and a third was searching him.

"What is it?" asked Cí, struggling.

"Where is it?" one of them said. "Where have you put it?"

"We saw the way you were hiding your hands under your sleeves," said another. "Thief!"

Cí looked to Xu for help, but Xu was keeping his distance, looking out for himself as always. His captors demanded he give back the pearl brooch he'd stolen. Of course, he hadn't stolen it, but Cí knew they wouldn't believe anything he said. They stripped him naked and found nothing—still they weren't satisfied. They threw his clothes in his face and told him to cover himself.

"You'd better tell us where it is; otherwise you're getting a beating."

A boy had already been sent into town to report him to the authorities, but the rest of the family didn't seem willing to wait. The two men twisted Cí's arms behind him.

"I didn't take anything! I barely even touched him!"

A punch to the stomach doubled him over. He gasped for air.

"Give it back. Or you're dead."

Another man approached with a noosed rope. Cí cried out, "It's a mistake. I haven't taken anything!" He felt a knot being tied around his throat. Then an imperious voice boomed out.

"Let him go!"

The men took their hands off Cí as the head of the family stepped forward.

"You don't know how sorry I am," said the man, bowing remorsefully. "I just found it in the coffin. It must have fallen off in transit."

Cí said nothing. He dusted himself off and walked away.

That night he lay on the roof of the houseboat and meditated on the incident, which was a reminder that he was walking a fine line in this work. The slightest slip—even paying more attention to hiding the burns on his hands than anything else—could mean serious trouble.

Not a good day. Soon it would be the New Year, and he'd turn twenty-one. The violence felt like a bad omen.

Two days later, things went from bad to worse.

He and Xu were polishing a coffin in the Eternal Mausoleum when they heard a strange murmuring outside. At first Cí attributed it to the man who hummed incessantly when he raked the leaves. Soon, though, he realized the sounds were coming from dogs. His hair stood on end; his last encounter with a dog had been with Sheriff Kao's hound, and people didn't typically bring dogs into the cemetery. He hurried over to the door and peeked out.

Kao was heading up the hill with a bloodhound. Instinctively, Cí crouched down.

"I need your help!" he implored Xu. "The man who's coming—go and stall him for me. I need to figure out what to do."

Xu looked outside. "A sheriff! You in some kind of trouble?"

"No! Just don't let him know I'm here."

"And what about the dog?"

"Please, Xu, I'm begging you!"

Xu went outside just as Kao reached the mausoleum entrance. Xu stood back as Kao restrained the dog.

"Lovely animal," he said, shutting the door behind him and bowing. "Is there anything I can help you with?"

"I suppose so," growled Kao. "Are you the man they call the fortune-teller?"

"Yes, Xu is my name."

"A couple of days ago a robbery was reported. Do you know anything about it? They said a brooch was stolen here in the cemetery."

"Oh, that! Let me see…Yes, it was all a big misunderstanding. There was a family, prickly they were, and they *thought* we'd taken a brooch from a corpse. But it was found—it had just fallen into the coffin. That was all."

"Yes, that's what I heard."

"So is there a problem?"

"The report mentioned a young man who was helping you. He was in disguise and had burn marks on his hands and torso. This fits the description of a fugitive I've been tracking: a young male, tall and slim, good-looking, hair tied up…"

"That little bastard!" spat Xu. "I've been cursing myself for hiring him. He vanished yesterday and took some money from me. I was going to report it at the end of the week."

"Mmm," grunted Kao. "So I suppose you have no idea where he is now?"

"No, I mean, he could be anywhere…What's he wanted for?"

"Stealing money. There's also a reward on his head."

Xu's tone changed. "A reward?"

Just then there was a noise from inside the mausoleum.

"Is there someone in there?"

"No, I swear—"

"Out of the way!"

Though he'd bolted the door, Cí could see Xu wasn't able to detain Kao. The cemetery suddenly seemed very small; even if he escaped through a window of the mausoleum and ran, the hound would surely catch him. There was no way out. He was trapped.

"Nothing in there but the dead!" he heard Xu cry, as Kao began battering on the bolted mausoleum door.

"I'll make sure of that," roared Kao.

The door was sturdy, and the bolt seemed as though it could withstand the pounding Kao was giving it. Standing back, Kao spied a large board on the ground. Grabbing it, he smiled at Xu. The first impact made splinters fly; two more and a large crack appeared in the door. Kao was about to strike again when the door opened from inside. A figure stepped out, dressed in a necromancer's outfit, arms raised and trembling.

"The mask, take it off! Now!" shouted Kao. The dog was straining at the leash.

The man's hands were trembling so much he couldn't undo the knots on the mask.

"Get on with it! The gloves, take them off!"

The man began taking the gloves off, peeling them away one finger at a time. First the right, then the left. Kao's face went from triumph to stupefaction in an instant.

"But...but you..."

The hands were wrinkled, but there wasn't a single burn on them. Overcome with rage, Kao ripped the mask off, coming face-to-face with an elderly, and clearly very frightened, man.

"Out of my way."

Kao pushed past the imposter and went into the mausoleum, kicking anything and everything in his path. He howled: the place was empty. He came back out and grabbed Xu.

"Damned liar! Tell me where he is or I'll stuff your head down your throat!"

Xu swore he didn't know.

"I'm going to have eyes on you day and night. If that boy comes back to you, I swear you'll regret it."

"He won't be coming back. He robbed me. If I do ever see him, I'll be the first to give him a beating."

Kao left the cemetery in a whirl of oaths and curses.

<hr />

When Cí told Xu how he'd paid the gardener to dress up in the outfit, Xu couldn't help but laugh.

"But how on earth did you manage to not be found?"

"Got the gardener to shut me in a coffin—and make it look like it was nailed shut."

Xu told Cí what had happened with Kao. "I think you're going to have to tell me why they're after you. He mentioned a reward,"

Xu said, smiling, "but I don't think it can be as much as you and I are making together!"

Cí hesitated—he knew his story was barely believable. He also sensed something in Xu he didn't know if he trusted.

"Maybe it's time for us to stop," said Cí.

"No way. We'll change the disguise to something that makes you stand out less. Pick the clientele better. And make it clear they can't go telling the world about us." He winked. "I'm not an ambitious man. We've got plenty of clients for now."

But Cí still had the feeling that Xu would do whatever suited him. He'd said that this was by far the most lucrative enterprise he'd been involved in.

"I'm not sure, Xu. I don't want you to get in trouble on my account."

"Don't worry. We're in this together. Really. But let's forget about our little shows for a while, do something else."

Cí nodded.

But two days later, Cí found out that he and Xu weren't really in it together at all.

<hr />

It was cold that morning, and Xu's wives began complaining that Third was nothing but a nuisance. She was a slow learner, her head was always in the clouds, she got the prawns and the shrimp mixed up, and she ate too much. Plus they always had to look out for her health, which Cí knew was getting worse.

"Maybe we sell her," shrugged Xu. It was a common thing to do when families were hard up, he pointed out. Of course, Cí wouldn't hear of it.

"Marry her off, then," suggested one of the wives.

Xu was all for it. He didn't see how Cí could object. It was simply a question of finding a man who liked that she was still so young. When it came down to it, Xu thought girls were a nuisance until the day they married.

"It's what we did with ours. Third's eight years old—just tart her up a bit so she doesn't look so sickly. I can think of plenty of guys who'd love a little puppy like her."

Cí went and stood by Third. It wasn't unusual for girls to be offered in marriage at a young age—sometimes it was their best chance in life—but Cí couldn't accept the idea of Third being slobbered over by some old man.

But Xu kept on pushing.

As always, Cí's only recourse was to offer money. But he was running out of that fast. Third's medicine seemed to be having less effect; she needed more and more all the time. Since Xu had taken over the necromancer duties, and since he had gotten numerous tellings wrong, their joint income was much lower. In fact, before this conversation started, Cí had been about to ask for a loan.

"You're going to have to go back to earning proper money yourself," said Xu, pointing to the necromancer's outfit. Cí looked at it; though Xu had said he would modify it, he had barely done so. Cí took a deep breath and frowned. He worried about Kao's coming back, but if he wanted to save his sister, he had no choice.

That afternoon a group of students and their professor came to the cemetery. Seeing them coming, Xu told Cí how they would sometimes have visits from Ming Academy. For a fee, they were allowed to examine any unclaimed corpses. Luckily, there were three there at the time. Xu was exultant.

"Get dressed," he said. "These youngsters are *so* easy to get money out of, if you don't mind groveling a bit."

Cí did as he was told, the thought of Third spurring him on.

He watched from a corner, waiting for Xu's signal. The professor, a bald man dressed in red who seemed somehow familiar, arranged the students around the first body. Before they began, he reminded them of their responsibilities as future judges: respect for the dead and honor in their judgments were of utmost importance. Then he lifted the sheet covering the corpse, revealing a baby girl, a few months old perhaps, who had been found dead in a canal that morning. The professor embarked on a round of questions for the students to discern the cause of death.

"Drowned, no question," said the first, a fresh-faced youth with a smug air. "Swollen belly, no other marks."

The professor nodded, inviting the next student to speak.

"A typical case of drowned child. The parents threw her in the canal to avoid caring for her."

"They might not have been able to," chided the professor. "Anyone else want to say anything?"

Cí saw that the professor noticed one of the students—Cí had overheard him called Gray Fox, a fitting name given his gray-streaked hair—kept yawning, but the instructor said nothing. He covered the baby's corpse and asked Xu to bring the next. Xu took the opportunity to bring Cí in and introduce him as the resident necromancer. The students looked at his outfit with disdain.

"We're not interested in tricksters," said the professor. "None of us here believe in necromancy."

Cí withdrew, disconcerted. Xu whispered to him to take off the mask and stay alert. The next corpse was an ashen old man who had been found dead behind a market stall.

"Death by starvation," said one of the students, looking closely at the corpse with its protruding bones. "Swollen ankles and feet. Approximately seventy years old. Natural causes, therefore."

Again, the professor agreed with the evaluation, and everyone congratulated the student. Cí saw how Gray Fox went along with it but was clearly being insincere in his praise. Xu and Cí brought the third corpse in a large pine coffin. When they removed the lid, the students at the front recoiled, but Gray Fox came forward, immediately quite interested.

"Looks like a chance for you to show your talents," said the professor.

The student replied with an ironic smile and approached slowly, his eyes glittering as though the coffin contained a treasure. Cí watched as the student took out a sheet of paper, an inkstone, and a brush. His approach was very similar to the one Cí had seen Feng take in examinations.

First Gray Fox inspected the corpse's clothes: the undersides of the sleeves, inside the shirt, trousers, and shoes. Then, having removed the clothes and scrutinized the body, he asked for water, which he used to clean the blood-spattered skin thoroughly. Next he measured the body and announced that the deceased was at least two heads taller than an average man.

He began examining the swollen face, which had a strange puncture on the forehead that exposed a bit of the skull. Instead of cleaning it, the student extracted some mud, saying the puncture was most likely the result of a fall, the head having struck the edge of paving stones or cobblestones. He made a note and then described the eyes, which, half open and dull, were like those of a dried fish; the prominent cheekbones; and the wispy mustache and strong jaw. Then he mentioned the long gash that ran from one side of the throat, across the nose, and all the way to the right ear. He looked closely at the edges of the cut and measured the depth. Smiling, he wrote something else down.

He moved on to the muscular torso, noting eleven stab wounds; then he scanned the groin; the small, wrinkled penis; and the thighs and calves, which were also muscular and hairless. Cí helped him turn the corpse over; aside from the bloodstains, the back was unmarked. The student stood back, looking ever more pleased.

"So?" said the professor.

The student took his time before answering, looking at each person individually. He clearly enjoyed performing. Cí raised an eyebrow but paid attention.

"This is obviously an unusual case," began the student. "The man was young, very strong, and ended up stabbed and with his throat slit. A shockingly cruel murder, which seems to point to there having been a very vicious fight."

The professor gestured for the student to continue.

"At first glance we might think that there were several assailants—there would have been several of them to overcome a hulk like this—and the many stab wounds attest to that. The number of injuries indicates the fight lasted some time, before someone delivered the decisive wound to the throat. After that, the victim fell forward, causing the strange rectangular mark on the forehead." Here the student paused for effect. "And the motive? Perhaps we ought to think of several: from a simple tavern brawl to an unpaid debt or old feud or even a dispute over some beautiful 'flower.' But the most likely motive is robbery, given the fact the body's been stripped of all valuables, including the bracelet that should have been...here," he said, pointing to a tan mark at the wrist. "A magistrate would have done well to order the immediate vicinity searched, paying particular attention to taverns and any troublemakers either showing wounds or throwing money around." The student closed his notebook, covered the corpse, and stared at the group, waiting for his applause.

Cí remembered what Xu had said about the possibility of tips if they groveled, and went over to congratulate the student, but the student looked at him with disdain.

"Stupid show-off," muttered Cí, turning away.

"How dare you!" Gray Fox grabbed his arm.

Cí shrugged him off and squared up to the student, ready to argue, but before he could reply, the professor was between them.

"So, it seems the sorcerer thinks we're loudmouths," said the professor. Looking at Cí more closely, his face changed. "Do I know you?"

"I don't think so, sir. I haven't been in the capital long," he lied. As he said it, though, he realized the professor was Ming, the man to whom he'd tried to sell his copy of the penal code at the book market.

"Are you sure? Well, anyway…I think you owe my student an apology."

"Or maybe he owes me one."

At Cí's impertinence, a murmur went around.

Xu stepped in. "Please, sir, forgive him. He's been quite out of sorts lately."

But Cí wasn't backing down. He wanted to wipe the smile off the conceited student's face.

He turned to Xu and whispered, "Put a bet on me. Everything you've got. It's what you know best, right?"

18

Professor Ming resisted betting at first, but once he admitted a bit of curiosity, his students urged him on, and he agreed to the challenge. Xu skillfully upped the bets, making a show of worrying that he'd lose everything.

"If you mess this up," warned Xu, "I swear I'll sell your sister for less than the price of a pig."

Cí wasn't daunted. He asked the group to give him some space and took out instruments for his examination: a small hammer, forceps made from bamboo, a scalpel, a small sickle-like object, and a wooden spatula. Beside these he placed a washbasin, gourds containing water and vinegar, paper, and a brush.

Cí had some doubts about Gray Fox's inspection, and Cí was ready to see if he was right.

He went first to the corpse's nape, working his fingers from there up along the scalp to the crown of the head, and then inspecting the ears with the help of the little spatula. Then he went downward from the neck, examining the muscular shoulders, upper arms, elbows, and forearms, stopping at the right hand and paying particular attention to something at the base of the thumb.

A circular callus.

He made a note.

He checked the spine, the buttocks, and the legs for injuries before cleaning the face, neck, and torso—properly, with water and vinegar. He spent a good deal of time on the stab wounds, measuring and probing, and then concluding that at least three were fatal.

Just as I suspected.

Then the terrible throat wound: shaking his head, he measured it and made a note of the tears at the edges. Last came the face. Using the forceps inside the nose and mouth, he extracted a whitish substance. He made another note.

"We're waiting," warned the professor.

But Cí refused to be hurried. A hundred facts were swirling in his mind, and he still hadn't quite come to the answer. He returned to the face, where, now that it was clean, he noticed some small scratches on the cheeks. He moved to the mark on the forehead, which he concluded couldn't have been caused by an impact at all; the edges of the rectangular mark were too neat to be anything but an incision. The mud stuck in the flesh was a red herring, he decided.

Now he was getting somewhere.

He went back to the arms and hands, finding new scratches, then again to the head, parting the hair very carefully and inspecting the scalp. His suspicion confirmed, he turned to the professor. The game was won, and only he knew.

Gray Fox smiled. "So, sorcerer, anything to add?"

"Not really," he said timidly, dropping his head and looking at his notes.

Laughter broke out among the students, who began clamoring for Xu to pay up. Xu looked nervously to Cí, who was still consulting his notes. Xu cursed and was about to begin paying on the bets, when Cí piped up.

"Not so fast."

They will be the ones to pay once I am done.

"What are you saying?"

Gray Fox came up to him. "If you think you can mock us and get away with it…"

But Cí ignored him and looked to the professor for permission to present his conclusions. Ming nodded, seeming interested to hear what Cí had to say.

"Your student has carried out a superficial examination. Blinded by his ego, he ignored the value of what seemed to him banal facts. Just as a race over a thousand *li* can only be achieved one step at a time, examining a corpse requires patience and attention to the most minute details."

Before his opponent could object, Cí continued. "The victim's name was Fu Leng. Convicted of serious crimes, he was condemned to serve as a soldier at the Xiangyang outpost, on the River Han border, but he recently deserted. He came to Lin'an hoping to embark on a new life, but his violent personality was an obstacle. Yesterday afternoon, as so often, he fought with his wife and then beat her. Later, when he sat down to eat, she came up behind him and slit his throat. The unfortunate woman, should you be interested in speaking to her, will be found in her house, which is close to the walls where the body was found. Ask at the Yurchen shop near the north jetty. They'll know where she lives—if she hasn't killed herself already."

Everyone was silent—even Xu, who just stared back when Cí told him to take their winnings. Gray Fox stepped forward and, out of nowhere, slapped Cí.

"I thought I'd heard it all, but this is unforgivable. You should be ashamed. Listen—"

"No, you listen. It isn't my fault you're inept. You even cleaned the body *before* checking for evidence."

Astounded, Gray Fox looked to Professor Ming, who instructed him to keep calm and told the others that it wasn't quite time to pay Xu.

"As I've said many times, having conviction is important in this line of work, but on its own it is never enough. That's why we have tribunals rather than just taking the word of an accuser." Ming turned to Cí. "Your words have a convincing edge, but you also show insolence, and above all, your assertions lack evidence. Without the evidence, the only conclusion can be that this is a flight of fancy. Either that, or you were actually present at the crime."

Cí had known this presentation would be different from one to a group of mourners. The best investigators were trained at the Ming Academy, but if he explained his logic, they'd know he had medical training, which could give away his identity.

So he said that if they really needed proof, all they had to do was go to the scene of the crime. At this, Ming threatened to report him to the authorities.

Cí pressed his fists together and bowed. The risk was worth taking to prove he was right.

"Very well, we'll begin with the cause of death. He didn't die in a fight; there were neither several assailants nor numerous beatings. He died when his throat was slit, and the incision point and direction of the cut demonstrate that this happened from behind. Given that he was so tall, he must have been seated when he died. Otherwise, the killer wouldn't have been able to cut down to up like this. The stab wounds on the torso were all delivered by the same weapon, from the same position, and with the same intensity—that is, by the same person. Three of them are mortal, which means that all the others, including the slit to the throat, were unnecessary. So we can discard the story of the attack squad."

"Pah! Pure supposition," said Gray Fox.

"You sure?"

Cí seized the wooden spatula as if it were a knife and rushed at Gray Fox. The student leaped backward, holding his arms up to parry the thrusts. Cí kept on coming, eventually cornering him. But as much as he tried to get at Gray Fox's torso, he never managed to get past the raised arms.

Then, just as suddenly as he'd begun his attack, Cí stopped.

Gray Fox didn't launch a counterattack, but looked around incredulously. No one had come to his aid, and Professor Ming had watched the whole thing impassively.

"Master!" squealed Gray Fox.

But the professor's only response was to give the floor to Cí once more.

"As you can see, for all I tried, I couldn't get past his defense. Now, picture the situation: If I'd had a knife, instead of this wooden spatula, your arms would have cuts all over them. If I had landed a blow on your body, the angles of the cuts, and how deep they went, would all have been very different."

To this Gray Fox gave no answer.

"But," said Professor Ming, "that hardly leads us to the idea that the killer was a woman, or his wife, or that he was an escaped convict—nor any of the rest of your conclusions, or fabrications, I should perhaps say."

Cí went calmly over to the corpse, inviting the group to look closely at the wound on the forehead.

"The result of a fall? Wrong. If your classmate had carried out his examination properly, he would have seen that this section of skin, which he thought came away because of an impact, was in fact pulled off with the very same knife that slit the throat. Look at the edges of the wound." Cí ran his gloved fingers along them. "He didn't bother to clean the wound, so he missed that the edges of the wound are sharp and clearly defined. The precise rectangular shape of the wound can mean only one thing."

"A demonic ritual?" asked Xu.

Please, Xu, not now.

"No," said Cí, clearing his throat. "It was an attempt to remove something that would have identified the corpse, because it was something that would have identified the man, beyond doubt, as a dangerous criminal, convicted for the worst of crimes." He paused, turning to Professor Ming. "It wasn't any old piece of skin that was removed; it was where the tattoo they put on murderers was placed. Fortunately, in this case, the killer either forgot or didn't know that murderers are also tattooed on the crown of the head."

From their expressions, Cí could see the students' attitudes were rapidly changing from disdain to astonishment.

"And the idea that he deserted Xiangyang?"

"It's well known that our penal code sets out execution, exile, and enforced labor as punishments for murder. This corpse was alive only yesterday, which leaves exile or enforced labor." He held up the corpse's right hand. "And the circular callus at the base of the thumb proves, without a doubt, that this man was wearing the bronze ring with which the flexor tendon is tightened."

"Let me see," said the professor, coming closer.

"It is also well known that our army forces are concentrated in Xiangyang because of the incursions by the Jin invaders."

"And that's why you think he deserted."

"Basically. In a state of war, no one is allowed to leave the army, but this man did so to return to Lin'an. And not long ago, either, judging by his tan."

"His tan?" asked Ming.

"Look at this faint horizontal mark," said Cí, indicating a line across the forehead. "There is a very slight difference between the color of the skin here, compared to a little higher."

The professor checked this.

"A head scarf," continued Cí. "In the rice fields, the workers call them two-tones. But here there is only a very slight difference in coloration, indicating he only recently began using the head scarf to hide his tattoo."

The professor frowned, seeming to weigh his next question.

"And the whereabouts of the woman? What were you saying about asking at the Yurchen shop?"

"Oh, I was lucky there. There was so much leftover food matter in his mouth that I could only deduce he died while eating."

"But—"

"The Yurchen shop, yes. Look." He picked up the gourd in which he'd deposited the leftovers. "Cheese."

"Cheese?"

"Surprising, yes? A very unusual thing to eat around here, but common among the northern tribes. As far as I know, the only place bringing cheese into Lin'an is Old Panyu's exotic food shop. I'm certain they'd remember the few customers who had recently bought such disgusting fare!"

"Which he perhaps developed a taste for during his time in the army…"

"Perhaps. They have to eat whatever they can find."

"But you still haven't explained the key element—that his wife killed him."

Cí consulted his notes. Nodding, he lifted one of the corpse's arms.

"These," he said, pointing to some faint scratches. "The same as on both his shoulders. They showed up when I washed the body with the vinegar."

"And these lead you to conclude…"

"That she'd been beaten badly earlier in the day and tried to fight back. She couldn't take the abuse anymore, so when he sat down to eat, she came up behind him and slit his throat. And when he was down, she went into a rage, straddled him, and stabbed him in the torso. When she calmed down, she removed anything that might identify the body or link it to her. But because he's such a big man, she wouldn't have been able to carry him very far. Therefore the killer is still in the vicinity of where the body was found."

"Truly fantastic," said Ming.

Cí bowed in thanks.

"No, I mean fantastic as in you've created a huge fantasy based on scant findings. Anyone could find any number of holes in your argument—for example, why the wife and not a sister? If the skin from the forehead is gone, there's no way of being certain it had a tattoo on it, let alone what it said."

"But—"

"Enough. You're smart, no question about it, but you're not as brilliant as you think."

"And…the bet?" said Xu.

"Mmm." The professor took out a purse and handed it to Xu. "That should settle it."

The professor signaled to his students it was time to go. As they filed out, he motioned for Cí to follow him. Leaving the students, Ming led Cí over to a hedged garden. Cí's heart raced as he waited for the professor to say something.

"How old are you, boy?"

"Twenty-one, sir."

"And where did you learn your skills?"

"Learn? I don't know what you mean."

"Come on," said the professor. "I can tell where your knowledge is from."

Cí pursed his lips.

"As you wish," said Ming. "If you don't want to take part, that's a real shame. In spite of your temerity, I'm impressed."

"Take part? What do you mean?"

"One of our students fell ill last week and had to go back to his province. There's a spot at the academy, and in spite of the long waiting list, we're always on the lookout for anyone with real talent." He paused. "But I see it isn't for you."

Cí could hardly believe it. The Ming Academy was the gateway for anyone who wanted to be anyone in the judiciary, an entry point into the elite—it even meant avoiding the Imperial exams, and the promise of regaining his family honor. It was beyond his wildest dreams.

But this offer was like the honey on a spoon before the bitter medicine; he could never afford the fees.

As if he'd read Cí's thoughts, Professor Ming said they might be able to offer him accommodation, and that there was a job in the library with wages that would cover his tuition. Cí pinched himself. He'd be able to learn all the new techniques and cutting-edge developments. It was a chance to earn his rightful place. Finally his life would be what he wanted.

But what about Third?

The professor was shocked when Cí rejected the offer.

19

Cí cursed his fate again—it built him up only to knock him cruelly back down.

He went back to the grave he'd been digging. He dug and dug until his hands bled. Even then, he didn't stop.

There was one insurmountable obstacle to Ming's offer: he wouldn't have been able to continue taking care of Third.

Ming had made it clear that Cí's costs would all be covered if he worked in the library, but Cí wouldn't have been able to afford Third's medicine, or food or lodging for her. He had asked if he could carry on with his job at the cemetery, for extra money, but Ming said no, he would have to be fully dedicated to his studies.

Night fell and still Cí was digging, but then he remembered he had to get back to Third. He found it impossible to sleep that night. Third was sweating and coughing. He twisted and turned next to her, trying to figure out what to do. She'd had the last of her medicine hours earlier, and he was completely out of money.

Xu had refused to share Ming's purse with him, claiming that since he'd put the money up, he alone deserved the winnings. Cí couldn't have hated Xu more.

When morning came and Xu headed out for work, Cí ignored him and spent a few more minutes with Third. Though it was already summer, she couldn't stop shivering.

"Don't you dare make her work today," he spat at the wives as he walked out the door.

As he walked along the port, past the swell of beggars scrabbling for something to eat, Cí realized that enough time had passed for Feng to have returned to Lin'an.

He was running out of options and time. While he knew that his fugitive status could tarnish Feng, he was Cí's last hope.

Crossing the city by taking one barge after another, he eventually came to the Phoenix area in the south. He passed a few mansions before getting to Feng's pavilion, a venerable one-story building with gardens in the front and back. Memories came flooding back of happier times spent among those apple trees. But as he got closer, he was shocked. The back garden, previously full of well-tended flowers, was tumbledown and overgrown. He rounded a pond that was now nothing but scattered rocks, and when he climbed the wooden steps they splintered beneath his weight. The house was completely abandoned. He knocked on the door, its bright red paint now dry and peeling. No one answered, so he tried the door and found it unlocked. As he stepped inside, he thought he caught a glimpse of a hunched figure moving through the rooms. A woman?

All the shutters were closed, so it was mostly dark, and as he waited for his eyes to adjust he noticed the strong smell of mold. He went into the empty living room and headed for Feng's private chambers, dumbfounded by the ghostly layer of cobwebs and dust.

A noise from behind him made him jump. He turned and caught another glimpse of the figure running from one room to another. Grabbing a piece of bamboo, he advanced slowly in the dark. Then he heard a scraping sound just a few steps away and stopped to listen. Suddenly, whoever it was tried to rush past him. He tried to intercept the figure, but it kicked him in the shin and he fell over. As he got up, hands were on him, trying to attack him, but the person was weak, and when he grabbed the hands, the skin was soft and dry.

The figure screeched terrifyingly—yes, a woman. He dragged her toward the window and opened the shutters. In the misty morning light, he saw that it was an old, bony woman dressed in a grubby sack. Her wide-open eyes showed she was just as terrified as he. She pleaded with him not to hit her and swore that she hadn't stolen anything. He asked what she was doing in Feng's home, and though at first she didn't answer, when he shook her by the shoulders she told him she'd been alone there for months.

This was believable; beneath the nest of white hair, her skin showed the ravages of old age and hunger. And her frightened eyes didn't lie. All of a sudden they opened wider still.

"By the gods!" she said. "Cí! Can it really be you?"

He knew those bright eyes: they were those of Gentle Heart, former head servant in Feng's house. The dirt and the wrinkles disappeared as he saw the woman he used to know so well. They embraced each other, and she burst into tears.

Cí remembered that toward the end of his time working with Feng, Gentle Heart had started to become senile. But Feng had kept her on, as far as Cí knew. She had still been there when Cí's grandfather died.

Through her tears she told Cí that she'd left Feng's service when "that woman" showed up.

"What woman?" asked Cí.

"The evil woman. Beautiful, yes, but she never looked you in the eye." Gentle Heart gesticulated wildly, as if tracing the woman on the air in front of them. She looked off into the darkness, as if she were still seeing everything that had happened. "She brought new servants. And bad luck."

"But where have they all gone?"

"It's just me. I hide away...but sometimes they appear in the dark, and they talk to me..." Once again, her eyes filled with terror. "Who are you? Why are you holding me?" She pushed Cí and backed away.

She turned back into a hunched, delirious bundle of rags. He tried to calm her, but she turned and ran off into the house as if devils were after her.

Poor woman. One foot in the house of spirits.

He tried to find clues to what had happened, but there were only the bits and pieces of rubbish accumulated by Gentle Heart. The place clearly had been abandoned a long while ago. Cí thought it strange that Feng hadn't said anything the last time they saw each other.

By the time he left, it had started to rain. On his way back to the houseboat there was a downpour, and he had to take cover at the slave market. Under an awning, he grew extremely cold, and desperation took over. His very last option—Feng—had disappeared. Feng could still be on his journey in the North, or he might even have established himself in another city. Cí had no way of knowing. Money for Third's medicine, work, a place to stay: all were things Cí desperately needed. A group of slaves came by, tied together like livestock. They looked pitiful, but they were no worse off than Cí—at least they had food and shelter.

He had to do something. He knew it might be the worst decision he'd ever made, but he ran through the pouring rain all the way to the Fields of Death.

He found Xu working on a coffin. He didn't seem surprised to see Cí, and he didn't stop what he was doing.

"You look like a drowned chicken. Get out of those clothes and come help me with this."

"I need money," said Cí.

"Don't we all!"

"I need it now. Third is so sick…she's nearing death."

"I know. It happens—look around!"

Cí grabbed Xu and was about to hit him, but he let him go. Xu brushed himself off and went back to what he'd been doing,

"How much would you pay for me?"

Xu dropped his tools and looked at Cí. Yes, Cí said, he wanted to sell himself as a slave. Xu snorted.

"Ten thousand *qián*. That's the best I can do."

Cí knew he could have bartered with Xu, but he was utterly drained—drained from all the nights listening to Third's coughing and cries, drained from trying to find solutions. What did it matter now? He was trapped, barely alive. Exhausted. And he accepted Xu's offer.

Xu got up and went for paper to draw up the contract. He licked the brush and hastily scratched something out, then called to the gardener to come and act as witness. He handed the sheet of paper to Cí to sign.

"It has the essential points. You'll render me all services, and you'll belong to me until you die. Here, here. Sign it."

"The money first."

"I'll give it to you at the boat."

"I'll sign once I see the money."

Grudgingly, Xu agreed, then put Cí to work assembling coffins. Xu began singing a song, an accompaniment to the best bit of luck he'd had in years.

They started back to the houseboat halfway through the afternoon.

Xu walked with a spring in his step, singing the same melody over and over. Cí dragged his feet, head bowed, aware that everything he'd ever dreamed of was vanishing. He tried to banish these thoughts by focusing on Third and the hope that now, finally, she could be cured. He'd buy her the best medicine, and she'd grow up to be a beautiful, healthy woman. This was his one remaining dream.

But still, as they came closer to the docks, his mood remained dark.

The houseboat came into sight, and Xu's wives were on the jetty, screaming at them to hurry. Cí flew toward them, jumped onto the deck, and ducked straight into the little shelter where Third rested when she felt ill. Cí cried out, but he didn't see her.

He whirled around. At the back of the space, next to a container of fish, lay Third's small, worn-out body. He covered her with a blanket—quiet, pale, sleeping forevermore.

PART FOUR

PART FOUR

20

At the burial, Cí felt that a part of him was being nailed inside the small coffin along with his beloved sister. And the other parts of him—blasted and messy—though they might be sewn back together again, would never shine as before. His spirit was in a worse place than his body, and it was as if the burns that disfigured him had become internal. They were painful, and he had no way of soothing them.

He cried until he couldn't cry anymore. First his other sisters, then his brother and parents, and now the little one.

The only other person at the funeral was Xu. He waited outside, and when Cí came back to the cart they'd hired to transport the coffin, Xu was impatient. Cí hadn't even finished arranging the flowers for the small grave, and Xu wanted to talk about the contract. He'd brought it with him. Cí turned on him, taking the piece of paper and tearing it up. Xu didn't bat an eyelid. He crouched down and began picking up the torn pieces.

"Are you sure you don't want to sign it?" he asked, smiling. "Do you really think I'm going to let such a good piece of business escape, just like that?"

Cí glared at him. He began walking off.

"Whoa!" shouted Xu. "Where do you think you're going? Think you'll survive in this city without me? You're nothing but a beggar with airs."

Cí exploded. "Where am I going? Anywhere you're not! You and your greed. I'm going to the Ming Academy." No sooner had he finished speaking than he regretted saying that much.

"Oh, really? But you do know that if you try to go, I'll go straight to that sheriff who was after you, right? And I'll go out whoring with the reward money, stopping by your bitch little sister's grave to piss on it—"

He was interrupted by a hard punch in the face; the next blow dislodged some teeth. Cí stood back. Xu spat bloodily on the ground and then smiled up at Cí.

"Listen: you'll work with me, or not at all."

"No, *you* listen! Put your stupid disguise on and scratch together whatever living you want. You're enough of a trickster to fool a few people yet. But if I ever find out you've spoken to Kao about me, you can be sure the whole city will know about your fraud business. And that'll be the end of you. And if I find out you've come anywhere near my sister's grave, I'll break you in two and, I swear, I'll eat your heart."

He dropped one last flower on Third's grave and went down the cemetery's hill.

It was raining and he was soaked to the bone, but he dawdled in the streets anyway. He spent the whole morning walking the same maze of alleys, head bowed, going over and over the question: Was it really worth it to go to the academy? If it would never bring back Third, or his mother or father, was there really any point?

Leaning back against a pillar, he became lost for a long time in a swirl of images, all of his family. They were never coming back.

A beggar boy with no arms came and sat next to him. He had two cloth bags for carrying sand slung over his stumps. He grinned toothlessly at Cí; he liked the rain, he said, because it cleaned his face. Cí leaned over and adjusted the boy's bags for him, and with a cloth wiped some of the dirt from his face. Third's constant smile sprang into his thoughts, her enthusiasm in spite of everything. He felt her there with him.

Getting up, he stroked the boy's head and looked out. Maybe it was clearing up. If he hurried, he might even make it to the Ming Academy before nightfall.

⁓⁓⁓❧⁓⁓⁓

From outside the academy, he could see silhouettes of the students in the classrooms. Their talk and laughter drifted out into the gardens and through the cloisters where, behind an imposing stone wall, there was a grove of plum, pear, and apricot trees.

A group of students came from the street behind him and passed by as they walked in the direction of the academy. They were discussing their classes, and behind them a couple of servants pulled handcarts overflowing with all kinds of food. A few of them glanced back at him as if they were worried he might contaminate them somehow. I probably would, he thought. They entered through the academy gate whispering.

Inside there was wisdom and cleanliness; outside, ignorance and baseness.

Summoning all his courage, Cí walked through the academy's entrance. But as he did, a guard stepped out in front of him brandishing a stick. Cí told him Professor Ming had invited him.

"Professor Ming doesn't give interviews to beggars," he said, advancing on Cí.

Backing away, Cí noticed the group of students watching and laughing. But he wasn't going to be diverted from the academy any more. He sidestepped the guard and ran through the gardens toward the main building. Shouts went up as he came through the door, and as he looked back he saw that the guard and several students were chasing him. He ran through the hallway and into a library. The students and the guard entered through another door and, together with students who had been studying in the library, quickly surrounded Cí. With his back against a bookshelf, he shut his eyes and waited for the first blow.

But then they all went quiet.

Looking up, Cí saw Professor Ming coming toward them, glowering. As soon as Ming heard what the guard had to say, he ordered that Cí be thrown out without even the opportunity to explain himself.

Cí was just outside the main gate, still dusting himself off, when he felt a hand on his elbow. It was the guard, and, after helping Cí to his feet, he gave him a bowl of rice. Cí was confused, but he thanked the man.

"Thank the professor. He said he'll receive you tomorrow if you present yourself with better manners."

Cí slept collapsed against the academy's outer wall. He was exhausted, but his thoughts churned so much he didn't sleep well. Every time he drifted off, he saw Third's smiling face. All he could do now, he knew, was honor her memory and hope her spirit would give him protection.

In the morning, he had to be shaken awake by the guard. He got up and tried to make himself look as decent as possible, hiding his matted hair under his cap. Following the guard, who Cí now noticed had a strange tottering gait, he went through the gardens, stopping at a fountain to splash his face.

Ming was in the library, and Cí bowed as the guard left them. Ming, who was wearing the same red gown that he'd worn at the cemetery, closed his book and told Cí to take a seat. Ming asked his name, and he only replied, "Cí."

"What about a full name? What should I call you, then?" he said, beginning to pace the room. "The Amazing Murder Guesser? Hmm? Or what about the Uninvited Academy Invader?"

Cí blushed. He hadn't considered this obstacle, but he couldn't reveal his full name because of the report about his father's conduct. Rather than have to field more uncomfortable questions, he said nothing.

"OK, Cí No Parents, tell me this. Why should I make this kind of offer to someone who rejects his parents by refusing to name them? I was certain the other day not only that you were blessed with talent, but that you might even be able to make a contribution to our complicated science. But I'm having doubts, given this and your conduct yesterday."

Cí considered saying he was an orphan, but that wouldn't stop Ming from asking more questions. Finally, he came up with a story.

"I was involved in an accident three years ago and lost my memory. All I remember is waking up in a field one day. A family found me and took care of me, but they were moving to the south, so I decided to come to the city. They always said they thought I must have been from here."

"Right," said Ming, stroking his mustache. "And nonetheless you have a wide knowledge of how to uncover hidden wounds, about where a prisoner is tattooed, about which knife wounds are mortal and which are not..."

"The family worked in a slaughterhouse. The rest I learned in the cemetery."

"The only thing you'd learn in a cemetery is how to dig graves—and tell lies."

"Please, sir—"

"Not to mention your disrespectful performance yesterday!"

"That guard's an idiot! I told him about your offer, but he wouldn't even listen to me."

"Silence!" said Ming. "How dare you insult someone you don't even know? In this institution, everyone follows orders, and that was all the guard was doing." Ming turned away from Cí and went over to his desk. "Recognize this?" he said, picking up the book he'd been reading before.

It was his father's copy of the penal code.

"Where did you find it?"

"Where did you lose it?" replied Ming immediately.

Cí avoided Ming's penetrating stare. It was no use trying to fool him.

"I was robbed," he managed to say.

"Mmm...Maybe the robber was the same man who sold it to me."

Cí said nothing; if Ming had the book, there was a chance he knew about Kao's tracking him. He got up to leave, thinking he should never have come. Ming told him to sit back down.

"I bought it from some ruffian at the market. When you and I met at the cemetery, I thought I recognized you, but I couldn't place you. But I went to the book market last week, as I do every week, and this unique edition caught my eye—it stood out at what was a fairly insalubrious stall. I had a feeling you'd show up here sooner or later, so I bought it." He frowned and put a hand to his temple, meditating on what to say next. "Dear boy. I have a feeling I might regret this, but in spite of your lies, the offer still stands." He picked up the book. "There's no doubt in my mind that you have exceptional qualities. It would be such a shame for them to be...dissolved among the mediocrity. If you are truly willing to do as you're told..." He handed Cí the book. "Here. It's yours."

Trembling, Cí took the book. He found it difficult to comprehend what was happening. Ming might know about his father, but he didn't seem to know about Kao. He got down on his knees to thank Ming, but Ming told him to get up.

"Don't thank me now. Now is when your work begins."

"You won't regret it, sir."

"I hope not, boy. I hope not."

<hr />

Cí met his classmates-to-be in the Honorable Debating Hall, the lavish auditorium where debates were held and exams were taken. When there was a new student, it was traditional to give the professors and students an opportunity to meet him and express any concerns about his entering the academy. Standing in front of what seemed like hundreds and hundreds of piercing gazes, Cí tried to stay calm.

The room was silent as Professor Ming entered, bowed to the other professors and the students in the room, and then took his place at a podium. He related the story of the encounter in the cemetery, the meeting that had allowed him to witness Cí's talents. He referred to Cí as the Corpse Reader and defined his practice as "an unfathomable mix of sorcery and erudition." Ming said that perhaps with training and study—stressing the *perhaps*—the boy might shine. These were his reasons for inviting Cí to join the academy.

When the professor was asked about the applicant's origins, Cí was surprised to hear Ming recount the story about his memory loss and his last few years as a butcher and gravedigger.

Then Cí was invited to the podium. He looked around in vain for a friendly face. There were only cold glares. He was asked about his knowledge of the classics, about law, and about what he knew of poetry. A wiry professor with bushy eyebrows led the comments.

"Our colleague, Professor Ming, was clearly dazzled by your reading of the corpse. He has heaped praise on you. And I don't blame him; it can often be difficult to distinguish the brilliance of gold from the radiance of base metal. It seems that the accuracy of your examination and predictions have led Ming to think you're some kind of visionary, and that qualifies you to stand alongside those of us who have spent our lives studying the arts. None of this surprises me. Ming's passion for bodily organs is well known.

"But what you have to understand is that to solve crimes and bring justice to the dead, it takes much more than merely knowing *who* committed a crime and *how*. Truth lies in *motivation*—what could motivate a man to commit crimes?—and an understanding of people's preoccupations, their situations. Their *reasons* are not to be found in wounds and entrails. They are to be found through an understanding of art and literature."

The professor had a point, but his absolute contempt for medicine was too much. There was some truth in what he said, but if a judge couldn't distinguish a natural death from a murder in the first place, how on earth could justice ever be done? Cí considered how best to express his opinion.

"Honorable professor, I'm not here to win a battle. I can't possibly hope to prevail with the little that I know, nor compare my knowledge with that of the masters and students here. I only want to learn. Knowledge itself knows no limits, no compartmentalizing. Nor does it know prejudice. If you allow me to join the academy,

I swear I will give everything to my studies, even leaving aside the question of wounds and entrails if I have to."

A pudgy professor with a pinched mouth raised his hand to speak. His breathing was heavy, and the few steps he took to come forward left him out of breath. He crossed his hands over his belly as he considered Cí for a few long moments.

"It seems that you tarnished this institution's honor yesterday, bursting in here like a savage. It brings to mind a saying about a man: 'Yes, he might be a thief, but he's also a wonderful flutist.' Do you know what my reply to that is? 'Fine. He might be a wonderful flutist, but first and foremost he's a thief.'" The professor licked his lips and scratched his greasy hair. "What part of this truth do you embody? That of the man who disobeys rules but reads bodies, or he who reads bodies but disobeys rules? Further, can you tell me why we should accept a vagabond like you into the empire's most respectable academy?"

These questions surprised and worried Cí. He'd thought that, since Ming was the director of the academy, his opinion would prevail. Given the circumstances, though, he decided to change his approach.

"Venerable master," he said, bowing. "I beg your forgiveness of my unacceptable behavior yesterday. It came out of feeling powerless and desperate. I know this is no excuse, and that the most important thing is for me to demonstrate that I'm worthy of your confidence. So, first, I must ask for your indulgence; I'm a country boy, and I'm eager to learn. Isn't that what the academy is about? If I already knew all the rules, if I didn't have the thirst for knowledge, why would I want to study? And how could I then avoid the things that make me imperfect?

"This is the greatest opportunity I've ever had. I promise you, I swear, I won't let you down."

The pudgy professor took a couple of wheezy breaths; then, nodding, he went slowly back to his place, giving the floor to the last professor. The old, stooped man with dim eyes asked Cí why he had accepted Ming's invitation.

"Because it's my dream."

The old professor shook his head. "Is that all? There was a man who dreamed of flying to the heavens, but after throwing himself off a cliff, he ended up a pile of broken bones on the rocks."

Cí looked in the old man's eyes. "When we want something we've seen, all we have to do is reach out for it. But when we want something we've only dreamed of, it's our heart we have to stretch."

"Are you sure? Sometimes our dreams lead us to fall—"

"Possibly. But if our ancestors hadn't dreamed of better things, we'd still be dressing in rags. My father said to me once"—Cí's voice quavered at this—"if I was striving to build a palace in the clouds, not to bother. That was clearly where I was meant to be. All I should do is try to build the foundations."

"Your father? How strange! Ming said you'd lost your memory."

Cí bit his lip and his eyes moistened.

"That's the single memory I have."

The auditorium was swarming with students whispering in excited circles. What was the Corpse Reader's full name? What was the secret that meant he didn't have to go through the usual selection process? Some talked about him as a sorcerer; others said he'd learned his skills in a slaughterhouse. But one student kept himself apart and didn't join in the discussions. When Cí came in with Professor Ming, Gray Fox spat his piece of licorice on the floor and, casting Cí a poisonous look, moved farther away.

Ming carried out the introductions. Cí would be living with these students from now on, all of them vying to join the Imperial Judiciary. Mainly they were aristocratic youths, though their long nails and neat haircuts reminded Cí of courtesans more than any-thing. There were some disdainful looks, but everyone greeted Cí courteously enough—everyone except the student who stood on his own in the corner. When Ming noticed, he called Gray Fox over. The youth with the distinctive gray-streaked hair approached apathetically.

"I see you don't share your peers' curiosity," said Ming.

"I don't see what there is to be interested in. I'm here to study, not to be seduced by some swindling beggar."

"Wonderful, dear boy, wonderful...because you're going to have the chance to observe Cí up close and check exactly how much truth there is in what he does."

"Me? I don't understand."

"You two are going to be roommates. You'll share books and a bunk."

"But Master! I can't live with some peasant!"

"Silence!" spat Ming. "In this academy, money, business, and family influence don't matter. Obey me and greet Cí, or go and pack your bags!"

Gray Fox bowed his head, but his eyes drilled into Cí. Then he asked for permission to retire. Ming said he could, but as Gray Fox reached the door, Ming had one more thing to say.

"Before you go, you can pick up that licorice you saw fit to spit on the tiles."

<hr>

Cí spent the rest of the day finding out about the daily routine at the academy. He'd be up early for classes all morning; then there would be a brief break for lunch followed by debates in the after-noon and evening. After dinner he'd work in the library to pay for his stay. Ming explained that although the university boards had closed the Faculty of Medicine, part of the program was still dedicated to medical knowledge and, specifically, to causes of death. Sometimes they'd go and sit in on judicial assemblies when they examined corpses, and sometimes they'd attend criminal proceedings to learn firsthand about criminal behavior.

"Exams are four times a year. We have to make sure students are advancing as expected. If not, we initiate proceedings for the expulsion of those who aren't showing themselves worthy of our efforts. Remember," said Ming, "your place here is entirely provisional."

"Don't worry; you won't catch me acting like some rich kid."

"Let me give you some advice. Don't be fooled just because the other students dress well; don't confuse their appearance with anything like indolence. Yes, they come from elite families, but they also study extremely hard. If you go up against them, I can assure you they'll shred you like a rabbit."

Cí acquiesced. Nonetheless, he doubted that the force of the other students' motivation was anywhere near as strong as his own.

That evening, the academy assembled in the Apricot Room for dinner, which was adorned with exquisite silks depicting landscapes with summerhouses and fruit trees. All the students had already sat down in groups by the time Cí arrived. He looked hungrily at the abundance of soups, fried fish, sauces, and fruits, but when he tried to sit down at a table, the students there shifted so that there wasn't any space for him. The same happened at the next table, and the next. It didn't take long for Cí to work out whose orders they were following; there, at the back of the room, he saw Gray Fox, glaring at him with a sarcastic half-smile.

Cí knew that if he backed down, he'd get this sort of treatment for the rest of his time at the academy. He walked over to Gray Fox's table and, before the students could do what the other tables had done, planted a foot in the empty place. The students on either side shot him ferocious looks, but he squeezed in between them and took the seat. As soon as he did, Gray Fox spoke up.

"You aren't welcome at this table."

Cí ignored him. He took some soup and began sipping at the bowl.

"Didn't you hear?" said Gray Fox, more loudly now.

"Oh, I heard," said Cí.

"The fact that you don't know who your father is," said Gray Fox, "must mean you don't know who mine is, either."

Cí put the bowl down, placed his hands on the table and stood up slowly.

"Now you listen to me," he said in a quiet voice. He had the whole table's attention. "If you value your tongue, my advice is that you prevent it from ever daring to mention my father again. If you do, you'll be speaking to the world in sign language from that point on." Then he sat down and carried on eating as if nothing had happened.

Gray Fox's face lit up with rage. Without a word, he got up from the table and fled the dining room.

Cí congratulated himself. His opponent had only made a fool of himself in front of everyone. He knew it wouldn't be their only encounter, but it had been no simple thing to overcome him in public.

By nightfall the tension had increased. The room they were supposed to be sharing was a small cubicle divided by a paper panel. The only privacy to be had was in the small amount of space where the lantern light didn't fall. There was barely room for the two beds, let alone the two small tables and two wardrobes, their personal possessions, and books. Gray Fox's side was overflowing with silk robes and a splendid collection of beautifully bound books. Cí's just had cobwebs. He brushed these aside and placed his father's book on his shelf. Then he knelt down and, under Gray Fox's disdainful gaze, prayed for his family. Gray Fox began changing into his night-clothes, and Cí did the same. Though it was hopeless in such a small space, he tried to hide his scars.

They both got into their beds without a word. Cí listened to Gray Fox's breathing and couldn't sleep. His head was buzzing—with thoughts of his family and this opportunity, which Gray Fox seemed determined to ruin. How could he quench this animosity between them? Maybe the best thing was to ask Ming's advice. With this decision, his thoughts calmed and he began to drift off, but then he heard a hiss from his roommate.

"Hey, freak! So this is your secret, eh? You might be clever, but you're also revolting like a cockroach." He laughed. "It's hardly surprising you read bodies, when your own looks like a rotten corpse!"

Cí didn't answer. He gritted his teeth and tried not to pay attention to the rage bubbling in his stomach. He wrapped himself in his blanket and cursed his disgusting scars and the condition that meant he never felt pain. Gray Fox was right—he was an aberration.

But just before finally dropping off to sleep, he suddenly had the thought that perhaps his burns might present some way of reconciling with Gray Fox. And with that hopeful idea, he was asleep.

❧❧❧❧

Every day, Cí got up earlier than anyone else and stayed up later, going over the day's lessons long after he finished work at the library. He spent his few moments of free time rereading his father's copy of the penal code, trying to commit to memory the criminal chapters in particular.

Whenever he could, he accompanied Ming on his hospital visits. There were always many herbalists, acupuncturists, and moxibustion practitioners, but very few surgeons, in spite of the obvious need for them. Confucianism prohibited interventions inside patients' bodies, and so surgery was permitted only in the most serious cases: open fractures, deep wounds, and amputations. Unlike his colleagues, Ming showed a rare interest in advanced medicine, and he complained bitterly about the closure of the Faculty of Medicine.

"They opened it twenty years ago only to shut it now," said Ming. "The traditionalists among the deans argue that surgery is somehow backward looking." He snorted. "They expect our judges to solve crimes using their knowledge of literature and poetry."

Cí agreed with Ming. He had attended classes at the Faculty of Medicine when he was working with Feng, and it was one of the things he missed most. But he had also been one of few who appreciated it. Most students preferred focusing on the Confucian canons, calligraphy, and poetics—these were what they'd need for the official exams, after all. And a lot of judicial work *was* paperwork. If you ever had to deal with a murder, most of the time you'd just call a slaughterman to clean the body and give his opinion.

But any change was a good change, considering Cí's life recently, and he felt in his element among the students, debating philosophy, examining wooden anatomical models, taking part in impassioned judicial discussions.

His peers were surprised to find that Cí's knowledge was by no means limited to wounds and corpses; he knew the sprawling penal code very well, and bureaucratic procedure and interrogation methods, too. Ming had put him in an advanced group of students who would have the chance to enter directly into the judiciary at the end of that academic year.

And as Ming's confidence in Cí grew, so did Gray Fox's envy—as demonstrated when Ming told them they'd be taking the November exam, and that they would be working as a team in mock trial at the prefecture headquarters. One of them would serve as principal judge, the other in an advisory capacity.

"You have to come up with a shared verdict," said Ming. "If you work together, you'll have a chance. But if you squabble, I can promise you the other teams will take advantage. Understood?"

Both Cí and Gray Fox kept their eyes lowered. Eventually they said yes.

"Good! Oh, and one other thing: the winners of this test will be in competition for the one Imperial official job with fixed tenure that we are allowed every year. Your dream job, both of you! So you'd better be well prepared."

Gray Fox wanted to play principal judge, and Cí didn't actually mind. What worried him, though, was that he didn't think Gray Fox was ready. Ming accepted Gray Fox's proposal of roles not because he made a particularly convincing case for being ahead of Cí, but simply because he had been at the academy longer.

Cí knew this was too much of an opportunity to let their animosity spoil it. He was also willing to admit that Gray Fox had a better knowledge of certain legal and literary subjects, and that they'd probably need these to stand a chance of winning. After dinner that evening, students were breaking off in pairs to get in some last-minute study time, and Cí suggested he and Gray Fox do the same.

"Tomorrow's a big day. Maybe we could go over some cases together."

"What makes you think I'd want to study with you? We're only together because Ming ordered us to be; I don't need your help. You do your job, I'll do mine, and that'll be the end of it."

Cí didn't follow him to their dormitory, but stayed up late going over his notes, and in particular the subjects Ming had suggested they concentrate on.

But there was something else worrying Cí. Going to the prefecture headquarters raised the specter of Kao once more. For all

Cí knew, if the sheriff had put a ransom on his head, he might well have distributed descriptions of him, too.

Still, it was the most amazing opportunity.

In the early morning, when the characters began swimming in front of Cí's tired eyes, he began preparing the equipment he'd brought from the cemetery. He added some large sheets of paper, charcoals, already threaded silk needles, and a jar of camphor from the kitchens. He placed his things next to the other students' bags and made one last check that he had everything he needed.

Next he began his transformation.

Taking great care, he stuffed his nostrils with cotton, then shaved his downy beard and hid his hair beneath a cap he'd borrowed. He looked at himself in the dull bronze mirror and felt satisfied; it wasn't a huge change, but every little bit would help.

He felt a pang of nerves as he ran to join the other students, putting on his gloves as he went.

When Ming caught sight of him, he shook his head.

"Where on earth have you been? And what's that in your nose?"

Cí said he'd prepared the cotton with camphor to help him stand the stench of a corpse. That was why he was late.

"I'm disappointed in you," said Ming, pointing to a stray lock of hair poking out from Cí's cap.

Cí didn't answer, but just hung his head and joined the others. Gray Fox looked immaculate.

<hr />

It didn't take long to reach the magnificent walled prefecture headquarters. Situated between the principal canals on Imperial Square, it took up the ground space of at least four normal buildings. It stood out pristine and enormous against the ramshackle buildings and market stalls. It also had something of a dead, desolate air. All of Lin'an knew and feared the place, but Cí perhaps more so than anyone.

When it came into sight, he couldn't help but shudder. He pulled the cap down over his temples and wrapped his robes around him. Once they were all inside, Cí tried to hide by staying close behind Gray Fox, and only when they came to the Room of the Dead did he dare to raise his head. The camphor didn't seem to help much; the smell of death was everywhere.

It was an oppressive room with barely enough space for everyone. To one side there was a small basin fed by a water pipe, and in the middle, the corpse, which reeked. A gaunt guard came in through the opposite doors to announce the arrival of the prefect and to give them the basic details of the case. It was a complicated case, he said, and one that required the utmost discretion: A man of about forty with a ruddy complexion had been found floating in the canal two days earlier by someone working one of the sluice gates. The corpse had been fully clothed and carrying a flask of liquor, but he had no identification card and had not been carrying any personal effects or items of value. His clothes indicated his office, but the guard wasn't permitted to divulge *which* office at this point. An examination had been carried out the night before under the relevant judge's supervision, but his conclusions also needed to remain secret.

Ming stepped forward and picked the three pairs who would be carrying out the examination. Each team would have an hour to draw its conclusions, and Ming would track time using incense sticks. He reminded them about taking notes, which they'd need for their summary. First up would be two Cantonese brothers who were experts in literary studies, then a pair advanced in the study of law, and finally Gray Fox and Cí.

Gray Fox complained that they'd be at a disadvantage if the others had already handled the body, but Cí wasn't worried about that. The other pairs, being less versed in anatomy, would be unlikely to touch the body very much anyway, and he and Gray Fox would have the advantage of observing the first two before their own examination. Taking out his paper, brush, and ink bottle, Cí prepared to take notes.

Ming lit the first incense stick. The Cantonese brothers bowed and removed the cloth covering the corpse, but before they could begin, there was a crash behind them. Everyone turned to see a shattered ink bottle and a pool of dark ink spilling across the floor. It was Cí's ink. He was sitting exactly as he had been—one hand still positioned as if holding the ink bottle, the other holding his brush—and staring at the corpse. There, on the examination table, lay the body of Sheriff Kao.

21

Everyone in the room shot scornful looks at Cí. Gray Fox spat on the floor and turned his back on his partner.

Cí apologized and, in spite of the shock of seeing Kao's corpse, gathered himself as best he could. He went up to the table to observe the other pairs at work. Whatever happened, he had to know how Kao had died.

The first pair pointed out the lack of apparent wounds, which led them to think the man couldn't have died violently; perhaps, they said to each other, it had been a mere accident. The second pair focused on the small bite marks on the lips and eyelids—most likely from canal fish—and on details like Kao's complexion and old scars, which Cí thought were unlikely to reveal the cause of death.

The second incense stick burned down, and it was their turn. Gray Fox approached the corpse as if he had all the time in the world—and as if the incense stick were measuring only his time and not Cí's as well. Gray Fox circled the corpse and began his examination at the opposite end from what was typical—with the bluish feet. He palpated the knotty, muscular legs all the way up to the penis, which also appeared to have been nibbled by fish. Cí was watching the time closely; by the time a quarter of the incense stick had burned, Gray Fox hadn't even examined the torso. Finally, he reached the head, and then asked Cí to help him turn the body over. Gray Fox was exasperatingly slow as he moved down the back of the body.

Cí glanced from the half-finished incense stick to Ming, but the professor was deep in conversation with one of the students and didn't notice. By the time Gray Fox had finished, there was hardly any time left.

Having seen there were no wounds on the body, Cí followed his instinct and used his time to examine the head. He looked closely at the nape of the neck, the mouth, the eyes, the nostrils; failing to find any evidence of note, he moved on to the ears. Instantly he found something in the left one. Aware that the incense was about to burn out, he hurried over to his instruments to grab his forceps. But as he got back to the corpse, one of the guards stood in front of him; for a moment, Cí panicked that he'd been identified.

"Time's up," said the guard.

"But, sir," Cí said to Ming, who had come back over. "Gray Fox used up much more than half our time."

"Nothing I can do. The prefect is waiting."

Cí looked around, desperate.

I have to find a way.

He bowed his acceptance and backed away, but left his forceps near the head. As everyone was filing out, he asked the guard if he could cover the corpse. Since Cí seemed to be acting out of respect, the guard let him.

As they left the Room of the Dead, Cí was satisfied.

On their way back to the academy, Ming apologized to Cí. "I wanted to give you more time, but it would have upset the prefect."

Cí nodded. He was fully focused on the consequences of his discovery. The prefect, a dumpy, sweaty man, had impressed upon them the extreme confidentiality of the case and sent them off to write up their reports. They had two days—two days in which Cí would determine his fate.

At lunch, he hardly ate. Afterward they had to present their preliminary findings to Ming, and he still didn't know what he should say. Surely the prefect knew what Kao's job had been, but Cí didn't know if the prefect knew—as he did—that Kao had been murdered. If he didn't know, and Cí announced his conclusions, that would alert the authorities to the existence of a murderer, and Cí believed he would be the prime suspect.

He tried to swallow some food, but it lodged in his throat. The second pair was already meeting with Ming; soon it would be his and Gray Fox's turn.

Gods, what should I do? What would father do?

A shove from Gray Fox jolted him out of his thoughts. It was time. Cí got up, straightened his clothes, and followed his partner.

It was Cí's first time in Ming's private study. He was surprised to find it so gloomy; there were no windows or paper screens to let in daylight. Old silks with anatomical pictures hung on the rosewood walls. Ming sat at an ebony desk consulting a volume in the semi-darkness, and from a shelf behind him a row of skulls peered out. The professor invited them to approach, and they both knelt down. Ming looked at them, and Cí noticed how weary his eyes were.

"I dearly hope you two have something useful to say. Your classmates haven't drawn one sensible conclusion. I don't think I've heard such a lot of nonsense in all my days. Well? What can you tell me?"

Gray Fox cleared his throat. He took out his notes and began.

"Most honorable Ming, I thank you with sincere humility for the opportunity—"

"Hold the sincere humilities and get on with it."

"Of course, sir." He cleared his throat. "But perhaps Cí should wait outside. As you know, a second judge shouldn't have his judgment...*influenced* by another's."

"By the gods, will you just get on with it?"

Gray Fox cleared his throat again.

"The first thing to consider is why the case is surrounded by such secrecy. This is highly unusual, and it leads me to think that the deceased must have been a man of some importance, or had links with people of importance."

"Go on," said Ming, nodding.

"If that is the case, the next question is why the authorities would be interested in students' opinions. We must assume that to ask us, they do not know the cause of death, or at least are unsure of their own conclusions."

"Yes, yes, it could be."

"Because he was already undressed, we lacked an important source of information, but at least we can surmise from the smoothness of his hands that he was no laborer. At the same time, his short nails tell us he wasn't a literary person."

"Good observation."

"I thought so, too," said Gray Fox, modest as ever. "And finally, as to the cause of death: The corpse showed no signs of violence, no bruises or wounds, nothing to suggest poisoning. Nor was there any excretion from any of the seven orifices that might have suggested the death was by unnatural causes."

"And so..."

"And so, we ought to conclude that his death was caused by having fallen in the canal. In my view, the fact that he died of drowning is not the important thing; it's that he died drunk, as indicated by the fact he was found clutching a liquor bottle."

"Mm…" Ming's interest gave way to a frown of disappointment. "Your conclusion, then?"

"Um…" Gray Fox was unsettled by Ming's response. "As I was saying, the unfortunate man undoubtedly had an important office…His death, clearly unexpected, appeared to them a mishap, and that was what they called us in to confirm."

Ming puffed out his cheeks. He thanked him and turned to Cí.

"What about you?" he asked, clearly not expecting much.

Gray Fox interrupted. "If we could see the deceased's clothes, or talk to the person who found him—"

"It's Cí's turn now," said Ming.

Cí stood up. Gray Fox had made the same decent observations he had planned to point out in order to withhold his own terrible discovery. Now, if he merely repeated what Gray Fox had said, he would seem like a dolt in Ming's eyes. Nonetheless, that was exactly what he decided he had to do.

Afterward, Ming raised an eyebrow.

"That's all?" he asked.

"That's all that could be surmised from the corpse. Gray Fox's observations were, in my opinion, well founded and astute. They match as much as I could determine."

"In that case you should have paid better attention. All of the students have come to the same conclusions. We don't keep you here to parrot the stupidity of others." Ming was silent a moment as he scrutinized Cí. "And even less to try and trick us!"

Cí blushed. "I don't know what you mean."

"Oh, really? Do you honestly think I'm stupid?"

Cí had no idea how much Ming knew he knew. "I don't understand—"

"By the gods! Stop acting, for once! Don't you think I was watching when you discovered whatever was in the ear? That I didn't see what you were doing when you covered the body over, or the satisfaction on your face afterward?"

Cí said nothing.

Ming snorted. "Get out of my sight, both of you! Out!"

As they scrambled out, they could hear Ming muttering, "Damned little liar…"

◈

Cí spent the rest of the day in the library meditating over what seemed an intractable problem. He kept coming to the same conclusion: he was going to have to renounce his dream and flee Lin'an. Finally he picked up a brush and began writing down every detail of what he had really surmised, without deciding what he'd actually do with the report. How he envied Gray Fox. He'd seen him laughing with some classmates, and they'd been drinking, too. It didn't seem as though the failure mattered in the slightest to Gray Fox. Before going in for dinner, he had come tottering over to Cí. His eyes shining and a stupid grin on his face, he'd offered Cí a drink.

"Come on, *partner*," he said when Cí refused. "Forget about Ming. Drink!"

Alcohol was an amazing thing, thought Cí; this was the first time in his months at the academy that Gray Fox had addressed him with something other than an insult. He declined the drink again.

"Know what?" said Gray Fox. "I hated you, right up until this afternoon. *Clever Cí, brilliant Cí…*But you weren't clever or brilliant today, were you? How did you put it? 'Gray Fox's observations were, in my opinion, well founded and astute.' Ooh, I liked that. Here." He thrust the drink at Cí again and laughed heartily.

Cí took a drink, hoping it would make Gray Fox leave him alone, and felt the heat of the rice liquor invade his throat and stomach. He wasn't used to drinking such strong stuff.

"Brilliant!" laughed Gray Fox. "A bunch of us are going out later for dinner at the Palace of Pleasure. We'll toast Ming's health! Why don't you come?"

"No, thank you. I wouldn't want Professor Ming to find out."

"What if he does? We aren't prisoners here, you know. Ming's just a bitter old man; nothing's ever enough for him. Come on, we'll have a great time! Meet us after the second evening gong, down by the fountain. All right?" He left the pitcher of liquor there and went swaying off, singing to himself.

Cí grabbed the clay pitcher. For all his contemplation, he still didn't know what to do. If he revealed what he knew, he'd rise in Ming's estimation again, but the risk was huge. If he kept his mouth shut, he'd forsake his dream of joining the judiciary...He took another drink. And another. There was something comforting in the liquor, and gradually his mind clouded over and his problems floated away.

The second gong struck, and Cí was surprised to find himself still in the library. How much longer would Ming let him stay at the academy?

And could he possibly care less?

He heard the sound of laughter from the gardens, got unsteadily to his feet, and went downstairs. Four students, each of them with a drink, stood around Gray Fox by the fountain. Cí stopped and watched them for a minute before heading toward his room. But he heard Gray Fox calling after him, his voice amiable and persuasive. Then Gray Fox was next to Cí with his arm around him, cajoling him, saying they'd have a great time. Cí reasoned that at least it would be a chance to iron things out with Gray Fox.

At the Palace of Pleasure, Cí encountered women more beautiful than he ever could have imagined. He and Gray Fox and the other students were seated at a booth. Cí looked around at the whirl of rich young men, students, merchants—and the dancers. The painted "flowers" gyrated like water lilies on an eddying pool as lutes whipped up the excitement further. The women went around the room, giving men glimpses of their small, bound feet and driving them wild. Gray Fox greeted friends and staff as if he owned the place. Soon two smiling women joined them, and Gray Fox was pouring more drinks.

"Nice, aren't they?" said Gray Fox as he stroked one of the girls' legs. "Listen," he told them, "this is Cí, the Corpse Reader, my new partner. He talks to ghosts, so be nice to him, very nice, or he'll turn you into donkeys!"

Cí wasn't entirely comfortable with his lusty thoughts when the two girls came and sat on either side of him. It had been a long time since he'd touched a woman, and he'd forgotten what their soft skin felt like, and what the caress of their perfumes could do to him.

The food arrived, and there was so much, and such variety, that the well-known saying about Lin'an—that here you could eat anything that flew except the comets, anything that swam except boats, and anything with legs except tables—seemed entirely apt. Snails in ginger, eight-gem pudding, pearl crabs, fried rice, ribs with chestnuts, freshwater fish, dragon-teeth oysters…The warm rice wine kept flowing, and Cí drank it all down. Gray Fox—the change in whom astonished Cí—kept encouraging Cí to indulge.

He hardly needed encouragement. The two "flowers" were seeing to that.

The first time he felt one of their hands slip between his legs, he spat out his drink. The second time, he tried to set them straight: their perfume and their red lips stirred him in all the right ways, but he didn't have the money to thank them for their attentions. They didn't seem to care, and they started kissing his neck.

Pleasure crackled down Cí's spine and goose bumps spread over his flesh. Gray Fox and the others were laughing and cheering for him to go off with the girls.

It didn't take him long to decide. The last couple of swigs of rice wine had transported him into a hazy, vertiginous world of caresses and sweet smells. He was about to kiss one of the girls when a hand clutched his shoulder.

"Let go of her and get yourself another one!" roared an older man carrying a stick.

Gray Fox intervened. "What? Leave him alone!"

But the man ignored Gray Fox, grabbing the girl by the arm as though he were going to rip it from her body and knocking the table of food over at the same time. Cí jumped up to stop the man, but in an instant the man struck Cí across the face with the stick. Cí fell to the floor, and just as the man was about to deliver another blow, Gray Fox leaped on him. Immediately five or six members of the restaurant staff dived in to separate them.

"Goddamned drunkard!" said Gray Fox, wiping blood from a cut on his hand. "They should be stricter about who they let in." He helped Cí to his feet. "Are you all right?"

Cí wasn't sure what had just happened, but whatever it was, it hadn't cleared the alcohol from his brain. Some staff helped the two of them over to a quiet corner; the others in the group stayed with the two women.

"Buddha! That imbecile almost wrecked our whole night. Want me to call over one of the girls?"

"No..." said Cí. "It's fine..." Everything was spinning.

"You sure? She seems to know what she's doing, and she has the most delectable feet. I bet she wriggles like a frying fish. Don't worry. We're here to have fun!" And he signaled to a waiter to bring more drink.

Cí was soon enjoying himself again, and he and Gray Fox chatted as though they'd been friends their whole lives. Their commentary on the ridiculous old men drooling over the dancing girls, and the way the girls made mocking faces even as they took their money, had Cí in fits of laughter. They drank on until eventually their conversation lost all sense.

Then Gray Fox's face changed, and he started talking about his loneliness. From a very young age he'd been sent to the best schools, so he'd always been surrounded by great wisdom, but he lacked the affection of his brothers, his mother's kisses, and the intimacy of friendships. He'd learned self-esteem but also never to trust anyone. His life had been like that of a prize horse, shut up in golden stables, ready to kick the first person who came near.

"You have to forgive me," said Gray Fox. "I've acted so badly toward you, but until you arrived at the academy the one thing I had was Ming's admiration. When you came, all that attention shifted to you."

Cí didn't know what to say; the drink was making his thoughts blurry.

"Forget about it," Cí said. "I'm not that good."

"Yes, you *are*. Like this morning, you found something in the corpse's ear—*no one* else noticed it. I feel like an idiot."

"Don't say that. Anyone could have found it."

"*I* didn't though," said Gray Fox, hanging his head.

Cí understood Gray Fox's feeling of defeat. He fished around in his bag and pulled out a small piece of metal.

"Watch this," said Cí. He slowly moved the piece of metal closer to a small iron dish on the floor until suddenly the dish leaped up to meet it.

"A magnet?" asked Gray Fox, trying to pull the dish off.

"Yes, and if you'd had one at the examination you would have found what I found: the metal bar inserted in the ear. The metal bar that killed the sheriff because it was pushed straight through to his brain."

"Killed? Sheriff? What are you saying?" Gray Fox became animated again and took another drink. "So…the flask of liquor he was clutching…"

Cí pointed to an old man passed out on a divan across the room from them. He had a cane.

"See how he isn't gripping it? The cane is just resting lightly in his hands. When someone dies, it's like that; their last breath takes all their life force with it. The only way he could have been gripping the flask was if someone had introduced it into his hands after death and waited for the onset of rigor mortis."

"A red herring?"

"Essentially," said Cí, draining the last of his drink.

"You really are a devil," chuckled Gray Fox.

Cí didn't know what to say. The drink was making him blurrier and blurrier. A toast, he thought.

"To my new friend," he said, lifting his cup.

"To mine," said Gray Fox.

When more drinks came, Cí said he couldn't possibly. Cups, customers, dancers—everything was spinning. But then he saw a svelte figure approaching and thought he recognized the almond eyes on the face that leaned down to kiss him. And the wet lips full of desire.

As Cí let himself be pulled in by the woman, Gray Fox got up.

If Cí had watched his new friend go, rather than abandoning himself to caresses, he would have been surprised to see Gray Fox suddenly seeming entirely sober as he walked with determination to the door, handed some coins to the man who'd attacked them earlier, and left the Palace of Pleasure.

22

By the time Cí woke, the sun was high over the rooftops of Lin'an.

The noise of passersby felt like a thousand lightning bolts piercing his tender brain. He got up gingerly, and when he saw the sign for the Palace of Pleasure above the pile of rubbish he'd slept in, a shiver went through him. Clearly his companions from the previous night had left without him, and he began the walk back to the academy alone.

When he got back, the guard told Cí that Ming had convened the pairs who had carried out the examination, and that they were to present their findings to a committee of professors in the Honorable Debating Hall.

"They began some time ago, but don't you even think of going in looking like that."

By the time Cí had washed up, changed clothes, and made it to the hall, it was Gray Fox's turn to present his findings. Everyone in the room looked at Cí as he came in. He nodded at Gray Fox, but his new friend looked disdainfully away. It must be nerves, thought Cí, taking a seat and avoiding Ming's disapproving gaze.

Gray Fox was at a lectern in the middle of the hall. Cí's thinking was still very cloudy, and he hadn't figured out what he would present, given Ming's reprimand the day before. Cí rummaged in his bag for the report he'd written in the library. It wasn't there.

Then he began *hearing* what he'd written, presented by Gray Fox. *It can't be.*

The extent of Gray Fox's betrayal became clear. The night out, the friendliness, the confessions about his loneliness—it was nothing but a ruse. How could Cí have trusted him? It felt as if he were being stabbed over and over again as Gray Fox spoke.

By the time he finished—having repeated Cí's findings word for word, right down to the conclusion about the flask of liquor and even saying that he hadn't mentioned the metal bar in the ear because of the need to keep his finding secret—Cí had to force himself not to jump up and clobber him. He couldn't call Gray Fox out, and he had no idea how he'd be able to prove that he himself wasn't copying Gray Fox. Luckily, the one thing Cí hadn't written in his report was *how* he knew Kao had been a sheriff. And that meant, when Ming began quizzing Gray Fox, the student hesitated.

"I...deduced his profession from the fact we were repeatedly told that secrecy was paramount."

"*Deduced?*" asked Ming. "Don't you mean *copied?*"

Gray Fox's eyebrows shot up. Cí held his breath.

"I...I don't know what you mean, sir," stammered Gray Fox.

"In that case, perhaps Cí could explain." Ming nodded for Cí to come forward.

Cí did as he was told, folding up and leaving his notes in his bag. Coming to the lectern, he noted the fear in Gray Fox's eyes. Clearly, Ming suspected something.

"We're waiting," said Ming.

"I'm afraid I don't know exactly what for, sir."

"You mean, you have no objections?" said Ming.

"No, venerable master."

"Cí! Don't play me for a fool. You don't even have an opinion?"

Cí saw Gray Fox gulp, and he considered his words.

"My opinion is that someone has carried out some excellent work," he said finally, gesturing to his partner. "The rest of us should all congratulate Gray Fox and carry on working for our goals." And without waiting to be told, he stepped away from the lectern and, awash with resentment, left the Honorable Debating Hall.

He cursed himself a thousand times for his stupidity, and a thousand more times for his cowardice.

He would happily have beaten Gray Fox to a pulp, but that would only get him expelled. He went to the library to look over his notes for anything he could use to prove Gray Fox's guilt without jeopardizing himself. Then someone came up from behind, making him jump. It was Ming. Shaking his head, the professor sat down across from him.

"You're leaving me no option," he said. "If you don't tell the truth, I'm going to have no choice but to expel you. What's going on with you, boy? How could you let him present your findings like that?"

"I don't know what you mean," said Cí, trying to hide his notes in his sleeve.

"What's that? Hand it over." He snatched the paper. As he scanned the notes, his face changed. "Exactly as I thought! Gray Fox would never have written a report using those terms. Don't you think I know his style by now? And yours?" He paused, expecting Cí to answer. "Gods! You're only here because I trusted you, so now you have to trust me. Tell me what happened. You aren't on your own in the world, Cí."

Yes, I am. Alone is exactly what I am.

Cí tried to take the notes back, but Ming held them out of his reach.

He hung his head and said nothing as rage swelled through him. How could he possibly explain that everyone he'd ever trusted had let him down, even his own father?

Over the following days, Cí did his best to avoid both Ming and Gray Fox—no easy task, especially with Gray Fox, given their shared room. Luckily, though, Gray Fox kept his distance, too. They ignored each other when they crossed paths in the hallways; at mealtimes, they sat at separate tables. Cí imagined Gray Fox must have been worrying about some sort of reprisal and would therefore be feeling like a caged animal that might be attacked at any moment.

As for Ming, he hadn't mentioned the report again, which also disconcerted Cí.

No news didn't feel at all like good news.

In the evening, after his classes, Cí began working on a document that he led his classmates to believe would prove Gray Fox's deceit, hoping word would reach his rival. Cí was certain he'd take the bait and succumb to the temptation to steal the notes, just as he'd done with the report.

When the notes were complete, Cí let it be known that he planned to present them to the council the next day; Gray Fox would be exposed. Cí went back to their room and sat waiting.

Not long after, Gray Fox came in. He collapsed on his bed as if exhausted, but Cí could tell he was only pretending to sleep. After a little while Cí got up, put the new set of notes in his bag—rustling them so his rival would know exactly where they were. Then he put his bag in his dresser and left the room.

Ming was out in the passageway, just as Cí had asked him to be.

"I don't know how I let you talk me into this," whispered the professor, stepping behind a pillar.

Cí bowed in thanks, then hid behind an adjacent pillar. The light from the only lantern flickered at the far end of the passageway. Moments passed slowly, but then Gray Fox's head appeared in the doorway; he checked to make sure no one was around and then went back inside, shutting the screen door behind him. Cí and Ming stayed hidden until they heard the dresser creaking open.

"He's going to do it!" hissed Ming, starting forward.

But Cí shook his head, gesturing for Ming to wait; he counted to ten.

"Now!" shouted Cí.

They burst into the room, catching Gray Fox fishing in Cí's bag for the notes.

He looked up, startled, and then cursed. "You!" He leaped at Cí, knocking him over. Gray Fox pinned Cí down, and though Cí managed to push him off, Gray Fox punched him in the gut. When Cí didn't flinch, Gray Fox hit him again and stood up.

"Surprised?" shouted Cí as he jumped up and punched Gray Fox in the face. "Weren't you trying to get my proof?" He hit him again, splitting his lip. Another blow knocked Gray Fox to the ground. Finally Ming managed to step between them.

Cí staggered, panting, his clothes and hair a mess; Gray Fox groaned, his face covered in blood. Cí couldn't have cared less; Gray Fox had done plenty to make his life a misery, and he wasn't going to take it anymore.

The next day, Cí went to watch Gray Fox leave the academy. No one had come to see him off, not even the students who usually hung around with him. There was a retinue waiting for him at the entrance, and their expensive attire was straight out of an imperial celebration. Cí gritted his teeth. Maybe he'd given up the chance of a lifetime, but at least he felt he'd gotten even. To his surprise, Gray Fox smiled when he saw him.

"I suppose you know I'm leaving…"

"Shame," said Cí, with all the sarcasm he could muster.

Gray Fox grimaced, then bowed, coming close to Cí's ear.

"Enjoy your studies, and try not to forget me, because I certainly won't forget you."

Cí watched scornfully as his rival departed.

<hr />

That same afternoon, there was a staff meeting to discuss the question of Cí's expulsion.

A number of the professors were of the mind that, no matter how talented Cí was, nothing could excuse his behavior. His presence reduced the academy's credibility, and it was costing them money. His latest outburst had jeopardized the generous donation given annually by Gray Fox's family.

"In fact," said one of them, "we had to guarantee Gray Fox's place in the judiciary to avoid losing all of their funding, which would have been a disaster."

Ming argued Cí's case. There was ample proof, he said, that Cí was the author of the report Gray Fox had tried to claim as his own. Others pointed out, though, that Cí had accepted his partner's authority, and that his subsequent lines of argument, and the way in which he had sought to uphold them, were unacceptable. The majority was clearly in favor of Cí's immediate expulsion.

But Ming was tenacious, and he expressed his conviction that Cí would eventually be more beneficial to the academy than all the grants in the world. He went further, suggesting that to save the academy money, the professors ought to take Cí on as a personal assistant.

A murmur of disapproval went around. One of the more outspoken professors jumped up and said Cí was a charlatan and that Ming's interest in the boy was anything but professional. Ming just hung his head at this; for quite some time there had been a faction seeking his dismissal. Before he could respond, the eldest member of the committee stood up.

"Such insinuations are entirely inappropriate." His voice was booming and authoritative. "Professor Ming is director of this academy and a laudable scholar whose scruples are unquestionable. He has always carried out his work impeccably, and any rumors as to his personal tastes, or anything that occurs beyond these walls, are matters for him and his family."

Tense silence filled the room. Ming requested the floor, and the elder master ceded it to him.

"It isn't my reputation, but Cí's, that we're here to discuss. Since the moment he arrived, he's worked night and day, he's carried out the lowest of tasks, and he's applied himself to his studies with great gusto. In a few months he's absorbed more knowledge than many of his peers learn in all their years here. He's rough, he's impulsive, but he is brimming with a special and rare talent. I agree that his behavior from time to time deserves our disapproval, absolutely, but the boy is also more than deserving of our generosity."

"He already benefited from our generosity," pointed out the elder master, "when we let him join the academy."

Ming turned back to the committee members.

"If you don't feel you can trust him, place your trust in me."

Aside from the four professors who were trying to see Ming dismissed, the rest of the committee eventually voted for Cí to stay—under Ming's strict supervision. They also agreed that the tiniest of infractions from the boy would lead to immediate dismissal of both Cí and Ming.

When Ming informed Cí, he could barely believe it.

Ming said that, from now on, Cí would be his personal assistant. He'd no longer sleep in the dormitory but would move up to Ming's private apartments, with access to the private library whenever he wanted. He'd continue to attend morning classes, but during the second half of the day he'd assist Ming in his investigations. Cí was overwhelmed; he genuinely couldn't understand why Ming had such faith in him or why the committee had approved these privileges.

The academy became a kind of paradise for Cí, and afternoons and evenings were the best. This was when he'd go to Ming's office and immerse himself in the books Ming had recovered from the Faculty of Medicine before its closure. The more he read, though, the more Cí realized how poorly organized the valuable information was. He came up with the idea of systematizing this chaos by compiling new volumes, organized according to ailments.

Ming thought it was a wonderful idea. He presented it to the committee and managed to win funding for the acquisition of more sources and to remunerate Cí.

Cí put his all into the project. To begin with, he compiled and organized information from the medical texts. As the months went by, he began to include some of his own ideas in the new volumes. He'd write at night, after Ming had gone to bed. In the yellowish lantern light, he described how to examine a corpse; in his opinion, an exhaustive contextual understanding was fundamental, but he also argued strongly for perfectionism, even in the smallest tasks. He created a step-by-step procedure, which involved beginning the examination of a corpse at the crown of the head, working down along the cranial sutures, the birth line in the hair, and down the forehead to the eyes—including lifting up and checking under the eyelids, ignoring the idea that the spirit might escape this way. Then one proceeded to the throat; the chest if dealing with a man or the breasts if a woman; the heart area; the uvula and navel; and the pubic region, including the penis, scrotum, and testicles, or the vagina. Finally, the legs and feet and the arms and hands were to be examined, not forgetting the toenails and fingernails. Once the body was turned over, the entirety of the corpse's back side required an equal amount of care; every part should be pressed on scrupulously to check for marks left by inflammation or beatings.

Ming didn't quite know how to react when he read the first pages. Much of what Cí had written, especially when it came to the forensic examinations, was clearer and more precise than many of the treatises in the library. And some of the procedures and experiences it detailed were new even to Ming, as were the innovative proposals on the use of surgical implements and the cold box, which Cí had dubbed the "conservation chamber," one of which he had acquired and modified for the long-term conservation of body organs.

Cí barely saw the other students. Perhaps it was his family's ghosts that urged him to work himself to the bone, but he didn't feel he needed much else in his life. He didn't have any friends, or companions even, but the isolation didn't bother him. He did his work as best as he could and was hard on himself. He had eyes only for his books, and his heart was set on achieving his dreams.

Ming kept reminding Cí of the importance of legal understanding, too.

"Remember, determining the causes of death won't be your sole function. What happens if a man is found to have been killed by several other men? Or, even worse, what happens if he dies over the course of a few days? How will you tell if his death was due to the wounds he received or a previous condition?"

While Cí knew how to classify deaths according to the instruments that had caused them, he was surprised when Ming taught him how the time elapsed since death was calculated. Wounds caused by blows from hands or feet would be certain to cause death within a period of ten days, Ming explained. In the case of wounds from any kind of weapon, including bite wounds, the time limit would be set at twenty days. Scalding and burns went up to thirty days, the time also allotted to gouged eyes, split lips, and broken bones.

Ming explained that if the deceased died within the amount of time that corresponded to the type of wound, it was determined to be caused by the wound, but if death came after the prescribed period, it was not due to that wound, and the person who inflicted it could not be accused of murder.

When Cí said he thought it was more sensible to treat each case individually, Ming shook his head.

"We have laws for a reason. Hasn't your rebellious streak gotten you in enough trouble?"

Cí hung his head to signal he had nothing more to add. But he wasn't so sure about the laws. Yes, they were surely crafted with good intentions, but the rules had also allowed someone like Gray Fox to become an Imperial official. The thought of it made Cí's stomach hurt, but he continued with his work, speculating about what exactly had become of Gray Fox.

Winter went by in a flash, but when spring arrived, Cí was in turmoil.

He began waking up from nightmares so vivid he would search for Third in the darkness. He'd then spend the rest of the night trembling, terrified and alone, feeling the absence of his family. Feng came to his mind at points, and he wished he could be under his wing again.

One afternoon he decided to seek solace and company at the Palace of Pleasure.

The girl he chose was kind to him; Cí would even have gone so far as to say she was sweet. Her caresses didn't avoid his burn marks, and her lips did things he'd barely imagined possible. In exchange for a few *qián* she gave him brief respite.

He began going back to see the same girl every week. And one cloudy evening as he was leaving, he ran into Gray Fox, who was drinking and being rowdy with a moronic little retinue but who sobered up when he saw Cí. The scar on Gray Fox's lip from Cí's punch had altered his face considerably. Cí made a dash for the door, but Gray Fox and the others got there first; they held Cí's arms as Gray Fox laid into him.

And because he couldn't feel the blows and didn't pretend to feel pain, they hit him harder and harder, until he could no longer move.

He woke up at the academy. Ming was mopping his brow with a cool cloth, showing as much care as a mother would show her child. Cí could barely move, and his eyes were swollen almost closed. Blackness swallowed him again. When he woke again, Ming was still with him.

Ming told him he'd been out for three days; a girl who seemed to know Cí had reported his situation. Ming and several students had brought him back to the academy.

"According to her, you were attacked by strangers. At least that's what I've been telling people here."

Cí tried to get up, but Ming told him to rest. The healer who had been to see him had recommended a couple of weeks' rest, at least until his fractured ribs were better. Cí's first thought was that he'd be missing important classes, but Ming told him not to worry and took his hand with all the sweetness of a "flower."

"What you need now are prayers, not classes," he said.

Ming cared for Cí through his recovery and praised him for all his hard work. But he reproached him too—his powers of analysis had made him aloof and isolated him from his peers.

At night, Ming's words, along with the doubts as to his father's honor, preyed on Cí's mind. If he really wanted to achieve his dream, he realized, he'd have to purge the ghosts from his heart.

He decided to confess everything to Ming.

When he was able to walk, he went to Ming in his private apartments. His master was shrouded in a cloud of incense smoke as he carried out his nightly prayers, and when he opened his eyes he looked far away, his face waxy and pale. He invited Cí to sit. Cí did, though then he didn't know where to begin.

"Whatever it is," Ming said softly, "it must be important if you've decided to interrupt my prayers."

Ming knew how to turn the burnt ends of a branch into a fine brush, just right for the job.

Cí poured out his heart, revealing everything: who he was, where he was from, the strange infirmity that prevented him from feeling pain, his time at the university, his time as assistant to Judge Feng, the deaths of his family members, his solitude. He told Ming about his father's dishonor. He confessed that he himself was a fugitive, and that the corpse from the prefect's test had been that of the very sheriff who had been tracking him.

Ming listened impassively, delicately sipping at his steaming tea. He looked as though he'd heard the story a thousand times. When Cí finished, he put his cup down and looked Cí firmly in the eye.

"You're twenty-two now. A tree must always be held responsible for the fruit it bears, but not the other way around. Nonetheless, I believe that if you look deep in your heart, you'll find reasons to be proud of your father. I see those reasons in you, in your wisdom, in the way you carry yourself, in your manners."

"My manners? Since I've been back in Lin'an, my life has consisted of farces and lies, one after another—"

"You're young and ambitious, and that makes you impetuous sometimes, but I don't see you as heartless. If you were, this remorse, which prevents you from ever sleeping properly, wouldn't be a factor. And as far as your lies go…" Ming took a sip of his tea. "This might not be good advice, but I would say you just need to learn to lie better."

Ming got up and made his way to the library, returning with a book Cí recognized only too well.

"A butcher who has memorized the *Songxingtong*? A gravedigger who, despite having only just arrived in Lin'an, knows where to buy something as rare as cheese? A poor country boy who's forgotten everything—except for a detailed knowledge of wounds and anatomy?" He looked Cí in the eye. "Did you really think you could fool me, Cí?"

Cí didn't know what to say.

"I saw something in you. Behind all the lies, I saw the shadow of sadness. Your eyes were innocent and helpless. And you were begging for help."

That night, for what felt like the first time in his life, Cí slept. But the next day, news came that overwhelmed him.

PART FIVE

PART FIVE

23

Cí was up early, honoring his dead and cleaning Ming's patio, like any other morning. After breakfast he hurried to the library and immersed himself in the compendium of forensic procedures he'd been working on, and which he was scheduled to present later that day. Halfway through the morning he realized he hadn't included certain passages from the *Zhubing Yuanhou Zonglun*, or *General Treatise of Causes and Symptoms of Illnesses*, and he wanted to be sure to add some of the information it contained. The volumes he needed were in Ming's apartments.

Unfortunately, Ming had been called away at the last minute to a meeting at the prefecture. If Cí waited for him to get back, he wouldn't have his compendium ready in time for the presentation, but he was strictly forbidden from entering Ming's apartments without permission.

This is a bad idea.

He pushed open the door to Ming's library and felt his way forward in the darkness. He ran his hands over the shelves, and then shuddered when he came to the place where he knew the volume should be. There was a gap.

It wasn't easy in the dark, but he didn't want to light a lantern. Cí kept searching, and finally he found the volume he was looking for on Ming's desk, underneath another silk-bound book.

This is a bad idea.

Just as Cí put his hand on the book, Ming entered. Startled, Cí dropped both books to the floor. The silk-bound volume fell open to some pictures of nude men.

"I...needed...the *Zhubing Yuanhou Zonglun*," stuttered Cí. "For the presentation."

They both looked down at the book with the naked men.

"It's...an anatomy book," said Ming, grabbing it up off the floor.

Cí nodded and dropped his head. He couldn't understand why Ming would try to pretend. They both knew full well what books of physiognomy looked like, and they never depicted men in sexual positions. Cí stuttered an apology and asked permission to leave.

"Strange," said Ming, barely containing his anger. "You ask me if it's all right to exit, but you didn't bother to see if I'd mind your entering."

"Please excuse me. It was foolish."

"Tell me," said Ming, ignoring Cí's request, "have you ever stopped to ask yourself why anyone would show you the kindness I've shown you?"

"Often."

"Do you think yourself worthy of it?"

Cí frowned. "Not really, no."

"And do you know where I've just come from? The prefecture. And they've just invited me to help on a case—an outrageous crime that even the sickest of minds would be hard pressed to execute. And when they asked me to go to court, do you know what I did? I said I wanted you as my assistant. I told them I have a truly exceptional student with unprecedented acumen when it comes to forensic work. I spoke about you as if you were my own son…and this is how you repay me? Betraying my confidence while I'm away? Snooping?" He slammed his hands on the desk. "After everything I've done for you!"

Cí was trembling and silent. Everything he should have said was tumbling through his mind: that he would never have entered without permission unless it had been of the utmost importance, that he'd wanted to present the compendium as completely as possible, precisely so Ming would be proud of him. He couldn't make the words come out, and he turned away, trying to hide his tears.

"Not so quickly," said Ming, grabbing him by the arm. "I gave them my word you'd present yourself at court. And so you will. But after that, don't bother coming back. Get your things and never show your face here again." And with that, Ming let go of Cí's arm.

<hr />

Under normal circumstances, Cí would have given anything for a chance to go to the Imperial Palace. But at that particular moment, all he wanted was to regain Ming's favor.

It was with deep sadness that he walked with the group making its way along Imperial Avenue. Two officials led the way, drumming on tabors to announce the presence of the prefecture judge, and a multitude of townspeople milled around them, looking up at the man on his litter and hoping for any bit of gossip to do with torture or execution. Ming was at the rear, looking despondent. Cí couldn't stop glancing back at him.

How could I have been so stupid?

Since their confrontation, they hadn't spoken another word, except for Ming to mention that Emperor Ningzong himself was awaiting their arrival.

Ningzong, the Heavenly Son, the Tranquil Ancestor. Very few were allowed even to kneel before him, let alone look at him directly. Only his most trusted advisers were allowed to approach him, only his wives and children could ever touch him, and only his eunuchs were permitted to converse with him. He spent his days inside the Great Palace, protected by its imposing walls from the rest of the city. Shut up in his golden cage, the Supreme Herald's time was taken up with interminable receptions, ceremonies, and rites that, according to Confucian strictures, would never change. It was well known that his position was one of great responsibility and sacrifice.

Now that Cí was about to cross the threshold, he was utterly intimidated. The group went through the entrance, and a world of sumptuous wealth opened up before Cí's eyes. Beautifully carved stone fountains were situated throughout the gardens, and he caught a glimpse of a leaping roebuck. Iridescent-blue peacocks roamed free. Streams trickled between clumps of peonies and wide, old trees. The columns, eaves, and balustrades of the palace buildings glinted gold, vermilion, and cinnabar-scarlet. Cí marveled at the roofs with their extravagant cornices curling skyward. The buildings were perfectly aligned on a north-south axis and had the presence of an enormous soldier so confident of his strength that he would spurn any offer of protection. Yet there were still seemingly countless ranks of sentries standing guard on either side of the entrance that separated the palace from the city.

The hushed group came to a halt at the steps of the Reception Pavilion—the first of the palace buildings, which stood between the Palace of Cold and the Palace of Heat. A stout man with a soft, wrinkled face waited impatiently for them beneath a glazed-tile portico; his cap identified him as the venerable Kan, Minister of Xing Bu, the much-feared Councilor for Punishments. As they came closer, Cí saw the man had one eye missing, and the remaining eye blinked nervously.

A sullen-looking official carried out the formal introductions. Following the bows of greeting, he asked the group to follow him.

They walked along a passageway that passed through several galleries and auditoriums. In one gallery, snow-white porcelain vases contrasted against purple lacquer walls. Another glowed so green it resembled a jade mine. After this they came to an impressive pavilion, where the official leading them stopped.

"Honored experts," he said, indicating the unoccupied throne behind them, "salute Emperor Ningzong."

They all prostrated themselves before the throne as if the emperor were really there. This ritual complete, Councilor Kan took the floor, climbing up onto a dais and scanning the room with his one eye. There was a touch of terror in the man's countenance.

"As you already know, you have been brought here on account of a truly shocking matter. A situation that I suspect will require you to summon more instinct than wit. It is a truly monstrous matter. I don't know if the criminal we are facing should be counted as a human being or some vermin aberration of nature. Whatever the case may be, your task is to try and apprehend this abomination."

He descended the dais and led them to a door where two colossal guards bore large axes. Cí couldn't help but be dazzled by the ebony doorway, its lintel wrought with depictions of the Ten Kings of Hell. Stepping through, he was hit by the unmistakable smell of rotting flesh. Each person in the group was given a piece of cotton soaked in camphor to hold to his nose.

They arranged themselves around a bloody bulk in the middle of the room. Horror immediately registered on everyone's face. The cloth was blood-soaked, particularly in the area of the chest and neck.

The head matron of the palace stepped forward at a signal and uncovered the corpse, drawing gasps. Beneath the sheet lay a mutilated, headless body. One member of the group vomited, and everyone else recoiled. Everyone, that is, except Cí.

Undaunted, he scanned the body of what appeared to have once been a woman but now looked more like a partially devoured animal. The tender flesh had been pitilessly defiled, the head severed completely, and bits and stumps of trachea and esophagus hung from the neck like a pig's entrails. The feet had both been cut off at the ankles. Two grievous wounds stood out among the many on the torso: The first, above the right breast, was a deep, messy cavity that looked as though some beast had sunk its maw in and tried to eat out the lungs. The second was even more atrocious: a triangular incision straight across the navel and then down on both sides over the groin that left only a bloody gap. The entire pubic area had been removed in some strange ritual. They were informed that the missing parts of the body, including the head, were yet to be found.

The sight filled Cí with sadness. He noticed, in a stark and poignant contrast to the violence done on the body, the woman's hands, which were very delicate, and a hint of her perfume, still discernible even amid the awful stink of decomposition.

Kan read out a preliminary report based on the matron's examination. It included a rough idea of the corpse's age (thirty or so), remarks on the state of the breasts and nipples (small and flaccid), and a note about the velvet texture of the pale, downy hair. The report also mentioned that the corpse had been found fully clothed, disposed of on a street near the Salt Market. There was a final speculation as to what kind of animal might have been capable of wreaking such havoc on a body: a tiger, a dog, or perhaps a dragon, it said.

Cí wasn't convinced of the value of the matron's comments. She was probably good at many things, but he seriously doubted she had much acumen when it came to corpses. The problem was, of course, that Confucianism forbade men from touching the dead bodies of women, and no one would disobey the law. They'd have to base their findings on those of the matron, and that was that.

With the reading of the report concluded, Kan asked those in attendance for their verdicts.

The prefecture judge went first, stepping forward and asking the matron to turn the body so he could look at the back. The rest of the group drew closer. The back itself was pale and free of wounds, the waist fairly thick, and the buttocks flabby and smooth. The judge began circling the corpse, tugging pensively at his goatee. He then went over to the clothes the corpse had been found in and held up a simple linen smock of the kind worn by servants. The prefecture judge scratched his head and addressed Kan.

"Councilor for Punishments," he said, "such a loathsome crime… In my opinion, it would be irrelevant for me to talk about the type and number of wounds. Given the strangeness of the wounds, I am in clear agreement with my colleagues on the idea that an animal might be responsible." He stopped and meditated on his next remark. "But the wounds also lead me to think that we might be dealing with the work of a sect: the followers of the White Lotus, Manichaeans perhaps, Nestorian Christians, or maybe the Maitreya Messianists. Driven by some abominable desire, the killers cut off the head and feet in some bloody ceremony and then allowed some beast to devour the lung. The motives could be varied, though, given how twisted the mind of a killer has to be: an initiation ritual, a punishment, a demon offering, an attempt to remove some elixir contained in a gland or an organ."

Kan nodded and seemed to weigh the judge's words for a moment before inviting Ming to take the floor.

Ming came forward. "Most worthy Councilor for Punishments, permit me to bow down in the face of your magnanimity," he said, bending low, and Kan gestured for him to continue. "I am only a lowly professor and therefore hugely grateful that you thought of me in relation to this awful event. I hope that, with the assistance of all the spirits, I might cast a little light on this dark affair. I would also like to apologize in advance to those who might be offended if my assessment differs from those given so far. Should that be the case, I commend myself to your benevolence."

Ming went over and looked at the corpse's back before asking the matron to turn it back over. Seeing the wound around the sex, he couldn't help but flinch, but he leaned close to the body and began examining this and the other wounds slowly and in turn. He then asked for a bamboo stalk with which to probe the wounds, and Kan gave his approval. After some final checks, Ming turned to the councilor.

"Wounds are always faithful witnesses. Sometimes they can help us establish the how, sometimes the when, and sometimes even the why. Having an understanding of corpses allows us to evaluate the depth of an incision, the intent behind a blow, or even the force of that blow. All of this is well and good, but if you want to solve a murder, the fundamental thing is to enter into the murderer's mind."

He paused briefly, and the room seemed to hum with the group's anticipation.

"It may be mere speculation, but I see the removal of the pubic area as indicative of a depraved mind, a lustful impulse that unleashed a rare feat of violence. I couldn't comment on whether these are the acts of any cult or sect, though the wound on the breast might suggest that. What I am absolutely convinced of is that the removal of the head and feet had nothing to do with any ritual—it was to make it difficult to identify the corpse. Someone's face, obviously, is the easiest way to tell who they were, and their feet contain the secrets of lineage and office."

"Would you mind elucidating?" said Kan.

"This woman was no peasant, let me assure you. The delicacy of her hands, her well-kept nails, and the vague hints of an expensive perfume all indicate nobility. The murderer tried to make us think otherwise by dressing her in a servant's clothes." Ming paced the room slowly. "I'm sure no one in this room needs me to tell them that, from a young age, the feet of upper-class girls are bound in order to prevent their growth and render them beautiful. What people might not know, though, is that with binding the big toe is often stretched back over the top of the foot, while the other toes are bent under the foot. This produces somewhat different, and painful, deformities in each woman. Though men never get to see them, the women's servants do, in private. Therefore the motivation to remove a woman's feet is to prevent her from being identified by a servant who knows her peculiar deformities only too well."

"That is certainly very interesting," said Kan. "What about the wound to the breast?"

"Well! The prefecture judge pointed to the indubitable cruelty evidenced there, and I'd agree that the wound looks very much like teeth wounds from a large animal. But we don't know that the wound was necessarily inflicted immediately after the moment of death. Any dog passing down the alleyway where the corpse was dumped could have stopped and devoured that part of her, and at any point."

Kan frowned and glanced at the hourglass standing on one side of the room.

"Very well," he said. "Thank you, in the name of the emperor, for your efforts. We'll call upon you if we have any further need of you. Now if you'll please follow my assistant, he'll show you out." And with this he turned on his heel.

"Excellency! Please!" It was Ming. "You've skipped the Reader... I spoke about him to the prefecture magistrate, who agreed that he should accompany us here."

"The Reader?" said Kan.

"The Corpse Reader," said Ming, pointing to Cí. "The best student I've ever had."

"Well, I wasn't informed." Kan shot a malevolent glance at his assistant. "And frankly, I wonder what he could possibly add that your expertise might have missed."

"It might seem strange, sir, but he has the ability to see things where, for any other person, whoever it may be, there is only darkness."

"Yes, I do find it strange." He muttered something but then turned to Cí. "Fine, but get on with it. Anything to add?"

Indeed I do.

Cí stepped forward, picked up a knife, and, before anyone could stop him, plunged it into the corpse's belly.

"I can add that what we have here is no woman," he said, lifting out innards and holding them above the corpse. "This body belonged to a man."

24

Further examination confirmed Cí's assertion: the corpse had no female reproductive organs. Kan was astonished. Seating himself on a bench, he asked Cí to go on.

With a confident tone, Cí went on to assert that the wound to the lung had been the sole cause of death. Though its edges didn't have the hard, pinkish patches produced when living flesh is cut—nor did the ankle and neck stumps, nor did the gash around the sex—Cí found definitive signs of collapse in the lung, which happened only when a living person's lung was punctured.

He rejected the idea that an animal had been involved. The lung had clearly been removed with a great degree of brutality, as if someone had been trying to access the heart, but, he pointed out, there were no scratches or bite marks, nothing to indicate the involvement of any large animal. And though the ribs had been broken, they were clean breaks, as if made by some kind of tool. It seemed, in any case, as though the murderer had been looking for something inside the corpse. And it would appear that whatever it was had been found.

"Why? What might he have been looking for?" asked Kan.

"That I don't know. Maybe an arrowhead broke off inside and the killer tried to remove it because, say, it was reinforced with some kind of precious metal or something else that would point to the culprit."

"As for the amputations…"

"I believe they were a red herring. Professor Ming's idea that the corpse belonged to a noblewoman, and that the feet had been removed to prevent her identification—though an excellent reflection—is, I think, what the murderer wanted us to believe. Add that to the smooth, feminine body, and the breasts above all—"

"Male genitalia, but also breasts? Should we be thinking about the victim as some kind of aberration of nature?"

"Not at all. The deceased was, in fact, none other than an Imperial eunuch."

But Cí's astuteness did not have the desired effect. From the way Kan clenched his fists and muttered under his breath, it seemed that he was kicking himself for not having drawn the same conclusion. Everyone knew that eunuchs often developed feminine features, especially those castrated before puberty. Kan glared at Cí as though he were responsible for the oversight, as if he had somehow caused Kan to misinterpret the evidence.

"That will be all," he hissed.

❧❦❧

On their way back to the academy, Ming asked Cí to explain his logic.

"I worked it out during your remarks, when you said it would have been easy to identify the woman by her deformed feet…"

"Yes?"

"Well, as you yourself pointed out, foot binding is only something the upper classes do. Kan would definitely have known that.

So we have to assume he'd already interviewed all the noble families about a disappearance. Since he asked you to help, it must have been because those interviews bore no fruit."

"But from there to saying the corpse was a eunuch?"

"Something just struck me. Right after I arrived in Lin'an I was unfortunate enough to witness a castration of a child whose parents wanted the boy to be an Imperial eunuch. That poor boy has stayed with me so strongly...And then all the details fell into place."

Ming didn't say another word on their way back to the academy. Cí tried to guess his mood, but his clenched jaw and hard eyes didn't bode well. Cí thought his pride might have been hurt by not figuring out the eunuch. The situation reminded him of when he'd tried to help Feng and it had ended worse than he could have imagined, with his brother being accused. Although Cí had already effectively been expelled, he had a feeling things were about to get even worse.

As they arrived at the academy, Ming announced that he had a meeting, and that Cí was to wait for him so they could talk. He said he would be back by nightfall.

No sooner had Cí crossed the academy threshold than the guard appeared and took him by the arm.

"A man came by earlier," he said, leading Cí into the gardens, "and claimed to be your friend. I told him you weren't here and he went into a rage, so I kicked him out." He lowered his voice, stopping to face Cí. "He said something about being a fortune-teller, about a reward or something. I thought you should know. Be careful. If the professors see you hanging around with his kind, they won't like it. Not one bit."

Cí flushed. Xu had found him, and it would seem he was ready to follow through on his threats. Cí felt his world crashing down. He was being kicked out of the academy, and Xu was going to be there waiting to report him the moment he set foot on the streets.

Even though Ming had told him to wait, Cí knew he had to pack his things and flee the city before things got any worse.

Cí wandered through the academy for the last time. The empty classrooms struck him as somehow desolate, as if the sorrow crushing him were contagious. The walls seemed like mute witnesses to his vain efforts; they were part of the dream from which he was now forced to wake. When he passed the library and its shelves lined with generations' worth of knowledge, it felt like a hammer's blow to his already dejected state of mind.

Night was falling as he made his way along the streets of Lin'an. He walked aimlessly through the city he knew so well. He thought that he would walk until he happened upon a wagon or a boat—anything—that could take him far away. He went to the house he'd lived in with his parents and Third in what seemed another lifetime, and he stopped, silently wishing that someone would come to a window, open it, call out to him. But no one came. He was about to continue on, when all of a sudden four soldiers came around the corner and ordered him to stop. He recognized one of them from the palace.

"The Corpse Reader?" said the highest-ranking soldier.

"That—that's what they call me," stammered Cí.

"We have orders to take you with us."

Cí didn't put up a fight.

<hr />

They took him to the prefecture building, where they covered his head with a hood and put him in the back of a cart. During the journey through Lin'an he heard insults being hurled by people who must have thought him a criminal being taken to the gallows, but gradually these subsided, and eventually the cart came to a stop somewhere extremely quiet. Cí heard the squeak of gate hinges followed by voices, but he couldn't make out what was being said. The mules were whipped into action and the cart continued on for a while. Suddenly the cart came to a halt and Cí, with the hood still on, was helped down. He was led along a paved path and up a slippery ramp. He began to smell mildew and earth, and he had a terrible feeling he wouldn't be leaving this place alive. He heard a key turn in a lock, and then a hard push to his back caused him to stumble forward. The lock turned again, and everything went quiet.

He thought he was alone, but then he heard footsteps, and the hood was suddenly removed.

"On your feet!" ordered a voice.

A burning torch was held up. Cí could feel its heat on his face and was blinded by it. The soldier holding it stood back, and Cí's eyes began to adjust to the dungeon darkness. There were no windows, only filthy walls, rank and damp and cold. The soldier pushed him into the next room, where torture instruments hung on the walls. At the far end of the room was a stout figure surrounded by a group of sentries. The man, who had only one eye, came forward.

"We meet again," said Councilor Kan.

"What a coincidence," said Cí.

"On your knees."

Cí cursed himself for not having fled the city more quickly. Hanging his head, he prepared for the worst. But instead of a deathblow, another figure stepped forward into the torchlight. Cí saw a pair of curved shoes decorated with gold and inlaid gemstones. As he slowly looked up, his eyes came to a mother-of-pearl belt, then a red brocade tunic, and a magnificent gold necklace. Before him stood a slim, ill-looking man with an intense gaze. He wore the royal seal that confirmed what Cí thought from the man's attire: this was the emperor. Cí began trembling.

To look upon the Heaven's Son without express authorization meant death. The first thing that occurred to Cí was that the emperor wanted to watch him executed. He gritted his teeth and waited for it to come.

"Are you the one they call Corpse Reader?"

"That is what some call me, Your Highness."

"Get to your feet and follow us."

Cí was helped up. This couldn't be happening…The emperor, and the Councilor for Punishments to his right, were immediately swallowed up by a coterie of attendants and guards. They went ahead down a dimly lit passageway, and Cí, escorted by two sentries, followed.

After crossing a narrow hallway, they came into a large, vaulted room, in the center of which were two pine coffins. A number of torches flickered in the darkness, casting a little light on the bodies inside. The guards and assistants departed, leaving Cí and his two escorts alone with Kan and the emperor. Kan nodded, and the escorts brought Cí closer to the coffins.

"His Imperial Highness requires your opinion," said Kan, with more than a hint of a grudge in his tone.

Cí stole a glance at the emperor, noticing how emaciated the man was, and turned to the first coffin. The corpse was an elderly man, of thin build and long limbs. The face was entirely worm-eaten, and the belly—which had a gash that looked familiar—had also been devoured by worms. Cí estimated that the man had been dead for five days, but he didn't say anything yet.

He turned to look at the second body, that of a younger man in a similar state of decomposition. Maggots spilled out of every orifice, and a wound above the heart teemed with them.

Cí had no doubt that both men had died at the hands of the eunuch's killer. He began telling Kan this but was interrupted by the emperor.

"You may address me directly," he said.

Cí turned toward him but was so overwhelmed that it took a moment for him to speak. When he was able, he managed to conjure a steady voice. His conclusion, he explained, was based on the unusual characteristics that were common among the three corpses.

"All three deaths were caused by a single type of wound made by the same weapon, a curved knife—and then a bloody excavation took place in an attempt to open up the torso and extract something. And the widths of each fissure, and the appearance of their edges, are very much alike."

This was the part that didn't make much sense to Cí. An arrowhead could snap off, but what was the likelihood of this happening twice, or three times, in exactly the same way?

Cí continued, "It is odd that none of the corpses show any sign of a struggle." And the most unsettling thing, he added, was that all three, in spite of the smell of rotting flesh, also gave off a distinct scent of perfume.

He explained that there were also differences. "As with the eunuch, the murderer clearly tried to eliminate any identifying signs of the corpse in the first coffin, though here by multiple slashes to the face. But if you consider the third corpse, you'll see that, despite all the worms, the face is still somewhat intact."

The emperor turned his own cadaverous gaze to where Cí was pointing. He nodded and gestured for Cí to continue.

"In my opinion, this isn't due to an oversight, nor has it come about because of some kind of improvisation. If we consider the hands, callused and dirty like those of a pauper, we also see that the fingernails are chipped, and the small scars all over the fingers suggest a lower-class working person. This is very much in contrast to the eunuch and the older man, whose hands were delicate and well cared for, which suggests their superior social status."

"Hmm...Continue."

Cí nodded. He took a moment to collect his thoughts before gesturing to the younger of the corpses.

"I'd say the murderer was either surprised in the act or didn't care about the possibility of some poor laborer being identified. But clearly, the murderer went to great lengths to make it difficult to identify the other two. If we could figure out who they were, there would be a clear link to the murderer."

"Your verdict, then?"

"I wish I had one," lamented Cí.

"I told you, Your Majesty!" said Kan. "He can't really read corpses!"

The emperor didn't react. He seemed entirely devoid of emotion.

"What would be your conclusion, if you *had* to make one?" he asked Cí.

"I wouldn't want to mislead Your Majesty. I suppose your experts said the murders were committed by some sect. If I had my normal materials and equipment, I might be able to comment more fully. But not having my tongs, my vinegar, my saw, or chemicals, I'd be loath to confirm or deny what has already been suggested. The only thing I can say for certain, given the level of decomposition, is that the murders occurred in the last five days, and that the older man was the first of all three to be killed."

The emperor stood preening his long whiskers, deep in thought. Eventually he motioned to Kan to come nearer and whispered something in his ear. Kan shot Cí a baleful glance and then withdrew, accompanied by an official.

"Very well, Corpse Reader," whispered the emperor. "One more question. You mentioned my judges before. In your opinion, is there anything they missed?"

"Have they painted him?" Cí asked, gesturing to the younger corpse.

"Painted him?"

"Because of the maggots, in a couple of days all that will be left is the skull. I'd have a portrait done. It might be needed for a future identification."

<hr>

Cí was taken out of the dungeon and led to a nearby room. Before leaving, the emperor spoke briefly with a white-haired, sallow-skinned official who bowed repeatedly. Then everyone but Cí and the official departed.

"The Corpse Reader, eh?" said the official, circling Cí and looking him up and down. "Interesting name! Choose it yourself, did you?"

"No—no, sir."

"Hmm." The official's eyes sparkled beneath his bushy eyebrows. "And tell me, what's it supposed to mean?"

"I suppose it's to do with my skills of observation when it comes to dead bodies. I was given it at the academy where I'm studying—where I used to study."

"The Ming Academy, yes…" The official's demeanor softened. "My name is Bo, and I'm going to be your liaison officer, it seems. Anything you need, but also anything you find out, from now on you'll communicate it through me."

Cí had no idea what the man was talking about. "Anything I find out?"

"Well, your performance impressed the emperor. It impressed everyone, in fact."

"Councilor Kan doesn't seem very impressed with me."

"Kan is a good man. Very traditional, very strict—he served the emperor's father—but he's an upright person. The problem was that you broke the rule about touching women's dead bodies, and you didn't even ask his permission. If there's one thing Kan doesn't like, it's rules being broken."

"The corpse was a man. I meant no disrespect."

"In any case," continued Bo, "you discovered things not even the palace judges had. His Majesty thinks you might be of use. But first of all, I need to fill you in a bit. Remember, though, this is not for general consumption. What I'm about to tell you, you have to listen to as though you have no tongue. Understood?"

Cí nodded seriously.

"For a number of months now, there has been a great evil in Lin'an. Something that threatens to devour us all. It seems to have become weaker just recently, but it still represents an awful threat. Our sergeants have done what they can, but every time they establish a suspect, that suspect disappears or winds up dead in an alley. We've been running out of ideas, but your observations have been most valuable."

"But I'm just a simple student, sir."

"A student, yes, but simple, clearly not. We've done our homework on you. We've heard about all the good work you've been doing at the academy and about your very ambitious, useful compendium."

Cí wasn't as convinced of his worth. He thought about all the mistakes he'd made at the academy, too. Before he could say anything, though, Bo cut him off.

"The best evidence is that you worked out the corpse was a eunuch. You saw it straightaway, unlike our judges."

Cí couldn't argue with that. He felt buoyed by it, but then immediately remembered that, no matter what, he was still a fugitive with a dishonorable father. If he became too involved, they'd surely find out who he really was.

"Don't worry about the other judges," said Bo. "And don't think you're going to be made solely responsible for large decisions. Your opinion will be sought, and that's all. You obviously have a very keen vision for these matters. We have also heard about your ambition to take the Imperial exams, but do well here, and the emperor might just see fit to give you a place in the judiciary regardless of the exams."

Though this was obviously more than Cí could ever have dreamed of, he wasn't wholly pleased.

"Maybe the palace judges aren't stupid after all," he said, half to himself.

"What's that supposed to mean?"

"Just that…everyone knows a judge can be punished for getting a verdict wrong."

"Yes, and?"

"Well, this clearly isn't a straightforward case. If you'll permit me to speak frankly, sir, it seems to me that they might have been reserving judgment so as not to risk that eventuality. Better to say nothing and be thought a fool than speak and confirm it, right?"

Bo squinted and was about to answer when Kan entered the room and ordered Bo to leave. Kan's knit brow and pursed lips spoke for themselves.

"From now on you'll be answering to me. If there's anything you need or want, you have to ask me first. You're going to be given a pass that gives you access everywhere in court, everywhere except the Palace of the Concubines and my private apartments. You may consult the legal archives, and you may examine the corpses further. You are also permitted to question any person at court. All of this, but you must ask me first. Bo will explain the rest."

Cí's heart was racing.

"Councilor," he said, bowing. "I don't know if I'm up to this…"

Kan gave him a cold look.

"No one's asking you."

Kan led the way to the legal archives. He seemed in a hurry, as if he wanted to rid himself of Cí as soon as he could. Gradually the dank, narrow passages gave way to tiled galleries. The Hall of Secrets took Cí's breath away; it was an infinite labyrinth in comparison with the academy library. Shelves full of all kinds of volumes stretched into the distance and went all the way to the high ceiling. Sunlight broke in through a high window. Kan took a seat at a black lacquer table on which a single dossier lay. He flicked through its pages for a minute and then invited Cí to sit.

"I happened to overhear some of what you were saying to Bo. I might as well spell it out: that the emperor has given you this opportunity does not mean I personally have any confidence in you. Our judicial system is inflexible with any who try to corrupt or violate it, and our judges have grown old in the study and application of that system. You might be vain enough to speculate as to the worth of these judges. Maybe in your eyes they seem like nothing more than obstacles, unable to see beyond the ends of their own noses. But mark my words: should you dare to doubt the abilities of my men, I promise you'll regret it."

Cí made a show of submission. Deep down, though, he knew that if these judges were any good, he wouldn't have been brought there in the first place.

Kan directed Cí's attention to the dossier.

"These are the reports on the three dead people. And here's a brush and ink. Read the reports and then record your opinion." Kan took out a square seal and handed it to Cí. "Any time you need access to any of the rooms, present this to the sentries for them to mark the registers."

"May I ask who carried out the examinations?"

"Their signatures are at the bottom of each report."

Cí had a quick look.

"These are the judges' names. I mean, who performed the physical examinations?"

"A *wu-tso* like you."

Cí frowned. *Wu-tso* was a derogatory term for someone who did autopsies and cleaned corpses. But he decided it was better not to argue. He nodded and returned to the reports. He soon put them aside.

"There's nothing here about the evil that Bo told me about. He mentioned that something terrible was happening in the city, but these reports are only about the three corpses. There's no mention of motives or suspects."

"I'm sorry, but I can't give you any additional information."

"But if you want me to help you, councilor, I need to know—"

"You? Help me?" Kan leaned across the table toward Cí. "It seems you've understood absolutely nothing. Personally, I couldn't care less what you find out, get it? It will be better for you if you do as you're told. That way, maybe, you'll help *yourself.*"

Cí bit his tongue. He looked through the reports again. There was nothing there. Any idiot could have written them.

"Councilor," he said, getting to his feet. "I will need a place where I can carry out a detailed examination of the corpses. And I need my instruments. As soon as possible. Also, I will need to consult a perfume maker, Lin'an's best."

Kan's face tensed and his one eye opened wide. Cí tried not to let Kan's evident surprise at his requests get to him. Determined to succeed at this new opportunity, Cí needed to make sure he had his instruments and as much information as possible.

"Should there be more murders, I must be informed immediately, regardless of the hour, or where the body is found. The body mustn't be tampered with or cleaned until I arrive, not even by a judge. Any witnesses should be detained. I'll also need the best portraitist in the city, not one of those who make the princes look nice, but someone able to capture reality.

"Also, I need to know any information there is on the eunuch who was killed: his role in the palace; his tastes, vices, and virtues; whether he had any lovers, male or female; if he kept in contact with his family; his possessions; anyone he fraternized with. I need to know what he ate and drank and how much time he spent in the toilet.

"A list of all the sects would be useful," Cí went on. "The Taoists, the Buddhists, the Nestorians, the Manicheans, anyone who has been investigated for practicing occultism, witchcraft, or any kind of illicit act. Finally, I want a full list of every single death in the city in the last six months that has happened under strange circumstances—any police report, anything about people disappearing, and absolutely any witness who, however distant the link may seem, could possibly be related to these deaths."

"Bo will take care of it."

"I would also appreciate a map of the palace including details on all the officials and their functions."

"I'll try to have an artist make one up."

"And one last thing."

"Yes?"

"I need someone to help me. I'm not going to be able to solve these cases alone. Master Ming could—"

"I've already thought of that. Someone I hope you'll be able to trust."

The councilor got up and clapped his hands twice. A door creaked open at the end of the hallway. Cí looked toward the light in the doorway and saw a slim silhouette coming toward them. As the person came closer, Cí shuddered. He'd know that condescending smile and gray-streaked hair anywhere: Gray Fox.

"Councilor," he stuttered, "excuse my insistence, but I really don't believe Gray Fox is the best person for this job. It would be better—"

"Enough of your demands! Gray Fox has my wholehearted approval, something you are far from achieving. The two of you will work together; anything you find out I want you to share with him, and vice versa. Gray Fox will be my eyes and ears during this investigation, so you would be better off working with him than against."

"But he betrayed me once. He never—"

"Enough! I won't listen to another word. Gray Fox is my brother's son!"

Gray Fox waited for Kan to leave before turning to Cí with a smirk.

"So! We meet again," he said.

"A bit of ill luck," shrugged Cí, not bothering to look at Gray Fox.

"And look how far you've come! The emperor's very own Corpse Reader." He took the dossier and sat down.

"Whereas you," said Cí, ripping the dossier from Gray Fox's hands, "are still clutching at whatever you can get."

They faced each other and stood so close their noses were nearly touching.

"Isn't life just full of coincidences?" said Gray Fox, eventually taking a step back. "In fact, my first job for the court happened to be investigating the death of that sheriff. The one we examined in the prefecture. Kao was his name."

A shudder ran through Cí.

"I don't know who you mean." Cí tried to keep his voice steady.

"Oh, that's odd. In fact, the more I find out about that sheriff, the odder the whole thing becomes. Did you know he'd traveled from Fujian in search of a fugitive? It seems there was a reward involved."

"Why would I know about that?"

"Apart from the fact you're from Fujian yourself? Wasn't that what you said at your presentation at the academy?"

"Fujian's a big province. Thousands of people must arrive from there every day. Why don't you ask them?"

"So suspicious, Cí! I only mention it seeing as we're such good friends." He sneered. "Still, quite a coincidence..."

"And you haven't found the name of the fugitive?"

"Not yet. It seems this Sheriff Kao kept himself to himself, barely talked about the case."

Cí felt as if he could breathe again. He considered trying to change the subject, but he knew he needed to appear interested.

"Strange, though. The judiciary doesn't offer rewards, does it?"

"Quite strange. Maybe the reward was from some rich landowner."

"Maybe the sheriff was close to solving the case and thought about taking the reward for himself," suggested Cí. "Maybe that was why he was killed."

"Could be." Gray Fox appeared to weigh his words. "For now, I've sent a post to the Jianningfu authorities. I expect to have the fugitive's name in less than two weeks. And then, catching him will be as easy as can be."

25

During dinner Cí could barely eat even a grain of rice. He was utterly exasperated by the prospect of working with Gray Fox again, but knowing he was on the Kao case was even worse. It would be two weeks until any word would come from Jianningfu that might link Cí to Kao, so he had to find out whatever he could at court. If he managed to solve the case, maybe he'd still stand a chance.

Gray Fox slurped his soup, but when Cí pushed his dish away and got up, Gray Fox was right behind him. They'd been advised that the corpses had been transferred to an examination room, and neither wanted to let them decompose more. Cí hurried ahead, but when he got there, it turned out that none of his materials or instruments had been brought. Bo claimed not to have received the request.

Damn Kan, he thought. Bringing out his pass, and without asking Bo's permission, he announced that he'd collect his effects personally and was on his way out the door in an instant. Gray Fox stayed behind, but Bo followed after Cí.

At the academy, while Bo and a servant collected Cí's instruments, Cí rushed around looking for Ming, eventually finding the old man bent over some books in his apartments. His eyes were red-rimmed, and Cí thought he might have been crying. He bowed and begged his old master to talk to him.

"Don't think I don't know the emperor's taken you on. Corpse Reader—the outstanding youth showing up his imbecile master." He smiled bitterly. "That's what everyone is saying."

Ming's resentment was clear, but Cí still felt he was in the man's debt. He'd raised Cí up from nothing and never asked for anything in return. Cí didn't think Ming would believe him if he said he needed his help; he thought it would sound insincere to say he'd asked for him to be brought to the palace—even though both were true. He was trying to find the right words when Bo burst in, urging him to hurry.

Seeing the servant weighed down with Cí's instruments and books, Ming said, "Oh, I see, *that's* why you came. Fine. Go on, get out of here!"

As the old man turned away, Cí thought he saw a tear in his eye.

❧❧❧❧❧

When Cí returned to the examination room, Gray Fox was nowhere to be seen. Apparently he'd left when a brief examination hadn't revealed any new information. Cí decided to make the most of Gray Fox's absence to carry out his own examination. Then he noticed a nervous-looking little man standing quietly by the door. It was the perfumer, Bo said, and his name was Huio.

Cí greeted the man, who was staring at the sentry's large sword as if he thought he was about to have his head chopped off.

"I already told them, I haven't done anything! I told the guards when they detained me, but they wouldn't listen!"

Clearly the perfumer hadn't been informed why he'd been asked to come. But before Cí could explain, Bo stepped forward and told the man to keep quiet.

"All you need to know is that you have to obey this young man."

Huio began whimpering and nodding. He got down on the floor and clutched at Cí's feet, begging not to be killed.

"I've got a family, sir…"

Cí helped him gently to his feet. Huio was trembling.

"All I need is your opinion on a perfume. That's all."

Huio didn't seem to believe he could have been detained by Imperial Guards for such a matter, but he began to calm down. That was, until they took him over to the three corpses, which, in their advanced stages of decomposition, immediately caused the man to pass out. Cí managed to bring him around with some smelling salts, and once Huio was calm again, Cí explained his task to him in more detail.

"I believe the perfume each was wearing might have halted the advance of the worms in the flesh."

Huio approached the corpses again. The stench was really dreadful, and he gagged. Recovering, he asked for three bamboo sticks to be brought; then he rubbed one against the edges of the wounds on each of the three corpses and put the sticks in jars. He rushed out of the room and Cí followed, shutting the door after them.

"I don't know how you can breathe in there." Huio gasped. "Awful!"

"How soon can you have answers for me?" asked Cí impatiently.

"Difficult to say. The perfume is obviously mixed up with the smell of the rotting flesh, so I'll have to separate the scents. Then I'm going to have to compare my findings with thousands of perfumes from around the city. Every perfumer mixes his own scents.

Perfumes are all based on similar essences, but everyone proportions them differently. And of course," said Huio, smiling, "every perfumer's proportions are his greatest secret."

"It doesn't sound hopeful," said Cí.

"Something has already stood out to me. Something that might make my job easier. The very fact that there are traces of perfume after several days tells me that the fixatives are of the highest quality. That already excludes quite a few. And, though this might not provide a definite answer, I'd also say, judging by the combination of fragrances"—he took the lid off one of the jars and sniffed it— "that we're *not* talking about a pure essence here."

"Which means?"

"We might, just might, be in luck. I'll get to work. I hope to have an answer within a couple of days."

❧❀❧

The reports from the other examinations of the corpses reminded Cí of one important thing that he'd already noticed himself: The corpse of the older man had a wound beneath his right shoulder blade. It was circular, about the diameter of a coin, and its edges seemed to have been ripped at and torn outward. Cí made a note and continued his investigation.

There were no signs that any of the victims had put up a struggle—either they'd been so completely surprised they didn't have a chance of defending themselves, or they had been familiar with the killer. It was something to bear in mind. The examination brought only one more detail to light: a strange corrosion between the fingers and on the palms and backs of the older man's hands. The skin, in spite of the decomposition, was slightly whiter on those parts than anywhere else. There was also a small, reddish tattoo of a flame at the base of the thumb on the right hand. Cí removed the hand using a saw, packed it in ice, and put it in the conservation chamber before going outside for some air.

Soon Bo returned, accompanied by the artist who would be drawing the portrait of the young corpse. Unlike the perfumer, the artist had had his job explained to him, but he shrieked when he saw the state of the corpse. When he recovered, Cí explained what he wanted drawn, emphasizing that the artist was to make his representation as accurate as possible.

As the artist took out his brushes and began, Cí started reading the information Bo had brought. The first was a report on the eunuch, whose name was Soft Dolphin. He had begun working in the Palace of Concubines at age ten. He'd acted as overseer of the harem and as a chaperone, a musician, and a reader of poems. His keen intelligence had apparently made him a favorite of treasury officials. Eunuchs were considered trustworthy with money because they would never have an heir to pass it on to, and at age thirty, Soft Dolphin had been made aide to the administrator. He'd kept the post until his death at forty-three.

According to the report, a week before Soft Dolphin's disappearance, he'd requested leave to see his sick father. Because he'd been given permission to take leave, there was no immediate alarm when he disappeared.

As far as the eunuch's vices or virtues went, the report only mentioned an unbounded passion for antiques, a small collection of which he kept in his private quarters. The report closed with notes on his daily activities and the people with whom he tended to have contact—primarily eunuchs of a similar rank.

Cí then studied the map of the palace grounds. His accommodations had been marked out, and he noticed that even though Kan said he wasn't allowed there, his room adjoined the Palace of the Concubines. He gathered his tools and glanced at the artist's half-finished sketch; it was turning into a very accurate likeness, and he thought it would be a great help. He gave Bo instructions for a small lance he wanted made, then left.

Cí spent the afternoon and evening exploring the areas of the palace where he was allowed to go. Walking the exterior of the imposing, squarish building, he realized just how isolated the palace was: its crenellated walls were at least the height of six men, and four watchtowers, situated according to the cardinal points, overlooked the four ceremonial gates.

Having completed his tour of the perimeter, Cí made his way to the lush gardens, where he let himself be bathed by the dappled light and the intense emerald tones of the damp mosses, the olive-brown of minerals, the muted reds and paler greens of fruit and leaves—a splendid and exuberant palette. Peonies, orchids, and camellias drew his eye toward groves of pine and bamboo. The fragrance of cherries, peaches, and jasmine scrubbed the stink of rotting flesh from Cí's lungs. He shut his eyes and breathed it all in. He felt life coming into him anew.

He sat down in a pavilion next to a stream. A goldfinch warbled nearby. He took out the map of the palace, which had with it the palace rules related to the number of workers allowed to remain on the premises after their day's work. The rules established the hour of *shen* as between three and five in the afternoon—this was when all workers were required to have their identity papers checked by an official. The same official made sure they all left via the same gates through which they'd entered. It was no light matter: workers caught on the premises beyond their allotted time would be subject to prison and then death by strangulation.

Cí couldn't understand why this warning was included with his copy of the map; the pass he'd been given meant none of these restrictions applied to him. Maybe it was to impress upon him that his stay wasn't permanent, or perhaps it was a warning to be careful. It occurred to him that, for all the beauty and opulence of the gardens and the architecture, this was really little more than a prison.

He got to his feet and made his way toward the palace's southern buildings, where the offices for the executive branch and many government councils were situated. Then he made his way to the *siheyuan*, the gigantic porticoed patio that formed the facade of the Interior Court, the Palace of Concubines, and the Imperial Palace itself.

He took in the majesty of both of these palaces, whose rooms— two hundred, according to the map—were hidden by the interior facade. The emperor resided in them along with his wives and concubines, the eunuchs, and a permanent detachment of Imperial Guards.

From his view from the portico, he was also able to locate the East Wing, opposite the Palace of Concubines, which held the warehouses and kitchens, and the West Wing, where the stables and grooming yards were located. He thought the dungeon could be beneath them, but given how labyrinthine the underground sections were, they could really have been anywhere. Finally there was the North Wing, which held the two summer palaces: Morning Freshness and Eternal Freshness.

Much as Cí thought it both enjoyable and productive to familiarize himself with the palace grounds and buildings, he knew it was time to get back to work. He sat on the portico and pulled out the reports to compare them again with his own notes. Soon enough he was gritting his teeth in frustration.

His only certainty was that he was up against a dangerous and cruel killer who was also brilliant in his ability to disguise his crimes. That Cí had identified the first corpse as a eunuch was in his favor because he presumed the killer wouldn't imagine that this would be discovered, but there remained considerable obstacles to the entire investigation. The first, as he saw it, was having absolutely no idea of motive. Given the advanced decomposition of the corpses, it seemed particularly important that he establish this. Then there was Kan's hostility. But these were mere grains of rice next to his worst problem, which was having Gray Fox around.

Cí went to his quarters, deep in reflection.

His room was clean and private, with a low bed, a desk, and a view of the interior courtyard. Cí liked the simplicity. He intended to put his thoughts in order and try to move the case forward, but he quickly realized that he was relying on others—the perfume maker and the portrait artist, in particular—for any real progress. The results of their tasks weren't guaranteed to lead anywhere. He had to take charge of the investigation and his own fate. He headed back to the examination room.

He took the corpse hand from the conservation chamber. Now that he had some proper light, he noticed that the fingertips were dotted with dozens of what looked like pinpricks, or perhaps marks from a *fu hai shi*, he thought, the bumpy Guangdong pumice stone. He guessed that these were old marks, but he wasn't ready to proclaim that. Then he turned his attention to the fingernails, under which there were several black fragments akin to splinters. When he removed them he found that, unlike wood, they crumbled under a small amount of pressure; they were actually tiny bits of carbon. Putting the hand back in the chamber, he turned his mind to the strange craters the murderer had left in the three main wounds. Why might he have applied perfume to these? Why that brutal scrabbling around inside the wounds? Could he really have been trying to extract something, or might Ming and the magistrate have been right when they said it was the result of some ritual or an animal attack?

He got up, shutting the folder. If he wanted to make any real progress, he knew he had to go back to the first murder and track down people familiar with Soft Dolphin.

An official told Cí that Languid Dawn could be found in the Imperial Library.

Soft Dolphin's closest friend turned out to be a confident-looking eunuch of no more than seventeen. Though his eyes were red from weeping, his voice was assertive and his answers calm and mature. But when Cí asked him specifically about Soft Dolphin, his tone changed entirely.

"I already told the Councilor for Punishments, Soft Dolphin was very reserved. We spent a lot of time together, but we didn't actually talk all that much."

Cí avoided asking him what he spent his time doing. Instead he asked about Soft Dolphin's family.

"He hardly ever mentioned them," said Languid Dawn, relieved Cí didn't seem to be treating him as a suspect. "His father was a lowly lake fisherman, and as with many of us, Soft Dolphin didn't like admitting it. He'd fantasize."

"Fantasize?"

"Exaggerate, go off on flights of fancy. He spoke respectfully and admiringly of his family—not out of familial piety but out of a certain conceitedness, I'd say. Poor Soft Dolphin. He never lied out of wickedness. He just couldn't stand to think about his miserable childhood."

"I see." Cí looked up from his notes. "It seems he was very diligent in his work—"

"Oh, yes! He kept careful notes, spent any downtime going over his accounts, and he was always the last to leave. He was proud of having been successful. That was why so many people were envious of him—and me, for that matter."

"Envious? Who was envious?"

"Everyone, pretty much. Soft Dolphin was good-looking, soft as silk, but also rich. He was careful with money and had saved up."

Cí wasn't surprised. Eunuchs who progressed in court often became quite rich. It all depended on how good they were in the arts of flattery and adulation.

"He wasn't like the rest," added Languid Dawn. "He only had eyes for his work, for his antiques, and...for me." At this, the young eunuch broke down.

Cí tried to console him. He decided not to push him further; he could always interrogate Languid Dawn again at a later date.

"One last thing," said Cí. "Who would you say, apart from you, *wasn't* envious of Soft Dolphin?"

Languid Dawn looked in Cí's eyes as though he appreciated the question. But then he looked down.

"I'm sorry, I can't tell you that."

"You've nothing to fear from me."

"It's Kan I'm afraid of."

Soft Dolphin's quarters were situated near the Council for Finance, where he'd worked. Cí had to go by a couple of sentries on the way there, showing his pass. Everything in the space was extraordinarily neat and orderly: The books lining the wall, all of poetry, had been covered in identical silk bindings; the clothes were folded immaculately; the writing brushes were so clean a baby could have sucked on them; the incense sticks were organized according to size and color. The only exception was a diary on the desk that seemed to have been carelessly left open at its midway point. Cí asked the sentry to check the register, and the man confirmed that no one had accessed the quarters since Soft Dolphin's death. Cí went back through and moved on to the adjacent room.

It was a large salon whose walls looked as if they had been invaded by an entire army of antiques. On the first wall were dozens of bronze and jade Tang and Qin dynasty statuettes. Four delicate Ruzhou porcelain vases flanked the windows that looked out over the Palace of Concubines. Refined landscape paintings on silk covered the opposite wall, and on the fourth wall a single canvas hung, an exquisite piece of calligraphy crowning the door. The vigorous, right-to-left brushstrokes of the poem were stunning. At the bottom were several red seals denoting the previous owners. Cí was drawn to the sloping curves of the frame, and he found himself scrutinizing the piece close-up. It was much too expensive for a eunuch, even a relatively wealthy one like Soft Dolphin.

Cí went through into the third and final room, finding a divan wrapped in chiffon and heavily perfumed. The quilt came very precisely to the corners, like a glove tightly over a hand, and framed silks hung on the pristine walls. Absolutely nothing in these quarters had been left to chance.

Nothing except that diary.

Returning to the first room to examine the volume, Cí found that it consisted of thin paper pages decorated with images of lotus leaves. Cí settled down to read it. He found that Soft Dolphin's work life wasn't mentioned in the slightest; he wrote about purely personal matters. It appeared that he and Languid Dawn had been deeply in love. Soft Dolphin wrote in delicate, praising tones about his young lover, as he did when mentioning his parents.

Cí finished reading and put the diary down with a frown. All he could really glean was that Soft Dolphin, in spite of his passionate love life, seemed to have been both sensible and honest.

But he could also infer, he thought, that Soft Dolphin had been tricked by his murderer.

❧❧❧❧❧

Cí went early the next morning to the finance records office. Gray Fox didn't sleep on the palace premises, and Cí knew he tended not to be an early riser. So he decided to take advantage of a bit more time without his so-called helper.

According to the files, Soft Dolphin had spent the past year dealing with accounts to do with the salt trade, the import and export of which the state had control over along with tea, incense, and alcohol. Cí had little knowledge of mercantile dealings, but simply by comparing the past year's reports against the previous year's, it was easy to see that profits were steadily declining. The downturn could have had to do with market fluctuations, or some illegitimate siphoning of funds, or perhaps even the hugely valuable antiques collection of a certain Soft Dolphin…

To get more information, Cí presented himself at the Council for Finance, where they told him that state profits had been down across the board for the duration of the conflicts with the northern barbarians. Now Cí understood that the Jin invasions had impacted the whole country in one way or another. He bowed, thanking the official, and left to go and clean the corpses.

❧❧❧❧❧

In the antechamber of the examination room, the stench hit him straightaway; he knew camphor swabs wouldn't be much good but stuffed his nostrils with them nonetheless. Just then, Bo appeared.

"Here it is; sorry it took a while," he said, bringing out the lance Cí had asked for.

He looked the lance over, checking its weight and alignment and nodding in satisfaction; it was exactly what he needed. Then he carried on with his preparations, mixing white thistles and bean-tree pods and setting fire to them—another way of counteracting the smell. He also had some ginger to chew, but that was about all he could do. He took a deep breath and entered the examination room.

The corpses were once again crawling with worms, in spite of having been cleaned only the previous day. He picked the larvae and worms off with a wooden stick dipped in vinegar and water and completed the cleansing by pouring bowls of water over the corpses.

He made no new findings with either the corpse of the older man or that of the eunuch; the decomposition had gone so far in both that the blackened flesh had begun peeling away from the muscles in stiff sheets. But on the face of the younger corpse, the one he'd had the portrait made of, he discovered a myriad of tiny pricks like poppy seeds. These scars looked to be old and were scattered across the face like tiny burns or pockmarks. There were also odd squarish rings around each of the eyes. He quickly sketched the marks in his notebook, and then found exactly the same marks on the hands.

Then Cí took the lance and went over to the older man's corpse, introducing it into the crater wound on the chest and carefully nudging and applying pressure. He asked Bo to help him turn the body and discovered that, as he had suspected, the wound went all the way through from front to back. So, there were not two separate wounds at all. He was about to remove the lance when something gleamed on it, catching his eye. Picking up his tongs, he removed the object; it turned out to be a stone chip. He couldn't tell where it might be from, but he saved it as evidence.

Cí turned to Bo.

"I need another corpse," he said in a serious voice.

"Well," said Bo, looking worried, "I'm not going to help with that!"

Cí let out a laugh and Bo a sigh; they weren't going to have to kill anyone, but Cí did ask if it would be possible to have access to a corpse so he could test a hypothesis. Bo immediately suggested they go to the Great Cemetery.

"No. It has to be from somewhere other than the Great Cemetery," he said, remembering Xu's threats straight away.

Next he took out two large sheets of paper, one with an anatomical drawing of a human from the back, the other from the front. Bo had never seen anything like them.

"I use them as a screen," explained Cí. "These black points indicate the places in the body where it is fatal to receive a wound, and the white points are where, though not fatal, wounds would have grave consequences." He spread them out on the floor and marked on them precisely where the wounds had been inflicted.

Cí cleaned the lance and put away the sketches. After giving the order for the three corpses to be buried, he and Bo left the palace.

<hr />

They went to the Central Hospital. People died there with such frequency that Cí was sure there would be some corpses on which he could practice. He wanted to find out what kind of wound the lance would make when passed through the body fully. However, the sanatorium director informed them that the most recently deceased patients had already been taken away by their families. When Bo suggested they use a sick person instead, Cí thought surely he was joking, but the director didn't see why they couldn't. Still, Cí rejected the idea.

"I don't know how I could have dared to suggest it," said Bo apologetically.

"What about convicts who have been executed?" asked Cí.

⊶⊶⊷⊷✶⊶⊷⊷

The prison was located just outside the city walls. Its director, a military man covered in scars, seemed to relish the idea of skewering a dead prisoner.

"We strangled one just this morning," he said brightly. "I know dead prisoners have been used in the past to test the effects of acupuncture, but nothing like this. At least the scum will be put to good use. And if it's for the good of the empire, all the better."

He showed them to where the body of the recently executed prisoner was being kept. It was sprawled out and in tatters.

"The bastard raped two little girls and threw them in the river," the prison head told them.

Taking out his drawings, Cí tried to mark on this corpse the exact locations of the wounds he had found on the other corpses. He decided against undressing the body so as to better reproduce the conditions of the other deaths.

"And it would be best to stand him up," he said.

The prison head ordered a number of soldiers to help, and they eventually hoisted the body up with a rope slung over a beam and then under the armpits. The dead man hung there like a rag doll. As Cí approached, wielding the lance, he felt a moment of compassion for the criminal whose half-open eyes seemed to issue a challenge from beyond death. Cí pointed the lance at the body and, bringing to mind the girls this man had killed, thrust the point into the body with all his might. There was a crack, but the blade snagged halfway through the torso.

Cí cursed. He removed the blade and prepared to thrust again. Summoning all his energy and bringing the girls to mind again, he struck harder this time but still didn't make it through the torso. He removed the lance and spat on the floor.

"You can take him down." He kicked a stone in frustration, shaking his head.

He didn't feel the need to explain anything to anyone there, but he thanked them for their efforts and said he was done.

❦

When he met up with Gray Fox later on in the afternoon, Cí had no qualms about keeping his findings secret.

"The only thing I've really managed to ascertain is that, in the eyes of his colleagues, Soft Dolphin was an honest person, a good worker," said Cí. "But that's about all. What about you?"

"Honestly, this case is a poisoned chalice. A body without feet or head! They haven't got the slightest idea, and then they're going to make it seem like you and I are totally inept."

"Any ideas how to move it forward?"

"I've decided to work on something else. The case with the dead sheriff. No way am I going to let these bastards smear my career in shit when it's only just getting started. I've decided to go to Fujian myself and hurry things along. I have a feeling I can work this one out, and that'll be a good early success to help me make my name."

"But what about our orders?"

"Oh, I've chatted with Kan; he's fine about it." Gray Fox smiled nonchalantly. "Blood's thicker than water and all that...You're going to have to work this one out without me, I'm afraid!"

Cí couldn't be happier that Gray Fox was going to be out of his hair, but at the same time he felt sure that Gray Fox would figure out that Kao had been tracking him, and that would be the end of everything.

"So, when do you leave?" Cí asked, trying to keep his voice level.

"Tonight," said Gray Fox. "The longer I stay here, the more of this disaster gets pinned on me."

"Well, good luck to you," Cí said, turning to go up to his quarters. He had a lot to think about.

26

The perfume maker arrived, breaking Cí out of his state of deep concentration. He had been thinking about the corpse with the tiny scars on its face and had come up with a few ideas but had yet to reach a conclusion he found satisfactory. So when the perfumer said they were in luck, he was delighted.

"Smell this," said the perfume maker, holding out a small vial. The fragrance was deep and sticky-sweet, almost like jelly; it had notes of sandalwood and patchouli, and its intensity intoxicated Cí's senses.

"Essence of Jade," said the perfume maker, replacing the stopper. "Which just happens to be a fragrance I've been making for the emperor for many a year now."

"It's what the emperor wears? I've had the privilege of being in his presence, but I didn't get close enough to smell him."

"No, no," said the perfume maker, as if it were common knowledge. "The emperor doesn't wear Essence of Jade."

The perfume maker explained how he made the fragrance using secret ingredients and in secret proportions. The only people allowed to wear it were the emperor's wives and concubines.

"And could anyone from your workshop have gotten hold of some of the fragrance?"

"Impossible!" He was genuinely offended. "I'm the only one allowed to have anything to do with Essence of Jade. I not only mix it myself but bring it to the court in person."

"And might anyone have tried to imitate your mix?"

"They might have, but it's punishable by death to do something like that with a product the emperor himself favors."

"And you're absolutely sure this is the scent on the corpses? Even with all the other odors?"

"Boy, I would know this smell if it were stuck in the middle of an army of elephants. But there was one other smell I picked up. An unusual smell, very acrid. But I'm afraid I couldn't work out what it was."

Cí made a note.

"All right," he said. "And what about this Essence of Jade? Who in the palace do you deal with when delivering it?"

"A woman…" The perfume maker's eyes opened wide as if he were imagining her there before them, naked. He cleared his throat. "A *nüshi*. She handles all of the emperor's encounters with his concubines. Generally I stock her up every first moon or so with thirty vials like this one. Don't forget, the harem's made up of more than a thousand women! I can promise you she keeps a close eye on the batches; she wouldn't let it be squandered."

Cí thanked the perfume maker and showed him out, then made his way toward the interior gardens.

Before long he was in the vicinity of the Palace of Concubines, which he knew full well he was forbidden from going anywhere near. He hid behind a tree and peeked out at the beautiful lattice-work stretching all the way to the end of the building. He imagined that the delicacy of the edifice mirrored the beauty of the women inside. Graceful silhouettes, apparently naked, moved behind the paper window screens. He couldn't help but stare; it had been a long while since he'd lain with a "flower." But he needed to purge the sensual thoughts from his mind and concentrate. Cí had to find a way to speak to the *nüshi*.

First, though, he needed to check on the artist's progress.

Cí was very pleased when he saw how lifelike the portrait of the young corpse was. The artist had perfectly reflected every single line and feature—except for one thing, a grave error.

"I should have been clearer with my instructions," said Cí. "I need you to render him with the eyes open."

The portrait artist was surprised and extremely apologetic, bowing repeatedly. Cí said the fault was partly his own. Fortunately, the artist said it wouldn't be too hard to remedy.

"Could you also add some scars?" asked Cí.

Cí described in detail the type, size, shape, and distribution of the scars, specifying that the artist should avoid painting around the eyes. He waited for the changes and additions to be made and, looking at the amended work, expressed his satisfaction.

"It's tremendous, really."

The portrait artist bowed proudly, handing Cí the silk canvas to roll up and put in its fabric container. Cí headed off to his quarters, where he took the portrait out and admired its lifelikeness again. The only problem was that it would be impossible to duplicate and distribute. But Cí still thought it would be useful in helping him understand where those scars had come from.

Cí had reached a point where he wasn't sure how to proceed. Ming was the one person Cí knew who always had new ways to approach a problem. Although he wasn't sure how the professor would receive him, Cí had to go and ask for his help.

When he tried to leave the palace, however, the sentry barred his way. Cí, holding out his pass, didn't understand.

"Take it up with the councilor," spat the unfriendly guard. "He's the one who said you weren't allowed to leave."

Cí clenched his jaw and kicked a pebble, picturing it to be Kan's head. He decided he had to address this with the emperor; if the case was going to progress even an inch, Cí needed someone above him who wasn't intent on obstructing his every move. Cí went to the office of the emperor's personal secretary. He introduced himself and asked how he might go about arranging an audience with the emperor, but the secretary, an old, sleepy-looking man, acted as though a fly had just landed in his eye. It was unusual, insulting in fact, that a worker would even imagine he might be able to speak directly with the emperor.

"People have died for less," said the secretary, barely deigning to look at Cí.

But Cí was convinced that if the authorities had really wanted him dead, he'd already be dead. Besides, he had already spoken directly with the emperor.

So he asked again but only managed to make the secretary more indignant. He ordered Cí to get out or he'd call the guard, but Cí was determined to get things straight. He didn't budge, though the secretary began to shout and he knew a guard would appear at any second. But just then Cí saw the approach of the Imperial retinue, including the emperor himself and Kan. He rushed past a guard and prostrated himself in the retinue's path. The group stopped, and Kan ordered for him to be arrested, but the emperor overruled him.

"Strange way of presenting yourself to your emperor."

Cí knew he was being extraordinarily improper, and he didn't dare look Ningzong in the eye. He pressed his forehead against the floor and begged indulgence. He stammered that it had to do with the crimes he was investigating, and that it was urgent.

"Majesty," said Kan, "this is unacceptable!"

"There will be plenty of time for punishments. Have you made progress?" he asked Cí.

Cí thought about asking to speak with the emperor alone, but he also didn't want to push his luck further than he already had. Still prostrate, he cast a sidelong glance at Kan.

"Your Majesty, with the greatest respect, I think someone's trying to sabotage my work."

"Sabotage?" He waved his sentries aside and came forward. "What on earth do you mean?"

"I've just been prevented from leaving the palace grounds," he said quietly. "The pass I was given by His Excellency the Councilor doesn't allow me to get on—"

"I understand," said the emperor, looking over at Kan, who seemed unconcerned. "Anything else?"

Perplexed, Cí opened his mouth, but it took him a few moments to speak.

"Yes, Majesty," he said finally, forehead still on the ground. "The reports I was given don't mention the palace judges' investigations. I've been given no information as to where the bodies were found or how, no witness statements or police reports, and if there have been any advances in terms of suspects or motives, none of this has been communicated to me." He glanced over at Kan again. "I interviewed one of Soft Dolphin's intimates yesterday. He was very forthcoming until a certain point. When I pressed him he said he'd been forbidden from saying too much. By the Councilor for Punishments."

The emperor was quiet for a few moments.

"And you think this is sufficient cause to importune me? To act like some savage in front of me?"

"Highness, I…" Cí realized how crassly he was acting, but he still continued. "Councilor Kan stated that no one had entered Soft Dolphin's quarters, but that was untrue. Not only did he himself go in there, but he swore the sentry to secrecy! Your councilor doesn't want the case to progress! He seems intent on preventing reason and method from coming to bear. I may not interview the concubines, nor am I allowed to see the reports, and I can't even leave the palace—"

"Enough of this insolence!" The guards were already stepping forward. "Take him to his quarters."

Cí didn't bother resisting. As he was taken away, he couldn't help but notice Kan's poisonous smile and the twinkle in his one eye.

<hr/>

The door slammed shut and Cí heard the sentries taking up position outside. He began gnawing his nails, but Bo soon burst in, and he was furious.

"You think you own the world, you youngsters!" He began pacing the room. "You come here with your new techniques, your expert analysis, so full of yourself, and you forget the most basic things. *Basic protocol!*" He stopped and fixed Cí with a look. "Mind telling me what you're up to? How could you think to accuse a councilor?"

"A councilor who's preventing me from doing the job the emperor asked me to do, shutting me up like a prisoner."

"That was the emperor's idea, not Kan's, and it's for your own good! Idiot boy! If you leave the palace without an escort now, you'll last about as long as an egg in a fox's jaw."

Cí was beginning to understand.

"It isn't that you can't leave, it's just that if you do, you have to have protection."

"But—so—"

"And of course Kan went into Soft Dolphin's quarters. What do you expect? Do you really think every single thing is going to be left up to you?"

"What you don't seem to understand," said Cí, "is that I'm not going to be able to help you unless you give me some idea of this danger we're up against."

Bo paused to think, going over to the window and looking out. Then he turned back to Cí with a different expression.

"I understand how powerless you feel, but you have to understand where they're coming from. You can hardly expect the emperor to confide in any old newcomer."

"Fine. But if I'm not going to be allowed to move the case forward, ask the emperor to relieve me of my duties. I'll tell you as much as I've found out, and—"

"You've found something out?"

"Less than I could have, but more than they let me."

"Enough of the sarcasm! I may not be a councilor, but I can still have you flogged any time I like."

Cí knew his impertinence was getting him nowhere. He dropped his head and apologized. Then he pulled out his notes, took a deep breath to calm down, and ran through his findings: the discovery of the tiny scars on the dead youth's face, the Essence of Jade perfume and the palace *nüshi*'s responsibility for it, and Soft Dolphin's deception.

Bo's eyes were wide with curiosity.

"Soft Dolphin lied to Kan. He never went to see his father because his father never fell ill. Soft Dolphin had to make something up so that no one grew suspicious about his absence."

"How can you be so sure? His father was often ill."

"Clearly. And Soft Dolphin mentioned it in his diary. He went into great detail: his fears, his preparations for travel, what presents he'd take. But in the last month there's not one single mention, not even of his father's having a chill."

"Maybe it was sudden," suggested Bo, who now looked uncomfortable. "Sudden enough that he didn't have time to write it down."

"It could have happened like that, but it didn't. The reports show that Soft Dolphin asked permission to leave the day after the first moon of the month but didn't leave until the following night. Plenty of time to write in his diary."

"And what does this lead us to, then?"

"Something that I think should trouble you. Soft Dolphin was killed by someone he knew, possibly someone he trusted. Remember, there weren't any marks to show he'd put up a fight, nothing to suggest he'd defended himself, which means he didn't expect to be murdered. His reason for lying to leave the palace must have been something very pressing—he would have known very well the penalty if he was found out."

"This is troubling, yes. Yes. I think the emperor needs to know."

27

As Cí went down into the Library of Hidden Archives, his heart contracted. The emperor had said Cí could be told about their suspicions but had made something very clear: Cí was allowed to consult the documents selected by Kan, but he mustn't touch any other volume, on threat of death—by the worst of torture methods. Kan would be watching over him the whole way.

He followed the councilor through gloomy passageways. The light from Kan's lantern had transformed the older man's face into a gruesome mask. Cí was frightened; he felt his actions had turned Kan into an outright enemy. He scanned the spines of books as they passed: *The Putting Down of the Yurchen Army Rebellion, Espionage Under the Yellow Emperor, Weapons and Armor of the Dragon Warriors, Systems for Causing Disease and Pestilence.*

Kan stopped and pulled out a volume titled *The Honor and Betrayal of General Fei Yue.* "Do you know who this man was?" he asked, handing the book to Cí.

Cí nodded. Fei Yue was a national hero. Born to a lowly family, he'd joined the army at nineteen and seen action on the northern borders. His bravery and strategic acumen repelling the Jin invaders had won him promotion, and he became the assistant chief to the emperor's private councilor. There was a popular legend that he and only 800 other men had fought off 500,000 on the outskirts of Kaifeng.

"But what's *betrayal* doing in the title?" Cí asked.

Kan took the volume back. "It refers to a little-known fact, one of the Tsong dynasty's most dishonorable episodes. Despite his devotion, at the age of thirty-nine Fei Yue was executed for high treason. It was years until it was revealed that the prosecution had been based on lies. Emperor Xiaozong, our current emperor's grandfather, restored Fei Yue's honor with the building of the Qixia Ling temple."

"I've been there," said Cí. "The one with the four kneeling statues, with their hands tied behind their backs."

"Those are effigies of Prime Minister Qin Hui, his wife, and their lackeys, Zhang Jun and Mo Qixie. They had created the lies and accusations." He shook his head disapprovingly. "Ever since then, we've been in conflict with those damned Yurchen. We still haven't managed to kick them out, and now it's *us* paying tribute to those barbarians! Thanks to them, our territories have been about halved. They're even occupying the old capital. All because we're a peaceful people—which is precisely the problem! *Now* we regret not having a proper army!" He slammed his fist down on the volume.

"Mm, it is bad..." Cí cleared his throat. "But what has any of this got to do with the case?"

"A lot." Kan took a deep breath. "The histories say that Fei Yue had five children whose destinies were marked by the same shame and dishonor that had been heaped on their father. Their careers, their marriages, their property—it was all like dust in a hurricane. Each of them was consumed by hatred and died before Fei Yue's reputation was restored. But, according to this book, there was another child, one who managed to avoid all the disgrace by fleeing to the North. He went on to prosper. Now, it's our belief that one of the descendants of that child has come back for vengeance."

"By killing three men with absolutely nothing in common?"

"I know what I'm talking about!" growled Kan. "We're about to sign a new treaty with the Jin. An armistice to ensure peace on the border—at the cost of more tributes." He reached out to take another volume down but stopped. "And that's where the traitor's motives lie."

"I'm sorry, but I really don't—"

"That's enough! There's a reception this evening in the palace; the Jin ambassador will be there. Be ready. Dress appropriately. There you'll meet your adversary, Fei Yue's descendant. The one you're going to have to expose."

⚜

As Cí was being outfitted by the Imperial tailor in the green silk robes worn by all of Kan's personal advisers, one question preyed on his mind: Why, if Kan already knew who the murderer was, would he be introducing Cí and not simply making the arrest? The tailor looked at Cí and adjusted the silver brocade of the cap. Cí raised an eyebrow at his reflection in the bronze mirror. Actually, he had one other question: How, without trying, did he manage to look like some music hall singer, the kind who tries to sneak into a banquet without an invitation? But he just shut his eyes and let the tailor get on with his work. He had to focus on what was ahead.

⚜

The ceremony at the Palace of Eternal Freshness began as the sun was going down. A servant had led Cí to Kan's private apartments, and then he'd followed the councilor in his flowing robes toward the Hall of Welcome. On their way, Kan filled Cí in on protocol: he'd decided to say Cí was an expert on Jin customs, by way of explaining his presence.

"But I haven't got the first clue about the barbarians—"

"Where we'll be sitting, you won't need to talk about them."

Entering the Hall of Welcome, Cí turned pale.

Dozens of tables brimmed with delicacies. The smells of stews, fried shrimp, and sweet-and-sour fish mixed with scents of peonies and chrysanthemums. The air was cooled by a series of intricate windmills that stood beside bronze receptacles mounded with ice brought down from the mountains. The walls were red, blood-bright, and the open latticework drew the eye toward Japanese pines, white as ivory; towering bamboos; and stands of jasmine and orchids. A man-made waterfall cascaded into a lake below.

Cí couldn't hide his astonishment. Even the greatest of imaginations would have struggled to dream of the luxury that spilled out around him.

An army of servants stood like statues—all cast from the same mold—in perfect lines, waiting for the ceremony to begin. Behind them, on a dais lined with yellow satin, was the imperial table, which bore ten roasted pheasants. Hundreds of beautifully dressed people stood milling and conversing at the foot of the dais.

Kan gestured for Cí to follow him, leading the way through the sea of aristocrats, well-known poets, senior officials, and their families. Kan told Cí that the emperor had elected to give the occasion a festive air so it wouldn't seem like a defeat.

"Really, he has made the reception coincide with the party, and not the other way around."

Their table was arranged according to the eight-seat custom. The seat situated farthest to the east would be occupied by the most important guest, and that was Kan. The rest sat according to rank and age, with the exception of Cí, who was told to sit next to Kan. Women sat at separate tables to allow the men to discuss business.

Kan whispered that he'd given up his seat at the imperial table so that protocol wouldn't be such an issue. Then he pointed out the other people at the table: two prefects, three lawyers, and a famous bronze maker.

Soon a gong sounded, announcing the arrival of the emperor.

Preceded by timpani and trumpets, Ningzong came in with a large retinue of courtesans and a group of soldiers. The guests rose. The emperor drifted forward like a distant ghost, seemingly unaffected by the admiration and splendor surrounding him. He took his seat on his throne and gestured for his guests to sit as well. Waiters swarmed forward, and soon the room was a busy dance of trays, drinks, and food.

"This is Cí, an adviser of mine," said Kan.

The other men at the table bowed their heads.

"And what kind of adviser are you?" asked the bronze maker. "Our Councilor for Punishments is hardly a man to take advice!"

Kan scowled, but the rest of the men, along with the bronze maker, found this exceedingly funny.

"I'm—I'm an expert on the Jin people," he stammered.

"Oh? So what can you tell us about those dirty dogs apart from the fact they do nothing but bleed us dry? Is it true they're set to invade?"

Cí pretended to have something stuck in his throat and glanced at Kan, but he wasn't going to help.

"If I tell you anything," he said finally, "Kan will have my throat cut, and we wouldn't want that. I'll get blood all over the nice table and probably lose my job to boot!"

Everyone at the table erupted in laughter—all except Kan. But Cí could see he was also relieved. At least their cover hadn't been blown.

"Well, young man," said the bronze maker, clearly pleased with him, "allow me to recommend the chicken; it's fragranced with lotus leaf. Or if you like spicy food, the Songsao fish soup is quite delicious. It's a little sour, but that's excellent in summertime."

"Or the butterfly soup, that should be excellent too," suggested one of the lawyers.

"Or the Dongo pork chop," said the other.

One of the prefects began serving drinks. "Grape liquor!" he exclaimed. "Better than that rice wine!"

"But with the food," said the bronze maker, "there's really no need to hurry. I've heard there will be one hundred and fifty dishes served tonight."

Cí thanked them for the suggestions but decided on some simple meatballs in ginger and the warm, spiced cereal wine to which he was accustomed. His attention was drawn to a tray of noodles with goat cheese, an unusual dish.

"It's a northern recipe," spat Kan. "In honor of the Jin ambassador."

One of the men proposed a toast, to try to divert the conversation, but just then the ambassador entered the room.

No one stood up.

Cí turned in his seat and watched the man come forward, with his earth-colored skin and unusually white teeth, flanked by four officials of a similar complexion. The ambassador reminded Cí of a jackal. The small retinue came to within five paces of the imperial table, got down on their knees and prostrated themselves. Then the ambassador motioned his men forward to deliver the gifts they had brought.

"Hypocrites!" murmured Kan. "First they steal from us, and now they pretend to honor us."

The Jin retinue was seated at a table not far from the emperor. A whole roast pig was brought to them, a dish favored by their kind. They might have been beautifully dressed, but when they began eating, there was no doubt in Cí's mind that they were indeed savages.

Though the food kept coming, Kan stopped eating, and Cí decided it might be a good idea to do the same. The rest of the men at the table soon turned to the desserts, which arrived on delicate bamboo plates. There was lotus rice in syrup, and frozen watermelons and other fruits that had been carefully emulsified; there was also a good deal more drink. Much of both ended up on the table or in laps. Kan whispered to Cí that, when the fireworks began, he would point out the suspect.

Cí's heart skipped a beat.

Moments later a gong sounded, and it was announced that the emperor had concluded the banquet. Tea and after-dinner wines would be served in the gardens.

The guests got up, many of them somewhat unsteadily. Cí had to support the bronze maker.

"A promising evening!" said Kan, suddenly pleased. "Time for the fireworks."

In the terraced gardens, Cí noticed how the sexes remained separate: the men gathered around the drink tables on the principal balcony, and the women were beside the lake, preparing the ceremonial tea. The reflection of the moon in the water was broken by the passage of elegant imperial swans. Lanterns lit the undersides of Japanese pine canopies. Cí thought that when the time came to face his enemy, the darkness might be his ally. His hands trembled as if he were heading into battle. When Cí asked about the presumed assassin, Kan whispered that he must be patient.

After briefly chatting with some strangers, Kan signaled that Cí should follow him.

Despite his considerable size, Kan skipped up stairs leading to the lake as stealthily as a cat. Cí followed, trying not to bump into groups of people socializing at the tables. They went over to the edge of the water. There, a cage filled with hundreds of fireflies lit a group of old men and courtesans who were seated and drinking tea.

"Don't mind if we join you, do you?" said Kan, kneeling in a gap without waiting for an answer.

The smile of one of the older women was their welcome.

"This is your home, after all," she murmured. "And who's this you have with you?"

She and Kan clearly knew each other. Cí was awed by the woman's serene beauty.

"This is Cí, my new assistant."

The councilor sat next to the woman and made space for Cí.

There were four men and six women, all having a good time and laughing. The men were quite elderly, but their good manners and expensive clothes seemed to compensate in the courtesans' eyes. Except for the woman who had welcomed them, who was perhaps forty, they all seemed very young, and none exhibited the more mature perfection of the first woman.

While the beautiful hostess served tea, Cí carefully observed the men, since he was expecting Kan to point out the murder suspect from among them. The man across from him was sinewy and looked lecherously at the youngest courtesan. Cí thought the man would swallow her down in one gulp if he could, not stopping to savor her—just as he was doing with the gourd of liquor he was slurping. The other three men didn't seem at all dangerous. Just a few drunken old men slobbering over girls young enough to be their granddaughters.

Cí sipped his tea and focused on the first man, who noticed him staring.

"What are you looking at?" he spat. "You like boys, do you?"

Cí stared at the floor. He knew he shouldn't be drawing attention to himself.

"I—I thought I knew you," he said, taking another sip of tea.

The men continued drinking, and the courtesans laughed as the men caressed them. Cí was uncomfortable. What was Kan waiting for? What did he have in mind? Cí glanced at the man he thought most likely to be the suspect, who just at that moment began getting rough with the courtesan next to him. Then he slapped her.

Cí got up to intervene, and the man turned on him.

Cí was alarmed and thought the man was about to attack him, but Kan held up his hands, gesturing for everyone to calm down.

The lovely hostess intervened. "How dare you?" she said to the violent man. Her voice was firm and commanding.

"What?" The man was infuriated.

Cí felt himself tensing up, but Kan held him back. Then the hostess brought a small vial from her lap.

"That's no way to woo a young girl," she said quietly. She poured the liquid from the vial into a cup and handed it to the man.

"What's this?" growled the man, sniffing it.

"A love stimulant. It'll do you good."

The man downed the drink and immediately spit it out.

"Gods! What filth is that?"

The hostess smiled a perfect smile.

"Cat piss."

Everyone laughed except for the man, who stumbled away from the table. The other men, who seemed perhaps to work for him, followed grumblingly, and behind them went the courtesans. Now it was just Cí, Kan, and the hostess at the table.

Kan, chuckling and wiping his mouth, turned to Cí.

"Allow me to introduce our hostess, the one and only Blue Iris, descendant of General Fei Yue."

The woman bowed her head. Cí was dumbstruck. He saw something truly terrifying in her eyes.

28

Finding out that Blue Iris was Fei Yue's descendant was shocking. But there it was. Kan suspected that this delicate, perfectly mannered, glacier-eyed woman was responsible for the death of three men.

Cí managed a "nice to meet you," but he was both transfixed and troubled by Blue Iris's serenity and disquieting beauty. There was a coldness to her that brought to mind a viper, so calm before it strikes.

Blue Iris, oblivious to Cí's sudden anxieties, asked what his job as Kan's assistant involved.

Kan answered for Cí. "This is why I wanted you to meet," he said. "Cí's working on a report on the northern tribes, and I thought you might be able to help him. You're still involved in your father's business affairs, isn't that right?"

"As much as I'm able. My life has changed considerably since I married, but of course, you already know about that…" She paused for a moment before addressing Cí. "So, you're looking into the Jin? You're in luck, then, aren't you? You can speak to the ambassador personally."

"Don't be ridiculous," said Kan. "The ambassador's a busy man. Almost as busy as me!"

"And is he busy with women's affairs, too?"

"Iris, Iris, always so ironic." Kan grimaced. "Cí doesn't want the words of a man versed in pure deception. He's after the truth."

"Can't he speak for himself?" asked Blue Iris provocatively.

"I like to be respectful of my elders," Cí said.

He saw she'd noticed the slight and allowed himself a wicked smile. Then he looked at Kan for some idea of where this was all heading. He was starting to sense that Kan and Blue Iris's connection might not be a straightforward one.

Suddenly Cí saw a silhouette outlined against the lantern light. Cí thought it was the bronze maker from dinner. When Kan saw him, he got up.

"Please excuse me," said the councilor as he headed after the bronze maker. "I have something to attend to."

Cí chewed his lip. He was unsure of what to say. He drummed his fingers against the side of the teacup before bringing it to his mouth.

"Nervous?" asked Blue Iris.

"Should I be?"

Just then, he had the thought the tea might have been spiked and decided against drinking more. When he looked up, he noticed Blue Iris seemed to be staring at him oddly, but he didn't know why.

"So," she said. "Respect for your elders? How old are you?"

"Twenty-four," he said, adding two years to his actual age.

"And how old would you say I am?"

Feeling protected by the darkness, Cí looked directly at Blue Iris. The orange light from the lantern softened her sculpted face and smoothed her few wrinkles. Her breasts were full under her silk *hanfu* robe, and her waist, which, since she was seated, was as far down as

Cí could see, was quite small. She didn't seem uncomfortable as he looked at her body. Her strangely gray eyes sparkled.

"Thirty-five," he said, though if he were being honest he would have said a few years older.

She arched an eyebrow.

"To work with Kan you need to be either fearless or stupid. Which would you say you are?"

Her bluntness surprised him. He didn't know what she thought of him, but she must have been very sure of herself to criticize Kan to one of his employees, particularly one she'd never met before.

"Maybe I'm the kind of person who doesn't insult people I don't know," he replied.

She grimaced and looked down, which Cí interpreted as a sort of apology.

"Sorry, but I've always had issues with that man." She spilled some of the tea she was pouring. "He knows full well I have scant knowledge of the Jin, so I'm not sure how I can be of assistance."

"Why don't you tell me about your work? You're clearly no housewife."

"It's low work," she said, sipping her tea.

"I find that hard to believe."

Blue Iris weighed her words for a moment.

"I inherited a salt export business. Dealings with barbarians are always tricky, but my father knew how to handle them and managed to set up some warehouses near the frontier. In spite of the obstacles the government put in his way, they became lucrative quite quickly. Now I run them."

"Government obstacles?"

"Unhappy tales shouldn't be told on happy occasions."

"But from what you say, it sounds like risky work for a woman on her own."

"Whoever said I was on my own?"

Cí, unsure how to respond, went back to his tea.

"Kan mentioned something about your husband. I suppose you mean him."

"Kan talks too much. My husband is involved in lots of things," she said bitterly.

"And where is now?"

"Abroad. He travels a lot. But why all the questions about him? I thought it was the Jin you were interested in."

"Among other things."

Cí felt the situation was getting out of hand. His fingers began drumming his cup again. The silence felt heavy, and he thought Blue Iris must be thinking the same. Time was against him, but he couldn't think how to get the conversation going. She took out a fan, and, as she began fanning herself, Cí could suddenly smell an intense and familiar fragrance.

"Essence of Jade?"

"What?"

"The perfume, it's Essence of Jade. How did you come by that?"

"That's the kind of question you can ask only certain types of women," she said, smiling coyly. "And an answer that can be given only to certain types of men."

"Even so," he said insistently.

Blue Iris's answer was to finish her tea and get up to leave.

Cí was going to try to make her stay when suddenly there was an explosion. Cí looked up. The night sky was filled with brilliant green and red bursts of light.

"Fireworks!" Cí was awed by the flowery forms. "Beautiful." He looked across at Blue Iris, expecting her to agree, but she wasn't even watching. "Look," he said.

At this, she turned toward him. Her eyes were motionless despite the explosions of light.

"I wish I could," she said.

Cí watched as she turned away, searching out obstacles in her path with the use of a walking stick.

⊱✦⊰

On his way back to the palace, Cí peered into the crowd—all the guests looked skyward, transfixed by the pyrotechnic display. He began searching for Kan, going to the balcony, the Welcome Hall, and the small annex rooms before trying the garden again. Cí sat and watched the fireworks until the display was over and the guests were swathed in a dense, acrid fog. Both the fog and the odor reminded Cí of the night Lu's house had burned down, killing his family…

Cí's thoughts turned to his father. Not a day passed that they didn't.

It must have been after midnight when he finally caught sight of Kan moving through the thickets at the periphery of the gardens. He had someone with him. Cí headed toward them, but when he saw who it was, he froze. It was the Jin ambassador, and the two of them were having an animated conversation. Cí decided not to approach them. He was confused about everything, and the hours of drinking had had their effect.

⊱✦⊰

The next morning another dead body was discovered. Cí was shaken awake by a surly official and led to the examination room. All he could tell Cí was that the body had been found just outside the palace walls. Kan was waiting for them when they got there, along with an inspector.

The body was laid out in the middle of the room. Like Soft Dolphin, it had been decapitated.

Cí scanned the superficial report that had already been filed—it noted little more than the number of wounds and the skin color. Then he asked permission to begin his own examination.

The first thing that drew his attention was the neck wound; unlike the eunuch's, the edges of this one were ragged. Cí concluded that the murderer must have killed in a hurry. The opening in the chest was shallower than on the other bodies. There were scratches at the nape of the neck that extended to the shoulders. The backs of the hands and the sides of the ankles had similar scratch marks. Cí pointed them out to Kan.

"The body was dragged along the ground," said Cí. It was dressed when it was dragged—otherwise the same scratches would have occurred on the buttocks."

He removed the traces of dirt from under the fingernails and on the skin with his pincers, depositing them in a small jar. Then, noting that the arms and legs were too stiff to bend at the elbows or knees, which meant that rigor mortis was setting in, he estimated that the murder must have occurred within the past six hours.

Suddenly he stopped. He caught a waft of a familiar scent.

"Don't you smell that?"

"What?" asked Kan.

"Perfume."

He leaned in close to the wound on the chest and smelled around there. Frowning, he stood up. Essence of Jade, without a doubt. The same as he'd smelled on Blue Iris the previous evening. This, though, he decided not to mention to Kan.

"And the clothes?" Cí asked.

"The body was found naked," said the councilor.

"No objects with him, or anything to help identify him?"

"No, nothing…"

"There were the rings," pointed out the inspector.

"What rings?" said Cí.

"Oh, I forgot about them!" said Kan, showing Cí over to a small table on which a number of rings lay. Cí could hardly believe it.

"Don't you recognize them?"

"No," said Kan. "Why should I?"

"Because they belonged to the bronze maker we sat with last night."

<hr/>

When Cí and Kan were alone, Cí expressed his reservations about Blue Iris's involvement.

"She's blind, for goodness' sake!"

"That woman's a devil, let me assure you," said Kan. "Or if I'm wrong, tell me, how long did it take you to work out she was blind? How long did she have you fooled?"

"OK, but can you really imagine someone who can't see cutting off heads and dragging bodies around?"

"Don't be stupid!" Kan's face hardened. "No one said it was she who was doing the actual dirty work."

"Ah! No? In that case, who?"

"If I knew that, would I be here helping you?" roared Kan, and he took a swipe at Cí's equipment, scattering it across the floor.

Blood rushed to Cí's face. He took a deep breath and began picking up his things.

"Councilor, everybody knows there are many kinds of killers. But let's put aside the kind who doesn't set out intending to kill: normal people who lose their grip on reason in a fight, or find their woman in bed with another man. Those are the people who would never murder if they were in their right mind." He finished picking up his equipment. "Let's turn our thoughts to the true murderers, the monsters.

"There are groups within this group. Some act out of a kind of lustiness, and they are as insatiable as sharks. In general they kill women and children, and they don't tend to be happy *only* killing. First they profane and destroy; later they massacre. Then there are the violent ones: men capable of taking a life at the tiniest provocation, like tigers who seem quite calm but then devour a person just for pulling out a whisker. Next are the visionaries: made fanatical by ideals or by their involvement in sects, they carry out the most execrable savageries; they are like fighting dogs. But the fourth group is the strangest: they take pleasure from killing. And they can't be likened to any animal; the evil that dwells in them is infinitely worse. Now, tell me, which group would you put that woman in? The lusty one? The violent one? The visionary one? Or perhaps the pleasure one?"

Kan looked sidelong at Cí.

"Cí, Cí, Cí…I don't doubt your abilities when it comes to bones, weapons, or worms. For all I know, you could write books, give lectures," he roared. "But for all your wisdom, you've neglected to mention one important group, more bloodthirsty than most, shrewd, calculating: the snakes. A snake is capable of waiting coiled up until just the right moment, hypnotizing the victim before unleashing the deadly poison. This kind of killer is motivated by the venom of revenge, a hate so strong it corrupts the very heart. And, I swear to you, Blue Iris is just such a person."

"And she hypnotizes her victims?" blurted Cí. "With her blind eyes?"

"There is no one blinder than the person who does not *want* to see." Kan punched the table. "You're so wrapped up in your absurd techniques, you've forgotten common sense altogether! I've already said she uses accomplices."

Cí had already decided not to mention that he'd seen Kan conversing with the Jin ambassador. He knew an argument with Kan would get him nowhere.

"OK, you could well be right. So who helped her with the killings? Her husband?"

Kan looked toward the door, on the other side of which the inspector would be waiting. "Let's go outside," he said.

Cí put away his equipment and followed. He felt less and less trust in Kan. Why hadn't he mentioned the rings? Why had he not reacted when Cí identified the corpse as the bronze maker—especially considering Kan was quite possibly the last person to have spoken to the man before he died?

"Forget about Blue Iris's husband." He frowned. "I've known him a long time, and he's a good man. A Mongol with a face like a dog but an upright man. His one mistake was marrying that harpy. I think we'd do better to consider him her servant. She brought him from the North to be with her."

Cí scratched his head. A new suspect.

"OK, but then why haven't you had him arrested?"

"How many times do I have to tell you? I'm convinced there are various accomplices. One person wouldn't be able to commit such atrocious crimes."

Cí was fed up with all the mystery; it seemed like everyone except him knew what was going on. If Kan's idea was correct, why wasn't he going after the Mongol? Or if that was already under way, wasn't Cí's own part in the investigation pure absurdity? It had to be a lie cooked up by Kan, he thought.

One thing still didn't fit: the perfume. Doubtless Kan, with his wide-ranging power, could have taken some and used it to implicate Blue Iris. But Cí failed to see how, if the perfume was exclusively for use by the emperor's women, Blue Iris might also have some.

This last part he communicated to Kan.

"Didn't she tell you?" said Kan in surprise. "Blue Iris was a *nüshi*. She was the emperor's favorite."

A *nüshi*. So *that* was how Blue Iris had become an intermediary between the nobles and the "flowers"; like a high priestess of pleasure, she knew better than any the art of courtship.

"The emperor likes to treat his guests well, so whenever he can he invites Blue Iris. She's pure fire, that woman. Despite her age, she'd swallow you up in a second, no question."

In spite of her blindness, Kan explained, word of her beauty had spread far and wide during the previous emperor's reign. He had ordered that she join his harem and that her family be compensated.

"She was very young then, and she cast a spell on the emperor. Ningzong's father no longer had eyes for any of his other concubines. He obsessed over Blue Iris, and he took pleasure in her to the point of exhaustion. When he became ill, he appointed her Imperial *nüshi*. He was old, and he suffered from numerous ailments, but she saw to it that he lay with concubines frequently—if anything more often than before—and that he had the queen once a month. She was in charge of leading them to the royal bedchamber, placing the ritual silver ring on their right hand, undressing them, spraying Essence of Jade on them, and then witnessing the act itself." Kan seemed to be conjuring the scene in his mind. "Though blind, they said she enjoyed being there."

Blue Iris had given up her position when Ningzong came to power, and she went on to run her inherited business with a fist of iron. The man she married, according to Kan, had also been bewitched.

"She's got something she can turn on to drive men wild. You never know, she might even decide to cast a spell on you!"

Cí considered Kan's words. He had no time for ideas of witchcraft, but it was true that he couldn't get Blue Iris out of his mind. There was something about her; he felt his thoughts begin to get tangled as he pictured her…He shook his head to clear his mind.

"And the bronze maker?" asked Cí.

"He seemed nervous when we said good-bye," said Kan. "I asked him about the new alloy he was working on, the one he kept going on about. You obviously noticed he was a show-off, but I had no idea someone would want to kill him."

"Not Blue Iris?"

"That's for you to work out."

29

You never know, she might even decide to cast a spell on you!

These words played on Cí's mind as he tried to concentrate on the job at hand. But he kept picturing Blue Iris's delicate features, hearing her sonorous voice, and, above all, feeling those gray eyes on him.

Maybe his fascination had something to do with how capable Blue Iris was in spite of her disability, or how well she hid what were essentially scars, or how cool she'd been with Kan...He had to focus on the murder cases. And the fact Gray Fox would be back any day now. The potential implications of his return immediately concentrated Cí's mind.

He decided to split the investigation into parts. He needed to address the remaining questions about the earlier murders, and he had to advance his investigation of the bronze maker's murder by visiting his workshop and the location where the corpse had been found.

First he would try for some answers about the earlier murders. He had the portrait of the younger corpse to use, but he could hardly take that around Lin'an. Where could those tiny, poppy-seed scars on his face have come from? They didn't look to him anything like the marks from an illness, so the only other thing he could think of was that they were scars from an accident. But what kind of accident? Surely, whatever the cause, the scars were a testament to pain. And if the man had been in pain, there was a good chance he would have gone to a pharmacy or a hospital.

That was it! A step forward! At least there were a finite number of pharmacies and hospitals. He just needed to ask if they remembered a man with such unusual marks on his face.

He called Bo and told him the plan.

❧❧❧❧❧

Cí took the disfigured corpse's hand from the conservation chamber and was pleased to see how well the ice had worked. The corrosion, like hundreds of tiny perforations covering the fingers, the palm, and the back of the hand, struck him as being similar to the holes of a tea strainer. He'd made a list of the jobs someone might have to handle the kind of acid that could make those marks—a silk cleaner, a chef, a housepainter, a chemist—but he hoped a pharmacist would be able to help him whittle it down.

They went to the Great Pharmacy first. There was a crowd at the entrance, and Bo sent his men ahead to clear a path. When Cí finally reached the main counter and took out the severed hand, he was mobbed again. Bo's men dragged the spectators away, and Cí placed the hand in front of the pharmacists, who were trembling as if they feared their own hands might be chopped off.

"I only need you to have a look and tell me if you've prescribed anything for anyone with a condition like this."

After examining the hand, the pharmacists didn't think there was anything remarkable about the slight corrosion. Cí demanded to speak to the head pharmacist. A tubby, distracted-looking man in a red gown and cap appeared and, having looked at the hand, agreed with his staff.

"No one would come asking for treatment for such a petty thing."

Cí clenched his fists. These men didn't seem to be trying very hard.

"How can you be so sure?"

The manager held out his own hands.

"Because I have the same corrosion. It's from working with salt. Sailors, miners, fish or meat salters, anyone who works with salt day after day will end up with these same marks on their hands. I handle salt every day to conserve compresses. It's nothing serious. I'm not sure this poor person actually needed his hand cut off," he joked.

But Cí wasn't laughing. He thanked the man for his help, put the hand back in the conservation chamber, and quickly left the Great Pharmacy.

One door opened and another shut. Discarding the idea of the marks being the result of acid eliminated several jobs, but there were as many, if not more, that had to do with handling salt. A quarter of Lin'an's population must have been in some way involved in fishing, and although only a fraction of those would go out to sea to fish, there were all the workers in the salting warehouses. Cí thought that could be at least 50,000 people…His hopes now rested on one last detail: the small flame tattoo by the thumb. Bo said he'd do what he could to try and identify it. He gave the conservation chamber to Bo's men with instructions to change the ice once they'd got it back to the palace.

Cí hoped his visit to the bronze maker's workshop would turn up some useful evidence. He and Bo made their way to the docklands on the south side of the city. But when they reached the address, Cí was shocked to find that, where yesterday had stood the most important bronze workshop in the whole city, there were now only its burned remains. Embers were still glowing among the scorched beams, burned wood, melted metal, and piles of rubble. Fire had reduced the workshop to nothing but a smoking, desolated strip, just as it had done with his family's home.

He made his way directly to the crowd nosing through the wreckage. Maybe someone could tell him something. A number of them spoke of a voracious fire in the early hours, others of the loud noises when the workshop fell. Everyone lamented how slow the firefighters had been to arrive; several adjacent workshops had also been damaged.

Then a beggar boy came over and said he had some firsthand information, but it would cost 10,000 *qián*. The boy was nothing but skin and bones, so Cí added a bowl of boiled rice from a nearby seller to the sum. Between mouthfuls, the boy said there had been some noises before the fires had started, but in fact that was all he knew. Disappointed, Cí got up to leave, but the boy grabbed his arm.

"But I do know someone who saw everything."

One of his fellow beggars, he said, always slept under one of the workshop awnings.

"He's a cripple, which means he never goes very far from where he always begs. When I got here this morning I found him over there, like a rat hiding in its nest. He looked like he'd seen the God of Death himself. He was saying he had to get away. If they found him, he said, they'd kill him."

Cí's eyes grew wide.

"Who?"

"No idea. But he was terrified, I know that much. As soon as the sun came up and people started arriving, he disappeared into the crowd. He even left his things," said the boy, pointing to a begging bowl and a ceramic jar. "But I bet I can find him."

Cí searched the boy's face—in vain—for the slightest trace of truthfulness.

"Fine, take me to him."

"But sir, I'm very sick. And if I'm helping you, I won't be able to beg…"

"How much?"

"Ten thousand, no, five thousand *qián*!"

Cí didn't feel he had much of a choice, but when he asked Bo for the additional money, Bo insisted it was a bad idea.

"He'll just vanish," hissed Bo. "He'll take the money and you'll never see him again."

"Just give it to me!" He knew Kan had given instructions for any costs to be covered. Bo shook his head in disapproval but eventually handed over the money.

The boy's eyes lit up as Cí began counting out the money. He stopped at 500 *qián*.

"You get the rest when your friend shows up. He'll get a reward, too."

The boy got up to go.

"One last thing: If you decide to disappear, I swear I'll find you, and it won't be pretty. There are plenty of other beggars I could give his money to, and I'm sure they'd be only too happy to help locate you—*and* beat you to death."

Taking with him a note of Cí's name and how to find him, the boy headed off into the streets.

Cí had a look around the wreckage. He was surprised to come across not a single bronze object, nor any solder remains, but it had likely all been taken by looters already. Before leaving, Cí asked

Bo to find out details about anyone who had been employed at the workshop in recent months, and to have any remains other than bricks and beams gathered and brought to the palace.

"I don't care how damaged they are. And make sure each piece is labeled with exactly where on the premises it was found."

"I'm not sure how much Kan will appreciate your turning the palace into a trash can."

"Just see that it's done," said Cí.

When he got back to the palace, Cí was pleased to find that the same sentry who had found the bronze maker's corpse was guarding the spot. The guard, who resembled a granite mountain, confirmed that, yes, this was where he had found the corpse, at the foot of the wall, and it had been headless and naked. Cí examined the dried blood on the stones and then sketched the scene, and the trail of blood, with charcoal. He asked the sentry if he always stayed in the same place during a shift.

"When the gong sounds, we all count out three hundred paces to the west of our positions, come back, do another three hundred paces east, and then return to our position until the next gong."

He asked the guard if, the reception and all the guests aside, there had been anything, anything at all, during last night's watch that had struck him as out of the ordinary.

Just as Cí expected, the man said no.

It didn't matter. Cí had made a discovery that definitely constituted an advance.

Back in his quarters, Cí compared soil samples from the palace gardens with the soil he'd removed from under the bronze maker's fingernails. The soil from beside the pond was moist, compact, and blackish; the soil from the edge of the forest was looser, brown, and had bits of pine needles in it; the third sample, from underneath the balconies, was gravelly; the last, which was from directly alongside the wall, was yellowish and sticky, probably due to the clay used as mortar between the bricks.

The soil from under the bronze maker's nails matched this last sample.

He labeled the samples and spent the rest of the afternoon going over his notes. At sundown, he threw his notes to the floor in frustration. He had yet to hear any results from the portrait's being passed around the hospitals and pharmacies, or from the interviews with the bronze workshop employees, but he didn't hold great hope for either. His idea with the lance in regard to the chest wounds hadn't worked out. His hypotheses suddenly seemed as foolish as the idea that a blind person would be capable of multiple murders.

Though he had his doubts, he hadn't put aside the possibility of Blue Iris's involvement. The link between the post of *nüshi* and Essence of Jade, though circumstantial, potentially placed her at the scene of every single one of the murders. And as Kan had been so eager to point out, she had ample reasons to hate the emperor. It was a deep-rooted hate, one her father would have fueled with stories of the bad treatment of their ancestor Fei Yue.

Cí's thoughts turned to the *nüshi*. Really, he hadn't stopped thinking about her since the moment they'd met. He didn't want to admit it, but there was something about her that had hold of him—something beyond the murders, something he couldn't fully comprehend, much less explain.

Gray Fox was also on Cí's mind. In spite of the danger represented by Gray Fox's return, the risks associated with failing to solve these crimes, and all the many reasons that seemed to be telling him to flee, he wouldn't consider leaving. He'd come too far to stop now. A place in the judiciary was almost within reach. The emperor had promised it, and however great the obstacles seemed, it was his dream, the dream Judge Feng had inculcated in him.

He owed Feng everything. He had only to shut his eyes and there Feng was. And if he kept his eyes shut a few moments longer, his father also appeared. Cí pictured himself receiving the title of judge.

He asked himself what could have become of Feng. He often thought of making another attempt to find him. But much as Cí didn't want to think about it, he was still technically a fugitive. He had no right to drag Feng into dishonor.

A knock at his door interrupted his thoughts. It was Bo. The transfer of remnants from the bronze workshop was under way, he said, and Blue Iris had sent word that she wished to meet Cí the next day at the Water Lily Pavilion.

She wants to meet me?

It was improper for a married woman to meet a stranger without a chaperone. Although Bo told him Blue Iris's husband would be there, too, Cí shivered. The norms calling for women to be seen and not heard, serving tea and doing not much more, obviously didn't apply to a *nüshi*.

He barely slept that night, so insistent was Blue Iris in his mind.

<hr />

Cí woke exhausted. It wasn't the first time his nerves had gotten the better of him, but he was annoyed; he'd wanted to be at his best when he saw Blue Iris again. He decided to wear the same robes as he had at the reception and was dismayed to find they were wrinkled, though Blue Iris wouldn't see them. He rubbed a few drops of sandalwood essence at his wrists and neck. He had a quick look over the notes he'd made on Jin history before setting out.

The Water Lily Pavilion was situated inside the Forest of Freshness, its walls running parallel to the Imperial civil servants' palatial buildings. Bo had described how to get there, and Cí had no trouble finding it.

He arrived early at the gleaming pavilion, a two-story structure surrounded by a lemon grove. The building's eaves curved proudly upward like the flight of a crane. Cí made sure his cap was straight and glanced down at his robes, annoyed to see the wrinkles were still there. Then he stepped forward and reached his hand up to knock, but the door opened before he made contact. A servant bowed and beckoned him to follow. They came to a light-filled room with tiles that appeared to have been freshly glazed, and continued until they came in sight of a woman, with her back to them, wearing a loose-fitting turquoise *hanfu* and with her hair up in a wide silk band. The servant announced Cí, and when the woman turned to face him, he blushed. Blue Iris was even more captivating in the light of day. He tried to get a hold of himself and glanced around for her husband, who was nowhere to be seen.

"We meet again," he said, immediately aware of how ridiculous he sounded.

Blue Iris smiled. Just to see her teeth felt to Cí like some kind of erotic invitation. Her *hanfu* was very slightly parted at the front, and Cí could see a glimpse of her cleavage beneath. In spite of her blindness, he still had a sense she'd catch him looking, and he averted his gaze. She invited him to sit and began serving tea. He was touched by the ease with which her hands seemed to caress the pot and the cups.

"Thank you for inviting me," he managed to say.

She nodded courteously and asked how he had found the reception. He answered amiably, avoiding any mention of the bronze maker's murder. Then there was an uncomfortable silence—Cí felt uncomfortable, at least. He was absorbed watching Blue Iris; he felt gripped by every blink, every breath. He wrenched his gaze away and took a sip of the tea. For some reason, perhaps to try and reassert an air of normality, he let out a gasp as if the tea was too hot.

"What is it?" she asked.

"Nothing. I burned my lips."

"Apologies," she said, immediately dipping a cloth in some cool water and dabbing at Cí's lips, which, despite her blindness, she found effortlessly. He trembled, embarrassed.

"It's nothing," he said, disengaging from her touch. "And your husband?"

"He'll be here soon," she answered, unperturbed. "So. You stay in the palace. Unusual for a simple adviser..."

"And it's unusual for a woman of your rank not to have her feet bound," he said before he could stop himself. Blue Iris hid her feet beneath the *hanfu*.

"Maybe you find it an abomination," she said, "but it's a custom my father rejected, luckily."

Cí couldn't believe he'd been so tactless.

"I haven't been here long," he said. "Kan invited me to stay for a few days, but I'd rather not stay too long. This isn't my place."

"Oh? And where is?"

He weighed his response.

"Academia."

"Really? And what is your specialty? The classics? Literature? Or poetry, perhaps?"

"Surgery."

A look of deep disgust wiped the beauty from Blue Iris's face.

"You'll have to excuse me," she said, "but I really don't see the attraction of opening up bodies. Or, for that matter, what that kind of work could have to do with Kan."

Cí kicked himself for being indiscreet. Far from gaining anything from the conversation himself, it could get out of hand if he gave too much away. He had to be more cautious with his answers.

"The Jin," he said, clearing his throat, "have quite different dietary habits from our own. The presence or absence of certain illnesses can be put down to this, and this is the focus of my current research, and the reason I'm here with Kan. Tell me, though, to what do I owe the honor of your invitation? The other night you didn't seem much interested in talking about the Jin."

"People change," she said with a sarcastic tone. She served more tea, then smiled. "I found your behavior the other night, when you defended that courtesan against that man, interesting. Very unusual for the kind of men you usually find in the palace."

"That's why you asked me here?"

"Or I suppose you could say I just…felt like seeing you."

Cí sipped his tea, feeling another blush spread across his face. He'd never had a women speak so informally to him before. She leaned forward, and he couldn't help but notice her *hanfu* fall open a little more. It was impossible to tell how aware she was, but Cí averted his gaze nonetheless.

"You have collected beautiful antiques," he said eventually.

"I don't collect them for myself, but to please the people around me. In many ways, a mirror for my life."

Cí wasn't sure how to respond to the unveiled bitterness in her words. He was racking his brains for a way to ask her about her blindness when they heard a noise outside.

"That will be my husband," she said.

She got to her feet and turned calmly toward the entrance. Cí followed suit and noticed as she tightened her *hanfu*.

At the end of the passageway Cí could make out the figure of an aged man, accompanied by Kan. The two were chatting. The older man had a bunch of flowers. The man greeted his wife and seemed pleased that their guest was already here, but when he came a little closer and looked properly at Cí, the flowers fell from his hands.

The old man was speechless. He simply stood and looked incredulous—as did Cí—while the servant hurried to pick up the flowers. Blue Iris stepped forward.

"Beloved husband, please allow me to introduce our guest, young Cí. Cí, may I introduce my husband, the honorable Judge Feng."

30

Cí and Feng were paralyzed. When he recovered, Feng started to ask Cí something, but Cí wanted to speak first.

"Honorable Feng," he bowed.

"What are you doing here?" asked Feng.

"You know each other?" Kan was surprised.

"A little," said Cí hurriedly. "My father used to work for Judge Feng." He could tell Feng was struggling to understand what was going on.

"Very good!" said Kan. "That should make everything a little easier. Cí is helping me with some reports on the Jin. I thought your wife's experiences might be useful to us."

"And I'm sure you thought right! But let us sit and celebrate," said Feng, still clearly confused. "Cí, I thought you were still in your village. How is your father? What brings you to Lin'an?"

Cí hung his head. He didn't want to talk about his father. Really, he didn't want to talk at all. He was overwhelmed with shame—and now not only at the possibility of bringing dishonor on Feng, but also at the fact he'd felt desire for his old master's wife. But there was no way of avoiding the conversation now.

"My father died. The house burned down. Everyone died...I came to Lin'an thinking I would take the exams." Again he looked down.

"Your father, dead! But why didn't you come to see me?" he said, and asked Blue Iris to serve more tea.

"It's a long story," said Cí, trying to make it clear he didn't want to talk about it.

"Well, let's put things right," said Feng. "Of course, when he mentioned this I didn't know it was *you*, but Kan told me you're staying at the palace. Now that you have business with my wife, I propose that you move here, with us. If Kan has no objections, of course."

"On the contrary," said Kan. "An excellent idea!"

Cí wanted to refuse. Gray Fox would be back any day now, and with him the knowledge of Cí's fugitive status. But Feng was very insistent.

"You'll come around. Blue Iris is an excellent hostess, and we'll have a chance to remember old times. You'll be happy here."

"Really, I'd rather not trouble you. I've got all my books, all my belongings over there—"

"Pish! Your father would never forgive me, nor I myself, if I let you leave. We'll have your effects transferred here immediately."

They went on chatting, but Cí wasn't listening. He gazed at Feng's much older face and felt sick at the thought of staying under the same roof as this great man. He breathed a sigh of relief when Kan got up and asked Cí to accompany him back to the palace. Feng and Blue Iris showed them to the door.

"See you soon!" said Feng.

Cí replied in kind, but was secretly praying it would be more like never.

On their way back to the palace, Kan was overjoyed with the for-tuitousness of it all.

"Don't you get it?" he said, rubbing his hands. "Now you'll have the chance to uncover Blue Iris's secrets. You can investigate without seeming to, and it will be much more straightforward to follow that Mongol, too!"

"With all respect, councilor, it's against the law for an investi-gator to live in a suspect's home."

"Against the law!" spat Kan. "That law is only there to protect investigators against corruption. But if the suspects don't know they're under investigation, how could they ever corrupt you? Plus there's the fact you aren't a judge."

"Apologies. I'm happy to carry the investigation forward, but I won't stay in that woman's home."

"What are you on about? This is a unique opportunity! We couldn't have planned it any better!"

Kan's predatory attitude only hardened Cí's resolve. He was unwilling to betray Feng's confidence, he said, and pointed out that Feng and his father had been friends.

"So you're willing to let that woman ruin him?" said Kan. "Her treachery will come out sooner or later. And it will destroy him."

"If you're so worried about Feng, why don't you just arrest Blue Iris?"

"You fool!" Kan's good humor vanished. "Haven't I already said we need her accomplices, too? Take her now, and they'd disap-pear before we could torture their names out of her. And there's far more than some old man's honor at stake here; we're playing for the emperor's very future."

Cí thought hard about what to say next.

"Do as you please, but I can't comply with this," he said firmly. "I won't put the emperor's future before that of Judge Feng."

Cí felt pierced by Kan's glare. The councilor said nothing, but at that moment Cí felt a new and unknown terror arise.

✺

Going back to his room, Cí realized he didn't know what he could do other than flee. If he hurried, he could still manage it. Since he'd told Kan he wouldn't move to Feng's, he needed an excuse so that Bo would accompany him beyond the palace walls. Once they were outside, he'd find a way to slip off and would escape Lin'an forever. He called a servant to go and fetch Bo.

As he packed, regrets rained down; he knew he'd never have another opportunity like this, and he'd come so close to achieving his dreams. His thoughts shifted to his family and he thought of his father and Third, too. He wanted so much to become a judge— to prove to the world that there were ways to uphold the truth. It was all a lost cause now.

When he heard Bo at the door, he put his melancholy aside and grabbed a small case for his notebooks. He told Bo he needed to go back to the bronze workshop, and Bo seemed not to suspect a thing. They left the palace precinct and made their way to the first of the walls, where they were halted by a sentry. Cí gritted his teeth while Bo showed their seals of passage. The sentry took his time looking over the documents and then looked Cí up and down—excruciatingly slowly, it felt like to Cí. The man let them pass. At the next post, Bo took out the documents again. The sentry looked at Cí oddly. Cí began chewing his lip. It was the first time while accompanied by Bo that there had been any delay at the checkpoints. He waited, trying to stay calm. After a short while the sentry handed Bo's documents to him, but when Cí reached to take his own documents from the sentry's outstretched hand, the man wouldn't let go.

"They have the Councilor for Punishment's signature on them," said Cí angrily.

"Follow me to the tower," the sentry ordered Cí.

Cí did as the man said. On entering, he was surprised to find Kan waiting for him there. The councilor stood, took the documents, and crumpled them up.

"Where were you off to then?" said Kan disdainfully.

"The bronze maker's workshop," said Cí, heart pounding. "There were some clues I needed to follow up on. Bo's coming with me."

Kan arched an eyebrow. "What kind of clues?"

"Um…clues," stuttered Cí.

"Maybe, maybe! Or, maybe, as I suspect, you're toying with the foolish idea of making your getaway." He paused and smiled. "And in case I'm right, I thought it might be worth mentioning that it would be very rude on your part if you were to go without saying good-bye to your master, Ming. He's in the dungeon. Under arrest. And that's where he'll stay until you decide to obey me and take a room in Feng's pavilion.

Cí was consumed with rage when he saw the state in which Ming was being kept. The old man was lying on a broken wicker bed. His face was impassive and his gaze distant. When he saw Cí come in, he tried to get up but was completely unable; his legs were bloody and bruised. When he spoke, Cí saw that his teeth had been bashed in, leaving a gory mess.

"They beat me…" Ming managed to say.

Cí could see he had no choice. He told Kan he'd go to Feng's, and he demanded that Ming be attended to and transferred to a better cell.

Several servants helped Cí take his belongings to the Water Lily Pavilion. When they'd left, Cí stood astonished by the loveliness of his new quarters, a large room overlooking the lemon grove. Putting his things down, he went to his appointment with Feng, who was brimming with satisfaction at the turn of events. Cí bowed, but Feng took him in his arms and hugged him.

"Boy!" he exclaimed, ruffling Cí's hair enthusiastically. "I'm so happy you've joined us!"

Once they were sitting and drinking a delicious black tea, Feng asked Cí to tell him about his father's death. Cí told him the story and went on to outline his difficulties in Lin'an, the dealings with the fortune-teller, Third's tragic death, his entrance into Ming Academy, and his later arrival at the palace. He told Feng everything apart from the circumstances that had brought him to this present juncture.

Feng could hardly believe all the things that had happened to Cí.

"All these hardships…I just can't understand why you didn't try to find me."

"I tried…" Cí thought about admitting to being a fugitive. "Sir, I really shouldn't be here with you. I'm not fit to share—"

But Feng shushed him. Cí had suffered quite enough, said the older man. He was just pleased they'd found each other now, so that they could share the good as well as the bad. Cí fell silent. Remorse gripped his throat. Eventually Feng broke the silence by asking him about the exams.

"You wanted to take them, didn't you?"

Cí nodded. He said he'd tried to obtain the Certificate of Aptitude but was denied because of his father's dishonor. Tears came to his eyes.

Feng lowered his head in sorrow.

"So you found out. Such a terrible thing, I couldn't bring myself to tell you. Not even when you were asking me about the changes in your father. You already had plenty on your plate at the time, what with your brother's arrest. But maybe I can help you now, use my connections. That certificate—"

"Sir, I'd really rather you not do anything more for me."

"You know how highly I've always thought of you, Cí. Now that you're here, I want you to think of yourself as family."

Feng went on to speak about Blue Iris, how they'd met, the difficulties of their courtship, and their happy marriage.

As Feng spoke, Cí glanced at the *nüshi*, who was relaxing in the gardens. Her sleek black hair was arranged in a bun, leaving her smooth, firm back in sight. Cí sipped at his tea, hoping the cup would hide his blushing. Finishing, he stood and asked permission to return to his room to study. The judge said he could go but stopped him to give him a sweet rice dessert.

"Thank you, Cí. Thank you for agreeing to come. You've made me so happy."

⧽⧼⧽✦⧼⧽⧼

Cí went and lay down on his feather bed and contemplated the richness of his surroundings. Normally he would have been delighted to find himself in such a place, but now he felt like a stray dog taken in by a kind master whom the dog would nevertheless turn on and maul.

Disobeying Kan would mean Ming's death; obeying him meant betraying Feng. He tried to eat a little of the sweet rice but immediately spit it out. He tasted only the bitterness in his soul. Was it really worth living like this?

He lay there, tormenting himself, blaming himself for the damage he was going to have to do—either to Ming or to Feng.

pirateANTONIO GARRIDO

Trying to focus instead on his work, he ran through the murders: Soft Dolphin, the eunuch, an elegant homosexual, a sensitive lover of antiques; the man with the corroded hands, in some way linked to the salt industry; the youth captured in the portrait, his face peppered with tiny wounds that Cí was yet to understand; the bronze maker, whose workshop burned down the same night he was decapitated…None of it added up, least of all how Blue Iris might be involved. She might have wanted revenge on the emperor, but how would she achieve that with these four seemingly unrelated deaths? What difference would they make to the emperor? When it came down to it, in spite of the similarities in the appearances of the murders, there was nothing yet to say the same person had carried them all out or even coordinated them.

When he was called down for dinner, he said he had a stomachache and sent the servant away. His dreams were inhabited by the seemingly inescapable image of Blue Iris.

The next morning he woke early and, after asking the servants to tell his hosts he'd be back to eat with them later, went to see how Ming was getting on.

Finding his old master in a cell that was no better than the last—damp, with rotten food and excrement in the corners—he couldn't contain his rage. Cí demanded an explanation from the sentry, but the man seemed about as merciful as a butcher going about his work. Ming was lying down and complained about his leg wounds. Cí gave him some water and, wiping the dried blood from the man's face with a wet cloth, tried to comfort him. The wounds didn't look good. A younger man might recover from such treatment, but Ming…Cí tried to stay calm, but he thought he was in more of a state than Ming. He swore to Ming that he'd get him out of there.

"Don't trouble yourself. Kan has never had much of a liking for effeminate men," he said sarcastically.

Cí cursed the councilor—and himself—for getting Ming into this mess. Then he told Ming about the bind he was in.

"What's the point in following clues in the investigations if I have no idea about the murderer's motive?"

"You've considered revenge?"

"Kan suggested that, too. But he also seems to think a blind woman could be responsible!" He outlined the situation with the *nüshi*.

"Could Kan be right?"

"Of course he could. The woman's rich enough to employ a whole army if she wants. But why? If revenge on the emperor is what she wants, why kill these poor swine?"

"And you haven't established any other suspects? The deceased didn't have enemies?"

"The eunuch, no, he just lived for his work. And the bronze maker, I'm making inquiries."

Ming tried to get up but immediately felt a stabbing pain in his legs and couldn't move.

"I wish I could help." He groaned, then, having recovered a little, he took a key from a chain around his neck. "But maybe there's something you can do for me. There's a false door in my library, after the last set of shelves. My life secrets are all behind there—books, drawings, poems, things that would have no significance to anyone else but mean everything to me. Please, should anything…happen to me, make sure that no one else gets their hands on those things."

Cí tried to say something, but Ming silenced him with a wave of the hand.

"Promise me. If I die, bury them alongside me."

Aloud, Cí agreed. To himself, he added one thing: if his master died, Kan would be next.

Cí went to Kan's offices. He didn't wait to be announced but burst in, surprising Kan, who was bent over a pile of documents at his desk. He began putting them hurriedly away, glaring at Cí. But Cí was more threatening still. He didn't allow the councilor to speak.

"Either you let Ming out of that dungeon right now, or I'm going to tell Blue Iris everything!"

Kan sighed.

"Oh, that. I thought they'd already moved him."

Cí didn't believe a word.

"If you don't have him moved, I'll tell her. If he doesn't recover, I'll tell her, and if he dies—"

"If he dies it will be your fault for not doing your job properly! And if you don't solve these murders, you'll both be put to death. Let's see: your findings so far might have satisfied the emperor, but not me. Boy, your chances are growing slimmer all the time, along with my patience. You'd better forget about that degenerate Ming and focus on your job. That is, if you don't want to end up like him."

Kan turned back to his work, but Cí wasn't going anywhere.

"Deaf or something?" said Kan.

"When you let Ming out."

Kan took a knife from his belt and was on Cí in a flash; the blade was at his jugular before he knew it. But Cí held firm, knowing that if Kan really wanted him dead, he'd be dead already.

"Only when you have Ming moved," Cí repeated.

He felt Kan's anger vibrate through the edge of the knife. Eventually, Kan released him.

"Guard!" he shouted, and the sentry appeared straightaway. "See that the prisoner Ming has his wounds attended to, and then have him brought up here. As for you," he said, bringing his face right up against Cí's, "you've got three days. If you haven't found out who the killer is by then, a killer will find you."

⋘⋙

Leaving Kan's offices, Cí found he could breathe again. He had no idea how he'd ever found the gall to challenge the councilor like that. The three days Kan had given him, he realized, corresponded with Gray Fox's return. Cí dug his fingernails into his palms. The only way to save Ming was to uncover the assassin, even if it meant betraying Feng.

Bo met him in the hallway, and together they stopped by the dungeon to check that Kan's orders were being followed. They found four servants and a doctor carrying Ming out on a stretcher.

Their next stop was the room where the remains of the bronze maker's warehouse had been deposited. Whoever had brought the remains had ignored his instructions. Nothing had been labeled, and it had all just been left in a pile. Cí kicked aside a singed beam and cleared some iron pokers out of his way. Bo apologized and began helping Cí organize all the wood and the molds. Reconstructing all the damaged equipment wasn't going to be easy. There were so many bits and pieces, many of them tiny, that the task seemed nearly impossible. But then Cí found a piece of a mold that struck him as promising.

"Forget the iron. Have you seen this?" He held up a piece of greenish ceramic. "It's different from all the others."

Bo considered the piece of ceramic with the same lack of enthusiasm he'd shown for all the other remains.

"Let's look for more!"

They managed to find eighteen pieces of the green ceramic. Cí gathered them up in a bag and put them to one side. Bo asked why, and something in his voice made Cí cautious, so he said casually that he planned to do the same with all the molds and went back to sorting through the wreckage. Soon it was lunchtime, and when Cí left for the Water Lily Pavilion he took the bag with him.

***

Back in his room at the pavilion, he took the fragments from the sack and began piecing them together. It wasn't only their greenish tone that had attracted his attention but the overall uniformity, which suggested they probably hadn't been used much. He was still assembling the pieces when he felt someone watching him from the door.

"The table's laid," said Blue Iris.

Cí cleared his throat and quickly put the pieces away, as though he'd been caught stealing. Glancing up, though, he saw how vacant Blue Iris's gaze was. It struck him how her figure was like an exquisitely crafted lute. He followed her to the dining room.

As they ate, Feng revealed to Blue Iris the extent of his and Cí's bond.

"You should have seen him in those days! He was a bundle of nerves as a child, and sharp as anything. His father worked for me, and I took him on as an assistant. I think he might have run from school to my offices; every day, he seemed to be there earlier and earlier waiting to join me on my rounds." Feng's face lit up at the memory. "He used to drive me crazy with all his questions! My goodness! A simple 'Because I say so' was never enough!"

Cí couldn't help but smile. Those had been the best days of his life.

"And he turned into a brilliant assistant. The best I've ever had." Before Cí could object, Feng went on. "The case in his village, for example."

"Oh?" said Blue Iris. "What happened there?"

Again Cí would have liked to stop his old master right there, remembering how things had turned out with Lu, but Feng was on a roll.

"Cí not only discovered a corpse but was absolutely key in solving the case. It seemed like a real dead-end case, but Cí never gave up. He helped me and eventually, together, we managed to break the deadlock."

Cí could remember clearly the moment when Feng had swished away the flies and they had swarmed around his brother's sickle, and how that had led to Lu's confession.

"I'm not surprised Kan decided to employ you, then," said Blue Iris, "although it seems a little strange he's got you working on the Jin. Their dietary habits, wasn't it?"

"Really?" Feng was surprised. "I would have thought he'd been making the most of your considerable talent as a *wu-tso*."

Cí choked, quickly blaming the rice wine. He tried to be as offhand as he could and said something about having studied the northern barbarians a little at the Ming Academy. Luckily, Blue Iris didn't pursue the matter.

For the rest of the meal, Feng filled Cí in on his successes since they'd parted, his move to the Water Lily Pavilion, and how he owed it all to Blue Iris.

"My life changed the moment I met her," he said, stroking his wife's hand, though she responded by retracting her hand and excusing herself, saying she'd bring the tea.

They both watched her make her way to the kitchen—without the aid of the walking stick she always carried. Cí began thinking about her skin; he couldn't help it. Feng broke the silence.

"You'd never guess she was blind," he said lightly. "She could run the length of this place and wouldn't bump into a thing, I bet you."

Cí nodded. He felt like a traitor on so many fronts. If he didn't tell Feng the truth, or at least part of it, he was going to burst.

First he made Feng promise not to tell anyone.

"Not even Blue Iris," Cí said.

Feng swore on his ancestors' souls.

Cí told him about the circumstances of his departure from the village. He told him he was a fugitive. He told him about Gray Fox's imminent return. Then he went on to detail the case he was really working on, and the progress he'd made, and Kan's conviction that it had something to do with a plot against the emperor.

"Interesting," said Feng. "I'm thinking how I might be of help…This other youth, Gray Fox was it? Hmm. I wouldn't worry about him. When he gets back, he and I are going to have a little talk."

Cí looked in Feng's eyes. All that trust—and Cí was on the verge of betraying it. He felt a pang in his stomach. He was just about to reveal the part of the story about Kan's suspicions of Blue Iris when they heard her coming back with the tea.

Again, Cí was captivated by her movements, even performing such a simple task as pouring drinks. There was a deep calm in her, and it acted on him like a balm.

When they'd drunk their tea, Feng issued some whispered instruction to a servant. "Here," he said when the servant returned, handing over a sheaf of papers to Cí. "These, I believe, are yours."

"But—but," stammered Cí.

Feng nodded.

It was the Certificate of Aptitude he needed to take the Imperial exams, and there was no mention of his father's dishonor, nothing about any obstacles. It was clean. He would be allowed to take the exams. Tears sprang to his eyes as he looked again to his old master.

Just then, the servant came in, saying a group of businessmen were there to see Feng. When Feng came back, he reported that one of his goods convoys had been attacked near the border.

"The attackers were repelled," he said, "but we've lost men, and some of the goods, too. I have to go immediately."

Cí felt even worse. He'd have given anything to admit the part of the story about Blue Iris, but he wasn't going to have a chance now. As they embraced, Feng whispered in his ear.

"Be careful with Kan," he said. "And look after Blue Iris for me."

And with that, he was gone.

31

Feng had said he'd be away for only a few days, but Cí couldn't imagine being alone with Blue Iris for any amount of time. He spent the afternoon trying to reassemble the bronze maker's green mold but couldn't stop thinking about her. And when the bell rang for dinner, he realized he'd made no progress whatsoever.

It would have been too much of a discourtesy not to attend dinner, so Cí quickly washed, shaved, and went down. Blue Iris was waiting for him. He sat across from her, not daring to look straight at her. He glanced up and couldn't help but admire the sight: her sheer blouse gave him a clear view of large expanses of her skin. When she handed him a plate of soybean shoots, it was her breasts in particular, or their outlines, that magnetized his gaze. He knew she couldn't see him drinking her in, so he looked, more intensely than ever before.

"What are you looking at?" she said.

"Nothing!"

"Nothing? Don't you like the food? There are even figs somewhere here…"

"Oh, yes!" he said, taking one of the strange, dark little fruits. "Of course."

"So would you like to hear about the work I used to do?"

"Very much," he said. Reaching for more fruit, his hand brushed hers, which sent shivers through his entire body.

"If you really want to hear about the life of a *nüshi*, you might want to drink a little more. It is a tale full of bitterness." She sighed, and there was anguish in her voice. "When I entered the emperor's service I was a child, but not for much longer; one doesn't stay innocent doing such work. He must have seen something in me, and he wasted no time seizing it. I grew up among concubines. They were my sisters, and they taught me how to live in those conditions, living only to please the Heaven's Son. They gave me all the necessary refinements, the subtleties, the arts. Instead of learning to play, I learned to kiss and lick...Instead of laughing, I learned how to please.

"Confucian texts? The classics? Not for me. The books that were read to me as a child were all about the art of pleasure: the *Xuannüjing*, or *Manual of a Dark Woman*; the *Xufangneimishu*, or *Preface to the Secret Bedroom Arts*; the *Ufangmijue*, or *Bride's Secret Formula*; the *Unufang*, or *Recipes of a Simple Lady*. As my body changed and I became a woman, a deep hate was also taking hold of me, as intense as my experience of blindness. And the more I hated him, the more he wanted me.

"I learned to be better than all the rest in pleasuring him. I honed my skills in the bedroom knowing that the greater his desire, the greater my revenge would also be.

"That was *my* desire." She seemed to turn her pupils on Cí. "I soon became his favorite. He longed for me night and day. He coveted me, licked me, penetrated me. And when he'd taken all of my body, when there was nothing physical left for me to give, his desire shifted to possessing my soul."

Cí contemplated her crestfallen face. He felt grief grip his stomach. The tears were flowing freely down her smooth cheeks.

"You don't have to go on," he said. "I—"

"You mean you don't want to hear more? You don't want to hear what it's like to feel used, empty, your self-respect in tatters?

"I became a husk of a person. My youth was a wounded time, and I hated it completely. The funny thing was the other concubines' envy. Any one of them would have changed places with me, even with my blindness. But, unlike all of them, I couldn't have children." She laughed bitterly. "I got what I'd set out to achieve, and the price was my dignity. When it reached the point where he called out my name in the night, when he needed me like life itself, that was when I began denying him. But the happiness I felt at that control quickly became sadness; my only desire had been achieved, and there was nothing left. He cried, he screamed, he beat me. He claimed to have fallen ill, but of course there was no cure any doctor could provide. His proud penis became nothing more than a soft silk sheet, and no concubine, no courtesan, not one prostitute in the whole kingdom was able to give him what I'd been giving him."

Cí listened dumbly. His hand hovered over hers and he strongly wanted to comfort her, but he stopped himself and was relieved, once more, that she couldn't have seen the gesture.

"Really," he said, "you don't have to go on if you don't want to."

"Even so, I stayed by his side. He made me *nüshi* so I'd teach the others my skills. I did as he asked because it meant I could watch his deterioration firsthand. I watched him grow old, and I watched him go out of his mind at the same time.

"When Ningzong came to power, I moved on to a different plan. Ningzong and I were indifferent to each other. I stayed until his father died. It was during that time I met Feng."

She stopped crying. Cí imagined that she'd cried most of her tears during the days she'd spoken about. She served two glasses of liquor.

"And then?" asked Cí.

"I don't want to talk about it." Her answer struck him like a hammer blow.

They both fell silent. Then she got up, begging Cí's pardon for her behavior, and retired to her room.

Cí stayed there with his drink, his head a whirlwind of desire and ideas. He found himself swigging straight from the bottle. He thought about Feng. He thought about Blue Iris. Everything was spinning. He grabbed the bottle and headed to his room.

Cí was woken by a noise in the middle of the night. Rubbing his pounding temples, he turned onto his back, and though the room was dark, he saw the liquor bottle empty beside him. He thought he heard footsteps coming down the hallway. He glanced up and there, silhouetted in the doorway, was the naked form of Blue Iris.

She came in and shut the door behind her. He shuddered as he watched her, this goddess, approaching him. She stopped next to the bed. Cí didn't move, but there was no way to hide his heavy breathing, his excitement.

Blue Iris moved the sheet aside and slipped in beside him. They were a hair's breadth apart. He could feel her warmth. The intensity of her perfume made it harder still to think. Then her hand was on his leg, moving slowly upward toward his waist. He didn't move, praying she'd leave him alone at the same time that his body was crying out for her to go on. Then she brushed her breasts against him, and it was all too much.

ANTONIO GARRIDO

He'd never experienced sensations like these.

He kissed her neck, burying himself in her. His lips sought the spaces in her, the soft corners, her clavicle and shoulders. She groaned with pleasure.

And when they kissed, it felt to him as though he were quenching a thirst that had been with him all his days.

She clung to him. Her panting breath goaded him. He wanted to be inside her, and he told her so in whispers. But she moved her lips down Cí's torso and belly—past his scars and to his erect penis. When she wrapped her lips around him, he thought he would die from pleasure. He shut his eyes, hoping he could record this moment, so it would be something he could always conjure. Then he felt Blue Iris wrapping her legs around him as if to say she needed him inside her. He tried to get up, but she prevented him and crouched over him instead. She placed a hand over his eyes, and with her other hand guided him inside her. He gasped and tried to move away the hand that was blinding him, but she insisted, coming close and licking his lips.

"Equals," she whispered.

"Equals," he whispered back, and left her hand where it was.

She lowered herself onto him. He was overcome by the heat of her. She moved, arched, kissed him as though taking her last breaths, as though she needed him if she were going to stay alive.

Then her body began shaking in a prolonged and pleasurable torture that became quicker and more violent. He felt her losing control, which prompted him to do the same, and he let go inside her.

Afterward she stayed beside him, as if they had been stitched together. Cí tasted the salty tears on her cheeks. He hoped they were tears of happiness.

But no.

When he woke in the morning, Blue Iris was gone. And when he asked the servants where she was, they had no idea.

He had breakfast alone, in the same little room where they'd dined together. He took a deep breath, trying to clear his hangover, but only seemed to inhale the bittersweetness of Blue Iris again.

Feng came into his thoughts; Cí knew he'd never be able to face his old master. He couldn't even look at himself in the magnificent bronze mirror that overlooked the space. He finished his tea and went to bathe, hoping the running water would cleanse these feelings: he wanted the pleasure he'd felt with Blue Iris, but he also knew for certain that he'd forfeited his soul.

He stopped on his way upstairs, captivated by the beauty of the antiques and the paintings adorning the walls. Soft Dolphin's collection paled in comparison. The exquisite calligraphies of ancient poems, whose curved frames offset the blood-red silk covering the walls, were particularly sublime. The texts were by the celebrated Taoist Li Bai, the immortal poet of the Tang dynasty. He slowly read one:

I think of night.
The moon shines in front of the bed.
Above the frost is the doubt.
I look up and there is a full moon.
I look down and miss my life.

He continued up the stairs, reading the other poems as he went until he came to a smaller text that said the composition was part of a series of eleven. But Cí noticed there were only ten. A crude portrait of the poet hung where the eleventh should've been; the mark left by the old picture frame was clear to see.

He gulped. It couldn't be.

He was about to confirm his suspicion when there came a noise from behind him, making him jump. He turned, coming face to face with Blue Iris, who was wearing a striking red dress.

"What are you doing?" she asked.

"Nothing…" When he tried to stroke her hand, she pulled it away.

"I hear you were looking for me," she said. "I was out for my morning walk."

Cí turned back to the place where the eleventh frame had been replaced.

"Amazing poems," he said. "Were there always ten?"

"I don't know. I can't see them."

Cí frowned. "Has something happened? Last night you were…"

"Night is darkness; day brings clarity. What are your obligations for the day? We still haven't discussed the Jin."

Cí cleared his throat. He didn't really know what questions to ask. Maybe he could consult Ming—that way, he could also check to see if Kan was continuing to make sure the old man was cared for. Cí excused himself, saying he had to visit a sick friend first, and then attend an appointment, but maybe they could meet at midday.

"Fine," she said. "I'll wait for you here."

⋙※⋘

Cí left feeling weighed down by worries. He didn't want to admit it, but he felt less and less convinced of Blue Iris's innocence.

Ming had been taken to a modest but clean room in the same part of the palace as Bo's offices. He looked somewhat improved, though the violet bruising on his legs was worrying, and when Cí asked if any doctor had been to see him, Ming shook his head.

"I don't need one anyway," he grumbled, straightening up between groans. "I've managed to wash myself, and the food isn't that bad."

Cí looked at the tiny bowl with leftover rice in it. He kicked himself for not bringing fruit and wine. He decided to tell Ming everything about the situation with Blue Iris and his growing doubts about her. He listed various suspicions about the ex-*nüshi*, but then defended her.

Ming listened attentively.

"From what you say, this woman seems to have ample motives."

"They're really only circumstantial, though. Also, why shouldn't she detest the emperor, given what she went through at his hands? But I know that from there to deciding to kill...it's quite a leap... You should meet her," he added, looking down.

"And who says I haven't? The strange thing is that while you've spoken at length about her charms, you don't see that you might be getting your thoughts and desires mixed up."

Cí felt his whole face turn red.

"What do you mean?" he retorted. "Blue Iris couldn't truly hurt someone."

"Really? So I suppose you know why Emperor Ningzong removed her from service?"

"Because she made his father ill. She drove him mad because she stopped sleeping with him."

"I wonder who gave you that version of events! I find it very odd that you don't know the story. It's common knowledge. The old emperor didn't go mad because she stopped allowing him to have her," Ming said, looking reproachful. "He went mad because she poisoned him."

Cí's stomach turned. He didn't want to believe it and cursed himself for falling for her charms. How stupid could he have been? His soul for one short night of pleasure? He was about to ask Ming for more details when a sentry came in and leaned up against a wall, as if to indicate he wasn't leaving. They wouldn't have any privacy now. Cí decided to give up, said to Ming that he must allow a doctor to look at his legs, and left the room feeling terribly confused.

He tried to look at the situation from another point of view. When it came down to it, her motive was strong, and she hadn't even tried to hide her hatred for the emperor's father. The perfume was a direct link to the victims. But he still hadn't found out why Blue Iris might have wanted to kill four people—three of whom seemed distant from the emperor. At least, he needed to find out why *one* of them had been killed; he was convinced that if he solved one case, the others would quickly follow.

He decided to go to Soft Dolphin's quarters again. There was something he needed to check.

Guards were still posted there, and, as always, Cí's pass was checked and his name recorded. Once inside, he headed straight to the room containing the antiques. The majestic poem that had first drawn his attention was in the same spot, and he wasn't wrong. It was by Li Bai, the one that had been missing from Blue Iris's collection: number eleven.

He noted that the white frame was curved, just like those he'd admired in the *nüshi*'s pavilion. Taking it down, he checked the mark it had left on the wall, and then did the same with the other canvases hanging there. This done, his face was a mixture of rage and satisfaction. On his way out, it occurred to him that it might be worth looking in the register, and the sentry let him. Cí didn't recognize most of the names, but he soon came across the one he'd been looking for: The calligraphy couldn't have been clearer. Two days after the disappearance of the eunuch, Blue Iris had visited these rooms.

His heart pounded. Suddenly the truth was within reach.

He still had time before his meeting with Iris to take another look at the remnants from the bronze maker's workshop.

Everything seemed to be falling into place. But when he reached the room where the remnants were being kept, there was no guard outside. He walked slowly into the darkness and thought he was being careful, but he tripped over something and fell. As his eyes adjusted, he saw that the objects he and Bo had so carefully sorted were scattered around. He cursed whoever had done it. He went back to the door and opened it wide to let in some light. What had been taken? He went over to where they had stacked the molds and was horrified to see they'd all been smashed up into tiny pieces. It looked like a club, now lying on the enormous anvil beside him, had been used. Suddenly there was a sound above him; he grabbed the club and peered up toward the attic where he and Bo had piled the pieces of iron.

Seeing nothing up there, he went back to inspecting the remains until he found a bag containing the plaster used to extract the positives from the molds. He put it aside and then heard another sound, a crack, louder this time. Again he looked up toward the attic and caught a glimpse of a crouching figure. And that was all he saw, because suddenly an avalanche of joists, railings, and pieces of wood fell on him, burying him.

Cí dared to open his eyes only when the dust started to settle. He could hardly see anything, but at least he was alive. He was thankful to have slipped under the anvil, which had sheltered him. But his leg was caught beneath an iron bar and he couldn't move, much as he tried. Gradually, rays of light began filtering from the doorway through the dusty air, and suddenly a figure was in front of him. Cí couldn't say anything. He was sure it was the same person who had caused the attic to collapse, and he couldn't get away. He gulped, his saliva thick with dust. He grabbed a metal bar and prepared to defend himself. He was about to strike out when the person spoke.

"Cí? Is that you?"

It was Bo. He felt a flash of relief, but he didn't let go of the metal bar.

"Are you OK?" asked Bo, beginning to clear the debris trapping Cí. "What happened?"

Bo managed to get Cí free and helped him out of the room. Cí sucked in the dust-free air. Still feeling suspicious of Bo, he asked why he had been there.

"A sentry came and told me the door had been forced open and the room ransacked. I came to see."

Cí was far from convinced. Whom could he trust? He had trouble walking, though, and asked Bo to help him back to the Water Lily Pavilion. He was worried his attacker might come after him again.

On their way, Cí asked what progress there had been in taking the portrait around.

"Nothing yet," said Bo. "But some news on the hand. The flame tattoo wasn't actually a flame tattoo."

"Meaning?"

"I had Chen Yu, a well-known tattooist at the Silk Market, examine it. He's thought to be one of the best, so I believed him when he said it."

"Said *what*?"

"The salt had erased part of the tattoo. There would have been a circle also. It wasn't a flame at all, he said, but a yin-yang."

"The Taoist symbol!"

"Exactly. But Chen Yu was even more specific," Bo continued. "In his opinion, the man must have been an alchemist monk, because the pigment was cinnabar, which can only point to occultists. They use cinnabar in their experiments to formulate the elixir of eternal life."

As soon as Cí got back to the pavilion, he pulled out the green ceramic fragments he'd been piecing together. What had just happened at the palace made it clear he was going to have to be careful with his evidence.

He shut the door behind him and took out the piece he'd found just now. He had a feeling it was going to complete the puzzle. He was putting the pieces away again when Blue Iris came in without knocking.

"They told me you'd been in an accident," she said, sounding worried.

"Yes, and a pretty unusual one, too. Actually, I'd say it was more like an attempt on my life."

Blue Iris's eyes grew wide, which emphasized their strange grayness.

"What—what happened?"

Cí thought it was the first time he'd ever heard her say something lacking conviction.

"I thought *you* might be able to tell me!" he said, grabbing her by the wrists and throwing her onto the bed.

"Me! I don't under—"

"No more lies! I wanted to believe Kan was wrong, but he was right all along!"

"What is this?" she cried. "Let go of me! Let go or I'll have you flogged!"

He let go and she leaped from the bed, backing away from him in the corner of the room. Cí pushed the door shut and went toward her, trapping her in the corner.

"That's why you seduced me, isn't it? Kan warned me about you. He told me all about your plot against the emperor. I wanted to believe he was wrong, and it nearly cost me my life. But your ruses are all played out now. Your lies won't help you anymore."

"You're crazy! Let me go!"

"The eunuch's work had to do with the salt monopoly. I haven't yet figured out if he uncovered something in the accounts and you bribed him, or if it was blackmail. But you knew all about his love of antiques, and you offered him one he couldn't refuse! And once you had him in your grip, that's when you had him killed!"

"Get out!" she sobbed. "Out of my house!"

"You were the only one who knew I was going to look at the remnants from the bronze workshop! You sent someone to kill me, too—probably the same person who took the life of Soft Dolphin and all the others!"

"I said get out!" she cried.

"You felt protected by what had happened to your ancestors; the emperor would never risk accusing the granddaughter of the betrayed hero. But your thirst for revenge knew no limits. You lied when you told me the emperor's father died of lovesickness. You poisoned him, the same as you did me yesterday with your seduction!"

Blue Iris tried to get past him to the door, but he blocked the way.

"Admit it!" he roared. "Admit that you lied to me. That you made me believe you felt something for me."

"How dare you! You were the one who lied to me! What's your real job? You who are so loyal to Feng that you slept with his wife."

"You put a spell on me!" Cí howled.

"Pathetic," she spit. "I don't know how I ever felt anything for you." Crying, she tried to push past him again.

"Think your tears will save you? Kan was right about you."

Blue Iris's eyes, wet with tears, were also inflamed with rage.

"I thought you were different," she said. "But you're not. You think I'm just a used-up *nüshi* whom you can condemn, use, despise. That all I'm good for is toying with in the bedroom. Yes, I seduced you, so what? You don't know me. You have no idea of the hell I've lived through."

Cí's mind turned to his own hell. He knew very well what it was to suffer, but that understanding certainly didn't make him think she wasn't guilty. She had no right to reproach anyone, especially after what he'd just found out.

"Kan warned me," he said again.

"Kan? He'd sell his own children if he thought it would benefit him. What did he tell you?" She slapped Cí on the chest. "That I tried to poison the emperor? Wrong! Much as I might regret it now, I didn't. Do you really think I'd have been allowed to live if I did something like that? Kan didn't tell you the real reason he despises me: the thousand times he tried to take me, and the thousand times I rejected him. I bet he didn't tell you he proposed to me! He didn't tell you what it means to a councilor to be refused by a lowly *nüshi*..."

At this, she fell to her knees, overcome with tears.

"I found your name in the registry for Soft Dolphin's quarters. I don't know how you managed it, but you gained access. There was a canvas there with the eleventh of Li Bai's poems—an antique *I know* belongs to you, an heirloom that belongs on *your* walls. The one on Soft Dolphin's wall is something he never could have afforded." Cí waited for her denial, but Blue Iris had fallen quiet. "I read the stamps of ownership. Those verses belonged to your grandfather."

"Ask Kan! He kept dozens of vials of Essence of Jade to woo me with. And the poem—my husband gave it to Kan, so again it's Kan you should be asking about how it ended up on Soft Dolphin's walls. Yes, I've been to Soft Dolphin's quarters. I went to retrieve some porcelain figures I gave him. Yes, he was a friend of mine. Which was why, I thought, Kan told me he'd disappeared. If you don't believe me, ask Kan."

Having let Blue Iris leave, Cí tried to get things clear in his head. Once he'd calmed down, he took out the mold again to try to finish piecing it together. He followed the numbers he'd written on the pieces to arrange them, but one of the pieces crumbled in his hands. His hands were shaking like those of a frightened child. He swiped the pieces across the floor.

He regretted pushing the woman who'd loved him so sweetly the night before. He'd felt so sure of her guilt, but then the way she'd reacted didn't seem like the behavior of someone who was guilty. Cornered, perhaps, but to blame? There was plenty of proof against her, but there were plenty of holes in the case, too.

What on earth could make her want to kill *those* men? He turned it over and over. Maybe the answer lay in the ceramic pieces. Or maybe Kan was the only one who really knew.

He went back to working on the mold, more carefully this time. Little by little, it took shape, becoming a prism about the size of someone's forearm. He moved a leftover piece aside, noting that it seemed to be some kind of internal spoke, then joined the two halves of the mold together with a belt. Then he mixed up some plaster and poured it in. Now he had to wait for it to harden. Eventually, when it seemed solid, he undid the belt and parted the mold.

It looked more like a scepter than anything: two palms in length and about as wide as a sword hilt. Cí could just about fit his hand around it. What could it be for? He decided to put it aside, hiding the scepter and the spokelike interior piece under a loose floorboard and the mold in his wardrobe.

<hr/>

Cí left the Water Lily Pavilion for some much-needed air.

His specialties were corpses and scars, not intrigue and rancor; he knew how to find invisible clues on dead bodies, not how to unpack madness and lies.

The more he thought about it, though, the clearer it became that Kan had manipulated him from day one. If what the councilor had said about Blue Iris contained any truth, he'd surely have taken action against her already. And now it seemed his dislike for her might have different motivations. Kan could easily have accompanied her to Soft Dolphin's rooms, and if he really did have access to Essence of Jade, it would also make sense for him to have left traces of the perfume on the corpses to incriminate her. Why he might have done so, thereby incriminating himself, Cí couldn't understand. And Blue Iris had made no secret of her resentment toward the emperor, which made her an easy person to frame. On top of that, Kan was the last to be seen with the bronze maker, he had kept an appointment with the Jin ambassador, and he offered only obfuscation when it came to giving explanations. Maybe the councilor really *was* the person to turn to for answers.

What to do? Cí clearly couldn't go to Kan, who would only try to get in his way. Maybe he was the murderer, or the one who had given the orders. Or maybe he had nothing to do with it and had just tried to take advantage of the killings to get back at someone who had humiliated him.

Maybe Cí needed to speak to the emperor. Perhaps that was the only way to get answers before it became far too dangerous. And for that he needed Bo's help.

"Protocol's protocol, Cí, and we all have to respect it."

Cí had gone straight to Bo's quarters, where he found the official just finishing his bath. Perhaps it was because he'd been interrupted, but Bo didn't seem very disposed to help.

"If you try and circumnavigate protocol, heaven help you."

The ritual nature of the emperor's every movement was well known. But what Cí also knew was that if he was going to solve this case, he couldn't have more delays.

"I've solved the crimes." The words were out of his mouth before he knew it. "It can't wait, and I definitely can't talk to Kan about it first."

Bo looked skeptically at Cí.

"Have you forgotten," asked Cí, "the attic's collapsing on my head? If you don't help me, I might not be around tomorrow to tell anyone what I've found."

Bo agreed, gritted his teeth, and went to his superior, who within a matter of hours had passed the request up the chain of command. Bo learned that, although there was consternation among the officials over Cí's request, one of the elders grasped its importance and took the petition to the emperor himself.

To Cí, the time passing felt like years. Then he was summoned.

The elder official's face was cold as stone as he considered Cí. Finally he spoke.

"His Majesty will receive you in the Throne Room." He lit a stick of incense the length of a fingernail and handed it to Cí. "This is the time you have allotted to speak. Not a moment longer."

As Cí followed the man to the Throne Room, he licked a finger and touched it to the side of the incense, hoping it would slow its burning a little. Suddenly the elder stood aside, and Cí was face to face with the emperor.

Cí was dazzled by the emperor's golden tunic. Before he could think of what to say, the elder official hissed at him to kneel. Cí, regaining his composure, got down and kissed the floor. The incense was already burning low, and the elder was taking an eternity with the formalities. When he was finally ushered forward, everything came out in a jumble: his suspicions about Kan, all the lies, and the councilor's blatant attempts to frame Blue Iris.

The emperor listened in silence. His pale eyes scrutinized Cí. His waxen face was utterly devoid of emotion.

"You are accusing one of my most loyal men of dishonorable acts." Ningzong's voice was slow and deliberate. "An Imperial Councilor who would willingly chop off his own hand if I said so. If your accusations turn out to be wrong, the penalty will obviously be death. And yet, you're still here. Keeping the embers of a tiny stick of incense between your fingers..." He brought his hands together and placed them over his pursed lips.

"Yes, Majesty."

"If I give the order for Kan to be brought here and he refutes your allegations, I'll be obliged to have you executed. If, on the other hand, you think better of it and decide to withdraw your accusation, I shall be magnanimous. I shall forget the nerve you have shown in coming here. I want you to think properly about this. Are you prepared to uphold your accusation?"

Cí took a very deep breath. The incense was all but gone.

"Yes," he said without having to think about it at all.

An official was sent to fetch the Councilor for Punishments. When he burst back into the Throne Room, he looked as if he'd seen a devil; he was bathed in sweat and shaking all over. He ran and threw himself at the emperor's feet, and the emperor recoiled as if touched by a leper. Several guards were on the man immediately, pulling him away. He was incoherent. His dilated pupils spoke pure terror.

"He's dead, Your Majesty! Kan has hanged himself in his room!"

PART SIX

PART SIX

32

Ningzong suspended all royal engagements immediately and ordered the Imperial Judges to be summoned. With them in tow, and surrounded by a large retinue and all his guards, the emperor went in semiprocession to Kan's rooms. Cí was allowed to go with them.

Kan's flabby, naked body, hanging from the rafters, stopped them all in midstep. His face looked like that of a burst toad. Ningzong ordered the body cut down, but the Imperial Judges advised against it; they all agreed the first thing was for the room to be inspected. Cí was asked to take part in this.

While the judges commented on Kan's appearance, Cí's mind turned to the fine layer of dust on the tiles, illuminated by a shaft of sunlight. He made a quick sketch of the layout of the furniture in the room, including the large dresser that Kan must have climbed on to reach the rafters. He was then granted permission to examine the corpse, and he was so nervous that it felt as if it were the first time he had ever performed such an examination.

Kan's neck was grotesquely disjointed, his one eye was shut, and his partially open lips and what could be seen of the gums were black. The teeth were clamped down on the tongue. There was dried spittle at the corners of the mouth, and the rest of the face was tinged blue. His fingers and toes were curled unnaturally inward. His stomach and lower abdomen hung lower than they normally would and had turned blue-black. His thick legs had little spots of blood below the skin—much like the marks made by moxibustion. A pile of feces was on the floor beneath him.

Cí asked permission to approach the corpse and hopped onto the dresser. The rope, he now saw, was made of braided hemp the width of a pinkie finger, thin enough that it cut deep into the skin. It had a slipknot in it and crossed around the back of the head, ear to ear, where it had left a deep, blackish groove just beneath the hairline. To everyone's surprise, Cí asked for a chair and stood on it on top of the dresser. Higher now, he was able to study the top of the rafter itself, over which the rope had been slung. Then he climbed down and announced he was finished.

Ningzong ordered that Kan be cut down and asked that the Councilor for Rites be brought so funeral preparations could take place.

Once Kan's body was down, Cí quickly checked the neck to see if the trachea was broken. As the body was being carried out, Bo found a handwritten note on a table alongside Kan's neatly folded clothes. He scanned it and brought it to the emperor, who read it to himself in a low voice. Then he crumpled the paper and threw it to the floor. When he looked up, his rage was plain for all to see. There would be no public ceremony, he announced, and the Councilor for Rites would not be needed. Kan's body would be buried nowhere special, he said, and he forbade the utterance of even one word of sympathy for Kan.

A murmur of surprise went around. As the retinue followed the quickly departing emperor, Bo picked up the note and passed it to Cí, who smoothed it out. Kan's handwriting was unmistakable, and his seal was there, too. He confessed to the murders and to an attempt to discredit Blue Iris.

Cí sat on the mahogany floor. He couldn't believe it was all over.

Eventually, Bo helped him to his feet. Cí said good-bye, unsteadily, and headed out into the gardens.

There was nothing keeping him here now. Ming would be freed; Blue Iris would be exonerated. Any accusations Gray Fox brought against him, Feng had promised to divert. The Imperial exams were within reach.

So why, as he wandered through the willows, was he filled with fear?

Because he knew, and couldn't have been more certain, that Kan's death hadn't been suicide, but homicide.

Cí made his way toward the Water Lily Pavilion determined to pack his bags and go. He'd made up his mind. He'd see to Ming's release, and that would be all. Whatever was going to happen next wasn't Cí's concern. They'd made him carry out an investigation; had threatened, tortured, and blackmailed him; they'd locked Ming up…What more could they ask? In Kan they had their scapegoat. If someone was going to find out what had really happened, let it be one of the palace judges who'd been so disdainful toward Cí all along. Or Gray Fox, if he ever bothered to come back. And if he'd managed to find anything out in Jianyang, Cí would be long gone by then.

He saw Blue Iris in the garden. Now he'd never get to find out whether she was guilty or not. He hoped she wasn't, but what did it matter? He'd been stupid to fall for a woman he knew he couldn't have, and to betray the one man who had ever really treated him like a son. He cursed the night they met. And yet, he could still taste her kisses on his lips.

He went up the entrance steps and straight to his room to begin packing. He had to decide what to do with the bronze maker's mold. If he really wanted to put the case behind him, he had to destroy the evidence. He took the plaster scepter and the spokelike piece from underneath the floorboards. Then he went to his wardrobe to retrieve the two parts of the mold. They were gone.

Clearly, this case wasn't going to be easy to leave behind, but he was resolved on his course of action. Maybe this was the best thing that could have happened. If someone had collapsed the attic and tried to kill him because he'd been sifting through the remains of the workshop and assembling the ceramic pieces, then whoever had the mold now should keep it.

He finished packing and turned his thoughts to the strange scepter. He picked it up and examined it closely. Its outside was decorated with flower motifs, and he still thought the spoke-like piece somehow went inside. Could it have been some kind of musical instrument, he wondered?

No. Why was he still trying to work it out anyway? He lifted it above his head and was on the verge of smashing it on the floor, but something stopped him. He couldn't help but think that, if it were relevant to the case, it couldn't be a bad thing to keep. He'd hide it, just in case there was a chance he could make use of it.

But where? Thinking, he absentmindedly scratched his chest, and his hand caught the key hanging at his neck. He'd forgotten about it. The key to the secret compartment in Ming's quarters at the academy.

That decided it. He hid the scepter in his clothes and left his room, luggage in hand. Blue Iris was in the main hall, standing beside the front door. She wore a silk dress beneath which he could make out her figure. He noticed, too, that she'd been crying and couldn't help but feel a pang at this. He managed only a shamed good-bye before leaving.

He decided to enlist Bo's help. He was concerned that by the time he returned from the academy, they might not allow him back into the palace. Bo eventually agreed, and together they walked to the academy.

When they arrived, Cí asked for Ming's assistant, Sui. When he appeared, the middle-aged man looked out from under his bushy eyebrows at Cí with astonishment. But when Cí showed him the key, his expression suddenly became one of concern.

"The Master…?"

Cí explained that Ming was weak but that he'd be better soon, adding that he had asked Cí to bring him a book to read while he recovered. Sui nodded and told Cí to follow him. Bo waited in the garden.

Up in Ming's quarters, Sui carefully removed a number of books from a shelf at the back, revealing a locked mahogany trapdoor. Cí waited for Sui to leave him, but the servant made no sign that he was going to do so.

Cí hadn't foreseen this. He took the key from the chain and unlocked the padlock. Cí cursed. It was only a small space, and already full to the brim. Where was he supposed to put the scepter?

"What's wrong?" asked Sui as Cí turned to face him.

Cí took out the scepter and a purse of coins.

"I need you to do me a favor. Not me, in fact. It's for Ming."

<hr/>

Now that Kan was dead, Cí's only reason to go back to the palace was to secure Ming's release. Bo went with him to speed the process along. When Cí was alone with Ming, he tried to cheer him. The wounds on his legs had improved, and the color had returned to his cheeks, so he'd be able to walk within a matter of days. He might as well recuperate back at the academy as in these lovely surroundings, joked Cí, making Ming smile. But when Cí recounted the circumstances of Kan's death, Ming turned pale again.

"What aren't you telling me?" he said, as if he could tell Cí was hiding something.

"Nothing," said Cí, glancing at the sentries.

Ming seemed to believe this, which in a way annoyed Cí. He hated deceiving Ming. And Feng and Blue Iris, too. He bid Ming farewell, saying he'd do his best to get him back to the academy as soon as possible.

Leaving the room, Cí couldn't shake his self-hate. Deceitfulness was precisely the thing he'd despised in his father these past months, but now he was acting just as unscrupulously. He was finding out firsthand what it was like to look the other way, to not be devoted to the truth, so he could look out for himself. Ignore the guilty, ignore the innocent. Feng and Ming—his compass points—were utterly against this kind of behavior. And his sister came to mind; she'd be far from proud.

What had he become? His head was telling him to flee, but something gnawed at him. He knew it was a feeling to which he had to pay attention.

And then there was Blue Iris, whom he could not forget. The warmth of her body, the sadness of her countenance…Suddenly, he knew he had to at least say good-bye to her. He headed for the Water Lily Pavilion, unsure whether he was obeying a carnal impulse or attempting to maintain a glimmer of dignity.

As he neared the pavilion, he could see Feng standing next to a carriage and horses while half a dozen workers rushed around. When Feng noticed Cí approaching, he stopped what he was doing and came toward him with a smile.

"Cí!" He hugged him warmly. "Iris told me you'd left, but I was sure you couldn't have."

Cí had never embraced someone whom he had deceived.

"You're back early," said Cí, sure Feng would pull away from the hug.

"Luckily, I managed to sort things out more quickly than I thought I could. Well! Give us a hand with the presents. Iris?" he shouted. "Have you seen? Cí's back."

Cí gazed at the *nüshi*, who was standing in the entranceway. He greeted her timidly, but she just turned and went back into the pavilion.

During lunch, Feng inquired as to events in his absence. He noticed that Blue Iris seemed distracted and said so, but she said she wasn't feeling well and went on serving the caramelized chicken. Feng changed the subject willingly, having only just learned the news about Kan.

"Suicide! What I'd give to know what was going through Kan's head! I always said he had secrets, but I never thought he'd do something like this."

Neither Cí nor Blue Iris said a word. So Feng changed the subject again.

"And you, Cí, what are your plans now that your employer isn't around anymore?"

Cí couldn't bring himself to look Feng in the eye, especially with Blue Iris right there.

"Go back to the academy, I suppose."

"Go and eat stale rice again? Not a chance. You'll stay on with us here. Right, Iris?"

She said nothing, except to order the servants to take away the empty plates. Then she stood up and said she was going to retire, and when Feng offered to accompany her, she flatly refused the offer.

"You must excuse her," said Feng as Blue Iris went off alone. "Women act oddly sometimes. But anyway, you'll have plenty of time to familiarize yourselves now!"

Cí found it impossible to swallow his mouthful and spit it into a bowl before getting to his feet.

"Apologies," he said. "I'm not feeling my best either." And with that, he went to his room.

Cí's thoughts were clouded—he felt awful about what he'd done, and Feng was being so generous by offering a place in his home. Feng didn't deserve this deceit. Could Cí just own up? No, because of the harm it would obviously cause Blue Iris. The worst part was that the damage had been done, and nothing could change it. Still, he needed to do something.

Cí left his room, determined to speak to Feng—he wouldn't go so far as to reveal what had happened between him and Blue Iris, but he would tell him absolutely everything else. He found Feng drinking tea in his library, a spacious, comfortable, high-windowed room. There were books everywhere, and the way they sat in neat piles seemed to mirror Feng's relaxed attitude. A light breeze was entering, carrying the smell of jasmine. Feng smiled when he saw Cí and invited him to sit.

"Feeling better? Would you like some tea?"

Cí accepted the tea Feng offered. He took a sip and then blurted out, "Kan employed me to spy on Blue Iris."

"On my wife?" Feng almost dropped his teacup.

Cí assured Feng that when he accepted the job, he had no idea who Blue Iris was. Then, when he found out, he tried to get out of the job, but Kan had blackmailed him.

"How?" asked Feng.

"By detaining Ming," said Cí eventually.

Feng was half dumbfounded and half indignant. His lips quivered.

"That man!" he roared, getting to his feet. "If he hadn't killed himself, I swear I'd rip him to pieces myself!"

Cí bit his lip, then looked Feng in the eye.

"Kan didn't kill himself."

"Eh? There are doubts? What about the suicide note?"

"Yes, I know. Even Bo said the handwriting was indisputably Kan's."

"Well?" said Feng. "So what are you saying?"

Cí said he might want to sit down for this. It was time for the truth. Then the emperor would have to be told.

He recounted the details of his examination of Kan's corpse, beginning with the rope around the councilor's neck.

"Plaited hemp. Slim but strong. The same as they use to hang up pigs."

"Very fitting," muttered Feng.

"Yes, but the thing is, I spoke to Kan the previous afternoon, and nothing that was in his demeanor fits the profile of a potential suicide."

"People change their minds. Maybe his guilt overcame him later in the day. He fell apart."

"And then went out before dawn to find a rope like that? If he'd really been overcome by anguish, he'd have used the first thing that came to hand. There were curtains, dressing gown ties, silk sheets—all kinds of things he could have knotted and used if he'd really been suddenly overcome. But no, in a moment of pure desperation, he goes out searching for this quite unusual plaited hemp rope…"

"Or sends someone to get it for him. It's hardly grounds for suspicion, particularly in the context of a full confession."

"Nowhere in the note did he actually say he was going to kill himself."

Feng cocked his head.

"Go on."

"It says he's guilty of the murders," continued Cí. "But that's all."

"I don't know. I'm not sure it would be a good idea to take something this flimsy to the emperor."

"There's more. His clothes, for a start. Beautifully folded and placed neatly on the table."

"Again, that might not mean anything. You know as well as I do that people often take their clothes off before hanging themselves. And, if you're saying you think it proves other people were in the room, I'm sure they were—at some point. After all, we're not talking about a commoner here, but an Imperial Councilor. Such a man would never deign to fold his own clothes."

Cí felt suddenly stupid but was heartened that at least it was his old teacher correcting him. And he hadn't finished yet.

"Forgive me if I seem arrogant," he said, "but what about the dresser?"

"What dresser?"

"Well, it *seems* Kan stood on a dresser before hanging himself. But it was so heavy. I tried moving it and couldn't! It would have needed at least two people, maybe even three, to shift it."

Feng frowned.

"It really weighed that much?"

"More than Kan. Why would you bother moving something as heavy as that when there are plenty of chairs?"

"I couldn't say. Kan was a large man; maybe he thought he would break a chair standing on it."

"A man who's about to kill himself is worried about the furniture?" Cí paused. "Anyway, there's more. The rope, OK, it was new. Never used. And yet, a stretch of it showed chafing. Two cubits, between the knot and the end. It just so happens, that's *exactly* the distance I measured between Kan's heels and the floor!"

"Sorry, you've lost me now."

"OK. If he really had hanged himself, he would have tied the rope to the beam, put his head through the loop, and then jumped from the dresser. But then the rope would not have had this chafing." Cí stood to try and present the scene as he saw it. "In my view, Kan was lying down, unconscious, before someone hanged him. In all likelihood, he'd been drugged. Two or three people lifted him up onto the dresser before introducing his head into the loop, then threw the end of the rope over the beam and pulled on the rope to lift Kan into the air. Kan's weight as he was lifted was what caused the chafing; that's why it's exactly the same length as the distance I measured between his feet and the ground. That's the distance over which his weight would have exerted pressure on the rope running over the beam."

Feng squinted.

"And what makes you think he was drugged first?" he asked quietly.

"An almost unarguable detail. The trachea wasn't fractured. Unthinkable in the case of a knot being situated beneath the Adam's apple and then supporting a very large weight thrown from such a height."

"Kan might have slipped rather than jumped."

"Might have. But if we enter into the scene as if it were a crime, there's no way Kan wouldn't have resisted, had he been conscious. No scratch marks, no bruising, no sign of any kind of a fight anywhere on his body. We might think about the possibility of a fatal poisoning. But his heart was still beating when he was strung up. How do I know? The skin at his throat reacted as only living skin does. The tongue was jammed hard against the teeth. The lips were blackish. He must have been drugged."

"Or they forced him to do it."

"I just can't see it. Whatever he was threatened with, when that rope was around his neck and he was hanging from a beam, his body took over. Instinctively, he tried to get free."

"His hands could have been tied."

"No marks to suggest it. Speaking of marks, I still haven't mentioned the most conclusive one." He glanced at the bookshelves and took down a dusty volume. Taking a cord from his shirtsleeve, he laid it along the length of the spine with the ends hanging free. "Watch," he said. He took both ends at once and stretched the cord abruptly, and then lifted the cord up for Feng to see. "See how the mark left in the dust by the cord is clearly defined? Now watch this." He repeated the action on another part of the broad spine, but this time shuffling it, making movements to simulate struggling. "See the difference?" The marks were wider and more diffuse. "When I climbed up to check the mark left by the rope on top of the beam, it was exactly like the first one. Clean, with no sign of any kind of agitation."

"This is all very surprising!" said Feng. "But why haven't you already told the emperor, since you've clearly already thought it through?"

"I wasn't totally sure," hedged Cí. "I wanted your opinion."

"The way you've related it, I can't see any doubts—well, maybe the note."

"On the contrary, it fits perfectly. Think about it! Kan lets two men into his quarters, men he knows and trusts. But once they're in, they threaten him and force him to admit guilt for the murders. Kan, fearing for his life, writes the note. There's no mention of his own death in the note because the men don't want him to know they're going to kill him. Once the confession is written, they offer him a drink to calm his nerves, a drink that's been laced with poison. This way they also avoid any noise from a struggle. Once he's passed out, they take his clothes off, drag the dresser over, and tie him up with the fine hemp rope—I'm thinking they brought such a fine one so it would be easier to conceal coming into the palace.

They lift him onto the chest and then hoist him up, technically still alive at this point."

Feng's jaw dropped. "Cí, this is exceptional work. We must communicate this to the emperor straightaway!"

But Cí wasn't so enthusiastic. He pointed out that it might bring attention back to Blue Iris.

"Remember what happened with the bloody sickle and the flies?" Cí found his voice turn tremulous at the memory. "I helped find the guilty party, yes, but I'll never forget that I lost a brother in the bargain."

"By the gods, Cí! That's in the past. Your brother condemned himself when he decided to kill a man. You only did what you had to, and anyway, I was the one who found the blood on the sickle; you're hardly solely responsible. As far as my wife goes, don't worry. I know the emperor, and I know how his mind works." Feng stood. "Oh, I forgot. I saw that new judge you were worried about in the palace this morning. Gray Fox, isn't it?"

Cí's heart fluttered.

"Forget about him," said Feng. "It's late now, but tomorrow we'll go to the emperor first thing, tell him about your discoveries and clarify your situation, too. I don't know what Gray Fox found out, but if he thinks he might use it against you, I'll see that he doesn't."

Cí thanked his old master. But he wasn't sure he should go with him to see the emperor. "Please don't be offended, but I imagine you'll also be talking about Blue Iris. That's private. I don't really think I should be there."

Feng admitted Cí had a point. But that didn't mean he was going to let him reject the offer of a room at the Water Lily Pavilion.

"There's no way I'm letting you go back to the academy," he said, adamant. "You'll stay with us here until your name is totally cleared."

Cí couldn't see any way of saying no.

Cí, Feng, and Blue Iris ate a light supper together, sharing an equally light conversation. Cí found it difficult to keep calm. Hard as he tried to control them, his hands kept bumping into Blue Iris's, and Feng's every smile felt like torture. As Cí chewed halfheartedly on the food, his mind turned again to the question of Kan's murder. Who might have done it? The *nüshi* sprang immediately to mind, and he couldn't help wondering if Feng would defend her so resolutely if he knew about her infidelity.

Before bed, Cí leafed through the *Ingmingji*, a manuscript on judicial process that Ming had written and which he'd borrowed from Ming's library. It contained descriptions of some of the most intractable cases in recent legal history. He was interested but soon found he couldn't keep his eyes open. He put the book away and immediately fell asleep, but not into restful dreams. Blue Iris was the only thing he saw.

And he saw her first thing in the morning, too. She came into his room without knocking. She placed a set of clothes at the foot of the bed and stood silently, waiting for something. Cí got out of bed. He was about to ask what she was doing, but she spoke first.

"You're going to need clean clothes, aren't you? If you're going to see the emperor."

Cí found himself so full of desire that he didn't even trust himself to speak. But she wasn't going away.

"What are you up to?" he asked.

"I'll wait for you in the dining room."

When he got downstairs, there was already food laid out: small, piping-hot rice cakes; cabbage salad; steamed vegetable buns. Cí was surprised that Feng wasn't there, but Blue Iris said he'd already gone to the palace. Cí nodded and sipped his tea. The light strained his puffy eyes. He glanced at Blue Iris. He had to get away from there.

He decided to go and see Ming, so he said good-bye to Blue Iris and headed to the palace. But on his way there he suddenly found himself surrounded by a group of soldiers. Before he could ask what was going on, one of them struck him across the face with a baton, drawing blood. The next thing he knew, he was on the ground being kicked and beaten. Soon his hands and feet were being tied, and then there was one last blow to his head—which meant that, by the time they announced he was being arrested for conspiring against the emperor, he was out cold and didn't hear a word.

33

Cí woke in a dimly lit cell with several filthy inmates, one of whom was on top of him, digging through his clothes as if to find a priceless treasure. Cí shoved the man off and sat up to get his bearings. There was something wet in his eyes. Blood, he realized, touching a hand to his sticky forehead. The ragged man jumped back on top of him, but a guard appeared out of nowhere and dragged the man off before hauling Cí to his feet. Cí, dazed, looked at the guard gratefully, but then the guard punched him across the face, knocking him to the floor.

"On your feet!" the guard ordered. Alongside him stood a giant of a man holding a club.

"He said get up!" said the man, hitting him with the truncheon.

Though he didn't feel the pain of the blow, and though he had no idea what was going on, Cí obeyed, bracing himself against the wall. Why had he been locked up, and why on earth was he being beaten like this? He began asking the men, but another blow came at him, this time to his stomach. He doubled over, winded.

Cí peered at them through the blood that had run down into his eyes. He could barely breathe. He wanted to ask for an explanation, but instead the first guard had a question for him: "Who did you have helping you?"

"Helping me do what?" he said, tasting blood as it dripped into his mouth.

Another blow with the club opened a cut in his cheek. Cí crumpled at the impact and fell to his knees.

"It's up to you: Tell us what we need to know now, and you can keep your teeth. Either that or we'll knock them out and you'll be on a porridge diet until they decide when to string you up."

"I don't know what you're talking about! Ask at the palace; I work for Kan!"

"You work for a dead man?" Another blow brought blood gushing from his mouth. "Well, then you can ask him yourself—in Hell!"

❦

When he came to again, someone was tenderly cleaning his head wounds. Through his blurry eyes, he saw that it was Bo.

"Wh…what's going on?" asked Cí.

Bo dragged him along the floor over to a wall, far from where anyone could hear. His face was etched with concern.

"What do you mean, what's happening? My God! You're all anyone's talking about at court. You're accused of Kan's murder!"

Cí blinked, trying to take this in. Bo dabbed at the blood on his forehead and gave him a sip of water. Cí gulped it down thirstily.

"They…they were beating me."

"I can see that! They almost killed you," he said, examining Cí's wounds. "Kan's body was examined this morning by Gray Fox, and in his view, it can't have been suicide. There was some fortune-teller with him who was willing to testify that you'd also killed some sheriff." Bo shook his head. "It's this Gray Fox who's accused you, but it's the emperor himself who ordered your arrest."

"But this is insane! You have to get me out of here. Feng knows—"

"Shh! The guards will hear."

"Ask Feng," hissed Cí. "He knows it wasn't me."

"You mean you've spoken with Judge Feng? What did you tell him?"

"The truth! Someone drugged Kan and hanged him." Cí buried his head in his hands.

"And that was all? You didn't say anything about the room with the bronze maker's studio remains?"

"What about the room? What's that got to do with anything?"

"Did you mention it to him or not?"

"Yes. No! Gods, I can't remember!"

"Damn it, Cí. If you're determined to be unhelpful, it will be a struggle to help you. You have to tell me *everything*."

"I have already."

"Stop playing dumb!" Bo threw the water glass to the floor, smashing it, and was silent for a few moments. "Sorry," he said. "Listen, Cí. You have to be completely honest with me. Are you sure you had nothing to do with Kan's death?"

"Of course I'm sure! What is it you want me to say?" he shouted. "That I killed him? On my parents' graves, no, but these animals are going to kill me whether I did it or not."

"Fine, have it your way," said Bo, getting to his feet. "Guards!"

The door opened immediately, and Bo left the cell.

Cí curled up on the floor. He couldn't understand why Bo seemed to think he was lying about Kan. He couldn't think straight. A deep tiredness consumed him, and soon enough he fell asleep.

When he woke, he didn't know what time of day it was, but he knew his shirt had been stolen. He glanced around, but none of the other prisoners were wearing it. He had no energy to try and look for it, and he crouched in the corner feeling ashamed, as always, at the scars and burns on his torso. After a moment, another prisoner came over and offered him a blanket. Cí accepted, and when he glanced over at the man, he noticed familiar marks on his face. When Cí peered closer, the man recoiled, confused. But Cí saw they were exactly the same kind of scars as those on the corpse of which he'd had the portrait made.

"What are they from?" Cí asked, gesturing to the tiny scars.

"It was New Year's," said the man when he realized Cí meant no harm. "I was…stealing from a rich home. Food. I was hungry. I was going through crates in the pantry, when all of a sudden, boom, they went off in my face! Just exploded."

Cí nodded for the man to continue.

"Fireworks! I was using a candle to see. Somehow I managed to light one. Never expected fireworks in the pantry…They nearly blinded me!"

Cí peered closer, shaking his head. The marks really were exactly the same. He wanted to ask if he'd ever met anyone else who had suffered the same injury, when two guards entered. The man moved quickly away, leaving Cí cowering.

"Up!" they said, but he was so weak they had to help him.

He shuffled behind them down a hallway so dark it felt as if they were at the bottom of a mine shaft. They came to a rusty old door, and when one of the guards stepped forward and knocked, Cí was gripped by a sudden certainty that this was his end. The door's creaking hinges sounded like a death sentence. He had a brief thought of attacking his captors to try and get away, but he had no energy to do anything of the kind. When they stepped through the door, the light blinded him, and it took a moment before he could see there was a person standing in front of him.

No…Could it be?

"Feng?" He fell forward into his old master's arms.

After the doctor left, saying Cí was lucky to be alive and instructing him to rest, Feng came and sat down on the bed beside him. It was Feng's own bed; he had insisted Cí be cared for in his private chamber.

"Those bastards," he said, shaking his head. "I'm sorry I didn't get to you sooner. I thought I'd gotten up early enough to see the emperor before anyone else could, but that Gray Fox fellow was there even earlier. It seems he came to the same conclusion as you about Kan's not killing himself, but it's also clear he's not very fond of you. He was so vehement in his accusations that they alone were enough to convince the emperor you killed Kan! He also had some flea-ridden fortune-teller with him, and there was some story about a sheriff you're supposed to have killed?"

"But—but I solved Kan's case!"

"That was partly what helped me get you free. I assured the emperor that only yesterday you had told me the very same details Gray Fox had brought up—the dresser, the marks on the rope, the confession note—and that we were going to tell him everything this morning. It wasn't easy to convince him, though. He made me swear on my name, and my honor, and only then did he say I could keep you in my custody. The trial's tomorrow."

"The trial? So he didn't believe you?"

Feng sighed. "Gray Fox has done everything to find motives and condemn you. He found out that the emperor had offered you a place in the administration if you solved the case, and his argument was that killing Kan was the simplest way for you to do just that. And that you're the only one who benefits from Kan's death. Then there's this fortune-teller."

"That man's a liar! You know full well—"

"It doesn't matter what I know. What matters is they currently believe Gray Fox. And I'm finding it hard to think of evidence, hard evidence, to prove your innocence. And apparently there are a number of witnesses who saw the two of you arguing recently—including the emperor."

Cí grimaced. His head was pounding. Feng left him to rest for a while, and he fell asleep in a whirl of fear. In his dreams, Lu kept appearing.

Waking to voices outside the window, Cí staggered over and braced himself against the ledge. He was so unsteady he thought he should lie down again, but then he saw two figures crouched down in the foliage. They glanced around nervously and spoke in sharp whispers. He couldn't make out actual words, but the tone was clearly accusatory. Carefully and quietly, he got on his tiptoes to peer through the plants and trees to try and see who was there. He could hardly believe it, but the two figures in the bushes were Bo and Blue Iris.

He went back over to the bed and lay down again, trying to clear his head, trying to figure out some way through the labyrinth he was stuck in. All he knew for certain, for now, was that Feng was the one person he could definitely trust. Several minutes later, there was a knock at the door, and in stepped Blue Iris.

"How are you feeling?" she asked coldly.

Cí said nothing. Blue Iris stood in the doorway looking impassive, emotionless, as if they hardly knew each other, before walking over to the bedside table and putting down a tray with a pot of tea and a cup. Her hands were trembling.

"Me?" he said. "I'm fine."

She began to pour a cup of tea.

"Oh, something I've been meaning to ask: How do you know Bo?"

She almost dropped the teapot.

"Sorry," she stammered, mopping up the spilled liquid. "That happens," she said, gesturing at her eyes to indicate her blindness. "Bo? I don't think I know anyone by that name."

Cí said nothing more; he was going to need every advantage he could get.

"We haven't had a chance to talk about the other night," said Cí.

"What about it?"

"Sleeping together. Though I suppose it's nothing out of the ordinary for you."

She went to slap him, but he caught her wrist.

"Let go," she cried. "I'll scream!"

Cí let go just as Feng walked through the door calling Cí's name. Blue Iris cleared her throat as she moved away from the bed.

"I spilled the tea," she explained.

Feng seemed oblivious to any tension. He simply helped his wife wipe up the tea and then held the door for her, seeing she got out all right. When she'd gone, Feng said Cí looked much improved, but he was still concerned; the trial the next day was only getting closer, and he hadn't been able to figure out anything in terms of Cí's defense.

It occurred to Cí to mention Bo's and Blue Iris's encounter, but he was sure that would only make it more likely Feng would find out that Cí had slept with his wife.

Feng put aside his own worry to reassure Cí. "Try to be calm. Think of the lake during the storm: its surface will be ruffled by the rain and wind, but there's stillness far down in the depths."

Cí looked in Feng's old eyes and found courage there. Then he shut his eyes and sought deep within himself the self-possession he knew he needed.

When he opened his eyes, he told Feng he was certain about one thing: It would be a mistake to let the whole case center on Kan alone. The real enigma still lay in the other murders, or, rather, what might link them together. The eunuch, the old man with the corroded hands, the young man of whom he'd had the portrait made, the bronze maker. There must be a connection more substantial than just the perfume and the strange wounds in their torsos. But he still hadn't found it.

Suddenly, everything around him disappeared. The room seemed to go dark. In his mind's eye, the four corpses stepped forward in turn.

First he saw Soft Dolphin, whom he imagined bent over the salt trade accounts, the same work Cí's father had carried out under Feng. The eunuch was making notes of consignments, surpluses, distribution, costs. At some point he came across something that didn't add up. And after that, the accounts changed and profits began to fall.

Next, the man with the corroded hands and the tattoo. Salt corrosion. Cí imagined him with his hands thrust into a pile of the pulverized mineral. But he'd also found fragments of carbon under his nails, hadn't he? So he must have worked with both products…mixing them together skillfully, with all the care of a Taoist alchemist.

Then the portrait man, whose wounds were the same as those of the prisoner who'd had fireworks go off in his face.

The last image was of the bronze maker, whose workshop had gone up in flames on the night he was killed. And there was that mysterious mold for a scepter. A bronze scepter…

Cí's mind lit up.

That was it! Salt, carbon, an explosion—he saw the link! The ingredients of an unusual and dangerous compound.

His heart was pounding.

"Feng!" he said excitedly, getting up from the bed and throwing on some clothes. "The key isn't whatever weapon the murderer used; it isn't the perfume used to cover up the smell! The corpses weren't disfigured only to hide their identities; it was also to hide their *jobs*! It's their *jobs* that hold the key!"

"Slow down, slow down," said Feng. "Tell me what you're thinking."

"Gunpowder! That's the key!"

"Gunpowder?" Feng looked quizzical. "For fireworks at New Year? What on earth could that have to do with anything?"

"How could I have missed this?" said Cí. He sat back down on the bed and started to explain everything.

<hr/>

"I came across a treatise named the *Ujingzongyao* while I was at the academy. It's all about wounds inflicted on combatants. Do you know it?"

"Never heard of it," said Feng.

"Ming said it probably wasn't very well known. It was commissioned by Emperor Renzong and compiled at the Zeong Gongliang and Ding Du Universities, and it was only meant for military eyes. Now that I think of it, I remember Ming saying something about the current emperor prohibiting further editions, yet neither of us could figure out why. Anyway—"

"And it has something to do with these murders?"

"Yes! Well, maybe. I remember there was a chapter about the possible *military* applications of gunpowder."

"As in...rockets?"

"No, not exactly. Rockets aren't much more than arrows with a bit of propulsion in their tail; they can go farther than a normal arrow, but try aiming them at a target! No, this chapter talked about something far more lethal." Cí pictured the illustrations from the *Ujingzongyao*. "Renzong's artillerymen found a way of using gunpowder in bronze rather than bamboo cannons. Before, they'd only been able to shoot bits of leather, grapeshot, excrement, that kind of thing; but the bronze meant they could send up rocks, boulders even, and in that way knock down battlements and so on. At the same time, the Taoist alchemists discovered that changing the proportions of the gunpowder—upping the amount of nitrate, I think—made a much bigger and more efficient explosion."

"OK…" said Feng.

"If I had the book here I could be more precise, but I do remember, yes, there were three types of gunpowder they used: incendiary, explosive, and propulsive, and it all depended on the proportions of sulfur, carbon, and saltpeter."

Feng looked bemused.

"Don't you see?" said Cí. "The scepter isn't a scepter at all; it's the most awful kind of weapon! It's like a cannon, but one you can carry around!"

"*What* scepter?"

"Sorry," said Cí, and he explained to Feng about the mold from the wreckage at the bronze maker's workshop, the positive he'd made from it, and how he'd thought, until now, that it was some kind of scepter. "Now everything makes sense. The unusual wounds on the corpses; the strange pockmarks on the face of one and on the hands of another. Some kind of hand cannon did all this!"

"It would explain a lot," said Feng, truly stunned. "And if we can present the mold in the trial—"

"I don't have it anymore. It was in my room, but someone came in and stole it."

"Here? In my house?"

Cí nodded. Feng pursed his lips.

"But luckily," said Cí, "I've still got the plaster positive I made. It's at the academy." He took the key from around his neck and handed it to Feng. "I must stay and write my defense. I hate to ask, but can you get it? It's in Ming's quarters. A servant named Sui knows where. I'll write a note to Sui authorizing him to give it to you."

Feng nodded. "I'll go later," he promised. As he headed out, he turned to Cí with a smile. "Try and get some rest."

Cí let out a massive sigh. This nightmare he'd been living finally felt like it was ending.

Having written the notes for his defense as well as a note authorizing Feng to retrieve the plaster cast, Cí tried to relax. But to no avail. He couldn't get Blue Iris out of his mind. Seeing her with Bo had sparked all kinds of questions. If the two of them were collaborating, it was very likely she had ordered the mold to be stolen and that Bo was the accomplice she'd needed for all the murders.

Cí felt his pulse quicken. Though he now had the plaster positive of the hand cannon as a part of his defense, he still felt danger was all around him.

While he waited for Feng to return, he asked a servant to bring him the copy of the *Ingmingji*, Ming's book on judicial processes, from his room. Given that he was going to have to defend himself in the court, he thought he should read up on similar cases.

The servant brought the book, and Cí skipped straight to the part about legal disputes. Ming had compiled lawsuits representative of every area of law: the first two-thirds of the book were taken up with inheritance disputes, divorces, commercial transactions, and disagreements over boundaries, but the last third was exclusively about prominent penal cases—notable either for the significance of the crime itself or for the brilliance of the judge's argument. These were the cases that interested Cí. Ming had provided extremely clear commentaries on the progress of each of the cases—beginning with a brief overview of the crime and continuing with the full crime report, the judge's investigations, any further fieldwork, the judgment and sentencing, and then any appeals and details of the execution of the sentence. Just as any attempt on the emperor's life—or the lives of any in his retinue—was punishable by death, so were arms trafficking offenses. This did little to calm Cí.

As he was running through these summaries, he came to one that stopped him cold:

> *An account of the inquiry carried out by the right honorable Judge Feng on the slaughter of a country peasant in a rice field and the surprising resolution of the case through the observation of flies around a sickle. Date: third moon of the seventh month, thirteenth year of the reign of Xiaozong.*

Cí checked the date again. He couldn't believe it.

In the account, Feng, then a new member of the judiciary, had won wide acclaim for the shrewdness he'd demonstrated in a case—a case that was all too familiar to Cí. The criminal had been flushed out from dozens of suspects by lining up all their sickles in the sun, placing a slab of meat nearby to attract a swarm of flies, and shooing them so that they flew over and gathered around the one sickle that had blood on it.

Cí shut the book. He felt as though demons had taken up residence inside him, and his hands trembled violently. Xiaozong was the current emperor's grandfather, and in the thirteenth year of his reign, Cí worked out, Feng would have been thirty. But this account was exactly the same as his brother's case. An exact replica.

His vision went blurry.

He read the case through again, all the while asking himself how he could have been so stupid. How could he not have seen it? His brother had been found guilty not because of the chance appearance of a swarm of flies, nor because of Feng's astuteness. On the contrary, thought Cí. The whole thing must have been a setup. Someone had used the exact same strategy before. And that someone was Feng.

But why?

Thinking Feng must still be somewhere in the pavilion, Cí headed out to find him. But when he came to the exit, a servant he hadn't seen there before blocked his way. Cí could see the man was a foreigner, and he looked familiar, but it took him a few moments to remember—he was the same Mongol aide who had accompanied Feng when he came to the village.

The Mongol stood in front of Cí. "Master says you are to stay here," he said.

Cí knew that even if he were at full strength he wouldn't have a chance against the well-built Mongol.

He went back to Feng's room and shut the door behind him. Then he went over to the window. Two sentries had been posted outside, and he didn't think he'd survive the jump anyway. Not in his state.

Aside from the desk and the bamboo sofa, all Feng's room had in it was books. Pacing around, Cí saw that not all of them were on legal matters, though. One corner was dedicated entirely to books on salt. He knew Feng had left the judiciary to concentrate on bureaucratic tasks related to salt, and he also knew, of course, that Blue Iris's family business was salt export, but such a collection of writing on one subject suggested far more than a merely professional interest. Cí took a closer look. Most of the books were on extraction processes, possible applications of the substance, and commerce, and there were a few on salt as a seasoning, for preservation, and in medicine. There was one book with a green cover that stood out to Cí, and when he pulled it off the shelf and saw the title, he could hardly believe it: it was the *Ujingzongyao*, the book on military techniques about which he'd told Feng just moments before—and about which Feng had claimed to have no knowledge. He ran a finger along the book spines until he came to one that was jutting out slightly. Cí wondered if this meant Feng had consulted it recently, and he decided to have a look.

At the very first paragraph, his blood froze. In fact, it was nothing but a list of accounts detailing the buying and selling of consignments of salt, but it was the handwriting, the distinctive style of the calligraphy, that caused Cí to shudder. He could have written it himself. But he knew that wasn't the case. The name and the signature at the end of each balance sheet were not his own, but his father's.

He went on reading the accounts, barely knowing what he was doing.

They went back over a five-year period. In fact, they contained the exact same numbers as the volume he'd consulted in the finance archives. This was some kind of parallel account, identical to the original. Cí closed the volume and ran his fingers over the page edges. Most of the pages were closed tightly together, but two parts of the book were less so—the parts Cí thought must have been consulted most often. He opened the book at the first of these sections, finding the numbers there had to do with the same strange fluctuations he'd found originally in Soft Dolphin's file. He went to the other well-thumbed section, examined the numbers closely, and found that the pattern was similar, with profits dropping to an all-time low. From that day on, it was no longer Cí's father's signature on the pages, but Soft Dolphin's.

He squeezed his eyes shut so tightly that he felt as if his eyeballs were going to burst. What could it all mean? He went over the numbers again but couldn't understand.

Suddenly there was a noise behind him; he hurriedly tried to return the book to its place but dropped it in his nervousness. In the very same instant that Cí picked the book up off the floor and slotted it back in place, Feng came in carrying a tray of fruit. Although Feng didn't seem to have noticed his hurried movement, Cí saw to his horror that a page had fallen from the book. With his foot, he slid it under the base of the bookshelf.

"Have you finished your notes?" asked Feng from the far end of the room.

"Not quite," lied Cí, hurrying over to the desk and stuffing the authorization he'd written into his sleeve. He began writing again, but Feng noticed that he was trembling.

"Has something happened?"

"Nerves," he said. "The trial." He rewrote the authorization for Feng to give to Sui and handed it to Feng.

"Here, have some fruit," said Feng. "And I'll go and get the plaster hand cannon."

On his way out, he stopped to ask again if Cí was all right. Cí murmured that he was.

As Feng turned again to leave, shrugging, Cí noticed that something had caught his eye—something in the library. Feng went straight over to the shelf where Cí had been. Alarmed, Cí noticed that the sheet he'd tried to hide was poking out from under the bookshelf. Surely that was what had drawn Feng's attention. But Feng lifted his hand to the book itself. Cí held his breath. The book was upside down. Feng frowned and put it back the right way up, leaving it, as before, jutting out a little from the rest. Then he bid Cí farewell and went out.

Once he was sure Feng wasn't coming back in, Cí went straight over and picked up the fallen piece of paper. He found it wasn't a page from the book, but rather a letter Feng must have slipped in there. Its stamp was his father's, from their village. He unfolded it and began reading.

Dear Feng,

Though there are still two years left of my mourning period, I wanted to let you know of my strong desire to return immediately and serve under you again. As I've said in previous letters, Cí is keen to take up his studies at the university, a wish I share.

In the name of both your honor and my own, I cannot accept being accused of these disgraceful actions. I am innocent. Nor will I stay in this village and leave you to endure or try to cover up these rumors of embezzlement. They who accuse me of corruption are themselves ignominious, and I am not afraid of them. I am innocent and want to prove it.

As luck would have it, I kept copies of the irregularities in your accounts. These constitute clear refutations of the accusations.

There's no need for you to come to the village. If, as you say, you are against my returning to Lin'an because you want to protect me, I beg of you, permit me to return so that I can bring this evidence forward and defend my own name.

Your humble servant.

Cí was utterly dumbfounded.

Cí's father believed himself innocent; Feng knew that Cí's father believed himself innocent. But when Cí had told Feng about the university's refusal to issue him a Certificate of Aptitude because of his father's dishonor, Feng had acted as though Cí's father *had* been guilty.

Cí took a deep breath, trying to get clear what might in fact have happened during Feng's visit to the village. If his father had his mind set on going back to Lin'an, why the change? What kind of terrible pressure would have been exerted for him to renounce his honor and accept the charges? Why did Feng even come to the village after Cí's father had said not to? And how did Lu's conviction fit into it?

The main thing Cí felt was regret. He'd distrusted his own father at the first opportunity. He felt himself, not his father, to be the real disgrace. A small cry escaped him.

Hateful thoughts threatened to swallow him up, but he tried to remain calm. What was Feng's role in all of this? He knew that this man, who had recently treated him like a son, was in fact a miserable traitor—that much was clear—but he still hadn't worked out Feng's exact place in the labyrinth.

Getting to his feet, putting the folded letter away in an inside pocket, he started looking for answers.

First he searched Feng's room from top to bottom—on shelves, behind paintings, under carpets—looking for other documents or anything else that might be of use, but he found nothing. Then he went over to the desk. The top drawers contained mainly writing materials, stamps, and blank paper. Nothing of interest—except for a drawstring pouch containing a small amount of black powder. Cí sniffed it and sneezed: gunpowder. A lower drawer was locked. He thought about smashing it but, not wanting to leave any marks, opted to remove the drawer above it and reach down through the gap. He found a wooden panel in the way. He looked around the room, his eyes alighting on the serrated fruit knife Feng had brought. He managed to saw a hole in the panel and squeezed his hand through this. His finger brushed against some kind of fragments. He thrust his hand further in, tilted the desk back so that the pieces would roll into his hand, and pulled them out. Here was another thing he could barely believe: In his palm lay pieces of ceramic, exactly the same green ceramic as the pieces stolen from his room. Among them was a tiny globe of stone covered in dried blood, and this was what truly astonished him.

He tried to leave everything exactly as he'd found it, then slipped out, taking the evidence from the drawer and the trial book hidden in his pockets and sleeves.

Safely back in his own room with the door shut, Cí took out everything he'd brought from Feng's room and began examining them.

The remnants of the mold weren't new to him, but on closer inspection he saw that the little stone globe that had been among them had small wooden splinters stuck in it. Its surface was cracked, as if it had undergone some kind of impact. His heart leaped. He hurried over to his tools and equipment, where he had the other objects he'd been collecting during the investigation, and took out the small bag containing the splinters he'd found in the wound of the man with the corroded hands. His own hands trembled as he held these shards up against the little globe. The splinters completed it. There was no mistake: They were of a piece.

For one brief moment, he thought he had sufficient evidence to unmask Feng in front of the emperor. But Feng was no amateur. As he now knew all too well, Feng was capable of manipulation of the highest order. It was possible he also had enough cruelty to murder several people. Moreover, Cí had already shown Feng all his cards. He needed more evidence. He needed help.

Who can I turn to?

Blue Iris…He still didn't know where Blue Iris fit into the puzzle, but at that moment she seemed like his only possible chance.

He found her sitting in the salon. She looked relaxed, her gaze in some far-off place only she knew; a cream-colored cat purred in her lap. Hearing Cí come in, she let the cat jump down and turned her head in his direction. Her grayish eyes looked more beautiful to him than ever.

"Do you mind if I join you?" he asked.

She gestured to the divan across from her.

"Have you recovered?"

"I'm much better," he said. "But there's something I'm much more worried about than my health. And I think it should be of concern to you, too."

"Go on," she said, emotionlessly.

"I saw you with Bo. This morning, in the gardens. I have to presume you were discussing something very serious for you to lie to me about not even knowing him."

"I see!" she shot back at him. "Not content with spying, now you dare to accuse as well! You should be ashamed. Since the moment you turned up in this house, all we've had from you is one lie after another."

Cí went quiet; this had gotten off to a bad start. His instinct was still that Blue Iris was the only person he could trust. He apologized for being so forthright, but he was desperate, he said.

"Strange as it might seem, my life is in your hands. I really need to know what you and Bo were talking about."

"And why would I want to help you? Lies, lies, and more lies, that's all I know about you. Now Bo accuses you and—"

"Bo?"

"Well, in a way," she said, and then went quiet.

"Tell me what happened!" he implored, getting to his feet. "Don't you understand? It's my life that's being played with here!"

"Bo said…Bo told me…" She was trembling now like a frightened child.

"What?" shouted Cí, shaking her by the shoulders. "What did he tell you?"

"He suspects Feng!" At this, she covered her face and broke down.

Cí let go of her. It was the best answer he could have hoped for, but he didn't know what to do with it.

He sat down next to Blue Iris and wanted to embrace her, but something stopped him.

"Iris...Feng is not a good person. You should—"

"And what do you know about good people?" She turned her teary eyes in his direction. "Were you the one who stood by me when the world rejected me? Who nursed me and looked after me all these years? No. You had me for a night, and suddenly you think that gives you the right to order me around. Just like all the rest! Get you in bed, treat you like a dog. No! You don't know Feng. He's cared for me. There's no way he could have done all the terrible things Bo was saying..." She broke down again.

It upset Cí to see her like this, and he imagined that perhaps her pain, which had everything to do with questioning someone she trusted, was somewhat similar to his own.

"Feng isn't who he says he is. And it's not only me who's in danger. Unless you help me, you will be, too."

"Me, help you? Wake up, Cí!" Her eyes, bursting with desperation, glanced from side to side. "I'm a blind, ill-fated, old whore—how can I possibly help you?"

"All I need is for you to come to the trial tomorrow and testify. Just be brave and tell the truth."

"That's all?" she said bitterly. "It's easy to be brave when you're young and you've got two seeing eyes! Do you know what I am, really? I'm nothing! Without Feng, I'm absolutely nothing."

"As much as you might want to ignore it, the truth will always be the truth."

"Which truth? Your truth? Because the truth for me is that I need him. That he's looked after me. What husband doesn't get it wrong sometimes? Who's perfect? You, perhaps?"

"Damn it, Iris! These aren't any old mistakes we're talking about here. We're talking about murder!"

She shook her head and began murmuring incomprehensibly. He knew he'd get nowhere by pressuring her.

"I can't make you do anything," he said. "It's up to you. You can come to the trial tomorrow, or you can tell Feng everything when he gets back. But nothing you do will change the truth. The reality is that Feng's a criminal. And your action, or inaction, will follow you wherever you go, your whole life—if being by that man's side is what you call a life."

He got up to leave, but Blue Iris grabbed his arm.

"Do you know what, Cí? You're right. Feng knows an infinite number of ways for a person to die. And be sure that you're going to experience the worst of them, when it's time for him to have you killed."

34

Cí barely slept. It was a long night, but not long enough to contain all the self-loathing he felt, or his newfound hate for Feng. With the first rays of sun, he got out of bed and started getting ready. He'd poured all his energy into preparing a case that would shine light on Feng's iniquity, but he still knew there was a very good chance the emperor wouldn't believe a word of what he said.

The time came for them to leave, and Feng was waiting for him at the door, dressed in his magistrate's robes and winged cap. He also wore an affable smile that Cí now knew was pure deceit. Cí managed a halfhearted greeting, saying he'd had a restless night. An Imperial escort awaited them outside. Seeing their weapons, Cí mentally ran through his own: the book of trials, his father's letter, the pouch containing the gunpowder, and the small, blood-spattered stone that he'd found in Feng's drawer. As they went out, he turned, hoping Blue Iris would be coming to support him. But as they left the Water Lily Pavilion, the *nüshi* didn't even wave them off.

As they walked, Cí did his best to avoid speaking to or even look-ing at Feng. He had to maintain his composure, but one more false smile from the old man and Cí didn't know if he'd be able to stop himself from pouncing on Feng and tearing his heart from his chest.

They arrived at the court and Feng took his place alongside the other members of the High Tribune, on the prosecution side. Cí came and stood beside Gray Fox. He wasn't surprised by his adversary's exaggerated look of triumph; he'd succeeded in having Cí arrested, and their colleagues in the judiciary were all there to see the humiliation. Cí was made to kneel before the empty throne. He was trembling as he touched his forehead to the floor. Then a gong signaled Ningzong's entrance. The emperor, dressed in a red tunic inlaid with golden dragons, came forward flanked by a large retinue, the Supreme Councilor for Rites and the new Councilor for Punishments foremost among them. Cí, still prostrate, waited to be told what to do.

Once the emperor was seated, an elder with a bonnet pulled down over his eyebrows and an oiled mustache came forward to announce the Celestial Majesty and outline the accusations.

"As the Official of Ancient Justice at the palace, and by consent of our most honorable and magnanimous monarch, Ningzong, Heaven's Son and Lord of Earth, thirteenth Tsong Emperor, on the eighth moon of the month of the pomegranate and the first year of the Jiading era, nineteenth of his dignified and wise reign, I hereby declare the initiation of the trial against Cí Song. He is accused of conspiracy, treachery, and the murder of Imperial Councilor Kan Chou, which—and this element is not open to appeal—entails the charge of treachery and an attempt against the emperor." The man paused, looking around the room. "In accordance with the laws set out in the *Songxingtong*, the accused has the right to defend himself. He may not have the assistance of any other person. And he may not be condemned until he confesses."

Cí, still prostrate, listened in silence and tried to weigh the allegations.

Next, the floor was given to Gray Fox. Cí's rival, after complimenting the emperor and obtaining his blessing, took out a number of sheets of paper and laid them out in an orderly fashion on the table he was sharing with Feng. Then, with a self-satisfied attitude, he presented Cí's personal details and outlined the numerous pieces of evidence that, in his opinion, demonstrated Cí's guilt.

"Before I go into detail," he said, "please allow me to give you an idea of the character of this con man we see here before us. I had the misfortune of studying at the Ming Academy at the same time as the accused. There he demonstrated, not once but repeatedly, his inability to respect rules and regulations. This led to his condemnation and expulsion. The only thing that slowed down this process was his defense by the director, a well-known homosexual."

Cí cursed under his breath. Gray Fox had decided to attack him by undermining the integrity of anyone who might stand up for him. He thought of a comeback but knew he'd have to wait a while until the floor was given to him.

"Cí Song has rebellion and hate deep in his soul. The professors who sought to expel him confirmed the meanness of his conduct. It was they who had been so kind in allowing an urchin like him into the academy in the first place. He repaid their generosity by biting the hand that fed him." Gray Fox's face hardened. "I want to illustrate for everyone present the true character of a young man possessed by egoism and evil, who used diabolical tricks and barefaced scheming to hook Councilor Kan and even cloud our emperor's mind. Who convinced the former to put him in charge of a very sensitive investigation and the latter to offer him a place in the judiciary if he solved it."

Cí began to have serious concerns that Gray Fox might turn the emperor fully against him. If Ningzong was convinced, it would be even harder for Cí to make his own case. But now came his turn to speak. He had kept his forehead to the floor throughout Gray Fox's diatribe, and he spoke his first word in that position.

"Majesty," he said, and was invited to stand. "Majesty," he said again, getting to his feet, "Gray Fox has seen fit to attack my person with unfounded conjecture that furthermore has nothing to do with the present case. This trial isn't about my academic record or where I might have learned my forensic skills. The only thing being judged here today is my innocence or guilt in the murder of Councilor Kan. No matter what Gray Fox may think, I never came up with a self-serving plan, nor did I lie to, trick, or cloud anyone's mind. Various people will be able to confirm that I was brought to the palace by Your Majesty's soldiers; my intention that day had been to leave Lin'an. You yourself were present that day, Majesty, when I was given the task of investigating these murders, so you know better than anyone that I had no choice in the matter. And I ask: Why would a man as wise as Councilor Kan, and the Heaven's Son himself, place their trust in an undesirable such as myself? Why, when they had the pick of so many magistrates, would they oblige a plain student who lacked anything like the appropriate qualifications?"

Cí knelt and touched his forehead to the floor again, allowing his last statement to settle. He knew it was important to be measured and calm, just as Gray Fox had been. He had to sow doubt in the minds of everyone present and allow them space to provide the answers. All he had to do was pose the questions.

The emperor was stone-faced; his pale eyes and his severe expression seemed to place him on a plane of existence above and beyond good and evil. With a gesture of his hand, he indicated to the official to give the floor back to Gray Fox.

Gray Fox looked over his notes before proceeding.

"Majesty," he said, bowing until he received authorization to speak again. "I am more than happy to keep to the subject at hand." He smiled, taking one of the sheets of paper and placing it on top of the others. "I see in my notes that on the day of Kan's murder, mere hours before the act, the accused brandished a knife at him. He did it in plain sight. Furthermore, he also appropriated and brutally stabbed Soft Dolphin's corpse, splitting it in two."

"A dead body," Cí whispered, but loudly enough that everyone in the room could hear. This won him a blow from one of the guards.

"Yes," said Gray Fox, "a dead body, but just as sacred as a living one! Or perhaps the accused has forgotten the Confucian precepts that rule over our society?" Gray Fox's voice grew louder. "No, obviously he can't have forgotten, because something we also know about the accused is that he has a powerful memory. He knew the Confucian precepts very well, but simply chose to disobey them. He knows that to cut up a body is to attack the soul that still resides in it until the moment of burial, and I would say that anyone capable of treating a defenseless spirit in such a manner would be more than capable of attacking an emperor's councilor as well."

Cí gnawed his lower lip. He felt he was being corralled by Gray Fox's argument, and his destination was like an abyss with only two bridges: one represented death, the other, damnation.

"I'm no killer," Cí muttered through gritted teeth.

"No killer, really? On that note, I'd like to ask His Majesty's permission to bring in a witness."

The emperor again signaled agreement via the official.

A graying, wrinkled old man came in flanked by two sentries. His sloppy gait belied the richness of his robes, suggesting the latter had been borrowed for the day. Cí recognized the fortune-teller Xu, the man he'd worked for at the cemetery.

Gray Fox invited Xu to come nearer, read out his name, and swear to be truthful in his answers. Then Gray Fox turned to glance at Cí. Xu, though, was unable to look Cí in the eye.

"Before his testimony," said Gray Fox, "so that we can all understand the irrefutability of the accused's criminal nature, I feel obliged to read out the reports that followed Cí Song to Lin'an. These facts will leave us in no doubt of the accused's familiarity with crime.

"Two years ago, in the village of his birth, which is in Jianyang, the accused's older brother was found guilty of beheading a farmer. Cí, being possessed of the same infected, criminal blood as his brother, went on to steal three hundred thousand *qián* from a local landowner, an honorable man. Next, he fled with his younger sister to Lin'an, not knowing that he was pursued by a sheriff named Kao. I will skip the various crimes committed during his flight to Lin'an and merely go on to state that, in spite of the large amount of money they had with them initially, the pair soon fell into poverty. And it was then that this poor but generous man," he continued, pointing at Xu, "took pity on the vagrant brother and sister, giving the accused a job alongside him in the city cemetery.

"And, as Xu will confirm, soon after taking the accused on, a Sheriff Kao turned up at the cemetery asking after a fugitive named Cí. Xu, knowing nothing of his employee's crimes, and having been tricked as to his identity, protected him. As is his way, Cí responded to someone who had been good to him with betrayal. He abandoned his rescuer when he was most needed.

"A number of months later, Xu thought the episode over again and decided to see justice done. He went and told Sheriff Kao that Cí was at the Ming Academy. But Cí found Kao first and murdered him."

Now Gray Fox invited the fortune-teller to speak. Xu prostrated himself before the emperor.

"It is exactly as the most honorable magistrate says. This sheriff, Kao, asked me to show him where the academy was. Said he'd take Cí down if it was the last thing he did. I said I didn't want to get caught up in anything, but he talked me around. The night before he died, after I showed him where the academy was, I saw him come out with Cí. The two of them were walking together toward the canal. I noticed the sheriff was carrying a jar of drink. To begin with they seemed to be talking normally, but suddenly the discussion got heated. When the sheriff wasn't looking, Cí came up behind him, cracked him on the head, pushed him in the canal, and ran off. I ran to try and drag Kao out, but when I got there he was already under."

Hundreds of accusing eyes turned on Cí, and an indignant murmur went around. Cí tried to think of ways to counter these claims.

"This fortune-teller is lying!" he cried. "Majesty, with your permission, I shall demonstrate that this is not only slander but a wholesale attempt to trick *everyone* in this room."

The official looked to his sovereign in search of a gesture of disapproval for Cí's having spoken out of turn. But just as Cí had hoped, his suggestion that the emperor himself could be duped prompted Ningzong to make a sign for Cí to carry on.

Touching his forehead to the floor once more, Cí glanced at Gray Fox.

"I can't prove it alone," he said. "I call on Professor Ming to testify."

⚜

The pause in the proceedings while Ming was summoned felt to Cí like a brief victory. Making the emperor feel as though he was implicated, sowing doubt in his mind, not only meant Cí would now have Ming alongside him for advice and his testimony, but also that he could initiate the second part of his plan. This involved Bo's also taking the stand. With Feng against Cí, Ming ill, and Blue Iris nowhere to be seen, his hopes now hinged on Bo, who had been with him for the entirety of the investigation.

While they were waiting for Ming to arrive, Cí took Bo aside. Bo, though surprised to be asked for help, agreed to do what he could. Cí outlined his case, telling Bo everything he now suspected. Ming was brought in, and Bo disappeared.

Cí quickly filled Ming in on the proceedings; this was the first Ming had heard of the charges against Cí, and he was clearly struggling to take it all in. Again Cí prostrated himself before the emperor.

"Majesty, as you well know, Ming has for years been director at the academy. Its prestige is on par with that of the university. In fact, Gray Fox studied there…though I think I'm right in saying it took him six years to obtain the title most people get in two."

Ningzong frowned, apparently troubled that the prosecution wasn't as competent as he'd been led to believe—precisely Cí's intent.

"Ming is the epitome of trustworthiness," said Cí, still with his forehead to the floor. "He always conducts himself uprightly and honestly, and has done a great deal to add to the wisdom of many of Your Majesty's subjects. He is a man who cannot be doubted."

"And your questions?" prompted the official.

"Apologies," said Cí, turning to face his old master. "Master Ming, do you remember the day when several of us, your students, inspected the body of a sheriff found drowned in Lin'an?"

"Of course," said Ming. "It was a very unusual case, and the one that formed the basis of Gray Fox's elevation to his place at court. Two days before the end-of-term exams."

"And in the week leading up to exams, are students allowed to leave the academy at all?"

"Absolutely not. It is expressly forbidden. If special circumstances obliged someone to have to leave, the guard would note it down, and I happen to remember there was no such case that week."

"I see. And tell me, how do your students tend to go about preparing for these exams?"

"In the preceding week they will be in the library all day, and after that, studying into the wee hours in their rooms."

"And do you remember if, in my case, I was put with a roommate when I joined the academy?"

"Yes, of course you were. The same as any other student."

"Which is to say, my roommate would be a reliable source of information as to whether I had left at any time leading up to or on the day of the crime?"

"In effect."

"And, Master, would you mind relating the robbery that took place not long after the inspection of the sheriff's corpse?"

"Robbery? Ah, yes, you mean the robbery of your report. A most disagreeable episode." Ming now turned to address the emperor. "Cí's report revealed that this sheriff had in fact been murdered. But the report was stolen by his roommate, presented as his own, and used to try and gain the place that had been offered at court for whoever solved the case."

"And," said Cí, "just one more thing: Do you happen to remember the name of my roommate?"

"Of course. Gray Fox."

Gray Fox, crumpling his notes, let out a curse that couldn't be heard over the clamor now filling the room. Feng, standing beside Gray Fox, looked unmoved. He passed the younger man a note and whispered something in his ear. Gray Fox quickly read the note and nodded, then stepped forward to ask permission to cross-examine the witness.

"Esteemed Master," he said, once the noise in the room had died down and the emperor had given his consent to proceed. "Can you be totally sure that everything you've just said is the truth?"

"Of course!" said Ming, shocked.

"I see…All right, now would you mind telling me if you consider *yourself* to be an honorable person?"

"Of course."

"Sincere? A person with integrity?"

"This is preposterous! Of course I am all of those things."

"Not a man with vices?" asked Gray Fox.

Ming hung his head and didn't reply.

"I'm sorry," said Gray Fox, "did you not understand the question? Shall I ask again?"

"No," said Ming in a small voice.

"No what? No, you're not a man with vices, or no I don't need to repeat the question?"

"I am not a man with vices!" Ming nearly shouted.

"Oh, really?" said Gray Fox. "So it would be incorrect to say that you have an all-consuming preference for men? It would be quite wrong to say that three years ago, a youth by the name of"—he glanced down at the note Feng had given him—"Liao-San reported you for making passes at him?"

"That was an abominable lie! Liao-San tried to blackmail me for a place at the academy, and when I refused—"

"But the two of you were found naked together."

"Slander, and again I say, slander! It was a summer's night, I happen to sleep without clothes, and that boy broke in looking to blackmail me."

"Of course. But I also see in my notes that, two years ago, you were witnessed handing money to a well-known homosexual as the two of you entered a house of ill repute. And that led your own staff to recommend that you step down from your directorship."

"Damn it! The man you are calling homosexual was my nephew, the place we were seen going into was his hostel, a perfectly respectable establishment, and, as for the money, his family had asked me to lend him some. All this was confirmed when the academy staff sought my dismissal."

"Blackmail, slander, lies…" said Gray Fox, shaking his head. "Are you married, Ming?"

"You know the answer to that question."

"Have you ever dated?"

Ming hung his head, his lips trembling.

"I am not a degenerate…I merely…"

"You merely find men attractive?"

"I never…"

"Let me try to understand," said Gray Fox, coming closer. "So if it isn't a vice to love a man, how would you define it? Love?"

"Yes, it is a form of love," said Ming, defeated. "Is love a crime?"

"No, I don't think so," said Gray Fox. "Love is unconditional. Love asks nothing in return. Right?"

"Yes, yes, that's it," said Ming, opening his tired eyes, his gaze far off, as if pleading for understanding.

"So you'd do anything for love?"

"Anything," he said.

"Thank you, Professor Ming. That will be all."

Ming, visibly shaken, nodded that he understood.

Ming looked broken, and Cí felt terrible for having put him through all this. Gray Fox was positively purring. Two sentries came forward to escort Ming back to the infirmary, but just then Gray Fox looked up as though he'd remembered something.

"Oh, one last question." He paused, looking deep in Ming's eyes. "Could you tell us honestly if you are in love with Cí?"

Ming turned to look sadly at Cí.

"Yes," he answered.

If such a thing were possible, Gray Fox had just gone down in Cí's opinion. Such low-down tactics. With no better argument to make, he'd fallen back on attacking Ming, playing into the disgust most people felt about homosexuality. Ming's admission of his feelings for Cí had damaged his credibility rather than demonstrating his commitment to honesty.

Cí asked if he could cross-examine Xu.

"Majesty!" said Gray Fox. "The accused is trying to insult your intelligence! Xu's testimony couldn't be clearer: he saw Cí kill the sheriff, and that's all there is to it."

Ningzong seemed swayed by this, and Cí cursed at not having the chance to undermine Xu's credibility. But he tried not to let it get to him.

"In that case, I would like the men who found the sheriff's body to testify."

It turned out that Gray Fox himself had planned to call the same two men. Since they were already present and there would be no delay, the emperor assented. The two men were led in and confirmed their identities, and Cí began.

"Your job consists of patrolling the canals, is that correct?"

The pair nodded.

"Would you mind describing precisely what this involves, where you go, the frequency of your rounds, and so on?"

The elder of the two men spoke. "We patrol daily, checking the canals' cleanliness, the moorings, and the sluice gates. Our area is the southern part of the city, between the fish market, the rice market, and the city walls."

"And how long have you been in this job?"

"Thirty years, me. Him, ten."

"That's a lot of combined experience. I'm sure that makes a man very conscientious in his work. Anyway, whereabouts exactly did you find Kao's body?"

"I found him," said the younger man. "He was floating face-down in the secondary canal, not far from the market."

"On the south side of the city?"

"Of course. Like my colleague said, that's our area."

"And what direction does the current flow along the canals?"

"Northward, with the River Zhe."

"So, in your opinions, and with your long years of experience in mind, would you say that a body thrown in the canal to the north could possibly drift against the current?"

"Impossible. Even if it got snagged on something and was carried along, the sluice gates would stop it from getting very far."

"Impossible?" repeated the emperor.

The two men looked at each other.

"Absolutely, Majesty."

Cí turned to the emperor.

"Majesty, everyone knows Ming Academy is in the far north of the city. Xu said I pushed Kao in the canal nearest to the academy. Don't you think it might be worth finding out what might have compelled him to lie?

Gray Fox was ashen. Xu was brought back in—he cursed the whole room and kicked and struggled until a blow from a guard's baton brought him to his knees in front of the emperor. He grumbled and spit on the floor, casting baleful glances at Cí all the while.

"When you're ready," said the official to Cí.

To everyone's surprise, instead of facing Xu, Cí turned to Gray Fox.

"Do you remember the causes of the sheriff's death? Since the report that gained you entry to the judiciary detailed them, I imagine they are imprinted on your brain."

Gray Fox pursed his lips and pretended to consult his notes.

"I remember perfectly well," he said sardonically.

"And?" Cí said, as if he didn't know already.

"He died from a rod inserted through his ear and pushed into his brain."

"A metal rod?"

"Yes," bristled Gray Fox.

"Like this one?" Suddenly Cí leaped at the fortune-teller and fished out a long needle that was hidden in Xu's robes. A hush fell across the High Tribune.

Again, the color drained from Gray Fox's face. Cí showed the needle around and, in a fury, Gray Fox excused himself from the courtroom. Cí didn't let this knock him off course. He proceeded to accuse the fortune-teller of the murder of Sheriff Kao.

"Xu wanted the reward Kao was offering for my capture. But Kao was a wary man and would have been unlikely to hand over any money until Xu handed me right to him. I don't know whether Xu thought Kao was trying to trick him, or if perhaps the two of them argued, but the fact is, Xu killed Kao for the money, using the same murder weapon as he always uses." At this, he held the metal needle up to the room once more.

"Lies!" yelled Xu, which won him another blow from the guard.

"Lies, you say?" said Cí, turning to address the fortune-teller. "Witnesses have confirmed that the corpse was found near the fish market, which happens to be a stone's throw from the houseboat you live on. As for the reward money, I wouldn't mind betting that if His Majesty's men were to ask in the taverns and brothels in that same area, any number of people could confirm that poor, impoverished Xu was there throwing money around in the days following Kao's death."

Overcome, the fortune-teller couldn't even stammer out a defense. The look he gave the emperor asked for pity, but Ningzong was unaffected. He ordered that Xu be detained and adjourned the trial until after lunch.

When the trial resumed, Gray Fox was clearly intent on showing that he was still a worthy opponent. Feng stood alongside him, and the irony of his serene expression struck Cí even more strongly. When the emperor reentered the room, everyone bowed—everyone, that is, except for the woman who had also just entered the room. It was Blue Iris. She'd come.

Gray Fox asked permission to speak and stepped forward.

"Divine Sovereign: The fact that the despicable fortune-teller Xu tried to abuse our trust does nothing to exempt Cí of the crimes of which he is accused. On the contrary, that there is now only one murder charge against him, as I see it, clears the way for his guilt to be unveiled." Gray Fox turned to face Cí with a wicked look in his eyes. "Clearly, the accused was hatching a diabolical plan to end Councilor Kan's life. His idea was to dress the murder up as suicide, and he carried out the execrable plan with great meticulousness. This is the true face of Cí Song: friend to homosexuals, fugitive, murderer's companion."

With a discreet raising of his eyebrows, Ningzong motioned for the proceedings to continue. It was Cí's turn to take the floor again.

"First, Your Majesty," said Cí, coming forward and bowing, "I would like to repeat the fact that it wasn't I who sought to work under Kan; it was under Your Highness's orders that I joined the investigation. Now, I want to emphasize something that we see again and again in all the different legal handbooks, and that is the necessity of motive. Crimes require motives. Revenge, fits of rage, loathing, ambition—whatever it is, there has to be something that drives a man to kill.

"With this in mind, let's think for a minute about what could have driven *me* to kill Kan. Let us not forget, Your Majesty had promised me a place on the judiciary if I were to solve the murders prior to Kan's death." Cí turned to Gray Fox. "So, I ask: Does a man who is starving chop down the only apple tree in his orchard?"

Gray Fox was completely composed, which unsettled Cí. It was Gray Fox's turn to speak again.

"This is no place for wisecracks. You want to talk about motives? Fine, let's talk about them. There's actually only one piece of what Cí Song has said that is definitely true, which is the promise of a place on the judiciary if he solved the murders. So? Did you actually manage to uncover the murderer? I can't remember having heard you talk about it." Gray Fox's expression was the epitome of self-satisfaction. "Revenge, loathing, yes. You refer to these things but neglect to mention they were precisely the feelings Kan stirred up in you when he threatened your *beloved* Professor Ming! Oh, and let's talk about fits of rage, such as when you maimed Soft Dolphin's poor corpse! And ambition, what about ambition? You also fail to mention the most blindingly obvious thing: that Kan's suicide, with that rather...*opportune* confession note, was the only sure way—considering you had failed to actually solve the case—to win what the emperor had promised. I don't know what everyone else here thinks, but your rather dramatic image of the orchard keeper would, I think, be more apt if we replaced the tree with a cow, and think about the starving man slaughtering it for meat rather than making do with drinking its milk.

"But anyway, since you also bring up judicial handbooks, yes, why don't we think about something else stressed again and again in the literature when it comes to murder: opportunity. Why don't you tell us, Cí, where you were the night Councilor Kan died?"

Cí's heart was pounding. He glanced up at Blue Iris; that was the night they'd slept together. He knew he couldn't mention that, but he also knew if he said he was alone in his room, neither Gray Fox nor the emperor would be satisfied.

"If you don't mind my saying so," Cí began, "your argument has about as much sense as a stampede of elephants." Laughter traveled around the room. "What you neglect to mention is that Kan was both feared and disliked—everyone here knows it. There must have been dozens of people with far greater motives than those you so cheaply confer on me. Why don't we think about this for a minute? What kind of imbecile would disclose his own crime?" Cí paused. "I'll make it simpler for you: If I had been the murderer, why would I have been preparing to tell the emperor that Kan's death was anything but suicide, when that would have been the perfect cover?"

Cí felt he'd knocked down the last possible strut of Gray Fox's argument, but then he saw that the emperor looked unconvinced. Eyebrows arched, he looked disdainfully at Cí.

"You told me nothing!" boomed the emperor. "Gray Fox came to me and explained how it couldn't have been suicide."

Cí looked straight at Feng; Cí now knew the judge's final betrayal.

⚜

The evening rituals meant another interruption in the proceedings, which were set to resume the next morning. But the emperor had ruled that Cí had to spend the night in the dungeon, lest he try to flee.

No sooner had the guard locked Cí in his cell than Feng walked into the dungeon. He gestured for the guard to leave him alone with the prisoner. Before going outside, the guard chained Cí to the wall.

There was a bowl of soup on the floor between Cí and Feng. Cí hadn't eaten all day but had little stomach for food now.

"You must be hungry." Feng pushed the bowl toward Cí. "I'll help you sip some."

Cí kicked the bowl, and the soup went all over Feng's robes. Feng jumped backward. Wiping the soup off, he gave Cí a resigned look, like a father whose child has just vomited on him.

"Calm yourself," he said condescendingly. "I know you must be upset, but there's still a way to clear everything up." He came and sat beside Cí. "This has all gone quite far enough."

Cí couldn't even look at Feng. How could he once have considered such a man a father figure? If he hadn't been chained to the wall, he would have strangled him then and there.

"Fine, say nothing. I can understand how you feel. I understand entirely if you don't even want to listen to me and you'd rather just wait for Gray Fox to finish shredding you." He asked the guard to bring another bowl of soup, but when it was put in front of Cí, he kicked it away again.

"You eat it, you bastard!" shouted Cí.

"Oh, so you have still got your tongue! Listen to me now. There are forces at work here you don't know about. This trial isn't really about you. Trust in me and forget about trying to win. Kan's dead; what does it matter how? Just keep your mouth shut and wait for me. I'll step in and discredit Gray Fox, and you'll be off the hook."

"Just forget about it? Like it's someone else here in this cell, someone else who's had his ribs cracked?"

"Damn it, Cí. All I wanted was to keep you out of this so Gray Fox would take over the investigation. It would have been far easier if he hadn't been so envious of you and dragged you into it with these accusations."

"Why would I believe anything you say? Gray Fox said *he* worked out that Kan's death wasn't a suicide. And you said nothing about how *I* had explained it all to you!"

"I would have, if it would have done any good. If I'd broken cover then, it might have made the emperor doubt me somehow. And the most important thing, if I am going to help you, is for the emperor to continue to trust me."

For the first time since Feng had come in, Cí looked him in the eye.

"The same way you helped my father?" he spit.

Feng's jaw dropped. "I—I don't know what you mean."

"There's a piece of paper in the pocket inside my jacket. Reach in and get it."

Feng leaned toward Cí, pulled the paper out, and unfolded it, astonished. His hands trembled as he read it.

"Recognize that, by any chance?"

"Where did you find this?" Feng stammered.

"Is that why you prevented my father from coming back to Lin'an? Just so you could carry on embezzling salt shipments? And is that why you did away with the eunuch? Because he figured it out, too?"

Feng backed away as if confronted by a ghost, his eyes wide.

"How dare you? After all I've done for you!"

"You duped my father, you duped us all!" Cí strained at the chains. "You really expect me to be thankful?"

"Your father should have kissed my feet rather than crossing me." Feng's face still had the contorted look. "I raised him out of poverty! And you, I treated you like a son!"

"You would dirty my father's name by even speaking it!" The chains shook as Cí tried to get free.

"You really don't get it!" Feng bellowed, his eyes smoldering madly. "I nurtured you like the offspring I could never sire. I protected you! With the explosion, I allowed you to live! Why do you think it was only the others who died? I could just as easily have waited for you to get back." He reached out his trembling hand to stroke Cí's face.

Cí felt torn apart by Feng's words.

"What explosion? Wh—what do you mean, allowed me to live?"

He felt his world crumbling around him.

Feng stood with his arms outstretched, inviting Cí to embrace him.

"*Son*," he sobbed.

Cí moved toward Feng for the embrace. The instant he was close enough, he wrapped his chains around Feng's neck and pulled them tight. Feng kicked and struggled but couldn't get free. Cí strangled his old master with all his might. Feng's face turned blue, and saliva frothed from his lips. Cí knew Feng was near death, but just then, the guard rushed in and delivered a hard blow to Cí's head.

The last thing Cí saw before he lost consciousness was Feng, on the floor, gasping for air, coughing violently, and promising Cí the most horrific of deaths.

35

From what seemed like very far away, Cí could hear the guard saying he didn't see the point in reviving a man who was about to be executed. But he did as he was told and emptied several buckets of water over Cí's bloody, insensate body.

Cí moaned, trying to open his swollen eyes.

"You should take better care of yourself," said Feng, handing Cí a cloth. "Here, clean yourself up a bit."

Cí's focus gradually came back. Feng stood over him like a man inspecting an insect he'd just crushed. Cí tried moving but found he was still chained to the wall.

"These guards can be so brutal sometimes!" said Feng. "Still, I suppose that's their job. Water?"

Cí didn't want to accept anything from Feng, but he was so thirsty he felt as if his insides were burning up, and he drank a little from the cup.

"I must say," said Feng, "I've always held your astuteness in high esteem, but today you really surpassed yourself. Shame, really, because unless you take it all back, that same shrewdness is going to get you hanged."

Cí managed to open one of his eyes, only to get a glimpse of Feng's insincere smile.

"Bastard," he muttered. "Same *shrewdness* you used to frame my brother?"

"Oh, you managed to work that out, too? Took you some time, didn't it? Well, from one expert to another," he said as he nudged Cí playfully, "you must agree it was a rather excellent play! Once Shang was out of the way, *someone* needed to be incriminated for it, and your brother, well, he was perfect. The three thousand *qián* one of my men *somehow* lost to him in a bet...the purse swap once we'd arrested Lu...the drug we used on him so he wouldn't be able to speak at his trial...and the best bit, the sickle, and the way we smeared blood all over it and waited for the flies to do the rest."

Cí was struggling to understand. His skull was still ringing with the blow to his head.

"So it seems that nosing around in other people's books runs in your family. Nasty habit," he said, shaking his head. "Your father wasn't even satisfied sticking his beak in my accounts; he had to go and blab about it to his little friend Shang! I didn't really have much choice after that. I tried to warn him, but when I visited that night, he really became *quite* unreasonable. Talking about reporting me to the authorities! Refusing to hand over the papers that would incriminate me! So we had to blow up the house. Should've done it sooner, really. Oh, and the idea of using the gunpowder rocket to mask the wounds? That idea came to me that evening, too; it was the thunder that made me think of it."

Cí couldn't talk. So that was why Lu had taken Cí's sickle when he hadn't been able to find his own—Feng had taken Lu's for the setup.

"Come on, Cí!" Feng suddenly roared. "Did you really think a bolt of lightning came down from heaven and finished your parents? Let me know when you decide to stop dreaming and join us in the real world."

Cí wished he could believe this was all some terrible nightmare. It was too much to absorb. He closed his eyes. When he opened them again, Feng was still in front of him with a nearly rapturous look on his face.

"What did your family ever do for you, anyway? Compared with me? You should thank me for having extracted you from that rat hole." He began pacing the room. "I made you! Ingrate. You'd have been the same as any other canal rat if it weren't for me… You were the one good thing about the Song family, its saving grace! And I thought, when you showed up, we could all be happy together—you, me, Blue Iris." He smiled at the thought of his wife before whispering, "You were like the son I never had…"

Cí felt numb watching Feng's demented display.

"We could still be that! A family!" Feng continued. "Let's put this all behind us! This is where you belong, with us! Anything you want, you can have. Wealth? To study? You can have it all! A little push from me here, and you'll be taking the exams like you always dreamed; a little shove there, you'll have a top spot in the administration. What you've always wanted! Don't you see what I could do for you? Why would I be telling you all this otherwise? I want us to be a *family*, Cí. Just the three of us!"

Not long before, Cí would have jumped at the chance of joining the judiciary, but now his only desire was to bring honor back to his father—and that meant unmasking this lunatic imposter, this murderer here in the cell with him.

"Get away from me!" Cí shouted.

Feng laughed.

"What? Do you really think you can turn me down? Think I'm going to tell you all this and then let you ruin me?" He laughed again. "Or maybe you think you can beat me!"

"I don't need you to tell me anything," muttered Cí. "I'm going to take you down anyway."

"I see! I wonder, what might you be thinking of saying about me? Hmm. That I killed Kan? That I embezzled money? Gods, boy. You must really have lost it if you think anyone's going to believe you now."

"I've got proof," Cí managed to say.

"Really?" said Feng, going to the far end of the cell and taking something from a bag. "You wouldn't mean this, by any chance, would you?" He walked back over to Cí with the model of the hand cannon. "You weren't hoping this could save you, were you? Oh, well." And at this, he threw the plaster to the floor, shattering it in a thousand pieces.

Cí shut his eyes as the fragments hit his body. He couldn't look at Feng. Not while he was still alive.

"What now?" sneered Feng. "Going to beg for mercy like your miserable parents before they died?"

Cí almost ripped the chains from the wall. Feng stood back and watched with enjoyment as Cí grappled with the shackles.

"Pathetic," said Feng, laughing. "Did you really think I'd be stupid enough to let you bring me down? I could have you tortured right now, and do you think anyone would hear your cries? Or bother to save you if they did?"

"Well, go on then!" screamed Cí. "Why don't you? What are you waiting for?"

"Hah! Just so I can get sentenced later? I don't think so. Clever boy." Feng shook his head. "Guard!" he called.

The guard came in with a bamboo staff in one hand and an implement resembling pliers in the other.

"Sometimes prisoners lose their tongues. Did you know that? Shame, it *does* make it awfully difficult for them to defend themselves."

These were Feng's final words before he went out, leaving Cí alone with the guard.

⟨⟨⟨✦⟩⟩⟩

Just as Cí doubled over from the first blow to his gut, the next one came down across his back. The guard grinned and rolled his sleeves up as Cí tried to protect himself from someone he knew would deliver as much pain as necessary to get paid. Cí had seen it all before. First the beating, then he'd have to sign the confession. Then his nails would be pulled out, his fingers broken, his tongue cut out. With all this done, no prisoner could write down or speak the truth. He thought about his family and the fact that, no matter how desperately he wanted to, he might not be able to avenge their terrible deaths.

The blows continued to rain down. His vision clouded over and he drifted in and out of consciousness. His parents whispered to him: *Fight*, they said. *Don't give up*. His mouth and throat filled with the iron-like taste of his own blood. What was left of his spirit was draining away. He could let himself die now and bring an end to this useless torment, but his father's spirit urged him on. Another blow. And another. Through his nose, he inhaled a mix of blood and air, and when he felt it reach his lungs, he exhaled as hard as he could, expelling the cloth that had been stuffed in his mouth. Finally he could say something.

"I'll confess," he mumbled.

This didn't stop the guard from hitting him once more, as though Cí's sudden decision had interrupted his fun. Satisfied, the guard removed the chains from Cí's wrists and handed him the confession document. Cí took the brush in his trembling hand and scribbled at the bottom of the page. Then the brush fell from his hand, leaving a trail of blood and ink on the page. The guard looked disgusted but said it would do. He gave it to another guard outside the door, told him to take it to Feng, then came back and stood over Cí with the pliers in hand.

"Now," he said, "let's have a look at those fingers of yours."

Cí was too weak to resist as the guard grabbed his right wrist and clamped the pliers on the edge of his thumbnail. He tightly squeezed the pliers and yanked. Cí barely flinched, which annoyed the guard. He prepared to pull off the next nail, but instead of yanking this one straight out, he ripped upward so the nail stood loose from the finger. Cí let out only a grunt.

Annoyed by this passivity, the guard shook his head.

"Well," he growled, "since you aren't using that tongue of yours to complain, maybe we should relieve you of that as well."

Cí felt his father's spirit coursing through him, spurring him on.

"Have you ever pulled out a tongue before?" Cí managed to ask.

The guard squinted his small dark eyes.

"Now you talk?"

Cí tried to force a smile, but instead found himself spitting bloody phlegm.

"Pulling out the tongue will bring the neck veins with it. I'll bleed out like a pig, and there will be no way to stop me from dying." He paused. "Do you know what happens to someone who kills a prisoner before he's been sentenced?"

"Save it," said the guard, but he let go of the pliers, knowing full well that it was a crime punishable by death.

"You really don't get it," said Cí. "Why do you think Feng left? So none of this could be blamed on him!"

"I said shut it!" He punched Cí in the stomach. Cí doubled over on the floor.

"Where are the doctors who are supposed to stop me from bleeding out?" he gasped. "If you obey Feng, you know I'll die, and he'll deny having given the order. You'll be signing your own death warrant."

The guard hesitated, and Cí was sure the guard knew Cí was right. Plus there had been no witnesses, so it would be Feng's word against the guard's. Still, he picked up the pliers again and turned on Cí.

"Stop right there!" came a shout from outside the cell.

Cí and the guard looked up in unison. It was Bo, accompanied by two sentries.

Suddenly Cí was being pulled, but in what direction he had no idea…Was he standing now? Salts were waved beneath his nose, and he was jolted into awareness.

"Come on!" said Bo. "We must hurry. The trial's about to begin again."

It was morning. Cí realized he'd survived a night of torture.

On their way to the courtroom, Bo told Cí everything he'd learned, but Cí was finding it hard to listen. His mind was that of a predator, and all he could focus on was the thought of Feng's jugular. But as the court came into sight again, he began to pay attention to Bo's discoveries. Bo stopped just before they went in, wiping Cí's face and giving him clean robes to put over his bloody, grimy clothes.

"Be careful," said Bo. "Try to make it look like you've got yourself together. Remember that accusing a court official amounts to the same thing as accusing Ningzong himself."

When the two soldiers made Cí kneel before the throne, the emperor himself let out a gasp. Cí's face was a mess of bruises and cuts. His two nailless fingers were bleeding. Feng smiled nervously. Bo stood a few paces from Cí, a leather bag slung over his shoulder. The gong sounded to announce that the court was in session again.

Feng took the floor first. He was wearing his old judge's robes and the mortarboard that indicated he was on the side of the prosecution.

"Some of you here, I'm sure, have felt the blows of disappointment from time to time—when unscrupulous colleagues have threatened to ruin you, or when a woman has betrayed you for a wealthier suitor, or when unfair claims are brought against you." Feng turned to the audience. "But I can assure you that none of those situations compare with the suffering and bitterness I now feel in my heart.

"Here before us, kneeling in front of our beloved emperor, you see the worst of imposters, the most ungrateful and insidious man alive. The accused has been living under my roof, and until yesterday I treated him like a son. I nurtured him, saw that he had an education, urged him to mature. I am childless, and I placed all my hopes in Cí Song. But to my deep, deep regret, I have learned that beneath that lamb's clothing there is the worst kind of vermin imaginable: perverse, traitorous, and, yes, even murderous."

"Once the proof was brought before me, I felt I had no choice but to support Gray Fox. It pained me to have to spill Cí's blood, I can tell you, but I knew we had to see this confession." He held the document up for all to see. "These are the hardest words a father could ever have to read. Unfortunately, though, it was the will of the gods, so that we might be saved the spectacle of more lies. Justice must now be served in regard to this despicable lowlife."

The emperor carefully read the confession note before handing it to the official to register its content. Ningzong stood and looked at Cí with a dark hatred.

"With this document in mind, I hereby—"

"Not my signature..." groaned Cí, spitting blood on the floor.

The astonishment in the room was palpable. Feng came forward, trembling.

"It's not my signature on that document!" cried Cí, the effort almost causing him to topple forward.

Feng flinched as if listening to a ghost.

"Your Majesty," he said quietly. "He confessed—"

"Silence!" roared Ningzong, peering around the room as he considered what to do next. "Maybe he did ratify this document," he said, pausing, "and maybe not. But in any case, every prisoner has the right to make his case."

He sat on his throne once more. His face couldn't have been more severe, or more regal, as he nodded at Cí to proceed.

Cí touched his forehead to the floor.

"Dear Sovereign," he said, but just these two words brought on a bloody coughing fit. Bo stepped forward to help him, but a guard stood in his way. Cí took as deep a breath as he could before continuing. "In front of all the people present here today, I should confess my guilt. A guilt that's eating me from inside." Another murmur ran around the room. "I'm guilty of ambition. Ambition blinded me, and I became unable to distinguish right from wrong. And in my blindness, I trusted a man who is hypocrisy incarnate, the very body and soul of evil. Just as he says he looked on me as a son, I once regarded him as a father, but I now know him to be the worst of criminals, a snake of the most poisonous kind."

"Hold your tongue!" warned the official who had been directing the proceedings. "You know that anything said against one of the emperor's men is a slur on the emperor himself."

Cí nodded to acknowledge that he knew the seriousness of his accusations, then fell into another coughing fit.

"Majesty!" shouted Feng before Cí could recover. "Are you really going to listen to this? Slander and lies! He knows it's his only chance to save his skin."

The emperor pursed his lips.

"Feng is in the right. Either show us some evidence, Cí Song, or I'll have you executed immediately."

"I can assure you, Majesty, there's nothing in the world I would like more than to prove my innocence." Cí shook his head, and when he looked up the determination had returned to his face. "And that's why I'll now demonstrate that I was the one, not Gray Fox, who worked out that Kan didn't commit suicide. I was the one who told Feng of the evidence. And it was Feng who, rather than bringing the news directly to Your Majesty, broke his promise to me and gave the information to Gray Fox."

"I'm waiting," said the emperor, clearly losing his patience.

"In that case, I need permission to ask *you* a question, Majesty." Ningzong nodded. "I suppose Gray Fox would have talked you through the details that led him to his conclusion."

"Yes," confirmed the emperor. "He did."

"Details so strange, so specific, and so obscure that no other judge could possibly have observed them beforehand."

"Exactly."

"Things that have not been spoken here."

"Get to the point!"

"In that case, Majesty, tell me, how could I possibly know those same details? Like the fact that Kan was made to write a false confession, that he was drugged and stripped naked by two people who then strung him up."

"What kind of nonsense is this?" said Feng. "He knows because *he* was the one who carried out the act!"

"I'm about to prove that is also not the case," said Cí, fixing Feng with a threatening look before turning back to Ningzong. "Dear Sovereign, did Gray Fox talk to you about the detail of the noose's vibration marks? Did he explain that Kan, drugged as he must have been, didn't struggle? That the mark left in the dust on the beam was neat rather than showing any sign of agitation?"

"Yes, yes, but what on earth has this got to do with—"

"Please, one last question: Is the noose still attached to that beam?"

The emperor glanced over at Gray Fox, who nodded in the affirmative.

"In that case, Gray Fox's lies can be checked once and for all. That mark isn't there anymore. I accidentally wiped it out when I was up there checking how the rope had moved. Which means by the time Gray Fox came to examine the room, the mark wasn't there. He only knew because I told Feng, and Feng told him."

Now Ningzong looked inquiringly at the prosecution. Gray Fox hung his head, but Feng, smiling, was ready with a retort.

"Nice try, but a bit predictable. Any idiot could tell that just by untying the corpse the dust up there would be rubbed out. Gods, Majesty! How long do we have to go on being insulted by this charlatan's stupidities?"

Ningzong merely stroked his whiskers and turned his attention to the confession paper. The process was stalling. He ordered the transcriptionist to be ready and stood to announce the sentence, but Cí stepped forward.

"Please, one last chance!" he said. "And if you're still not convinced, I swear to you I will stab myself in the heart."

Ningzong frowned and glanced at Bo, who nodded.

"One last chance," Ningzong said, seating himself once more.

Cí wiped the blood from around his mouth. He signaled to Bo, who came over and handed him the leather bag.

"Majesty," said Cí, holding the bag up so Ningzong could see it. "Inside this bag there is a piece of evidence that will both prove my innocence and unmask a terrible plot. A scheme hatched through heartless ambition and based on an awful invention: the most dangerous weapon ever dreamed by the minds of men. A cannon so lightweight that it can be shot without the normal support a cannon requires, so small that it can be concealed in a person's robes, so lethal that it can be used to kill, time and again, at a distance and with great accuracy."

"More nonsense!" roared Feng. "Is he going to try and bring witchcraft in here?"

Cí's only answer was to reach his hand deep into the bag and pull out a small cannon made of bronze. Ningzong looked astonished. The blood drained from Feng's face.

"I found the remains of an unusual ceramic mold at the bronze maker's workshop after it burned down. I managed to piece the mold together, but then it was stolen from my room at Judge Feng's. Luckily, though," Cí said, and at this, he couldn't help but turn a smile in the direction of Feng and Gray Fox, "I'd already made a plaster cast, which I hid at the Ming Academy. Before I knew of Feng's deception, I asked if he would retrieve it and look after it. But I found out about his trickery just in time and changed the note of authorization, telling Ming's servant, who was guarding the evidence, only to give Feng the plaster cast...but not this replica!" Cí paused, looking around the room. "Feng destroyed the mold to try and save himself, but little did he know I'd already ordered Ming's servant to have another made from the plaster cast. A true replica of the original weapon." He held it aloft again. "This very one."

The emperor seemed fascinated by the hand cannon.

"But," he said, "you still haven't explained what this strange contraption has to do with any of the murders."

"This contraption, Your Majesty, was the cause of all those deaths." Cí brought it forward, bowing and handing it to the presiding official, who then handed it to the emperor. "Feng," continued Cí, "whose only motivation in life is money, designed this perverse instrument and had it made. Furthermore, he was planning to sell the secret to the Jin. And how did he finance all this? By embezzling state funds from the salt trade. The eunuch, Soft Dolphin, as many people here today know, was an honest and scrupulous auditor, and at the time of his death his job was to keep accounts of the salt trade. Feng began siphoning off so much money for himself that it began to show in the books. And when Soft Dolphin confronted Feng, Feng had him eliminated."

"Slander!" cried Feng. "This is all pure—"

"Silence!" said the official before nodding to Cí to carry on.

"Like my father before him, Soft Dolphin also noticed that some of the embezzled funds were being used to buy up a very specific kind of salt—it's known as saltpeter. An expensive product, difficult to manufacture, and used primarily to add to the mix that makes up gunpowder. Soft Dolphin's accounts also show that he'd figured out something else: a considerable increase in the earnings of three men who apparently had nothing in common. An alchemist. An explosives expert. A bronze maker. And I think most people in the room can probably guess what ended up linking those three men together: they all ended up dead. Soft Dolphin's final act was to cut the funds, which prevented Feng from making progress in his research. And Feng couldn't have that."

Now Cí took another document from Bo and handed it forward.

"However, Soft Dolphin was not actually the first victim. That unfortunate honor went to a Taoist monk by the name of Yu. As you'll see in the report, his salt-corroded hands, the carbon under his fingernails, and the small yin-yang tattoo on his thumb showed he worked in the manufacture of gunpowder. When Feng didn't pay what he'd promised, the old alchemist objected and ended up being shot dead by the very weapon he'd been helping Feng create."

Cí turned a defiant look Feng's way.

"The hand cannon shoots a scaled-down cannonball. It entered through Yu's chest, broke a rib, and came out through his back, ending up stuck in a nearby wooden beam of some kind. Feng, wanting to hide any incriminating signs, recovered the small cannonball and tried to conceal the nature of the chest wound, enlarging and scraping it out to make it look like the result of either an animal attack or a macabre ritual.

"Next—the very next day, in fact—the young explosives expert was killed. I was able to identify his work due to the highly unusual scarring to his face, which I subsequently saw on a living man who told me gunpowder had exploded in his face. Feng's motives were similar, but this time it was a stab to the heart that killed the victim. Bo has since found out that such specialists work wearing visors, which matches with the fact this corpse had none of the scarring immediately around his eyes. Again, Feng worked on the wound to try and make it look like the first one and the result of another attack or ritual murder.

"Now we come to Soft Dolphin. Since his disappearance would inevitably draw suspicion, Feng first tried to pay him off. He knew of Soft Dolphin's passion for antiques and tried to buy the eunuch's silence with a framed poem of incalculable value. At first Soft Dolphin went along with it, but when he found out Feng's true intentions, he tried to renege on the deal. He was stabbed to death and, like the others, his wound was tampered with.

"Last to die was the bronze maker—the man who actually built the mold and cast the hand cannon for Feng. The murder occurred the night of the Jin reception, in your very own gardens, Majesty. I found soil just like the soil around the palace walls under the bronze maker's fingernails. Feng stabbed him, and with somebody's help dragged the not-yet-dead body to the walls, where the bronze maker struggled before his head was chopped off.

"So you see, Feng planned and carried out every single one of the murders, beheading or disfiguring the corpses to make their identification difficult and to suggest the involvement of some criminal sect."

To this, the emperor said nothing, but merely stroked his beard for a time.

"So..." he said eventually, "what you're saying is that this small piece of artillery has great destructive potential."

"Imagine every soldier having one. The greatest power a human mind has ever conceived."

Feng was visibly shaken as he stepped forward to try and formulate a reply. But the anger etched in his face was still fearsome— as fearsome as the weapon that Cí had just described, if not more so. He pointed at Cí and yelled.

"Majesty! I demand that this prisoner be immediately punished for these foundless accusations! They are an insult to you, dear Sovereign. This court has never heard such disrespectful lies. None of your antecedents would ever have permitted such a thing."

"Leave the dead in peace," said Ningzong. "First, you ought to worry about your own impertinence."

Feng's anger quickly turned to a blush.

"Imperial Highness...this insolent fool, the one they call Corpse Reader, is in reality nothing more than an expert in dissimulation. Where's the proof? Where, I ask you? His words are like fireworks, as explosive as this supposed gunpowder he speaks of. Hand cannons? All I see is a bronze flute. What would it shoot anyway? Rice? Cherry stones?" He turned to face Cí.

The emperor squinted. "Calm yourself, Judge Feng. I am not yet pronouncing your guilt, but much of what young Cí says seems logical. The question is, why might he want to accuse you, if not to uncover the truth?"

"Majesty, is that so difficult? Spite! Sheer spite! As you know Cí's father was once in my employ as an accountant. I hadn't intended to bring this out in public today, but I found out that his father had been falsifying accounts and stealing from me. I had to fire him. Out of affection, I hid the truth from Cí himself. To protect him. But the Songs are all the same! When he found out, he went crazy and somehow decided it was all my fault.

"With respect to these murders, I don't see how there can be any doubt: Kan killed these unfortunate men, but Cí, unable to solve the case and burning with ambition, made it look as though Kan also committed suicide. Simple. All the rest is the result of Cí's feverish mind. Pure invention."

"And I invented the hand cannon, too?" howled Cí.

"Quiet!" ordered the emperor.

The emperor got to his feet and whispered something to one of the officers near him, who signaled to Bo to come nearer. Bo hurried over and kneeled, before being ordered to follow Ningzong through to an antechamber. The two emerged after a few minutes, and as he came over, Cí could clearly see the concern on Bo's face.

"The emperor has asked me to talk with you," Bo whispered.

Cí was surprised at how firmly Bo took him by the arm, leading him into the antechamber and shutting the door. Once they were alone, Bo hid his face in his hands.

"What?" said Cí.

"The emperor believes you."

"No...really?" Cí whooped with delight. "Amazing! Feng's finally going to get what he deserves, and—" But Cí could see how worried Bo looked. "What? What else? You've just told me I've won the case, so..."

Bo wouldn't look Cí in the face.

"What's going on?"

Bo took a deep breath.

"The emperor wants you to say you're guilty." He sighed.

"But...but why? What for? Why me and not Feng?"

"He's offering a comfortable exile if you just say you're guilty," said Bo. "He'll give you a lump sum and an annual stipend. You'll never have to work again; you'll have plenty to pass onto future generations even. You'll receive no punishment whatsoever. It's a generous offer."

"And Feng?"

"The emperor has assured me he'll take care of him personally."

"Meaning what? And you, you agree with all this?" Cí began backing away from Bo. "You're in on it, too, aren't you?"

"Be calm, Cí! I'm just the messenger—"

"Be calm? You know what I'm being asked to do? I've lost everything—my family, my dreams, my honor. And now you want to strip me of my dignity? No, Bo! I won't give up the one hope I have left! I couldn't care less about anything else, but there's no way I'm going to let that bastard Feng get away with killing my father and shaming my family. No way."

"Gods, Cí! Don't you get it? This isn't a request. The emperor can't allow this kind of scandal. It would be far too damaging to him. His critics already say he's too weak, so if they hear of intrigues at court, if word of treason gets out, if people see he can't even control his own officials, what will they think of his ability to deal with the country's enemies? Especially with the Jin on our doorstep, Ningzong has to show an iron will. Councilors and judges killing each other? He can't allow that to get out."

"So let him show he's firm—but fair, too!"

"Damn it, Cí! If you reject his offer, what do you think he'll do? Condemn you anyway, of course! You'll be executed, or sent to the mines for the rest of your days. What would your father have you do? If you agree, you'll have somewhere to live, a stipend, a calm life—away from all this. With time, you might be able to repair your reputation and reenter court life. I don't see what more you can ask for or, really, what choice you have in the matter. If you try and oppose the emperor, he'll crush you. Your evidence is circumstantial at best."

Cí tried to find his conviction and fight reflected in Bo's eyes, but what he saw couldn't have been more different.

"Please," begged Bo. "It's your best—and only—option."

Bo put his hands on Cí's shoulders. Their weight was the weight of sincerity. Cí's thoughts turned to his dreams, his studies, his desire to become a great forensic judge. This had also been his father's dream for him…He nodded his head, resigned.

"Come on," said Bo.

⚜

Cí approached the throne with his head hung low and dragging his feet as though they were in shackles. He fell to his knees before the emperor, who glanced at Bo. Bo nodded. The emperor, pleased, calmly gestured to the scribe to prepare the deed.

Once the deed was written, an officer stepped forward to read it out. Everyone listened, and the emperor watched intently, as the officer slowly read the words. Cí's culpability was established, and the charges against Feng were dismissed. All that was left was for Cí to sign it.

When the deed was handed to Cí, the ink wasn't yet dry—as if offering some hope it might still be rewritten. Cí's hands trembled violently. He tried to pick up the brush, but it fell from his fingers to the floor, leaving a black dash across the red carpet. Excusing his clumsiness, Cí picked up the brush and then stopped to reflect. There was no doubt: sign the deed and he would be admitting sole responsibility, and Feng would be off the hook.

Bo's argument ran through his head. But could this really be what his father would have wanted? Cí could barely think straight.

He gripped the brush and wet it on the inkstone. Then, slowly, he began painting the lines that made up his signature. Again, though, his grip seemed to loosen on the brush; it was as if his ancestors were there in the room, knocking it away. When he reached the part of his signature that was his family name, something rose up inside him. And at that moment, he looked up and saw Feng's triumphant smile. Cí saw his parents' bodies buried in the rubble, and his brother's tortured form, and his little sister in agony. He couldn't leave them like that. He looked Feng steadfastly in the eyes until a grain of concern entered the older man's face. Cí jumped to his feet, threw the ink and brush to the floor, and tore up the deed.

Ningzong's wrath was immediate and terrible. He ordered his men to come forward, put manacles on Cí, and whip him ten times. When it was over, the emperor said the time had come for the verdict, but Cí demanded to be allowed his final defense. Ningzong bit his tongue. This was a centuries-old tradition, and Cí knew the emperor wouldn't dare prevent him his rights in front of the whole court. Eventually the emperor signaled for Cí to go ahead.

"You have until the water clock runs out!" he said as it was brought forward.

Cí took a deep breath. Feng still stood looking defiant, but a glimmer of fear was in his eyes.

The water began to drop.

"Majesty, more than a century ago, your most venerable great-grandfather allowed himself to listen to poor counsel with regards to the case of General Fei Yue, which led to the condemnation of that man. Nowadays, we know Fei Yue was in fact innocent and we celebrate him as a great man. That abominable verdict has gone down as one of the darkest chapters in our history. Fei Yue was executed, and though his name has subsequently been cleared by the efforts of his family, the damage was never fully repaired." Cí paused, glancing around for Blue Iris. "I wouldn't dare to compare myself with such a figure...but I do dare to ask for justice. I am also the son of a dishonored father. Now you ask me to declare myself guilty of the very crimes I have shown you that I am innocent of. And I can prove the truth of my assertions."

"Just as you've been saying right from the start," said Ningzong, glancing at the water clock.

"Allow me, therefore, to show you the terrible power contained in the weapon." He lifted up his chains so they could be taken off. "What if such lethal force should fall into enemy hands? Think on that. Think on our nation."

Cí allowed his statement to settle in Ningzong's conscience. The emperor muttered something to himself, turning the weapon over and over in his hands. He looked to his councilors. And then back at Cí again.

"Take off the chains!" he ordered.

The same guard who unchained Cí then stood in his way as he tried to approach the emperor, but Ningzong said to allow him. Cí staggered forward, his stomach gripped by fear. Coming up a few steps to the same level as the throne, he knelt down. Then he got up, as best he could, and held his hand out. The emperor handed over the weapon.

Facing the emperor, Cí took the small spherical stone from his robes along with the small bag of gunpowder he'd taken from Feng's dresser.

"The projectile I have in my hands is the very one that ended the alchemist's life. As you can see, it isn't perfectly round; a sliver has broken off of it. This fragmentation occurred on impact with the alchemist's spine, matching a sliver I extracted from the corpse when I examined it."

Without another word, and following what he'd read in the treatises on conventional cannons, he poured the gunpowder into the mouth of the weapon and then used the handle of a brush to stuff the small cannonball down into it. Then he tore a strip from his own shirt, twisted it into a sort of fuse, and inserted this into a gap in the side of the contraption. He then handed it to Ningzong.

"Here you have it. All that remains is to light the fuse and aim."

The emperor looked as though he was holding in his hands some great wonder. His small eyes shone with perplexity.

"Majesty!" Feng said. "How long am I going to have to put up with this disgrace? It's all lies, every single word—"

"Lies?" screamed Cí, turning on him. "Do you mind explaining how the remains of the mold you stole from my room, as well as the gunpowder and the small cannonball that killed the alchemist, were *all* in the drawers of *your* desk?" He turned back to the emperor. "That's where I found them. If you send your men to look in the same place, I'm sure they'll find many more projectiles."

Feng, though stunned, was quick with a reply.

"If you took them from my office, you could just have easily planted more there."

Cí wasn't sure what to say to this. His legs felt weak. He'd assumed Feng would crumble against this last onslaught, but the old man seemed firmer than ever. Was there ever going to be a way out?

"Very well. In that case, answer me this," Cí said finally. "Councilor Kan was killed on the fifth moon of the month, a night when you've already stated you were away from Lin'an on business. But we have the testimony of a sentry who allowed you into the palace that very evening." Cí looked across at Bo, who was nodding in confirmation. "So, you had motive, you had the means… and from what we now know, despite your lies, you also had the opportunity."

"Is this for certain?" asked Ningzong.

"No!" erupted Feng. "It's anything but certain!"

"Can you prove it?"

"Of course," snorted Feng. "I returned from my trip that night. I was at home with my wife, enjoying her company."

Hearing this, Cí's jaw dropped. That was the night he and Blue Iris had been together.

He still hadn't recovered when Feng came at him with a question.

"And you?" said Feng. "Where were you the night Kan was killed?"

Cí went deep red. He looked at Blue Iris, trying to find something in her face to suggest she might throw him a lifeline to get him out of this quickening whirlpool. But Blue Iris was impassive as ever. The submissive wife. Cí knew then that he'd never beat Feng, since he couldn't condemn Blue Iris by revealing their secret. He wouldn't destroy her life.

"We're waiting," said Ningzong. "Do you have nothing further to add before I deliver the verdict?"

Cí, glancing at Blue Iris again, was quiet for a moment.

"No," he said.

"In that case, I, Emperor Ningzong, Heaven's Son and Sovereign of the Middle Kingdom, declare Cí Song to be—"

"He was with me!" came a resounding voice from the back of the room.

Everyone turned around to see who had spoken. Blue Iris was on her feet, and she looked unshakable.

"I didn't sleep with my husband," she said firmly. "The night Kan was killed, I lay down beside Cí Song."

Feng stammered helplessly as hundreds of eyes turned to look at him. He stumbled backward in shock, his eyes fixed on Blue Iris.

"You—you couldn't!" he shouted, but he was clearly out of his mind now. He turned and tried to run for the door.

He continued to stammer and cry, "You couldn't! After all I've done! You snake!" as guards dragged him back into the middle of the room. He managed to get free of the men holding him and leaped up the steps to the throne, seizing the weapon from the astonished Ningzong.

"Get back, all of you!" he shouted. Before anyone could react he struck a flint and lit the fuse. "Back, I said!" The soldiers, who had begun to creep forward, stopped as Feng turned the weapon on the emperor. "You bastard," he said, lifting the muzzle and putting it to Ningzong's head. "I gave up everything. I did it all for you." The flame was advancing up the fuse. "How could you?"

The people next to Blue Iris crouched down. Feng was holding the contraption in two hands. It was shaking, just as Feng was. Cí held his breath. The flame was almost there. Feng cried out, turning the weapon around and pointing it at his own head. A dry report rang through the room; instantly Feng was down on the floor and blood was pooling around him. The guards leaped on him and looked up when they were sure he was dead. Ningzong stood, his face flecked with Feng's blood. Wiping at it, he muttered a few words: The trial was over. Cí was free to go.

EPILOGUE

Cí woke feeling stiff. It had been a week since the trial, and, though he was starting to feel the lack of exercise, he also felt his wounds were healing well. He rubbed his eyes and looked around his dormitory room, feeling content. Early-morning light streamed through the orange paper blind. Outside, there was the sound of students clamoring to get to class; he was home again, surrounded by books.

The doctor who had been monitoring him the past week came in, medicinal tea in hand, but before he could say anything, Cí asked how Ming was feeling.

The doctor's sparkly eyes lit up.

"He won't stop chattering! His legs are healing better than a lizard's." He examined Cí's scarring. "He is particularly keen to see you, and…I think the time has come for you to try walking!" He gave Cí an encouraging pat on the back.

Cí couldn't have been more pleased; he'd been lying down for a week, and his only news of Ming had come from doctors and servants. He swung his legs over the edge of the bed and stood shakily, then went over to the window. He had a sense that the orange brilliance of the paper blind contained something of his ancestors' spirits and that they were encouraging him to feel proud of his surname once more. For the first time, he felt at peace with them. He lit incense and, breathing in its aroma, said to himself that, wherever they all were, they might now also be at peace.

He dressed and left the room, using Blue Iris's red stick for support. She had sent it to him along with a get-well message; he'd been dreaming of getting better partly so he could use it. On his way to Ming's quarters he passed a number of professors who greeted him as though he were one of them. Cí found this surprising, bowing back to each in turn. It was a warm day, and the warmth was comforting.

Ming was in bed, and the skin on his arms and face still looked very bruised. The room was in semidarkness, but Ming's face lit up at seeing Cí.

"Cí!" he exclaimed happily. "You're walking!"

Cí came and sat beside him. Ming appeared tired, but his eyes were still full of life. The doctor had said it would do Ming good to see Cí, and they chatted about their wounds, about the trial, and about Feng.

Ming asked for tea to be brought and told Cí there were several things he still didn't fully understand.

"The motives, for one."

"It was very complicated to pull apart. The bronze maker was a vain man, both talkative and egotistical. Feng invited him to the Jin reception only because of the pressure he was exerting. We found out from Feng's Mongol aide that the bronze maker was desperate to enter high society and had no qualms about trying to squeeze Feng for it. But he had no idea how dangerous Feng was. According to the Mongol, the bronze maker was becoming so greedy and indiscreet that he might have compromised Feng's interests; at that point, Feng couldn't allow him to go on living. With the Taoist alchemist and the explosives maker, Feng simply preferred to kill them rather than risk delays in the development of the weapon because he couldn't pay them. It seems he owed them both a lot of money."

"But why kill the councilor? Killing some unknowns could have passed unnoticed, but he must have known he'd never get away with killing such a high-ranking official."

Cí arched an eyebrow.

"I can only imagine Feng felt he had no choice. Kan was obsessed with the idea that Blue Iris was guilty of something, and Feng was worried this might lead him close to the truth. And he thought the staged suicide would fool everyone. So when I told Feng I'd worked it out, he went and told Gray Fox, calculating that I'd then be accused."

"And what about the perfume?" asked Ming. "Earlier on, I remember you thought it must have been sprinkled on the victims to try and incriminate the *nüshi*. But why on earth would Feng have wanted to do that if the *nüshi* was his wife? Everyone says he was madly in love with her."

"This part I'm not totally sure of, but Kan had something to do with it. Just because Kan was killed doesn't mean he was entirely innocent. He really was obsessed with Blue Iris, to the point that he somehow began mixing up the results he wanted to find with the actual evidence. Apparently, Kan proposed to her once, and her rejection was more than his pride could bear. I think he tried to incriminate her. He had access to the Essence of Jade, and he, or his men, were among the first to have any contact with the corpses. False evidence."

"Nonetheless, it must be said that Kan wasn't very far wrong. Feng was guilty, after all." Ming took a sip of the tea. "Strange business! Feng seemed like such a cultured man! I really can't understand what could have driven him to all this."

"Who can? Isn't the problem that we try to apply sane logic to conduct that is far from being sane itself? Feng was disturbed, so only from the point of view of a disturbed mind could we ever find the justification for his actions. Bo says that when he was interrogated, the Mongol put it down to greed; he confirmed he'd helped Feng and said it had all been motivated by sheer avarice in his master."

"Greed? Avarice? Feng was already a very rich man. His wife's salt dealings—"

"It seems the business had been going downhill for a long time. The frontier wars meant Ningzong was cutting off trade links with the Jin, and they were Feng's main buyers. He'd lost almost everything already."

"But what was he going to get from killing people?"

"Money. Power. Feng had taken over the business from Blue Iris, and it was his management that led them to ruin. Feng began seeing Blue Iris during the time my father was still working for him, and, although her being a *nüshi* meant they had to keep it a secret, Feng also started to have a hand in her business affairs that early on. Feng began creating a network with the Jin, planning to sell them the weapons; the promise of the hand cannon may even have had a part in the Jin's decision to invade. This is speculation, but in his delirium, Feng might have thought a victory for the Jin would give him a monopoly over the salt trade. We can't be sure. Bo is still looking into the matter."

"Any idea how Feng got access to the secret, and such a terrible weapon?"

"I've asked myself the same question. I think Blue Iris's family must have had something to do with it. After all, Fei Yue wasn't only a sensational general, he pioneered the use of gunpowder, didn't he? In fact, I found a copy of the *Ujingzongyao* in Feng's office. Bo's research also seems to support such an idea."

"And all for the love of a beautiful woman…a woman who ended up betraying him."

"And who saved me." Cí's heart began beating harder.

He got to his feet, suddenly unwilling to continue the conversation. He told Ming he was tired and said good-bye, promising to return the next day.

Cí had dreamed of Blue Iris constantly during his recovery and couldn't wait to see her. Though his body was still battered, now that he was on his feet, he longed to be outside. And there was only one place he wanted to go. He headed to the Water Lily Pavilion.

He began picturing the meeting. He'd thank her for helping at the trial; he'd take her in his arms and show her how much he loved her; he'd tell her how sure he'd always felt about her. He couldn't care less about her blindness or how old she was. But as he approached the building, a trembling erupted in his heart.

There were dozens of soldiers at the entrance to the Water Lily Pavilion, shouting and running about. Cí broke into a hobbling run, going as fast as his aching legs would carry him. The soldiers stopped him at the entrance and would not tell him what was happening. Suddenly Bo emerged from the pavilion's main door.

"It's Blue Iris," said Bo, descending the stairs and leading Cí a little way off. "We were searching for documents we still need. She was ordered not to go anywhere while we conducted the search, but she's vanished."

"What do you mean, vanished?" Cí pushed Bo off and dashed past the soldiers into the pavilion.

Consumed by worry, he hurried along the hallways, Bo close on his heels. Cí passed one empty room after another. Could Blue Iris really have fled? He went into the main bedroom, and his stomach churned. Clothes and possessions were everywhere, as if Blue Iris had left in a panic. Next, Cí went to Feng's office, where several of Bo's assistants were taking down books from the shelves. Cí looked around distractedly before noticing a gap where Feng's copy of the *Ujingzongyao* had been.

Looking closer at the gap, he caught a glimpse of something red hidden behind the books and files. He pushed some books aside and reached his hand through. He couldn't believe it: it was his father's red lacquer chest, the one that had disappeared in the fire. Cí pulled it out, and with a quivering hand, as though his father's very spirit might be inside, he unclasped it and opened the top. He recognized his father's handwriting on the documents inside. They were the copies of the accounts, the ones showing Feng's embezzling activities.

Cí left the pavilion. Nothing made sense. He couldn't even believe his own incredulity; the truth was astonishing, but he knew he'd been a fool not to see it. He walked slowly using Blue Iris's stick and eventually found himself back at the academy. The porter came out and told Cí someone was waiting to see him; Cí's heart skipped at the thought that maybe Blue Iris had come, but instead two little beggar boys popped out from where they'd been crouching. He couldn't remember having ever seen them in his life, but the younger of the two reminded him.

"The day of the workshop fire," the boy said, "you told me I could come and claim my money when I found my friend, the cripple who saw what happened."

"You've come late, boy. The case has already been solved."

"But you promised, sir! If I brought the other boy you said you'd pay me the rest of the reward."

Cí considered the child; he looked genuinely hard up. Cí took out his purse, but he didn't take out any money yet.

"Fine. What did your friend see?"

"Come on, then," the younger boy said to the cripple, "tell him!"

"There were three people," said the cripple. "One was telling the other two what to do. They never saw me because I was hidden behind some crates, but I could see and hear everything. The one in charge waited outside while the others searched for something inside the building. Then they poured oil everywhere and set the place on fire."

"Right," said Cí, not entirely convinced. "And do you think you'd be able to recognize them if you saw them again?"

"I think so, sir. One of the men was called Feng. The other one looked like a Mongol."

Cí was startled. He came closer to the cripple and knelt down. "And the third man?"

"It wasn't a man! The person telling them what to do was a woman."

"What do you mean, a woman? What woman?" Cí shook the cripple.

"I don't know! All I saw was that she looked sort of clumsy, and she was leaning on a strange stick. The stick was like…" Suddenly the cripple fell quiet.

"Like what? Damn it, speak!"

"The stick was exactly like yours," said the cripple.

<hr />

Cí locked himself in his room for three days and wouldn't eat or allow the doctors in to look at his wounds. Time seemed to fall away as he agonized over whether Blue Iris could truly be as culpable as the facts suggested, if Feng really had been nothing but a puppet in her quest for revenge, or if she might have had wholly different motives. Cí also tried to come up with a reason why she would have betrayed Feng to save him.

In the evening of the third day, Bo came to see him. There was no news of Blue Iris, but Bo said Cí should consider himself fortunate. In fact, when the emperor offered immunity and a comfortable exile, he'd already decided to have Cí executed, false confession or no. Feng's suicide had saved him. Bo also reported that the Being of Wisdom from Jianningfu Prefecture had been arrested on charges of embezzlement and corruption. Cí thanked Bo, but none of this information alleviated the bitterness he was feeling.

On the fourth day he decided to put his lamenting behind him and get up. He'd come to Lin'an with a plan, after all, and what he needed to do was start working again to achieve it. His mind was still sharp and ready to be applied to his studies. He headed to the library, where his peers would be.

That afternoon he bumped into Ming, who had improved considerably. Cí was gratified to see him walking again, just as Ming appeared pleased to see Cí once more surrounded by books.

"Studying again?" he said.

"Yes. I have a lot of work ahead." He held up the bright red treatise on forensics he'd begun compiling.

Ming smiled. "Bo came by," he said, taking a seat next to Cí. "He brought me up to date on the investigation. It seems that the fortune-teller will be executed, and he told me about Blue Iris's disappearance, and about what happened with you and Feng in the dungeon. He also mentioned that the emperor has reneged on his offer of a place for you in the judiciary."

Cí nodded.

"But at least he hasn't said anything to stop me from taking the exams, and that's still all that matters to me."

"Mmm…" said Ming, not seeming convinced. "But it won't be easy. There are still two years until the next round of exams. I'm not even sure you need to carry on as a student. Your forensic knowledge is exceptional. If you want, I could get you a professorship. You wouldn't have to struggle so hard."

The look Cí gave Ming was full of determination.

"I appreciate it, sir, but I just want to study. All I want is to pass those exams. I owe it to myself, I owe it to my family, and I owe it to you."

Ming smiled, nodding. He got up to leave, but hesitated.

"One last thing that's been troubling me, Cí. Why did you reject the emperor's offer when it was still on the table? Bo told me that Ningzong said he'd give you everything you could possibly desire: a generous stipend, your reputation to be restored in the future, maybe a place in the judiciary. Why didn't you accept?"

Cí looked warmly at his old master.

"Blue Iris once said to me that Feng knew of countless ways to kill a man. And maybe that was true. And maybe there are infinite ways to die. But the one thing I know for certain is that there is only one way to live."

AUTHOR'S NOTE

I can still remember the day when, coffee in one hand, bundle of papers in the other, I sat down in my office to begin work on my new novel. At that point only two things were clear to me: first, that the plot had to move readers as much as it moved me; second, that until I found my theme, I could not begin.

I have to confess that I spent more than two months marking up dozens of pages. I was in search of a vibrant, captivating story, but in all my scribbling I only managed to come up with ideas that felt unoriginal. This was precisely what I didn't want. I wanted something more intense, more impassioned.

By chance—which tends to be the way with these things—luck came to me by way of an invitation, in January of 2007, to attend the eighth annual meeting of the Indian Congress of Forensic Medicine and Toxicology in New Delhi. Although not a forensics expert, I have nevertheless always followed such matters out of literary interest. For a number of years, I had been attending similar meetings and formed friendships with some of the members. Dr. Devaraj Mandal invited me to the conference in New Delhi.

For a number of reasons, I was unable to attend, but Dr. Mandal was kind enough to send me an extensive report summarizing the main talks. Primarily these were on toxicology, forensic pathology and psychology, criminology, and molecular genetics. But the one that immediately drew my attention was on the most recent advances in spectrophotometry, or findings in the field of mitochondrial DNA analysis, focusing mainly on its historical origins. Specifically, it was an in-depth study of the person considered worldwide to be the founding father of this forensic discipline. A man from medieval Asia. The Chinese Cí Song.

Immediately, I knew I had it. My heartbeat quickened. I abandoned what I'd been working on and gave my all to a novel that was truly worth the trouble. The extraordinary life of the world's first forensic scientist. An epic and fascinating story set in exotic ancient China.

The documentation process was exceedingly arduous. There were no more than thirty paragraphs in about a dozen books on Cí Song's life, and these, though they opened the door for a fictional account, limited the chances of a biographically accurate rendering. Luckily, the same could not be said of his own output; his five treatises on forensics, all published in 1247 as the *Hsi yuan lu hsiang I* (*The Washing Away of Wrongs*), have endured through translations in Japanese, Korean, Russian, German, Dutch, French, and English.

With the help of my friend Alex Lima, a writer and adjunct professor at Suffolk County Community College, I obtained a facsimile of the five volumes edited by Nathan Smith of the Center for Chinese Studies at the University of Michigan, from a translation by professor Brian McKnight that includes a useful preface from the Japanese edition of 1854.

The first volume listed the laws affecting forensic judges, the bureaucratic procedures employed, the number of investigations to be carried out per crime and who was in charge of carrying them out, jurisdictions, behavioral protocol for inspectors, the drawing up of forensic reports, and the punishments forensic experts might receive if they made incorrect judgments. This first volume also advocated using a standard procedure when it came to examining corpses, including stipulating the necessity of sketching the various findings on palimpsest sheets.

The second volume detailed the stages of corpse decay, the variations in these according to the time of year, the washing and preparation of corpses, the examination of disinterred corpses, the exhumation of corpses, methods for examining corpses at an advanced stage of decomposition, forensic entomology, the analyses to be carried out in the case of a strangling or suffocation, the differences when looking at female corpses, and the examination of fetuses.

The third volume looked in depth at the study of bones, wound traces on skeletons, bodily vital points, suicides by hanging, simulated suicides, murders, and drownings.

The fourth volume covered deaths caused by punches or kicks or by blunt instruments used for stabbing or for cutting, suicides committed using sharp objects, murders by several wounds in which the death blow needed to be identified, cases of decapitation or cases in which the torso or the head were not present, burn deaths, deaths caused by spillages of boiling liquids, poisoning, deaths caused by hidden illnesses, deaths caused by acupuncture or moxibustion, and the registration of deaths by natural causes.

Finally, the fifth volume dealt with investigations into the deaths of prisoners; deaths caused by torture; deaths caused by falling from great heights; deaths caused by crushing, asphyxiation, horse or buffalo stampedes, and crashes; deaths by lightning strikes; deaths caused by wild beast attacks; deaths by insect, snake, or reptile bites; deaths due to internal wounds because of overeating;

deaths due to sexual excesses; and, finally, the procedures for the opening up of corpses as well as the methods for dispersing stench and carrying out resuscitations.

All in all, it was a veritable array of techniques, methods, instruments, preparations, protocols, and laws, added to the numerous forensics cases solved by Cí Song, which enabled me to construct a story that not only had passion but also would be absolutely faithful to reality.

I spent a year researching and compiling information on contemporary political, cultural, social, judicial, economic, religious, military, and sexual mores; and conducting extensive research in the fields of medicine, education, architecture, diet, property, dress, measurement systems, money, state organization, and bureaucracy during medieval China's Tsong dynasty. Once this was all organized and compared, I discovered several astonishing things, including the convulsions undergone by Emperor Ningzong's court during the constant hostilities from the northern barbarians, the Jin, who, having conquered some northern regions, were threatening to move south; norms governing family behavior, which were strict and complicated but ultimately required complete obeisance by younger members to their elders; the importance of ritual as both axis and motor of daily life; the omnipresence of violent punishments for even the most petty of crimes; the massive penal code regulating every aspect of life; the absence of monotheistic religions and the coexistence of philosophies such as Buddhism, Taoism, and Confucianism; the triennial exams, which in many ways were ahead of their time in promoting social equality; the general air of antimilitarism; and the stunning scientific and technical advances—the compass, gunpowder, mobile printing presses, bank notes, refrigeration, watertight vessels—hatched during the Tsong dynasty.

Strange as it may seem, once I had vaguely sketched my plot, my first difficulty was giving characters their names.

When westerners read books with foreign characters, we can memorize their names and surnames and identify them with the individuals they represent because, in general, their names have Hebraic, Greek, or Latin roots, which are basically familiar to us. So family names that are unusual today (for example, Jenofonte, Asdrúbal, Suetonio, or Abderramán) are not only easily recognized but also easy to differentiate and remember. Something similar happens, for Spanish speakers, at least, when it comes to Anglo-Saxon names. Eric, John, or Peter are almost as familiar to us as Juan, Pedro, or José. Unfortunately, this is not the case with Asian names, especially Chinese ones.

The Chinese language—or languages—is extremely complex. Most of the words are monosyllabic, but a syllable can be articulated with five distinct intonations. So let's imagine a novel with characters with the following names: Song, Tang, Ming, Peng, Feng, Fang, Kang, Dong, Kung, Fong, and Kong. There does not exist a reader who would not have given up on the book by page three.

To negotiate this, while maintaining the names of the principal historical characters, I had to change others that were too similar and might create confusion. For the same reason, I gave secondary characters nicknames representing their personalities, which was also a custom at the time.

But the difficulties didn't end there. Pinyin, the phonetic rendering of Chinese, is an extremely useful system allowing the expression of complicated ideograms in alphabet-based words that can be spoken and written by any westerner. Nonetheless, the tonal diversity in spoken Chinese has meant that words can be transcribed differently to reflect the hearer's perception. This means that, depending on the source, we might find Song Cí written as Tsong Cí, Tsung Cí, Sung Cí, Sun Tzu, or Sung Tzu.

Also, in China, the family name precedes the given name, and the latter is rarely used. So our protagonist, referred to throughout the novel as Cí Song or just Cí, in reality would have been referred to by contemporaries as Song Cí and, very often, just Song. So why did I change this? For three main reasons. First, to make something that resembled western naming conventions, with given name first and family name last. Second, to avoid problems of comprehension that might arise when sons and fathers are referred to in the same paragraph (Song and Song). The third reason was to get around the strange coincidence that Cí's surname was the same as that of the dynasty to which the emperor belonged—the Tsong dynasty, sometimes also rendered as Song.

The next problem was larger. One of the greatest pitfalls for writers of historical fiction is to establish how much truth—and how much fiction—is contained in their sources, which should (but may not always) show scrupulous respect for the facts.

I have attended many discussions on the concept of the historical novel, debates which, with varying levels of vehemence, tend to turn on the degree of quality and quantity of facts a novel should contain if it is to be considered a novel of historical significance. Panelists tend to employ the semiologist Umberto Eco's typology of three modalities: First, there is the romantic novel with a fantastical setting, in which characters and the historical background are purely fictitious, but are overlaid with the appearance of veracity (for example, Bernard Cornwell's *Warlord Chronicles* novels). Second, there are what Eco terms "cloak and dagger" works, novels whose historically real characters are placed in fictional situations that never actually occurred (for example, works by Walter Scott, Alexandre Dumas, and Leo Tolstoy). Last, there are the historical novels that Eco considers to strictly adhere to the term, with fictional characters in historically veracious situations (including his own iconic *The Name of the Rose*).

Many would say that this typology leaves out biographical novels, false memoirs, and essays that are more or less rigorous.

In any case, my belief is that a historical novel should be a novel first and foremost. We should work from the principle that the novel is fiction, as that is the only way its magic and power to captivate can come through. Once this difficult process is complete, the key should be in the rigor and honesty with which the author deals with historical events; it is just as historical to write a novel about an anonymous slave who lost his life building a church as it is to write about Julius Caesar in Gaul. Rigor is everything. In Caesar's case, the character is historical, but that doesn't guarantee that our story will deal with his behavior, feelings, or thoughts. In the case of the former, the fictional character who is the slave didn't exist, but someone like him did. And if our fictional character acts as that slave might have acted, then the story will be vivid.

Obviously, the author's duty is to write a novel in which Caesar thinks, feels, and acts more than historians tell us to be the case; if we did otherwise, we'd be writing an essay, a biography, or a documentary. But the author also has a duty to make sure that the fiction is plausible. We would also be wrong to scorn the historical novel that employs fictional characters acting in a real world, because that world and whatever happens around the character also make up part of our larger history.

It is obligatory, in this sense—though larger events may be the only ones recorded—to point out that small, daily happenings are those that make up our lives, our highs and our lows, the things that make us believe and dream, the things that make us fall in love, reach decisions, and even, sometimes, fight or die for what we believe. The great historian Jacques Le Goff was the first to claim the history of the everyday: of medieval fairs; of the less well-off living in villages; of sickness, punishment, and pain; of the reality of the forgotten lives, in contradistinction to the brilliance and resonance of battles whose stories are related by the victors.

To anyone interested in looking into the subject further, I would highly recommend the essay "Cinco miradas sobre la novella histórica" ("Five Views of the Historical Novel") by Carlos García Gual, Antonio Penadés, Javier Negrete, Gisbert Haefs, and Pedro Godoy, and published by Ediciones Evohé. These prestigious authors not only contribute clear perspectives on the question, but also manage to do so in an entertaining and enlightening manner.

In the case of *The Corpse Reader*, the protagonist is a real person, albeit one little known for his work, despite his copious writings. With that in mind, I have endeavored to reflect exactly the protagonist's methods of working, his innovative forensic techniques, his difficult beginnings, his daring, his intellect, his love of academia, and his thirst for truth and justice. All the processes, procedures, laws, protocols, analyses, methods, instruments, and materials I have described are real. Other real people, including Emperor Ningzong and his retinue, the Councilor for Punishments and old Professor Ming, add to the cast of characters. I was also aided by historical facts such as the widely documented existence of the academy, the political instability on China's borders, and, above all, the appearance, for the first time in history, of the hand cannon, a wholly new, and wholly deadly, innovation.

But I also added fictional elements that enabled me to re-create, with verisimilitude, the society, intrigue, and evolution of the time. In this sense, I wove together a complicated plot in which I speculated on how the top-secret formula for explosive gunpowder might pass into the hands of China's enemies, the Mongols, and finally make its way to Europe.

The scientific name for Cí Song's unusual condition is congenital insensitivity to pain with anhidrosis (CIPA) and is consistent with an unusual mutation of the gene that controls the neuro-trophic tyrosine kinase receptor, which inhibits the formation of nerve cells responsible for transmitting pain, heat, and cold signals to the brain. I admit that there is no evidence that Cí Song suffered from it; this is dramatic license. But this infirmity, a marvelous ability allowing him to overcome certain difficulties, also has its downside—changing, toughening, and damaging the protagonist, making him feel like an accursed monster.

As a final remark, I would like to offer a personal reflection on literary genres. Everyone knows about the innate human tendency to classify, and it is only logical in an information-rich—sometimes overly rich—society. Something similar can happen with literary genres: so much is published that publishers have to decide which genre books fall under, booksellers need to know which shelves to place them on, and readers want orientation to help them choose a book to fit their tastes.

So far, so good. "Genrefication" is a way of organizing, and organization is necessary. But maybe the human tendency to give fixed labels to genres is less so. We label genres "great" or "minor," but these labels never depend on an objective classification of each individual book.

I say this because I have often heard the historical novel referred to as a "minor" genre. Every time I hear this, I wonder whether the person making this point is talking about a specific novel or, really, is just following common opinion. To illustrate my point, let's imagine for a moment a writer of unusual skill writing a tragic love story about two youths whose families, the Capulets and the Montagues, hate one another. Just because it is set in sixteenth-century Venice, should *Romeo and Juliet* be called nothing more than historical fiction, rather than the greatest love story ever told?

This leads us to the ineffable Jose Manual Lara's definition of genres: "In reality, there are only two types of novels, those that are good and those that are bad."

BIOGRAPHICAL SUMMARY
OF CÍ SONG

Cí Song was born in 1186 in Jianyang, a subprefecture of Fujian. His father, Kung Song, was not an outstanding student but managed, due to the facilities provided by Emperor Ningzong, to pass the governmental exams. Obsessed with his son's future, Kung had Cí take lessons with a follower of Hsi Chu before entering the *t'ai-hsue*, the National University at Lin'an (current-day Hangzhou). In 1217, after taking courses in medicine, law, and criminology, Cí Song obtained a *Chin-shih* doctorate, which qualified him to become a sheriff in Yin, in the subprefecture of Chekiang. But his father's sudden death prevented him from taking the post, as he had to withdraw from public life to observe the customary mourning period. Almost a decade later, Cí Song became a registrar in Hsin-feng, in the subprefecture of Kiangsi. His successes in forensics made his quartermaster envious, and the latter had him demoted several times until Cí Song gave up the life of an official. After the death of the quartermaster, though, Cí Song took up his former post and went on to rise through the administrative ranks, including subprefect, prefect, and judicial intendant. He dedicated himself to forensic study and analysis, discarding several ancient, esoteric, and magic-based practices. Some of his innovations are still in use today. He died in 1249, two years after completing the first and most important scientific treatise on forensics in history, the *Hsi yuan lu hsiang I.*

GLOSSARY

Alchemy: *Jindanshu*, or "gold and cinnabar technique," is the term most commonly used to refer to external Taoist alchemy, or *waidan*. The first alchemical techniques are mentioned in works such as the *Huainanzi* using the term *huanbaishu*, or "white and yellow technique," colors that designate silver and gold or their substitutes. Cinnabar also took on considerable importance in the manufacture of pills or long-life elixirs. This operation is known as *liandanshu* ("cinnabar refinement technique") or *xiandanshu* ("cinnabar immortality technique"). Numerous chemical and botanical discoveries were made in the application of these procedures, with various therapeutic uses. During the Han dynasty, Taoist alchemists, in trying to formulate an immortal elixir, created numerous fires by experimenting with mixes of sulfur and saltpeter (potassium nitrate). One of these alchemists, Boyang Wei, wrote a text on alchemy called *The Kinship of the Three*, pointing to the explosive properties of certain materials. Many of the early mixes of Chinese gunpowder contained toxic substances such as mercury and arsenic and can therefore be considered a form of early chemical warfare. From the time of the Tsong dynasty, the term *dandingpai*, or "cinnabar and crucible," began to be used to refer to alchemy in general.

Bialar: In Cí Song's time, men always went out with their heads covered by a cap, a mortarboard, a bonnet, or a skullcap, and with their hair tied in a bun underneath. Clothes, and in particular a person's hat, reflected social status. A winged cap might "fly" horizontally over the ears or have a turned-down brim, depending on the rank of the wearer. Poor people bundled up a threadbare strip of cloth and placed it on their heads.

Birthdays: The Chinese count people's ages differently from how it is done in the West. In the West, the birthday is the anniversary of one's birth, but in China people are considered one year old at birth, and turn two years old at the first lunar new year (the first new moon in January or February) of their life. For example, a child born in November will be two years old by the end of February, even though only three to four months have passed. The date of birth was recorded only to determine the person's horoscope rather than to measure age.

Conservation Chamber: Also known as *tong bing jian*, or "bronze icebox," this was a small metal chest with ice-filled compartments for conserving food, ice cream, or drinks. One of the first proven refrigerators was found in the province of Hubei and dated to around 300 BC.

Coolie: A lower-class worker or servant or an unqualified peon. The term has been used in the West as a pejorative reference to the Asian labor force that immigrated to the Americas in the nineteenth century. It is associated with the English word *coolie* as used in reference to a stevedore or longshoreman. The word originated as *gŭlí* or *kŭlì*, which translates as "the bitter use of brute force," and has cognates in the Bengali *kuli* and the Hindu *qŭlī*.

Hanfu: The traditional clothing worn by the Han tribe, which has made up the majority of the population throughout China's history. The *hanfu* consisted of a loose-fitting white gown with wide sleeves that crossed the chest and attached to the belt. Beneath this, men wore pantaloons. Homeless or destitute people wore hemp jackets and scruffy pantaloons and turbans. Women and men wore black silk caps and long-sleeved silk tunics dyed turquoise, vermilion, and purple, and fastened with jade, gold, or rhinoceros horn buckles. The outfits were regulated by sumptuary laws, provisions that restricted the wearing of the most luxurious garments to the upper classes. These laws were ineffective in practice. Imperial fashions were blatantly imitated by the socially aspirational mercantile classes, and nine out of ten people ignored the law. The *hanfu* influenced traditional dress in other countries, such as the kimono in Japan, the *hanbok* in Korea, and the *áo tú than* in Vietnam.

Hourglass/Water Clock: These were used in China for thousands of years BC. In AD 1086 the Chinese scientist Su Song invented an astrological clock powered by water, outdoing the contemporaneous mechanical European clocks for precision. This clock, in the form of a six-meter-tall tower, used a tank from which water flowed out over paddles on a wheel to put mechanisms in motion. These mechanisms made various figures appear to indicate the hours and, with the accompaniment of a gong and tabors, moved a celestial sphere with stars and constellations. On a daily basis, this clock was accurate within two minutes.

Jin, Yurchen: An Asian people inhabiting the area around the River Amur, located on what is now Russia's border with China.

Antecedents of the Manchu people, in 1127 they sacked Kaifeng, which had until then been the Chinese capital, leading to the abdication of the Northern Tsong dynasty. After the Chinese fled the capital, a new dynasty arose to the south, making its center in Lin'an. The Southern Tsong continued to battle the powerful Jin for more than a decade until a peace treaty was signed ceding all of northern China to the invaders. Despite several attempts, the Southern Tsong never regained these territories.

Li: A measure of distance equivalent to 560 meters, or 1,837 feet. Punishments by exile sometimes varied from 2,000 to 3,000 *li* in distance, that is, between roughly 1,000 to 1,500 kilometers, or 600 to 900 miles.

Lin'an (current-day Hangzhou): The Southern Tsong dynasty's capital city. After the Jin invasion, the Tsong retreated south and made their capital in Hangzhou, renaming it Lin'an. The city has since taken back its previous name.

Moxibustion: An Eastern medicinal therapy using the root of a sage plant pressed into the shape of a cigar, or moxa. The end is lit and either pressed against the patient's skin, producing a controlled burn, or placed next to acupuncture holes to pass heat into them.

Mu: A measurement of land equivalent to 666 square meters, or 2,185 square feet.

Neo-Confucianism: Three philosophies peacefully coexisted during the Tsong dynasty: Confucianism, Taoism, and Buddhism. However, within the bureaucratic elite, neo-Confucianism gained in popularity. This movement upheld the moral standards and traditional policies of Confucianism but joined them with Taoist and Buddhist concepts, including ideas extracted from *The Book of Changes (I Ching)* and yin-yang theories associated with the *taiji* symbol. A typical neo-Confucian motif is contained in the painting known as *The Three Masters Are One*, which depicts Confucius, Buddha, and Laozi drinking from the same pitcher. But many neo-Confucians declared themselves opposed to such trends, rejecting Buddhism as a faith system and condemning the adoration of Buddha. In spite of this, neo-Confucian texts adapted Buddhist thinking and beliefs as a way of enhancing Confucianism. Neo-Confucianism was the official creed in China from the time of its development during the Tsong dynasty until the beginning of the twentieth century. Among its many strictures, neo-Confucianism prohibited the opening up of corpses, though it allowed the examination of those already opened as a cause or consequence of death. Homosexuality was also considered libidinous and reprehensible.

Palanquin: A kind of chair or litter, usually closed and covered, used in the East to transport royalty and high-ranking officials.

Poisonous Waters: An encyclopedia from the time of the Chin dynasty containing what is possibly the first recorded reference to dengue fever. The volume was written between 420 and 265 BC, edited formally in AD 610 during the Tang dynasty, and reedited in AD 992 during the Northern Tsong dynasty. Dengue fever is a severe illness transmitted by the *Aedes aegypti* mosquito, which breeds in fetid or polluted water. A particularly life-threatening variety is dengue hemorrhagic fever, which causes loss of liquid and blood due to coagulation problems, which can bring about shock and death in as little as four hours.

Prefecture: During the Southern Tsong dynasty, China was divided, for administrative purposes, into sixteen circuits (*lu*) or provinces (*tao*), each roughly the same size as Ireland, and with a governor who was the judicial intendant. Each circuit was subdivided into ten to twenty prefectures, locally governed administrative units with a certain number of officials and assistants. Every prefecture was then divided into subprefectures, or districts (*hsien*), between two and twenty per prefecture, each usually overseen by two or three officials. The subprefect (*chih-hsien* or *hsien-ling*), who acted as judge and magistrate and carried out other administrative functions, had under him a registrar (*chupu*), who was in charge of tax collection, as well as a sheriff or chief of police (*hsien-wei*), who was responsible for keeping the peace and ensuring laws were upheld.

Punishments: *Lingchi*, or death by one thousand cuts, was the worst punishment in the penal code. But there were many other forms of punishment. Whipping with bamboo canes was one of the most common; the length, width, and weight of the canes were strictly stipulated and categorized. The *jia* was a yoke made of a square piece of dry wood that could be separated in half and had a hole in the middle for the head. Handcuffs, also known as wives, were made of dry wood and could only be used on men; foot shackles were made of metal.

Qián: The principal monetary unit in China was a thin coin that had a hole in the center so it could be hung from a cord or attached to one's belt. A cord with a thousand *qián* would weigh around five kilos, or eleven pounds, and be equivalent to one *tael* (approximately forty grams of pure silver). During the Tsong dynasty, there was also paper money. Initially, paper bills were similar to credit notes that could be changed for quantities of money deposited with wealthy merchants; in later years there were credit certificates and a regularized paper money unit. Forgery was punishable by death and informants were offered generous rewards; both notices were printed on the bills themselves alongside the image of a hanged or quartered forger so that illiterates would understand the warning. Also for the benefit of illiterates, bills had a picture of the number of pigs roughly equivalent to the value of the bill.

Ritual and Filial Piety: Rituals organized society and were structured according to a rigid hierarchy: a man was not defined by his personality but by how well he observed the rites—that is, by behaving in a regulated way with respect to his social rank. As with their biological fathers, inferiors owed respect to their "father emperor," a virtuous, benevolent being who had the right and duty to rule others. In traditional Chinese culture, ceremonial specialization was a constant theme between court members and aristocratic families, above all in the Confucian period. The *Li Ji* and the *Bohutong* (*Book of Rites*) both stipulated that the mourning period after the death of a father was three years and that the most orthodox way of observing this was to withdraw from public life, wear burlap, and live in a hut near the burial site. Poor people unable to cease working observed the mourning period by refraining from participation in festive occasions, marriage, and sexual activity. Chinese people offered sacrifices to their dead during funeral rites—whether Taoist, Buddhist, Confucian, or a combination of the three.

Sampan: A plain sailing vessel without a keel between 3.5 and 4.5 meters long, or 11 feet to 14 feet, used either for fishing or as a residence. *Sampan* literally means "three planks," in reference to the simplicity of making such a vessel, which requires one plank for the bottom and two for the sides. The sampan is possibly the oldest known sailing boat and has kept its original design since it came into existence in AD 600. It came to be known as the "junk rig."

Time: Year 1 corresponds in the West with the birth of Christ, and in Muslim countries with Mohammed's flight from Mecca in AD 622. But in Imperial China there is more than one initial date—every time a new emperor comes to power. Each emperor may also decree new eras within his reign, sometimes according to the zodiac. In Ningzong's reign (1194–1224), four separate eras occurred. The first, lasting from 1195 to 1200, was named the Qingyuan; the second, from 1201 to 1204, Jiatai; the third, from 1205 to 1207, Kaixi; and the fourth, from 1208 until Ningzong's death in 1224 at the age of fifty-six, Jiading.

A year was divided into twelve moon months, usually beginning in February (first moon month) and finishing in January (twelfth moon month). Every year was separated into twenty-four climatic periods.

Days were broken up into twelve hourly intervals known as *shichen* (one Chinese hour is equivalent to two western hours). Each *shichen* is divided into eight *ke* (fifteen minutes), each containing fifteen *fen*, so a *fen* is equal to a minute. An hour is known as a *tshuco*, and a *jike* is a quarter of an hour.

This difference is particularly relevant when considering the death periods. The law stated that no more than four *shichen* could elapse between the time a death was reported and the time a relevant judge examined the corpse. Because I wanted to make the novel easier to read, I used "hour" instead of *shichen*; the maximum time allowed before beginning an examination would really have been eight western hours. The nighttime hours were not included, so in practice the time allowed before beginning an examination extended to sixteen Western hours.

The denomination and classification of the hours were as follows:

Zi	Hour of the Rat	11:00 p.m.–1:00 a.m.
Chou	Hour of the Buffalo	1:00 a.m.–3:00 a.m.
Yin	Hour of the Tiger	3:00 a.m.–5:00 a.m.
Mao	Hour of the Rabbit	5:00 a.m.–7:00 a.m.
Chen	Hour of the Dragon	7:00 a.m.–9:00 a.m.
Si	Hour of the Snake	9:00 a.m.–11:00 a.m.
Wu	Hour of the Horse	11:00 a.m.–1:00 p.m.
Wei	Hour of the Sheep	1:00 p.m.–3:00 p.m.
Shen	Hour of the Monkey	3:00 p.m.–5:00 p.m.
You	Hour of the Rooster	5:00 p.m.–7:00 p.m.
Xu	Hour of the Dog	7:00 p.m.–9:00 p.m.
Hai	Hour of the Pig	9:00 p.m.–11:00 p.m.

The denomination and classification of the months were as follows:

February	First month
March	Month of the Apricot
April	Month of the Peach
May	Month of the Cherry
June	Month of the Pomegranate
July	Month of the Lotus
August	Month of the Orchid
September	Month of the Olive
October	Month of the Chrysanthemum
November	Good Month
December	Winter Month
January	Last Month

Since the introduction of Buddhism to China, years have also been named after signs of the zodiac and repeat in twelve monthly cycles corresponding with the hourly denominations.

The months are organized into three groups: *Meng* (first), *Zhong* (middle), and *Ji* (last). The seasons are named *Chun* (spring), *Xia* (summer), *Qiu* (autumn), and *Dong* (winter). The names of the months are formed using both concepts; for example, *ki-tsin* is the last month of autumn. Months can also be denominated in the same way as the hours and the years and are made up of three ten-day weeks.

University: Like the leaders of preceding dynasties, the Tsong advocated that the most virtuous and capable citizens, regardless of their social or economic extraction, should hold public offices. This idea was supported by a system of exams for civil service: any citizen could take the extremely difficult exams, and if he passed, he became a government employee, a career that could even lead one to become prime minister.

The Tsong set up elementary schools in every prefectural city. Even rural villages had basic universities, and these, along with the reduction in the prices of books due to the spread of the printing press, virtually brought illiteracy to an end.

In the capital, Lin'an, the proximity of the university to the court meant many students became involved in political activities that were criticized by senior government officials, who in turn didn't hesitate to boycott classes. The situation became sufficiently alarming that Emperor Li-tsung's notorious chief of staff, Chia Su-tao, began infiltrating student networks with spies.

The private academies, known as *shu-yüan*, were the only way to gain access to specialized higher learning in subjects like medicine; they included the Hanlin, the Bailudong, the Yuelu, the Chingshan, the Shugue, and the Yintianfu. In contrast to state schools, the masters at these academies taught more than the classics. Their teaching methods also included research, and masters would often present their own findings to students and then base further advances on the students' work. Many academies—with grants from senior officials, wealthy merchants, and sometimes the state—could provide accommodations for both teachers and students. The most exclusive and influential academy, the Hanlin, was founded to train high-ranking court officials and archivists. The upper classes had easier access to such academies, and the large numbers of cultivated women in the higher echelons of society reflected the fact that females were also highly educated.

Violence: Physically violent punishments, often in the form of canings, were part of the fabric of medieval Chinese society. This was because physical pain was such a strong deterrent and because most of the population was not in a position to pay fines. Imprisonment always meant forced labor, either in the salt mines or in the army. Physical punishment was the usual recourse and was employed for any kind of ill conduct, including in the private or familial spheres.

Wu-tso: Before judges' responsibilities were extended to include forensics, or corpse reading, these duties were carried out by the *wu-tsos*, poorly educated assistants who had to perform the most unsavory tasks, such as cleaning corpses, opening them up, and extracting and examining organs, while the judge would take notes. Generally, *wu-tsos* had other jobs as well, often as healers, butchers, or slaughterhouse workers.

Xylography: A primitive printing method using woodblocks carved with words and pictures. The carving was carried out by hand, and then watercolor paints were used as ink. The ink was transferred to the page by means of strong rubbing. The first printed book was the *Diamond Sutra*, stamped by Chieh Wang on May 11, 868, in China.

The first mobile printing press, made from complicated pieces of porcelain, was made in China by Sheng Bi between 1041 and 1049.

ACKNOWLEDGMENTS

Last, but by no means least:

After years of intense work, dozens of discarded drafts, exhausting days in which the word *rest* lost all meaning—when, finally, you come to the last page and look on the complete manuscript—you breathe for a moment before being gripped by a painful uncertainty. You feel satisfied because you've given your best, but inside you something says maybe it wasn't enough. You'd like to have studied more, revised more, made your text more vibrant and surprising. For a moment you think perhaps all this effort won't add up to an enthusiastic readership. And in that moment you remember everyone who helped you along the way. You remember your parents' phone calls, urgent and caring, asking, "Son, how are you? And the novel…?" You remember your brothers, the best people in the world. You remember your daughter.

You remember friends old and new. Those who have always been with you and those you've recently met. Friends like Santiago Morata, Fernando Marías, Antonio Penadés, Alejandro Noguera, Lucía Bartolomé, Manuel Valente, Anika Lillo, and Carlos Aimeur. Friends whose help, closeness, and care you appreciate.

You remember the editors, within your country and internationally, who had confidence and bet on you. You remember Ramón Conesa, your agent at Carmen Balcells, always ready with sage advice.

They all share a space in my memory next to my readers—those who have written to me to applaud or criticize, those whose spirits I managed to lift for a few days, and even those who haven't yet read my work, because they push me to keep going day after day. I fight for them; they make writing worth it.

A special mention for Lixiao Zhuang, cultural adviser at the Chinese Embassy in Spain, for her selfless work putting me in touch with the directors of the Chinese National Museum in Beijing, the Huqing Yutang Museum of Chinese Medicine in Hangzhou, and General Fei Yue's Mausoleum. And I couldn't forget Dr. Phil A. R. Hill, a bookseller in White City, London, who advised me on a wide range of books and bibliographies. I must also mention doctor of forensics Devaraj Mandal and the eminent sinologist Jacques Gernet, without whose wisdom I would have been unable to make this book as credible as it needed to be.

It is not enough to simply mention my wife, Maite. Thanks be to God, I enjoy her presence each and every day. My lighthouse when times are good and bad. She is my life's greatest gift.

I want to dedicate my final words to someone missed by all who knew him. A quiet person, but someone from whom I learned a great deal. His behavior, humility, and honesty all taught me things that books can't teach.

For him and in his memory.

Thank you, Eugenio.

ABOUT THE AUTHOR

 A native of Spain, a former educator and industrial engineer, Antonio Garrido has received acclaim for the darkly compelling storytelling and nuanced historical details that shape his novel *The Corpse Reader*. This fictionalized account of the early life of Song Cí, the Chinese founding father of forensic science, represents the author's years of research into cultural, social, legal, and political aspects of life in the Tsong dynasty, as well as his extensive study of Song Cí's own five-volume treatise on forensics. In 2012, *The Corpse Reader* received the Zaragoza International Prize for best historical novel published in Spain (Premio Internacional de Novela Histórica Ciudad de Zaragoza). Antonio's previous novel, *La Escriba*, was published in 2008. Garrido currently resides in Valencia, Spain.

ABOUT THE TRANSLATOR

Thomas Bunstead is a writer and translator based in East Sussex, England. In 2011 he was one of the British Centre for Literary Translation's mentees, working with Margaret Jull Costa. His translations include the acclaimed *Polish Boxer* by Eduardo Halfon, *Anton Mallick Wants to Be Happy* by Premio Nadal winner Nicolás Casariego, and "From now on, according to Schopenhauer," an essay by Enrique Vila-Matas, which was chosen by dOCUMENTA and featured in its Book of Books. Thomas's own writing has appeared at *3:AM Magazine,* >kill author, *daysofroses,* ReadySteadyBook, the *Paris Review* blog, and in *The Independent on Sunday* and *The Times Literary Supplement.*

BIBLIOGRAPHY

Bailey, Alison, Ronald G. Knapp, Peter Neville-Hadley, J. A. G. Roberts, and Nancy S. Steinhardt. *China.* Madrid: Akal, 2008.

Birge, Bettine. *Women, Property, and Confucian Reaction in Sung and Yüan China (930–1368).* New York: Cambridge University Press, 2002.

Chaffee, John W. *Branches of Heaven: A History of the Imperial Clan of Sung China.* Cambridge, MA: Harvard University Asia Center, 1999.

Confucius and Mencius. *El Chu-King, El Ta Hio, El Lun-Yu, El Tchung-Yung, El Meng-Tseu: Los cinco grandes libros de política, moral y filosofía de la antigua China.* Madrid: Clásicos Bergua, 1969.

Davis, Edward L. *Society and the Supernatural in Sòng China.* Honolulu: University of Hawaii Press, 2001.

Ebrey, Patricia Buckley, and Peter N. Gregory. *Religion and Society in T'ang and Sung China.* Honolulu: University of Hawaii Press, 1993.

Fenby, Jonathan. *Las setenta maravillas de China.* Barcelona: Blume, 2007.

Folch, Dolors. *La construcción de China*. Barcelona: Península, 2001.

García Menéndez, Silvia, and J. R. González Huertas. *Historia de China*. Madrid: Libsa, 2006.

García-Noblejas, Gabriel. *Mitología de la China antigua*. Madrid: Alianza, 2007.

Gernet, Jacques. *Daily Life in China on the Eve of the Mongol Invasion, 1250–1276*. Palo Alto, CA: Stanford University Press, 1962.

———. *El mundo Chino*. Barcelona: Crítica, 1991.

González de Mendoza, Fray Juan. *Historia del gran reino de la China*. Madrid: Miraguano, 2008.

Haskew, Michael E., Christer Jörgensen, Chris Mcnab, Eric Niderost, and Rob S. Rice. *Técnicas bélicas del mundo oriental, 1200–1860. Equipamiento, técnicas y tácticas de combate*. Madrid: Libsa, 2009.

Hymes, Robert. *Way and Byway: Taoism, Local Religion, and Models of Divinity in Sung and Modern China*. Los Angeles: University of California Press, 2002.

Layma, Yann. *China*. Barcelona: Lunwerg, 2008.

Lee, Thomas H. C. *Government Education and Examinations in Sung China*. Hong Kong: Chinese University of Hong Kong, 1985.

Mcknight, Brian E. *Village and Bureaucracy in Southern Sung China*. Chicago: University of Chicago Press, 1971.

———, *Law and Order in Sung China*. New York: Cambridge University Press, 1992.

——— and James T. C. Liu. *The Enlightened Judgments: Ch'ing-Ming Chi. The Sung Dynasty Collection*. Albany, NY: State University of New York Press, 1999.

Moretti, Marco. *China: El reino del dragón*. Madrid: Libsa, 2008.

Nancarrow, Peter. *La antigua China y la gran muralla*. Madrid: Akal, 1990.

Polo, Marco. *Libro de las Maravillas*. Madrid: Suma de Letras, 2000.

_____, Ricci, Dampier, Hunter, Huc, Claudel, et al. *Viaje por la China imperial*. Barcelona: Abraxas, 2000.

Preciado Idoeta, Juan I. *Antología de poesía China*. Madrid: Gredos, 2003.

Qizhi, Zhang. *Cultura tradicional China*. Madrid: Editorial Popular, 2008.

Ríos, Xulio. *China: De la A a la Z: Diccionario general de expresiones Chinas*. Madrid: Editorial Popular, 2008.

Scarpari, Maurizio. *Antigua China*. Barcelona: Folio, 2005.

Schafer, Edward H. *La China antigua*. Amsterdam: Time Life, 1972.

Shaughnessy, Edward L., *China: El mundo Chino, creencias y rituales, creación*

y descubrimientos. Barcelona: Blume, 2008.

Sung, Tzu (Song, Cí). *The Washing Away of Wrongs*. Ann Arbor, MI: University of Michigan Center for Chinese Studies, 1981.

Theroux, Paul. *En el gallo de hierro: Viajes en tren por China*. Barcelona: Ediciones B, 1997.

Time Life Books. *Vivir la historia de la China imperial, 960–1368*. Barcelona: Folio, 2008.

Tse, Lao. *Tao Te King*. Barcelona: Edicomunicación, 1994.

Van Gulik, Robert H. *La vida sexual en la antigua China*. Madrid: Siruela, 2005.

VV. AA., *Ta-Tsing-Leu-Lee. Las leyes del código penal de la China*. Madrid: Imprenta de la Revista de Legislación, 1884.

Virchow, Rudolfo. *Técnica de las autopsias*. Madrid: Administración de la Revista de Medicina y Cirugía Prácticas, 1894.

Wang, Yinglin. *Sanzijing: El clásico de tres caracteres*. Madrid: Trotta, 2000.

Wetzel, Alexandra. *China*. Barcelona: RBA, 2008.

Yoshinobu, Shiba. *Commerce and Society in Sung China*. Ann Arbor, MI: University of Michigan Center for Chinese Studies, 1970.